D0456879

behindlings

ALSO BY NICOLA BARKER

Wide Open
The Three Button Trick and Other Stories

behindlings
A NOVEL

NICOLA BARKER

An Imprint of HarperCollinsPublishers

First published in Great Britain by Flamingo, *an imprint of* HarperCollins*Publishers*, 2002.

BEHINDLINGS. Copyright © 2001 by Nicola Barker. All rights reserved. Printed in the United States of America. No part of this book may be used or reproduced in any manner whatsoever without written permission except in the case of brief quotations embodied in critical articles and reviews. For information address HarperCollins Publishers Inc., 10 East 53rd Street, New York, NY 10022.

HarperCollins books may be purchased for educational, business, or sales promotional use. For information please write: Special Markets Department, HarperCollins Publishers Inc., 10 East 53rd Street, New York, NY 10022.

FIRST ECCO EDITION

This novel is entirely a work of fiction. The names, characters and incidents portrayed in it are the work of the author's imagination. Any resemblance to actual persons, living or dead, events or localities, is entirely coincidental.

Library of Congress Cataloging-in-Publication Data

Barker, Nicola, 1966-
    Behindlings : a novel / Nicola Barker.—1st American ed.
        p. cm.
    ISBN 0-06-018569-4
        1. Friendship—Fiction. 2. England—Fiction. I. Title.

    PR6052.A64876 B44 2002
    823'.914—dc21

02 03 04 05 06 PDF/RRD 10 9 8 7 6 5 4 3 2 1

For dear Charles Edward Johnson,
who slammed his way out of that damn velvet factory—
smashing the glass door behind him—never, ever to look back again.
And for his beautiful, blue-eyed wife, Betty,
who, at the grand old age of 84,
discovered that the pylons could love one another.

behindlings

One

Wesley glanced behind him. Two people followed, but at a sensible distance. The first was familiar; an old man whose name he knew to be Murdoch. Murdoch, Wesley remembered, had been robust, once. He'd been grizzled. *Huge.* Frosty. A magnificent, clambering, prickly pear of a man. He'd been firm and strong and resolute. *Planted*; a man-tree, if ever there was one.

Recently, however, Murdoch's body had begun to curve, to arc (they all called him Doc, although he hadn't even seen the inside of a hospital until his sixty-third year – he was a home birth, people invariably were, back then – when necessity dictated that a small reddish hillock, a mole, on his right shoulder blade, should be surgically removed. He was a scaffolder, by trade).

But the curving was nothing medical. It went deeper. And along with this – initially – almost imperceptible transmutation (Wesley noticed details. It paid him to notice), Doc's colours had begun to alter: his bodily palette had changed from its habitual clean, crisp white, to a painfully tender pink, to a pale, dry, crusty yellow. Up close he smelt all sweet and sickly, like a wilting honeysuckle tendril.

Now, when Murdoch walked, it was as though he carried something huge and weighty within him, something painful, thudding, wearysome. His *heart*. It was too full and heavy. Stuffed but tremulous, like a chicken's liver.

Mmmm. Wesley felt hungry. I could devour him, he thought, smirking. But he knew – must I know everything? He wondered briefly, the smirk dissipating – that the thing Murdoch carried so heavily in his heart was grief. Yes, grief. And possibly, just possibly, a tiny, shrew-footed, virtually inaudible, pitter-patter of rage.

Unwieldy burdens. Wesley understood. He'd carried them himself, and badly. But Murdoch was strong, and he supported them fearlessly, he slung them – like an ancient holdall with rotted handles – firmly and evenly between his two old arms.

Doc was accompanied by a little dog. A sandy-coloured terrier. A plucky cur, a legendary ratter. The dog was called Dennis. Wesley knew Dennis well; the stout push of his legs, the familiar bump of his vertebrae, the inquisitive angle of his ears, his horribly intrusive nose, his fur wiry as poor quality pot scourers.

He remembered, once, staring briefly into Dennis's eyes and seeing a wild loop of fleas tightening in a crazy insect lassoo around the bridge of his snout. *Ah.* He was a good dog.

And the other person? The second follower? A woman. Wesley peered. She rang no bells. She wasn't familiar. She did not compute. Young. She seemed young and gangly, fine but big-boned with a delicate, tufty, parsnip-shaped head. Not unattractive, either. She was plain but wholesome, like a small, newly dug, recently scrubbed tuber. She was dressed like a boy.

Wesley turned, smiling grimly to himself. They were a bane. Yes. A bane. But only so long as they followed him (and this had to be some kind of compensation), only so long as they stalked, surveyed, trailed, pursued, could he truly depend upon his own safety. They were his witnesses. *Unwitting?* Certainly. *Witless?* Invariably.

But they were his witnesses. And Wesley knew (better, perhaps, than anybody) that he was a man who desperately needed watching.

Early. It was too damn early. Wesley paused for a moment in front of a bakery and glanced through the window. They'd just opened. He drew close to the glass and touched it. He left a perfect thumbprint. I'm leaving traces, he thought.

He stared down into a tray of speciality doughnuts. They were not the round kind, or the ring. They were not creamy zeppelins, apple-filled or cinnamon-sugar-rolled. No. They were shaped like people. Like gingerbread men.

In Canvey – because that was where he found himself on this

2

teeth-achingly cold, brutally bracing January morning – their wild and resolutely wool-infested island history was intertwined with the stamp of spicy ginger, with sweetness, with men (as late as the eighteenth century this precarious domain's unhealthy air – the interminable *dampness* – brought the fever like an unwelcome wedding gift to raw hordes of eager new brides.

Malaria. Concealed in the perilous but stealthy fog which constantly tiptoed around this fractured isle like a ravenously phantasmagorical winter mink, slipping, unobserved, between plump and tender post-nuptial lips, slinking, unapprehended, through the spirited flair of passionate nostrils.

Making itself at home. Rearranging the furniture. Infiltrating. Infecting. Conquering. Killing. In those days one stout and ruddy shepherd could take ten wives and think nothing of it. Some, it was rumoured, took as many as thirty-five).

Wesley knew his stuff. Or enough stuff, at least – he told himself tiredly – to be getting on with.

The doughnuts he took to be a local peculiarity. He gazed at them. He was hungry. Each doughnut had an ugly red scar where its jam had been pumped in the sweetest transfusion. Generally, the wound was located under the right armpit. Sometimes, but rarely, in the chest.

He glanced up. Instinct. A shop assistant watched him. She was tying on her apron but staring at his hand, her dark eyes, her clean mouth, battling instinctively against a wide tide of revulsion. On his right hand Wesley had only a thumb, and a mass of shiny scar tissue which glimmered a bright bluey-violet in the cold.

He removed his hand and tucked it into his pocket. But the assistant didn't stop her staring. 'I know you,' she said, the light of recognition gradually dawning. He could see her lips moving. 'I *know* you.'

Wesley stared at her, blankly, then turned and walked on.

The old man reached the bakery seconds later. Murdoch stopped in Wesley's tracks and peered through the window. He put his thumb where Wesley's thumb had been. His old eyes fed upon the trays of sweet iced fingers, sticky currant buns, cold bread pudding.

The small dog sat at his heels. Doc looked down at the dog,

fondly, and then up into the face of the shop assistant. Her expression was no longer hostile, but pitying. 'I'm sorry,' she said, her brown eyes suddenly unconscionably round and tender. The old man nodded, frowned, paused, blinked, nodded again, then hurried swiftly onwards.

The young woman wore baggy jeans, a pale blue sweatshirt, a quilted grey Parka and a solid pair of flat, brown walking shoes. Her hair was cropped. Like the old man before her, she carefully placed her thumb where Wesley's thumb had been. The assistant was standing behind her counter now, arranging french sticks into a wicker display basket. She didn't appear to notice her.

The girl – Josephine – went into the shop.

'I'll have a doughnut,' she said, raising her soft voice over the sound of the door bell jangling, then added, 'No. Two. I'll have two. Thank you.'

She took a wallet out of her pocket. She opened it. She glanced over her shoulder. She was plainly in a hurry.

'You did my smear,' the assistant smiled, hastily brushing sugar from her fingers, passing over the doughnuts and then punching the appropriate three keys on the till. 'Remember?'

'Did I?' Jo clutched the doughnuts to her chest. For some reason she'd believed herself quite invisible. A wisp. A shade. A wraith.

'Yes. Southend Hospital. I was *dreading* it. I actually have – if you don't mind my saying so – I actually have an unusually tight . . .' she lowered her voice to only a whisper, 'an unusually tight *vagina*.'

Josephine – having leaned forward a fraction to catch what the assistant was saying – nodded sympathetically as she handed over her money.

'I understand,' she whispered back, 'I understand *completely*.'

The assistant smiled, relieved.

'My GP was absolutely bloody useless,' she continued, taking the money, 'so I demanded a referral to Southend after I heard you on the radio talking about your campaign for environmental sanitary products . . .'

'Ah. *Dioxin* pollution,' Jo intervened, automatically, 'a dangerous by-product of the chlorine-bleaching process . . .'

As she spoke, she craned her neck slightly to try and peer down the road a way. From where she was standing, Wesley was well out of her range already, but Doc . . . Doc . . .

'Unfortunately, some women are chronically allergic,' she continued, doggedly, 'and it can play total havoc with coastal marine . . . uh . . . coastal marine . . .'

Had Doc just turned left or right? Or was it . . . ? Hang on. There was a van, a dirty white van . . . The van pulled off.

Damn. Now there was a stupid bus shelter in the way. She blinked. *Wow.* Was that fog? It suddenly seemed foggy. Or was it just her eyes? She usually wore glasses. Short-sighted. But she'd gone and sat on them, stupidly, first thing this morning, in her hurry. Needed sticky tape to . . . needed . . . early this morning. She'd been up since two-thirty. A full . . . she glanced down at her watch, squinting slightly . . . a full five and a half hours already.

Jo sighed, frustratedly, then slowly turned back around to face the counter again, her expression blank. Three long seconds ticked by. 'Oh . . . uh, sorry . . . coastal marine *biology*,' she concluded, then smiled distractedly.

'That's it,' the assistant nodded, '*Dioxin* pollution. I remember now. And you were great.'

'Well thank you.'

Jo's money tinkled into the appropriate compartments. Fifty. Ten. Two. She took a small step backwards.

'And I know this might sound a little bit peculiar,' the assistant continued, plainly undeterred by Jo's blatant inattentiveness, 'but you actually have a real . . .' she paused, thoughtfully, 'a real *knack*.'

Jo inhaled, but not – she hoped – impatiently, 'It's only a system. Everything depends upon identifying the precise angle of the womb . . .' she flapped her free hand around in the air (a furiously migrating Italian finch, caught in the cruel swathes of a huntsman's netting) in order to try and demonstrate, 'and then the rest is all just basic common sense, really. Your GP should get hold of my pamphlet. It's available free from the Health Authority. Tell him to send off for it.'

She smiled brightly and turned to leave. Jesus Christ, she was thinking, how absolutely fucking *excruciating*. To be caught out. Like this. And *here* of all places.

The assistant, for her part, smiled back at Jo, nodded twice, perfectly amiably, then slammed the till shut. Nothing – at least superficially – out of the ordinary there. But as the coins in their compartments shifted and jangled in a brief yet acrimonious base-metal symphony, Jo could've sworn she heard something. Something else. Something beyond. Something *extra*. Three words. Half-muttered. Virtually inaudible over the surrounding clatter.

Don't follow him.

Jo froze. Her professional smile malfunctioned.

'Did you just say something?'

She spoke over her left shoulder, her hackles rising. The assistant's brown eyes widened, 'Me? No. Nothing.'

Josephine walked quickly and stiffly to the door, put out her hand, grasped the doorhandle, was about to turn the handle, was *just* about to turn it, when, Oh God, how *stupid*. She simply couldn't help herself. She spun around again.

'You've got me all wrong,' she wheedled defensively, her head held high but her voice suddenly faltering on the cusp of a stammer, 'I'm hon . . . I'm honestly *really* only out shopping.'

It was barely 8 a.m. A pale and freezing January morning on Canvey Island.

Outside the distant fog horns blew, like huge metal heifers howling and wailing in an eerily undefined bovine agony.

Don't follow him.

Two

Broad as the whole wide ocean, I,
Empty as the darkest sky,
False as an unconvincing lie,
Invisible as thin air.
Others found me in the sweet hereafter –
Look hard,
Look harder,
You'll find me there.

'Behindlings.'

Arthur Young spoke this word quietly in his thin but rather distinctive pebble dash voice, and then abruptly stopped walking.

His companion (who was strolling directly behind him) veered sharply sideways to avoid a collision. But although he executed this sudden manoeuvre with considerable agility, he still managed to clip Arthur's scrawny shoulder as he crashed on by.

'What did you just say?'

He hurtled around to face him, slightly exasperated, his arms still flapping with the remaining impetus of their former momentum. Arthur stood silently, his eyes unfocussed, massaging his bony shoulder with a still-bonier hand, frowning. He was apparently deep in thought.

They were pretending to hike through Epping Forest together, but they weren't fooling anybody. A local woman walking a recalcitrant basset had already turned her head to stare after them, curiously. And a well-muscled young man on a mountain bike had peered at them intently through his steamed-up goggles.

'That's the special name he invented for the people who follow him,' Arthur finally elucidated. 'He calls them *Behindlings*.'

After a second almost indecently lengthy pause he added, 'We've actually been walking for almost an hour now . . .' he tentatively adjusted his baseball cap, 'and whether you choose to believe it or not,' he continued tiredly, his gentle throat chafing and rasping like a tiny, fleshy sandblaster, 'I'm really quite . . . I'm honestly quite *weary*.'

His companion – a portly but vigorous gentleman who was himself sweating copiously inside his inappropriately formal bright white shirt and navy blue blazer – also paused for a moment, pushed back his shoulders, and then slowly drew a deep and luxurious lungful of air.

He looked Arthur up and down. His eyes were as bold, bright and full of fight as a territorial robin's, but his overall *expression* – while indisputably combative, perhaps even a touch contemptuous – was not entirely devoid of charity.

That said, his immediate and instinctive physical assessment of the strangely angular yet disturbingly languid creature who stood so quietly and pliantly before him (speckled as a thrush by tiny shafts of morning light pinpricking through the dark embroidery of the thick forest canopy), plainly didn't inspire him to improve his long-term, critical evaluation one iota.

Arthur. Thin. Gaunt. Frayed at his edges; on his cuffs, at his collar. Wearing good but old clothes: nothing too remarkable, at first glance . . . Well, nothing, perhaps, apart from an ancient brown leather waistcoat (carefully hidden away under his water-proof jacket) with rotting seams and bald patches, a strange, waxy garment which effortlessly conjured up entire spools of disparate images: visions of a primitive world; the sweet, mulish stink of the traditional farmhand, the implacable fire and sulk of the Leveller, the fierce piety of the knight, the rich, meaty righteousness of Cromwell.

It was a curious thing. Ancient. Aromatic. Romantic. Almost a museum-piece.

Although superficially loose-limbed and listless, Arthur was actually exceedingly precise in both his movements and his manner. He was gentle but absolute. He was unforgiving. His mouth was unforgiving. The deep furrows from his nose to the corners of his lips were unforgiving. His hair – trapped under an old, plain, khaki-coloured baseball cap – was thinning. His skin was tight. They had not walked quickly but he seemed exhausted. *Shrivelled.*

They inhabited entirely different worlds. His companion was ripe and unctuous; as grand and imposing as a high-class, three-tiered wedding cake. And although – in view of his recent exertions – his icing had a slight tinge of parboiledness about it, he remained, nevertheless, disconcertingly well-configurated.

After a moment he drew a clean cotton handkerchief from his blazer pocket, mopped his brow and then exhaled heartily. For some reason he seemed inexplicably enlivened by Arthur's frailty. Buoyed-up by it.

'So you finally stopped drinking?' he asked.

Arthur twitched, then smiled, uneasily, 'Yes. I finally stopped.'

'And your family? Your wife?'

Arthur glanced up into the sky. It was a cold, clear day. It was midwinter. Everything was icy. His lips. His teeth. His fingertips.

'I never married.'

His companion frowned. This was not the answer he'd anticipated. He'd imagined he knew everything he needed to know about Arthur. He'd investigated. He'd peeked, poked, connived, wheedled. The rest – the polite enquiries, the stilted conversation, the walk, even – was little more than mere etiquette. He continued to inspect Arthur closely – yet now just a fraction more aggressively – with his hard, round eyes.

'There was something in your background . . .' he began slowly, carefully unfastening his blazer, 'which I never knew before, and it was something which absolutely *intrigued* me.'

'Really?' Arthur was unimpressed but he was nervous, and nerves alone rendered him obliging. As he spoke, he noted – with a sudden feeling of inexplicable dismay – how his companion's plump thumbnail was split down its centre. Sharply. Cleanly. Cracked open like a germinating seed.

9

'I did a little nosing around. It appears you once had a famous relative who wrote a book about walking. Or farming . . .'

'Both,' Arthur sounded off-kilter, 'a very ancient, very distant relative.'

He tried to make it sound insignificant.

'Well I found it fascinating. And you have his name?'

'Yes. But that's just a coincidence. My parents had no particular interest in either history or travel.'

Arthur cleared his throat nervously, then tried his utmost to change the drift of their conversation by suddenly peering over his shoulder and into the undergrowth, as if to imply that something infinitely more engaging might be silently unfolding, right there, just behind them, partially hidden inside that deep and unwelcoming curtain of winter green. Perhaps a badger might be passing. Or a woodpecker – lesser-spotted – undulating gracefully through the boughs just above them.

It didn't work.

'Your father . . .' his companion paused, as if temporarily struggling to remember the details, 'I believe he was a foreman with Fords at Dagenham?'

Arthur nodded, mutely, closely scrutinizing his own middle and index fingers. He wished there was a cigarette snuggled gently between them. He would kiss it.

'And your mother worked on the cold meats counter in the Co-op . . . But you did. You had an interest.' Almost imperceptibly, his companion's mellifluous voice had grown much flatter, and was now maintaining a casual but curiously intimidating monotone. 'Which was why you attended agricultural college in the early seventies, before undertaking what, in retrospect, might've seemed a slightly ambitious attempt to retrace the exact footsteps of the original Arthur Young, but a whole . . . now what would it be, exactly . . . ? A whole *two hundred* years later.'

Arthur said nothing. What might he add? The forest shouldered in darkly around him. A short distance away he thought he could hear horses. His companion noticed something too. He glanced off to his left, sharply.

'They're on an adjacent track,' Arthur murmured, cocking his head for a moment then walking to the edge of the path and sitting down on a wide, clean, newly-cut tree-stump. His companion remained standing, as before.

'So I *retraced*,' Arthur eventually volunteered, and not without some small hint of bile, 'I re-visited, I re-appraised. I intended to publish a book, but things didn't quite pan out. I found myself working for a London bank, and then, like you, in the confectionery industry. It wasn't . . .' he had the good grace to shrug apologetically, 'a particularly *sweet* experience. I encountered some . . .' he stumbled, 'a *portion* of bad luck. I became unwell. *Unfit*. I received a pension. I still receive it. And you . . .' he struggled to enlarge his focus, 'you probably got promoted after I left?'

'Yes. I had your old job in marketing for a while. Then I moved up a level.'

Arthur nodded. He inspected his hands again. They were looking – he had to admit it – just a little shaky.

'If you don't mind my saying so,' his companion suddenly observed, his voice worryingly moss-lined and springy, 'you got your breath back awfully quickly, for such an avowedly *unfit* man.'

'What?' Arthur's sharp chin shot skywards a few seconds after he spoke, in a slightly farcical delayed reaction. His companion chuckled, 'I'm not here about the *pension*, silly . . .'

His fastidious tone made Arthur feel grubby. It was a nasty feeling, but extremely familiar.

'Apparently,' the glare of his companion's hard smile continued unabated, 'you sometimes like to walk distances of up to two hundred and fifty miles during an average seven day span. Although last week, for some reason, you only clocked eighty-nine.'

Arthur was silent. In the weak morning light his sunken jowls glimmered like the writhing grey flanks of a well-hooked bream. The truth engulfed him.

'Can you guess what it is that really gives you away?'

Arthur didn't speak. He didn't move. He couldn't. He was a neatly snapped twig. He sat, rigid, hardly breathing, blankly appraising his several scattered parts from some crazily random yet inconceivably distant vantage point. From a cloud. From a swift's eye.

'Your *shoes*. High quality walking boots. Well worn to the extent that any moderately inquisitive person might easily find themselves wondering why it could be that a man claiming long-term disability allowance should be wearing such fine, strong, functional footwear.'

'I was given them,' Arthur whispered.

'No,' his companion interjected calmly, 'you have a private deal with a large shoe manufacturer. I believe the formal term is *sponsorship*.'

Arthur gazed down at his boots. He could smell his own guilt as patently as the shrill tang of disinfectant bleeding from the pine needles crushed under his soles.

'Which was actually rather . . .' his companion pondered for a moment, 'rather *audacious* on your part, come to think of it.'

Arthur considered this. He considered the word. *Audacious*. He paused. *Audacious*. Yes. He drew a deep breath. His back straightened. His chin lifted again. He stopped pretending.

'So,' he said, his voice hardening, 'does moving up a level – I believe those were your words – does moving up mean that you're to be held wholly responsible for that boy drowning recently?'

His companion stiffened; his beam faded. 'He wasn't a *boy*. He was twenty-eight *bloody* years old. Don't you read the papers?'

Arthur shrugged. He looked down, modestly, his insides warming. His companion walked to the opposite side of the path, leaned against a Scots Pine and then peered up tentatively into its branches, as if expecting to see a wild little monkey dangling among its boughs.

Arthur strung his fingers together. His confidence burgeoned.

'I did read the papers,' he muttered eventually, but without any hint of brashness, 'I read about the Treasure Hunt. I followed the clues.'

'*No*,' his companion interjected, unable to help himself. 'No. Not a Treasure Hunt exactly . . .'

'Oh God. But how . . . how *imprecise* of me,' Arthur's mean lips suddenly served up the thinnest of grins, 'and how *stupid*. Of course not. You called it a Loiter, didn't you? A *Loiter*,' Arthur unstrung his fingers and then hung them, instead, slack and loose between his bony thighs, 'because our good friend Wesley invents special words for things, doesn't he? He thinks words *make* things special.

He wants every action to be particular, to be . . . to be individual in some way. And you know what?'

No time for a response; Arthur rushed on, regardless, 'I honestly – I mean I *honestly* – believe that Wesley is actually self-obsessed and arrogant and *vain* . . . and *vain* . . .' Arthur lunged after this word hungrily, and when his mouth finally caught up with it, his tongue literally wriggled with the physical pleasure it accorded him, 'and *vainglorious* enough to seriously think that this curiously irritating custom of his – this silly habit, this novel facility – gives him some kind of special premium on originality. Not just that, either, but on . . . but on *morality* itself, even . . . You know? Some kind of God-given . . . some kind of . . .'

Arthur's fingers were now twitching so violently as he struggled, a second time – and failed, quite notably – to find the word he was searching for, that he actually looked as if he was playing scales on an invisible *Steinway* (right there, in the forest), or practising something impossibly fast and fiddly by Liszt or Stravinsky.

And while he continued to grasp – helplessly – for this infernal word that evaded him so absolutely, his eyes – previously glazed and grey – seemed to moisten and widen (their pupils dilating), his cheeks (previously sallow and sunken) grew ripe as sugared plums in an autumnal pudding (a crumble, a fool, something tart, something hot, something sticky), until he looked like a man who'd swallowed down a large lump of gristle much too quickly – without chewing properly.

But Arthur was still breathing. He was not halted or suffocated or silenced by what was happening. He was still vital. He was still active and still functioning. If anything, he'd been *galvanised*. He'd been enlivened. He'd been pinched – slapped – spanked – thrashed by an intoxicatingly hard *whack* of righteous propriety. An exquisitely addictive, high-minded, bare-fisted, low-church-style sanctimony. His rage was not only pious, it was borderline *biblical* – it was Abraham's wife Rachel, trapped, temporarily, in a violently impotent maternal frenzy.

Arthur's companion (still leaning against his tree), observed Arthur's long, lean fingers racing, the deep colour in his cheeks – his lips – and a tiny quirk of satisfaction began to lift his brow a way. Yet before it was completely risen, before it could settle, unequivocally, Arthur's fingers abruptly stopped their fluttering. They fell back between his knees again. He suddenly grew still, the colour draining from his face – at speed – as if somehow repenting the too sensual flush of its former flowering.

'The sad truth of the matter . . .' finally his voice re-emerged from the icy depths of his sudden stasis, 'the sad truth is that Wesley's been brainwashed by his own publicity. Brainwashed to the point that he actually, honestly believes in all that rubbish he's been spooning out over the years. All the lies. All the humbug. All the ridiculous *chic . . . chic . . . chicanery.*'

Arthur stumbled, quietly, on his final delivery. But even this stutter couldn't trip him up. It couldn't silence him. Not utterly.

'The bald truth is that he's watched too much bad TV,' Arthur spoke almost regretfully, inhaling again, eventually, with some difficulty. 'Yes. That, and he's been lucky. He's landed on his feet a few times when by rights he shouldn't have. He's milked his opportunities. And finally, to top it all off, he's jumped – and so . . . so *wholeheartedly*, with such flagrant, such obvious, such embarrassing *rapaciousness* – onto this whole, madly convoluted, New Age environmental bandwagon. All that ludicrously pat *Third Wave* jumble. All that Alvin Toffler "Small is Beautiful" crap.'

Arthur sniffed, somewhat haughtily, 'I mean it's all been very timely. No point denying it. And he's certainly taken the opportunity to read up on a little bit of pretentious French philosophy. He's sharpened his act. He's honed it. And I'm sure . . .' Arthur's voice was growing louder, his hands were picking up tempo again, were playing again – *The Death March* now, real-time, then double-time, then just plain madly, 'I'm certain he thinks he's a thoroughly modern hero. Like something from Rousseau. Or Nietzsche. Or, better still, an *anti*-hero. In fact I'm positive he thinks he's a genius. And there are plenty of fools out there more than happy to go along with his delusions. But not me. I'm not one of them. Because he *isn't* a genius, and I'll keep on saying it. He isn't a genius. Far from it. He's puerile. He's a shithead and a fathead and a peacock. He's . . . He's . . .'

Arthur stopped again, mid-flow, swallowed hard, twice, as if to keep something down, to push it back, ripped off his baseball cap (as if longing to keep his fingers distracted) and then continued talking, but glancing up now; connecting, engaging, projecting, speaking more carefully, more plainly, 'A *Loiter*,' he rotated his cap in his hand, pulling gently at the lining, as if testing its solidity. 'It's a movement – a violation, of sorts – but slow and calm and casual. It's an *invasion*, isn't it? Or an infringement? A trespass. It's slippery. It's untrustworthy. It's stupid and it's pointless. In actual fact it's just like . . . it's *just like* Wesley. It expresses him perfectly.'

Arthur shook his head, slowly, as if in wonder, 'A *Loiter*.' He rolled the word around on his tongue, 'It's actually quite pathetic, when you really come to think about it. It's unformed. It's adolescent . . . And yet,' he looked up, keenly, 'didn't the company end up adopting the phrase? Didn't *you* adopt it, I mean *personally*?'

Arthur's companion grimaced, as if taken aback by his pointed ferocity, but then he shrugged, 'We might've used it in the initial publicity, for a price, but – and let me emphasise this fact quite categorically – in this particular context it had nothing *whatsoever* to do with either mischief or risk. That was our proviso. And obviously there had to be a worthwhile prize at the end of it all, an incentive, a reward . . .'

'So you called in Wesley,' Arthur, in turn – even against his better judgement – seemed drawn into himself again, 'a man infamous as a prankster, as a joker. An out-and-out wildcard. Someone with enough of a reputation for piss-taking to make your average level-headed businessman run a mile. Which – oh dear God – *inevitably*, from your corner, must've made the whole deal feel so shocking, so seductive, so exquisitely . . . well, *transgressive*.'

'Yes. We called him in,' his companion quickly interrupted Arthur's unhelpful little river of adjectives, as if in the vain hope of somehow re-routeing it, 'and initially – I'll make no bones about it – to start off with, at least, it *did* all feel rather . . .' he paused, nearly sneering, 'rather *audacious*. Yes. So we called him in. And eventually – with a little prompting, obviously – he came.'

Arthur didn't have to try too hard to picture it. 'At first . . .' he placed his cap onto his knee and scratched at his prickly, wheat-coloured chin, 'knowing Wesley – I mean his *type* – he was probably fairly reticent. You presumably had your work cut out in persuading him. But you obviously,' he smiled tightly, 'you patently rose to the challenge.'

His companion simply shrugged his aquiescence.

'And in so doing,' Arthur continued, barely restraining his anger at the very notion, 'I can only suppose that you told him . . .' he held up his hands and counted off each of the virtues he subsequently listed, one by one, on his bony fingers, 'how much you admired his boldness, his imagination, his *integrity*, his amazing knack for acquiring publicity. And of course he has his followers – a large and wonderfully gullible ready-made assembly . . .'

'Of course. The Behindlings.'

'And if I know Wesley . . .' again, Arthur was forced to qualify himself, 'I mean if I *did* know him, I imagine he would probably have demanded complete control. Absolute autonomy. Because only Wesley can hold the reins.'

'So we hand them over,' his companion continued, amiably, 'we give him his autonomy. We let him work out a route, prepare clues . . .'

'And it's all terribly secretive.'

'Terribly.'

'But then two short weeks after you release the third clue . . .'

'Yes.'

Suddenly his companion's bold voice wavered, just a fraction, 'Yes. The drowning.'

Silence.

'*Fantastic!*'

Arthur clapped his hands. They flew together so rapidly, so violently, that they knocked his cap clean off his knee. But he didn't seem to have noticed. His eyes were moist. His cheeks were taut. For the first time during their lengthy meeting he seemed deeply and unreservedly happy.

'If you don't mind my saying so,' his companion muttered thickly, 'that's a somewhat insensitive choice of word, under the circumstances.'

'I know,' Arthur looked momentarily abashed, 'forgive me.'

'Forgive you?' His companion smiled, cheerlessly, '*Why?* You hate him. And it's a perfectly natural reaction.'

Arthur started, looked slightly surprised, and then, seconds later, almost guileful, 'Me? Why should I hate him? I've never even met Wesley.'

His companion snorted. 'There's a *history*,' he said, 'why the hell else would I be standing here today?'

Arthur said nothing. He was unhappy again. Deflated. Some things were unmentionable. Histories, especially. 'So he hurt somebody I knew once,' he offered, finally, 'that's all. It was only carelessness. And it was a long time ago.'

'Of course. A very long time. And you probably might prefer to try and forget all about it . . .' Arthur's eyes flared. To *forget?* How could he? 'But I'm afraid,' his companion's rich voice dropped, effortlessly, to almost a murmur, 'that's not quite what I'm anticipating.'

'Why not?' Arthur spoke normally, but the question reverberated on the quiet, tree-lined path with an almost unnatural clarity, sending up a blackbird from a low branch behind him. The bird chattered its fury.

'Why not?' His companion's eyes followed the angry bird. 'Because lately I've become the unwilling recipient of a certain amount of . . .' he paused, '*pressure*. From colleagues who aren't at all happy about how things have been panning out – with Wesley – with the Loiter. Perhaps they feel, in retrospect, that Wesley was a rather poor bet. These are people – as I'm sure you can imagine – who don't at all value adverse publicity.'

Arthur grimaced. He did not need to imagine. He knew these people. Their complacency. Their serenity. Their *ease*. He loathed them.

'So I've come under a certain amount of pressure . . .' as his companion spoke he left the shelter of his tree, drew slightly closer to Arthur, then closer still, 'and naturally, after a while, it seemed expedient to diffuse this pressure by contacting a man who had a history with the company, a man who might reasonably be said to have had a history with Wesley, a man with a grudge, an *unfit* man. I resolved to contact this man in order to quietly suggest that he might conveniently decide to renew his interest.'

'And if he doesn't?' Arthur's voice sounded flimsy. This was not a good question. Even he could sense it.

'If he doesn't? Well, then I suppose I might be tempted to make certain *discrepancies*, certain *inconsistencies* in his very private life a matter of more public concern.'

17

Arthur was scowling. But he said nothing.

'Okay . . .' his companion suddenly crouched down before him, his knees groaning and creaking like a brand new, high-polished leather saddle, 'you don't need to know everything, but what you *do* need to know is that Wesley was entrusted with something very valuable. For obvious reasons I cannot tell you what that thing was. And yes, while he did relate certain strategic points on the Loiter to a small group of us, and provided us with some basic outlines of his general intentions, he by no means told us everything.

'The final clue, as you probably already know, was announced only three weeks ago, after a certain amount of procrastination. At first we'd considered cancelling the whole thing – as a tribute to the dead man, as an apology – but then the father became involved. The old boy. The scaffolder. You'll have seen him in the papers.'

Arthur nodded. Yes. He'd seen the old man.

'So press attention at that point was obviously intense. It still is. But we were handling it. Unfortunately, Wesley then decided to raise the stakes. He broke off all communications with the company. He grew uncooperative. Three days ago he travelled to Canvey . . .'

Arthur clucked, shrewdly, 'Ah. *Candy* Island. Daniel Defoe. The first clue.'

His companion shrugged this off boredly. 'Of course. It's a very famous linguistic corruption. But that's not what concerns you. What concerns you is that I have recently developed some misgivings about Wesley's intentions. His motivations. His reliability. In short, I have stopped trusting him.'

Arthur sniffed, dismissively, then touched the cuff of his coat to the tip of his nose. A small droplet darkened its khaki. 'If you suspect fraud you could have him arrested.'

'Oh yes, before some poor, deluded fool went and killed himself, very possibly. But now it's much too fucked up. It's too complicated.'

Arthur still seemed befuddled.

'I need you to help me,' his companion continued, 'I need you to . . . to *involve* yourself in some way. I'm surrounding him. I'll need information. You'll have to be circumspect. My ultimate

18

ambition is to defuse the situation. I need to understand it. I need to distract Wesley. To . . . to *debilitate* him.'

He paused for a moment, then continued on again, silkily, 'Naturally, you're not the only person I'm involving. There will be others. They will know different things, but they won't know everything. Overall, my intention, my *need*, is to distance the company from the drowned man, from the old boy, and, ultimately, from Wesley. To keep things *clean*.'

Arthur was silent. But his mind was working.

His companion watched him, benignly. 'Here's some advice for you,' he whispered, 'I know about the history. I also know that you're screwing countless different sources for money. I know why. I *understand*. And if you help me I will ensure that nobody finds out. And I mean *nobody*. I will do things for you,' he paused, 'but if you go to the papers, if you act indiscreetly, there's sufficient ill-feeling between you and Wesley for me to manipulate that and to use it against you. At this particular point we have no way of knowing what it is exactly that Wesley's planning . . .'

Arthur's eyebrows rose. 'Perhaps he's not planning anything. Perhaps he's just . . . just . . .' he struggled, 'just plain *mooching*. Have you even considered that possibility?'

His companion nodded, unmoved by Arthur's cynicism. 'Of course we have. But it's unlikely. This is *Wesley*, after all.'

Out of the blue, he swung himself forward and moved his two lips right up close to Arthur's ear. 'The air around you,' he whispered gently, 'it smells of death. Hospitals. Disinfectant. Why? Who is responsible? Will you tell? Will you enlighten me?'

Arthur stiffened. He struggled to stop his hands from trembling. It was just a misunderstanding, that was all. Eventually his companion pulled away again and the warmth of his breath – on Arthur's cheek, his ear – transformed, gradually, into something quite different; a thing no less intimate, but cool now, and lingering.

Arthur sat and watched quietly as he stood up, slowly, pushing his hands onto his knees for leverage. Those strangely vocal knees, Arthur thought, and listened to them protesting. Perhaps he had room to protest himself? But he did not.

Instead, he remained mute, sucking his tongue and staring

dumbly ahead of him, down the path, into the distance. He could not bring himself to speak again. It was simply not necessary. His mouth was so thick and full now with the taste of Wesley.

Three

'What you did back then was unforgivable. It was mean, it was self-ish, it was thoughtless, it was just . . . it was just plain *wrong.*'

The man who spoke these stern words – his name was Ted, and he was a fresh-faced but avuncular small town estate agent – did so without the slightest hint, the slightest note, the slightest *tremble* of disapproval in his voice. His absolute lack of ire was not merely striking; it teetered, it lurched, it practically tumbled head first into the realm of remarkable.

Wesley, to whom this speech had been principally directed (but who didn't appear to have digested a word of it), acknowledged as much – internally – as he swung himself from left to right on an ancient and creaking swivel chair in Ted's Canvey High Street office. He was inspecting property details. He was considering renting.

'Which bad thing in particular?' he asked idly. There were so many bad things.

'*Which* thing? The Canvey thing. In the book. The Katherine Turpin thing.'

Wesley stopped swivelling and glanced up. 'What? In the walks book? All the stuff about perimeters? That was years ago.'

He liked this man. Ted. He liked his wide mouth, his charming effervescence, his loopy sincerity, his almost-silliness. Wesley appraised Ted's thick lips as they vibrated, like two fat, pink molluscs performing a shifty rhumba.

'Two years ago. Twenty-seven months, if you want to be precise about it,' Ted calculated amicably.

'Two years? Fuck. Is that *all*?'

21

Wesley frowned – as if this was a vexatious detail that had not previously occurred to him – while Ted waved to a passer-by through the agency's large, exquisitely high-polished picture window. It was the third time he'd done so in as many minutes.

'You seem to know everybody around here,' Wesley observed drily, turning his head to peer outside, 'it must be very trying.'

'Trying? Why?' Ted didn't understand. 'I find people their homes. It's an essential . . . it's a *quint*-essential service.'

'I get your point,' Wesley puckered his lips slightly, to try and stop an inadvertent grin from sneaking out and plastering itself – with unapologetic candour – all over his mouth. Then, in a bid to distract Ted's attention, he suddenly pointed, 'There's a woman. Do you see her? Over in the Wimpy. Sitting in the window, directly opposite the Old Man.'

'The sun's in my eyes,' Ted squinted, then moved to the left a fraction. 'Ah . . . Yes. The one in the sweatshirt? Short hair? Eating a doughnut? Looks like a boy?'

'That's her.'

'Who is she?'

Wesley shrugged, 'I don't know. That's why I asked.'

He glanced around him, momentarily non-plussed. It was a neat office. Ted was neat. In fact he was immaculately presented. He wore a dark grey suit from Next, a spotless white shirt and a silk tie with an image of Sylvester the Cat spewed repeatedly in full technicolor onto a noxious, salmon pink background. His two shoes shone like heavily glacé'ed morello cherries.

'So . . . *Ted*, was it?'

Ted nodded.

'So Ted, are you the boss of this agency?'

Ted did a humourful double-take, 'Do I *look* like the boss?'

'I don't know. How does the boss look?'

'Different. Older. Shorter. Brown hair. Glasses. *Huge* moustache.'

Ted was a strawberry blond.

'I knew a man like you once,' Wesley observed, rather ominously, casually flipping through the sheets of property details again. 'He looked like you, had the same cheerful . . . no, *altruistic* notions. Always beautifully turned-out. Then one day he became fascinated by pigeons' feet, and that was the end of him.'

22

Ted tried to look unfazed by this strangely baroque influx of information. He almost succeeded.

'He'd travel around,' Wesley elucidated, 'catching stray pigeons and giving them pedicures. He made special splints from old lolly sticks. Eventually he even began constructing his own, tiny, perfectly executed false limbs. Somebody made a documentary about his work and tried to sell it to Channel 5, but I don't think they bought it. He was involved in radical causes. It frightened the shit out of them.'

Wesley glanced up. Ted was rubbing his clean-shaven jaw with his nimble fingers in such a way as to indicate a certain want of credulity. Wesley scowled, irritated. 'I'm perfectly serious. He simply couldn't abide the sight of a bird with a limp. He was mad about feet. Birds' feet. *Loathed* human feet, though. If you pulled off your socks in front of him he'd break out into a sweat. It was tragic.' Wesley gave the forefinger and thumb on his good hand a cursory lick to improve his turning power. 'Pigeons aren't indigenous to Britain,' he observed, helpfully, 'and that was his beef. His argument was that they were kept domestically, originally, but then they strayed or were abandoned. Yet somehow they were canny enough to adapt and survive. That was partly why he felt such a powerful connection with them. He was temporarily fostered himself as a kid . . .'

Wesley paused for a moment to inspect a particular sheet, frowned, then continued turning the pages, 'People think factory farming is a modern phenomenon, but pigeons were kept by the Romans in the fourth century BC inside these huge, airless towers. They had their legs broken and their wings clipped to prevent them from moving . . .', he cleared his throat. 'This friend of mine waged a campaign against lime-use. People put it on their windowsills. Extremely common in the 1970s. Very cruel. Melts the bird's toes . . .

'The point I'm making . . .' Wesley stopped leafing and paused for a minute, 'is that he was actually ridiculously *sensitive*, underneath all that other stuff. Underneath that thick layer of poise and helpfulness and affability . . .

'*Right*,' he passed Ted a sheet, 'this is the place.'

Ted took the sheet and glanced at it, his mind still fully occupied by images of lime and feet and feathers. After a few seconds, though, his eyes cleared and widened. He shook his head. He began to snigger, nervously. 'You *can't* be . . .' he managed eventually, shaking his head and trying vainly to hand the sheet back again.

Wesley scowled. He would not take it. 'What's so funny?'

Ted's mirth slowly evaporated. He stared intently at Wesley for a moment, struggling to tell if he was sincere. But he couldn't tell. Wesley's expression was completely unreadable. He was a human hieroglyphic.

'This is *her* house,' Ted said, finally. 'She's renting out the spare bedroom. Shared use of bathroom and kitchen facilities. I'm only handling it as a personal favour.'

'Whose house?' Wesley sounded perfectly innocent. Benign. Casual.

'*Whose* house?' he repeated, after a pause.

Ted pointed at the printed details: 'This is Katherine Turpin's house. This is the house of the local woman whose life you ruined.'

A short silence followed, punctuated, briefly, by Wesley's stomach rumbling.

'Blow me,' Wesley finally expostulated (almost convincingly), 'that's some crazy coincidence. I suppose we'd better go and take a look, then, hadn't we?'

He stood up. Ted didn't move a muscle.

'Take me there,' Wesley ordered, reaching over to grab Ted's jacket from the back of his chair, bundling it up into a compact ball, and throwing it at him.

'You don't know me . . .' Josephine said, squeezing her way between the plastic bench and its table.

'I *don't* know you,' Doc affirmed, not even looking up at her, but applying all his energy to dissolving the foam on his coffee by stirring at it vigorously with the back end of a knife. The foam wouldn't dissolve though. Too dense. Too soapy.

He was occupying a window kiosk in the Wimpy. Dennis sat outside, tied to a lamppost, his snout pushed mournfully against the glass, his breath steaming up the window in small, cloudy patches.

'My name's Josephine,' she said, sitting down.

'Why all this foam?' Doc muttered, not anticipating an answer.

'That's a cappuccino. I believe it's prepared with frothy milk.'

Doc finally glanced up and inspected Josephine. He frowned slightly. He couldn't pretend to understand this irritating modern phenomenon of girls who dressed like boys. Did it mean she hated men? Was she sexually deviant? Was she frigid? Was she frightened? Was she predatory? Either way, she made him feel old and alienated and uneasy.

'Who made *you* an authority?' he asked curtly.

Josephine didn't respond at once. First, she picked up a napkin and neatly turned over each of its four corners – double-checking the sharpness of the fold, in each instance.

'I'm hardly an authority,' she murmured, unfolding the napkin again, smoothing it out with the flat of her palm and then shoving it away. Doc ignored her fidgetings. He occupied himself instead by staring out of the window and over the road towards the estate agency.

'Do you think he's only after information,' Josephine queried, leaning forward, pushing both elbows onto the table, cupping her neat chin inside her two immaculately clean hands (her short, white nails thin as ten tight crescent moons; bright as albumen) and glancing over herself, 'or do you reckon he might actually be planning to stay here awhile?'

Doc took a quick sip of his coffee. It was hot. He cursed under his breath and hastily put the cup down again.

'I bought your dog a doughnut,' Josephine said, indicating towards the paper bag she'd been holding, already dark with grease stains, 'I hope you don't mind.'

'He's diabetic,' Doc growled, clumsily wiping away his foam moustache with the back of his hand and then staring, bemusedly, at the remaining slick of cocoa-splattered residue, like it was some kind of toxic extra-terrestrial slop.

'A diabetic? Really?'

Doc – still refusing formal eye contact – gritted his teeth and then muttered gutturally through them, 'I hardly think it'd be worth my while to lie about such a thing.'

25

'No.'

Josephine frowned and leaned back, somewhat unnerved by Doc's pugnacity. She grabbed hold of the offending bag, removed a doughnut from inside (glancing, guiltily, towards the service counter), then sat and stared at it.

'It's shaped like a man,' she observed, biting off both of its arms in quick succession.

Doc didn't respond. He was concentrating on the estate agency again. Inside he thought he could see Wesley standing up and throwing something. He roughly pushed his cup aside (the coffee pitched then spilled, still steaming, into its saucer), fastened a couple of buttons on his cardigan, grabbed his oilskin jacket from the bench beside him, and clambered to his feet.

But before he beat his hasty retreat, Doc paused – almost regretfully – shifting his weight heavily from his bad leg to his better leg like a small child anxiously queuing to collect his Good Conduct certificate at school assembly.

'Look,' he spoke quickly, his voice – Josephine noticed – fractionally less abrasive than it had been previously, 'I've made it my business to follow Wesley for well over three and a half years now,' Doc inadvertently clenched then unclenched his left fist as he spoke, testing the joints for any hint of arthritic stiffening, 'and what I want you to understand . . .' his bleary brown eyes were already focussing beyond Josephine, out of the window, over the road, 'what I *need* you to understand is that for me this isn't just a game or a hobby. It's actually like a kind of . . .' he paused, struggling, his eyes briefly flickering towards the ceiling, 'a kind of *pilgrimage*.'

Still he wasn't satisfied, 'A way of *life*, if you will . . .'

He scowled, temporarily incapable of encompassing the complex landscape of his emotions verbally of fully *encapsulating* The Following and all its myriad implications.

'I truly, fully appreciate the depth of your commitment,' Josephine butted in, quickly snatching her opportunity, trying her utmost to sound sufficiently submissive, 'I mean I know you're quite the expert . . .'

'There are some people,' Doc rapidly continued, almost as if he hadn't heard her, 'who have Followed him even longer than I have, in terms of actual years, but none so intensively. There are many – especially since the big confectionery Loiter – who Follow him mostly at the weekends or perhaps for a day or two when they're on holiday, and others who simply turn up, at the drop of a hat, whenever the fancy takes them. We call these people,' Doc allowed himself a wry smile, 'we call such people *Fleas*, because their . . . because their *infestation* is almost always very temporary.'

Josephine inspected her armless sundry – a rather unwieldy wodge of dough still tucked inside her cheek – all too fully aware of which horribly capricious category Doc had already slotted her into.

'You see, to me, as yet,' Doc observed, pushing home his point rather more blatantly than was necessary, 'you are just another one of those people. Those Fleas. And while I would hate you to take this the wrong way, *Josephine* . . .'

(Her name. He'd remembered. He'd snatched it from the ether, quite arbitrarily.)

'. . . I'd much prefer it if you'd refrain from questioning me or talking to me, bothering me or pestering me. Because any information I may have gathered is *my* information. I have worked for it. I have *earned* it. I use it as I see fit. I don't . . .' he thought hard about the word he needed, 'disseminate. I do not disseminate it,' he paused. 'Well, I do, sometimes, but only when I want to, when I choose to,' he smiled briskly (old teeth. Yellow teeth. Wonky). 'I hope that settles things.'

The smile stopped (Doc turned it off in a flash – with a small click in his jaw – like the neat switch on a wall-socket) then he nodded abruptly and strode to the door.

Outside, Dennis dashed joyously forward until his elasticated leash stretched to capacity – like a horizontal bungee – and jerked him – ears flying, claws scrabbling comically – all the way back again.

Inside, Josephine grimaced, swallowed her cheekful of masticated doughnut, then savagely bit off the head from what remained of the torso.

'You miserable old *bugger*,' she muttered, her mouth still full, but a careful hand gently shielding it, for the sake of propriety.

As she spoke, dark raspberry jam slowly oozed through one of the now-truncated armholes and trickled down stickily onto the front of her sweatshirt. She didn't notice. Her wide hazel eyes were already swivelling, expertly, across the road, and fixing, hungrily, on the estate agency. There she saw the door swinging open, a blond man in a suit emerging, and just behind him, Wesley.

Four

The beautiful yet unspeakably wronged Katherine Turpin lived in a
bungalow just off the Furtherwick Road; a prime, centrally located
Canvey address which conveniently situated the property at an
exact halfway point between the town centre and the beachfront.
Ted might easily have shared these salient details with Wesley as
they covered the short distance together – on foot – between the
agency and the address, yet for some reason he refrained from
doing so.

In fact he failed to communicate even the most perfunctory of
observations during their journey (no mention of the weather – it
was foggy but still dry – no reference to the purported length of
Wesley's stay – as yet, indeterminate – no discussion as to the
quality of local amenities – uniformly high) preferring, instead, to
maintain an unswervingly ruminative silence.

Wesley tried his utmost to breach it, but to no avail. Twice
he reiterated a rather tedious enquiry about the opening hours of
the local library and its location relative to the property under
scrutiny. Twice his question was left hovering in the air like
an undernourished kestrel hopelessly scouring the scant grass
of a busy central reservation whilst being perilously buffeted by
speeding heavy goods vehicles.

This relentless taciturnity was in no way intended to imply
either indifference or any want of geniality on Ted's part. He
certainly meant no harm by it. He was simply in a temporary
state of absolute moral panic. His mind was unsuccessfully engaged
in a pitiful attempt to comprehend the various pernicious ethical
permutations of his present situation: the countless obligations

and commitments inherent in his role, his *duty*, as the honourable curator, the careful doorman, the kindly overseer of Katherine Turpin's home.

But even while his mind strove to consider the endless tortuous ramifications of his present inadvisable course of action, he still managed to maintain an image of external composure by dint of persistently jangling a huge bunch of house keys in his free hand, and feeling – if only briefly – just slightly comforted by their hair-raisingly discordant metallic clatter (the other hand, meanwhile, supported a very snappy, imitation crocodile-skin briefcase, containing, Wesley suspected – and correctly – nothing more than Ted's driving licence, a free handout about a carpet sale and two back copies of *The Southend Gazette*).

Perhaps, Ted pondered anxiously, this infamous Wesley truly was a bad man? *But who the hell am I to judge?* he countered modestly, shooting a sneaky sideways glance at him. Wesley did not have an especially bad face. His profile (already scarred – perhaps permanently – by the ongoing assault on his delicate senses from Ted's relentless key-shaking) was nevertheless reassuringly unhawkish, his skin unpocked, his eyes unhooded. He seemed at once friendly and unaffected but hearteningly reined-in. He was surely no wild man.

Clever? Possibly. Smart? Never. Physically speaking he bordered on the unkempt. He was rangy and casual in his old, olive green corduroy trousers (so well-scuffed at the knee that the fabric's corrugated indentations had been smoothed clean away), a terrifyingly plain – in Ted's eyes – brown, roundnecked lambswool jumper, with a cheap, scruffy, tweed jacket thrown over the top.

Each of his pockets was ridiculously full. They bulged, uniformly, reminding Ted – in essence – of his old school gerbil, a creature so dedicated to storage that the fullness of his pouches often rendered spells inside his compact mouse-house or runs on his exercise wheel an absolute inviability.

Wesley did not even wear walking boots (as Ted might quite reasonably have anticipated of a man in his line of business), but instead sported an exceedingly dirty pair of ancient black Hi-Tecs, the laces of which were knotted, frayed and extended to only two thirds of the available holes.

He was a sorry sight, Ted decided, but he did have a pleasingly round face: gappy teeth, snub nose, keen but bloodshot (and strangely unfocussed) anchovy-paste eyes. He needed a shave. He looked like he'd never troubled to brush his hair in his life. To the front it seemed fine, but at the back it stood up in a sleepy ridge like a misshapen muddy-brown tidal-wave.

A confident woman with a good vocabulary might easily have described his appearance as 'tousled', but Ted couldn't really find it in himself to be quite so articulate or so forgiving. He sniffed. Wesley smelled of old milk, dirty dishcloths and tobacco. The fruity kind.

'Will she be home by any chance?' Wesley wondered out loud as they finally turned into the driveway (at this late stage hardly anticipating a reaction).

'No,' an active, genial presence suddenly re-ignited inside Ted's eyes, 'she works.'

Wesley started, glanced over briefly towards Ted's newly-inhabited profile, then nodded. He felt almost relieved. He was finding some difficulty in recalling the *exact* details of what it was that he'd written about Katherine Turpin in the book – although there was one thing of which he was absolutely certain: whatever he'd said, it must've been necessary.

He had an unshakable confidence in the multifarious decisions made on his behalf by his former selves. How could a fundamentally decent and honourable man ever really seriously regret his past actions? How pointless would that be? How lily-livered? How inconsistent? How *slack*?

'She works,' Ted reiterated, 'growing beansprouts on a farm. But only part-time. I have a key.'

'A beansprout farm?' Wesley smiled caustically. 'How unique.'

Ted didn't respond. But he was deeply perturbed by Wesley's tone. Beansprouts? He pondered quietly, jangling his keys with a renewed determination. Beansprouts? *Unique*?

It was a pretty little property. A white bungalow, satisfyingly angular, with a small, friendly picket fence to the front, directly backed by a staunch and rather less welcoming row of well-tended shoulder-high evergreens. The garden was covered in a neat red-brick parquet. The overall effect was private, stately, and quite exquisitely anal.

'Grand,' Wesley said, peering around him intently. Ted stood on the doormat, struggling to locate the correct key. Wesley glanced behind them. The Old Man was following.

'You went to school here in Canvey, Ted?' Wesley asked.

Ted nodded, 'Furtherwick Park School. We just walked past it.'

'And what about her? What about Katherine?'

Ted finally selected a key. 'Yes. But she was two whole years older.'

'Two *whole* years?' Wesley grinned. 'Was she beautiful?'

'Not exactly,' Ted's cheeks flushed a sharp bullfinch pink as he turned towards the door and shoved the key into the lock.

Wesley had teeth like a pony. Indomitable teeth. Very gappy. Very square. Very strong.

'Did you have a crush on her?'

'Everybody liked her,' Ted mumbled, 'if that's what you're getting at.'

Wesley chuckled and then half-nodded his concurrence, although this was patently not what he'd intended by it at all.

He looked behind him again. The boy-woman had joined Murdoch on the opposite pavement. They stood a distance apart. Murdoch was holding a pager. He was tapping into it with his large, slightly arthritic middle finger. Wesley scowled. It seemed improbable that Doc should've already made the Katherine Turpin connection . . .

But if he had? Wesley's jaw stiffened at the thought. This possibility plainly jarred him.

Ted turned the lock, pushed the door, removed the key and entered.

'By the way,' he said, laboriously wiping his feet on a second doormat inside, 'I hope you don't have a problem with rodents.'

Wesley paused on the threshold and inhaled deeply. 'Sawdust . . .' he murmured, and then, just a fraction more quizzically, '*brandy* . . . ?'

'She keeps chinchillas,' Ted explained, 'in the lean-to behind the kitchen. I should've mentioned that back at the office.'

The bungalow's interior belied the neatness of its exterior. Where outside all had been cleanliness and order, inside, all was mess and mayhem.

'This woman is a slut,' Wesley observed, stepping carefully

over the doormat and calmly appraising the state of the hallway. 'Perhaps you should've specified that back at the office.'

'She's an artist,' Ted countered primly, slamming the door shut and then shoving a group of carrier bags up closer to the wall so that they could proceed unhindered. The bags clanked and tinkled. Wesley frowned. 'What kind?' he asked, bending over to peer inside one of them (it contained seven empty peach schnapps bottles). 'A *piss* artist?'

Ted merely growled, but not fiercely. It was the subterranean grumble of an old labrador in the middle of having his toenails clipped: sullen, irritable, mutinous even, but nothing serious. He led Wesley through a half-stripped pine door and into the living room.

'*Jeepers*,' Wesley immediately exclaimed, pushing a thumb down the neck of his jumper and yanking it outwards, 'it's *tropical* in here.'

He rotated his head with a quite startling, hawk-like facility, 'Does this woman have a different biological classification from the rest of us, Ted? Is she amphibian?'

Ted didn't bother responding. Instead he busied himself plumping up a couple of pillows on the sofa, minutely adjusting the stained antique embroidered throw on a chair.

'I'll certainly be keeping my eyes peeled,' Wesley continued, affecting an air of intense paranoia, 'for any suspicious grey scales on the bathroom floor . . . reinforced glass walls . . .' (he performed a dramatic trapped-forever-behind-a-glass-wall mime), 'those pathetic part-digested insect husks . . . the give-away imitation jungle-look paper back-drop . . .'

Ted carefully placed the second pillow back down onto the sofa. 'Underfloor heating,' he acquiesced stiffly. 'Costly to run but extremely effective.'

'Wow,' Wesley crouched down and touched one of the shiny black tiles with his fingers. It was warm. He kicked off his trainers and planted his stockinged feet firmly onto the floor.

'Oh I like it,' he said, 'this is wonderful. My toes have been numb since the New Year. I took a quick dip off Camber Sands for a bet. The sea was absolutely fucking *freezing*.'

'Your socks are steaming,' Ted frowned fastidiously.

'Damp,' Wesley smiled, moving around a little and enjoying the dark prints his feet elicited. While Ted watched on, he silently heel-toed a design onto the floor. A bad circle. A lop-sided splodge.

'So if that's Canvey,' he indicated towards the shape with a wide gesture of his arm, 'North . . . South . . . East . . . where would you say we are now, exactly?'

'Uh . . .' Ted walked to the southern-most tip, then marginally to the east of it, 'about there,' he said, 'approximately.'

'Where?'

Ted crouched down. 'About . . .' he pointed, 'although the industrial headland actually forms a slightly more exaggerated . . .'

He looked up. Wesley was no longer paying him any attention. He was peering around the room, absorbedly.

It was a large room; hot, yet airy. There was a bay window to the front swathed in heavy nets, but what remained of the watery Canvey sun still glimmered through in fine, silvery trickles. The room was crammed with *stuff* in industrial quantities. Every available surface was covered in practical detritus: glue, wire, beads, bags of sand . . .

Behind a huge, ancient, tiger-skin draped sofa (the big cat with its whole head still intact, eyes, teeth, everything) stood a workbench covered in a large mound of yellow-white, fibrous objects. Wesley moved towards them, 'What are these?'

Ted clambered to his feet again.

'Stones.'

Wesley picked one up. It was the approximate size and weight of a large mouse after a steam-rollering accident.

'From a mango,' Ted expanded, 'the furry stone from the middle of a mango.'

'Mango stones. *Ah.*'

Wesley stared at the stone closely.

'She gets them in bulk. I believe she has some kind of deal with a juice manufacturer in Kent . . .'

Ted was still speaking as the doorbell sounded. He jumped, guiltily, turning automatically towards the hallway.

'Hang on a minute,' Wesley moved over to the window and peered out from between the nets. After a couple of seconds he grunted, swatted a dismissive hand through the air and returned to the workbench. 'Relax,' he muttered, 'it's nothing.'

'Why? Who is it?'

Wesley picked up another mango stone. 'Nobody. Just some kid who follows me.'

The doorbell rang again, rather more insistently.

This time Ted went to the window and peered out.

'If he sees you looking he'll come over,' Wesley warned him, putting the mango stone up to his nose, inhaling. It smelled of old hay. Of wheat. Of corn dollies.

'*Damn*,' Ted quickly withdrew, 'I think he *did* see me . . .'

Sure enough, after a few seconds, the window was darkened by a small shadow, then a nose – pushed up hard against the glass – with two inquisitive hands pressed either side of it.

'Gracious,' Ted murmured, backing off still further, 'you weren't kidding.'

'Just ignore him,' Wesley counselled boredly, 'he'll go away eventually.'

'Who is he?' Ted was mesmerised.

'I already told you. Some kid.'

The right shadow-hand suddenly peeled itself away from the glass, formed itself into a tight fist, and began knocking.

'How do you know him?' Ted whispered.

'I don't,' Wesley shrugged, 'he just follows me around.'

'What's his name?'

'Pete. Patty. I can't remember.'

The knocking continued. It was loud and persistent yet maddeningly unrhythmical. After thirty seconds it grew mildly irritating, by fifty it was unbearable.

'I think he might be stepping on Katherine's hydrangea,' Ted stuttered.

'Then go out and yell at him.'

'Should I?' Ted looked appalled at the thought. 'Will he become aggressive?'

Wesley chuckled, 'No. He'll love it. He'll lap it up. He'll interrogate you. He'll molest you. He'll bend your ear. That's all.'

Ted didn't move. 'For some reason,' he said, 'that banging's really . . . it's making me . . . I think it's just the . . . I think it's the *irregularity* or something.'

'Calm down. He'll tire soon enough.'

35

As if on cue, the knocking abated.

'Thank *God*,' Ted shuddered, yanking his tie askew, his professional veneer denting like the tender skin of a ripe nectarine.

'Come over here for a minute,' Wesley commanded (the very image of icy unperturbedness), 'and fill me in properly on these mango things.'

Ted joined Wesley at the workbench. Wesley idly noticed that his forehead was glistening. He was sweating.

'She makes these strange little creatures out of them . . .' Ted said, fishing around inside his jacket pocket for a handkerchief, pulling one out and patting his brow with it.

He glanced around him, 'Here . . .'

He moved to a set of shelves behind the TV and picked something up, but before he could bring it back over, a loud discussion commenced next to the window, where the small, intrusive boy had now been joined by a second, much larger figure.

Ted froze. Wesley observed his reaction but said nothing, simply shrugged and then silently pushed his index finger into a soft heap of sand on the workbench. He made gentle, circular patterns with it, watching raptly as the fine granules flattened and dispersed. Ted remained glued to his spot by the bookshelves, anxiously rubbing his right palm onto his opposite elbow, listening apprehensively.

What are you doing? the larger figure demanded.

Who are you? the smaller figure responded.

Who are you? the larger figure countered. *And what are you doing in Katherine's garden?*

Katherine? Who's she? the smaller figure asked.

This is her house. Does she have any idea that you're here?

I rang the bell, the smaller figure explained, *but nobody answered. Well if nobody answered then she isn't around, is she? Use your common sense. You're treading on her hydrangea. You're damaging it.*

So who the fuck is Katherine when she's at home? the smaller figure enquired as the larger began firmly steering him away.

How old are you? Shouldn't you be at school or something?

Christmas holidays, thank you very much, the smaller figure explained cordially.

36

Their voices faded.

'Welsh,' Wesley noted, glancing up from the finely-granulated patterns he was forming, 'is he local?'

Ted nodded. 'It's Dewi,' he spoke softly, 'he owns the property opposite. He puts down wooden flooring. He did mine, actually. He's very good at it.'

'Why are you still whispering, Ted?'

'Was I?' Ted spoke louder again.

'Yes.'

He was just preparing to respond when Wesley noticed the object he was holding.

'*Fuck*,' he butted in, 'pass it over.'

Ted returned to the workbench and gave Wesley a small, plain, wire-legged, pearl-eyed, mango stone creature. Wesley took it and carefully balanced it onto the flattened palm of his fingerless hand. 'Holy Moly,' he murmured

'I think it's a lion,' Ted explained. 'See the way she's brushed up the natural strings and fibres on one end of the stone so that it resembles a mane?'

As he spoke, Ted concentrated – almost too fiercely – on the inconsequential little mango stone creature, yet all he was really seeing was the badly truncated hand below. He hadn't noticed it before . . . he . . .

But how was that possible? How on earth could something so patent, so profound, so *grotesque* have escaped his attention formerly?

His mind rapidly flipped back to a full hour previously:
The initial meeting . . .
Shaking Wesley's hand . . . (they did shake, didn't they?)
Making him a cup of coffee . . .
Wesley, sitting on the swivel chair, efficiently turning over the printed sheets of property details whilst chatting away, amiably . . .

He was suddenly very warm. Unsettled. Almost queasy. He clenched his hands together and tightened his buttocks, his gentle brown eyes clambering over Katherine's white walls like a couple of stir-crazy arachnids.

Warm? He was *boiling*. And it was no mere coincidence. Because the heat was one of Katherine's trademarks –

The heat

– well, the heat and rodents, more particularly. No. The heat and rodents and peach schnapps. She literally lived on the stuff. Locals joked – and it wasn't funny – that she took it intravenously.

Antique clothing, too, of course. And beansprouts, obviously. And mahjong (Chinese backgammon, to the uninitiated), and sex, and basic engineering. Yes. But mainly the heat. It was her thing. Always had been.

It was just so . . . just so *Katherine*.

Ted swallowed. Tried to clear his throat. Couldn't. Because it . . . it agitated him –

The heat

– he'd always found it disquieting. In fact he was currently feeling more than a little off-colour – uncomfortable – sticky – out of sorts –

No

– out of *place* – that was it – like he was trespassing or gatecrashing or sneakily intruding . . .

Of course she'd given him the key –

Yes

– he was here legitimately –

Yes

– but wasn't he . . . wasn't he *facilitating* something, just the same? Something improper? Something unscrupulous? Something . . . something unseemly?

Ted's mind began clicking. He felt over-wound and jerky. His skin was damp but the air in his lungs seemed horribly scant and thin and dry. His head felt all cotton-woolly. So did his tongue. Sweat trickled into his right eye. It stung. He blinked repeatedly.

Wesley finally broke the protracted silence between them. 'This is *twisted*, Ted,' he murmured, continuing to stare approvingly at the mango-stone creature. 'Does she actually sell these things?'

'Yes. Yes she does sell them, occasionally,' Ted's voice was flat. His tongue struggled to juggle with the weight of its syllables. He drew a deep breath, 'and if you don't mind my asking,' he paused, frowned, 'where did your fingers get to, exactly?'

(Where did they *get to*?

Oh Lord)

After he'd spoken, he couldn't quite believe what he'd said. He sounded drunk to himself.

Wesley's eyebrows rose a fraction, but his eyes did not shift from the mango-lion. 'I fed them to an owl,' he said, matter-of-factly, 'an eagle owl. Years ago. In an act of penance. I trapped my brother in an abandoned fridge. Christopher. Chris. When we were kids. A prank. He died. He was my right hand.'

They both stared for a moment, in silence, at Wesley's right hand.

'And you know what? I *like* this house,' Wesley continued calmly, as if these two thoughts were somehow naturally conjoined. 'Will I be able to move in immediately?'

Ted was still dreamy, 'Absolutely not,' he said.

Wesley's head jerked up so sharply on receipt of Ted's answer that it was almost as though – Ted thought idly – it was being operated from above by strings. He very nearly glanced at the ceiling to test the validity of this theory, but instead found himself noting – distractedly – how tall Wesley suddenly appeared and how tight his mouth seemed. Tight as . . . tight as . . . Tight as two navvies after ten pints. Tight as the lid on the only free jar of peanuts in a well-stocked hotel mini-bar. Tight as a good lie. Tight as a gymnast's thighs. Still *tighter*.

One. Two. Three seconds passed by, and then . . . *Fuck*. What on *earth* was he . . . ? Ted blinked and came to as the sharp and piercing gaze of Wesley's disfavour focussed full upon him; piranha-mouthed, marlin-nosed, pike-eyed . . . Wesley's face suddenly seemed as barbed and impenetrable as a razor-wire fence around a missile silo.

Oh bollocks.

Ted allowed himself a single, small, involuntary judder before the inestimably professional estate agent inside him stood to attention, clicked his high-polished heels together, smiled, saluted, and snapped straight back into action.

He rapidly re-assessed the situation. 'What I *mean* is that I'd have to run it past Katherine first, before I could actually promise you anything . . .' he spoke obsequiously, 'and you'd be wanting to take a look at the spare room, of course?'

What have I done? he thought. *Katherine Turpin will roast me on a spit, cut me into small pieces and devour me . . . if I'm lucky.*

Then . . .

An owl? An eagle owl? Is he crazy?

'Fine. So run it past her.'

Wesley shrugged – as if he believed no process so mundane as this could hinder the immense rolling stone of his destiny – then slowly began to deflate again, like a cheap plastic paddling pool at a children's party.

'And I don't need to see anything else,' he added, 'I'll just bring the rest of my stuff over later,' he smiled, 'about three . . . three-thirty.'

He held the mango stone creature aloft and inspected it once more, very thoroughly, his cheeks lifted and reddened by a spontaneous glow of good humour. Then his focus shifted.

His expression remained constant – calm, cheerful, *insistent* – but his eyes now held Ted's hostage in a penetrating gaze, as his other hand moved down slowly – deliberately – towards his bulging jacket pocket. He rummaged around inside it for a while until he located the particular thing he was searching for and carefully removed it: a clean, white, newly truncated, ten-inch-long lamb's tail.

Wesley removed the tail with a small flourish, and laid it out gently – almost reverently – onto the workbench. Then calmly, brazenly, he nested that strange mango-stone creature where the tail had formerly been: deep and safe within its own dark stable of itchy tweed.

In a perfect parallel, Ted's own dear heart gradually descended – down into his shoes, where it continued to beat faithfully, just as before, but closely bound now, and constricted by laces.

Five

Look for love
Where liquid is solid,
Where 62 fell
(46 still to fight for)
From Beaver to Antelope,
From Feather to Bear,
Kick your heels, sucker,
And find nothing there

Dewi came back early for lunch, each weekday, just so that he could watch her. She arrived home at twelve fourteen – twelve seventeen if she stopped to buy smokes on the way – twelve nineteen if there was a queue at the newsagents. She rode a fold-up bike. A Brompton. Tiny wheels. Bright red. It was three years old.

In winter she wore brown lace-up boots and grey woollen mittens: an irresistible combination which never failed to bring the sting of tears to his eyes. He could not think why. It was just one of those things.

She made him feckless and emotional. He was her fool. But he took strength from the fact that he was nobody else's. In every other respect, he told himself – and others told him – he was a rational man of poise and depth and stature.

Floors were his business. Wooden floors. He prepared them. He restored them. He laid, sanded and varnished them. And he had a sideline in wooden decks, and sheds and verandahs, all of which he designed and then built himself, single-handedly.

41

He worked hard. Like a demon. He worked until his shoulders locked, until his knees buckled, until his feet swelled and his palms blistered. He *believed* in work and his work sustained him. It gave him purpose. It gave him nourishment. It gave him reason. And he, in turn, gave it everything.

He embraced activity the way a hungry man embraces his first cup of tepid soup in too many days: with both hands and great satisfaction. He took what he could and was always grateful for it. He had been raised that way: to be proud yet never haughty; to be particular yet never fussy.

He was an old-fashioned creature, by and large, but with exquisitely modern parameters. He liked to do things simply and well, using the same traditional techniques his father had taught him, but twisted, very gently, into the realm of the contemporary. His father had been a boat-builder, just west of Rhyl. His grandfather, too, before him.

He understood wood completely: sheathing, siding, clapboard, cord; walnut, ebony, hickory, beam. He *understood* wood.

He liked to recycle. He could rip the back and the belly out of an old house (he had deals with local demolition men; they knew his number), the doors, the bannisters, the stairs, the pelmets even (he'd pick the corpse clean and leave it shining – he was meticulous as an ant), and then he'd transform what he'd retrieved into something new.

He tolerated the fashions in flooring, the fads: the pale finishes, the beeswax, the crazy veneers. He was no wood snob, although he knew perfectly well what he preferred, what his tastes were. But he kept his opinions to himself. He was subtle and enigmatic; as discreet as a shadow.

He did not smile secretly over the things people did or said, desired or demanded. He could not sneer. He had mouth and cheeks and chin, like other folk, but no spare space on his face for duplicity. He was straight as the shortest distance between two points.

And yet, for all of his sensitivity, he was not an especially sad or bleak or ruminative character (although others might well consider he had reason to be). He did not mull or muse or muddle miserably through. He was quiet, often. He was calm yet never vacant. He was as sweet and clear as pure rainwater in an ancient well. But it took a special little pail, a strong rope, care, steadfastness, persistence and an awful, long, deep, hard drop before you might finally discover him.

Occasionally, others' voices echoed down his walls, their cries reverberated, and sometimes pebbles or pennies disturbed the still calm of his surface, made him ripple, briefly. But true and natural light never reflected on his heart. Not a glimpse of it. Not even a glimmer.

He was dark inside, although not in a bad way. He was plain, brown and clean; like peat or coya bark, or fine, rich, fertilizer.

He was just a man, in other words, and nothing less.

They'd been joined by a fourth. The third had been a boy who – Jo couldn't help thinking – had dramatically overstepped the mark by strolling into the small paved garden, ringing on the bell and then repeatedly hammering with his fist at the window. She'd been alarmed by this behaviour. She'd presumed some invisible rule-book. She'd anticipated complex codes of practice, margins, restrictions, limitations. She'd expected *restraint*.

Doc also watched the boy closely – a submissive Dennis sitting morosely at his heels – but said and did nothing. When a fourth man arrived though (in his fifties and looking – Jo couldn't curb the crassness of her assessment – an absolute bloody Trainspotter with his long, grey face, thick glasses, waterproof beanie bearing a preposterous logo – a little fat koala-like creature with the word *Gumble* written underneath it – plastic rucksack and binoculars), she finally heard Doc mention the boy's impropriety, and in tones of fairly severe disapproval. They called the boy Patty.

'Will you say anything, Doc?' the fourth man asked, gazing over towards Patty bemusedly. 'He's absolutely *trashing* that hydrangea.'

Doc shrugged, 'Not my responsibility, Hooch. I'm hardly the boy's keeper.'

The two of them dumbly ruminated upon Patty's continuing antics for a while, before, 'Ay *ay!*' the fourth man whispered, clumsily adjusting his glasses on the flat, elongated (almost turtle-like) bridge of his snout and squinting furtively across Doc's right shoulder blade. 'It looks like somebody else might be squaring up to take the initiative.'

As he spoke he yanked off his rucksack and shoved his hand deep inside of it. He withdrew a pad and a pen.

The enterprising person to whom Hooch referred had silently emerged from the small, rather scruffy-looking mint-green bungalow behind them. He was a man; stern-seeming, handsome, sallow-skinned. A big, brazen creature. Wide-jawed. Gargantuan. A *moose*.

As they watched, he emerged fully into the sharp morning light, squinting antagonistically into the high winter sky like some kind of hostile, nocturnal organism, turned and slammed his front door (it clicked shut, then immediately swung back open) clumped rapidly over his large, well-constructed American-style verandah, banged down some thick, wooden steps, marched across his wildly Amazonian front garden, out through his gate (again, although he closed it with a satisfying clatter, only seconds later it was yawning insolently behind him), strode along the pavement – passing literally within inches of the three of them – and dashed straight over the road, narrowly avoiding a scooter and a small, battered yellow Volkswagen (the Volkswagen swerving and sounding its horn) without so much as a word, a squeak, a *grunt* of acknowledgement.

As he moved, Jo noted, a spray of something chalk-like – a fine, dusty aura – seemed to follow in his wake. When she looked harder, she noticed that he wore ancient trousers and a threadbare jumper, both of which were saturated with a diffuse, pale, powdery substance. Flour? She frowned. No. Not white enough. Grit? Nope. Something infinitely lighter. She sniffed the air, cat-like, after his passing. Ah. That was it. *Sawdust.*

The man-moose, meanwhile, was entering the bungalow's garden. He was marching across the brick parquet. He was grabbing Patty by the arm. He was towering above him.

Jo drew a deep, gulping breath – as if she'd just been shoved from a mile-high diving board – then gazed down at her shoes, slowly exhaling. *Birkenstocks.* Brown plastic leather-look. Square-toed. Lace-ups. Cruelty-free.

She found herself inspecting the heel of her left shoe (abstractly observing how the tread was far more worn on the right hand side), while simultaneously straining her two sharp ears for any vaguely audible scraps of conversation.

What could he possibly be *saying*?

Initially a couple more cars passed by, drowning out everything, and then – *damn* him, what *timing* – Doc started talking.

'Well that's certainly gone and done it,' he murmured, turning to Hooch conspiratorially. 'Happen to know whose house that is?'

Doc's voice, Jo felt (perhaps even for her benefit), was slightly louder than it had been previously.

'I don't know,' Hooch answered, staring wide-eyed at his mentor, opening his pad and priming his pen in sweet anticipation. 'Should I, Doc?'

Jo silently noted the obsequious way in which Hooch repeatedly used the Old Man's name in conversation.

'Katherine. Katherine Turpin. Remember her?'

Doc pronounced this feminine appellation only seconds before the huge, dusty, moose-like man echoed the self-same three syllables himself during the course of his own conversation.

Jo glanced up from her shoes.

'Katherine who?' Hooch quizzed.

'Katherine *Turpin*.'

'Turpin?'

'As in *Dick*,' Doc said.

'It rings a bell, Doc,' Hooch muttered, glancing sideways at Jo for the first time, as if supremely protective of the information he was gleaning. He suddenly lowered his voice, presumably hoping to encourage Doc to do the same, 'And the connection?'

'The walks book,' Doc announced, sounding justly proud of his coup, 'the section on Canvey. All that crazy stuff about boundaries. I never understood a word of it . . .' he chuckled, 'nor did Wes himself, more than likely. But this is where she lives. That much I am sure of.'

Hooch chewed on the end of his finger for a moment, frowning, then suddenly his monolithic mien brightened. 'Of *course*,' he squeaked, jabbing his biro into the air with a quite savage delight, 'of course of *course*. You mean *Katherine*. You mean *the* Katherine

Turpin. What on earth was I thinking? You mean Katherine the *whore* . . .'

Hooch proclaimed this slanderous defamation with all the uninhibited joy of a miserly man who unexpectedly finds his long-lost gold cap tucked inside a three-week-old carton of pasta salad.

'*Sssh!*'

Even Doc had the good grace to seem embarrassed by Hooch's complete want of delicacy. Dewi and the kid were currently well within earshot, standing on the opposite kerb, impatiently waiting for a van to pass. He scowled, quickly pushing his pager into his coat pocket – as if to free his hands for something (combat, possibly) – but then held them limply by his sides, open, loose.

They crossed the road. Dewi roughly yanked Patty up onto the grass verge in front of them. 'Is the boy with you?' he asked Doc, proffering the child, who dangled as weakly in Dewi's huge grip as a faded old bathrobe on a big, brass doorknob.

'The boy? *Mine*? Good Lord, no,' Doc exclaimed, lifting his hands and smiling as if this was possibly the most preposterous supposition he had ever yet been party to.

The boy, *his*?

Patty stared up at Doc, unblinking, his head yanked sideways by Dewi's tight grip. He was just a boy. He had no agenda. There was nothing unspoken or sly or resentful in his gaze. But even so, almost out of nowhere, Doc's smile suddenly faltered. His hands froze, mid-air. His lips twisted. Because he had indeed been the father of a son, once.

A father. This strangely alien yet acutely painful notion hit him like a karate kick. Two kicks. In the kidneys. It winded him. How on earth could he have forgotten? Even passingly. His own flesh and blood, his *boy*, dead. A too short life, curtailed, emptied, drained, exhausted . . .

Doc's loose hands clenched, just briefly, as if he was seriously considering doing something wild and magnificent – venting his rage. Perhaps calling death or fate or destiny to task. Going five rounds with the bastards. *Pulping* them – but then they unclenched again and hung inertly.

Dewi didn't notice Doc's distress. It was all much too subtle. He was far too irritable. He turned to Jo. 'What about you?' he asked,

46

then paused for a moment to inspect her face more closely. He had mistaken her for a boy, possibly a brother. But she was a girl, and as if to prove it categorically, a fierce blush – like two clumsily upended measures of sweet cherry brandy – slowly stained the impeccable cream cotton tablecloth of her soft complexion.

Jo shrugged, burning inside, burning outside, utterly mortified, yet still silently mesmerised by the layers of dust which – close up – coated Dewi's features and hung above either eyebrow like precarious hunks of soft, pale honeycomb.

'Why should the kid belong to anybody?' Hooch butted in – observing Doc's temporary state of disquiet and feeling bad for him. 'Why can't he simply be here under his own steam?'

Dewi loosened his grip on the child – he couldn't be much past eleven, at best, Jo calculated – and slowly drew closer to Hooch. Soon he stood only inches from him. He was a good foot taller, even hatless (if they'd suddenly begun slow-dancing, Jo couldn't help imagining, then Hooch's flat pate would've fitted with a reassuring snugness under Dewi's jutting chin).

As it was, Hooch's mean streak of a nose pointed with an almost stoat-like determination towards Dewi's left nipple. Eye contact was not maintained – it was not desirable – it was barely even feasible.

Patty, for his part, instantly busied himself in trying to eradicate a large smear of dust from the arm of his cheap, shiny green bomber jacket. He slapped away at it, vigorously.

Doc, in turn (and somewhat to his discredit, under the circumstances), stared fixedly off to his left, towards the distant smudge of sea at the road's end, as if he'd just received urgent word of an Armada.

Dennis – who'd stood up, initially, to sniff at Dewi's trouser leg – sat down again, glanced up at Doc, tightened his eyes, drew his lips back into an apprentice snarl, shook his head and then *sneezed*.

'It's very plain, my friend,' Dewi murmured softly into the crown of Hooch's slightly dented beanie, the curling vine of a Welsh accent suddenly twisting into audibility and looping with an almost unspeakable sincerity around each and every syllable, 'that there are some things, some *important* things, which you don't yet seem to know about Katherine Turpin.'

47

He inhaled deeply. 'The first of these,' he continued calmly, his voice deep and smooth as a stagnant loch, 'is that I am her friend. I am her guardian. I am her self-appointed foot-soldier. It is a service that I perform for her out of loyalty and love and veneration. And while you're at liberty to interpret my guardianship in any way you please,' he smiled (it wasn't friendly), 'you might benefit from knowing that my name is Dewi and that I live in this bungalow . . .' he pointed (somewhat gratuitously), 'directly opposite her bunga-low, and that if she ever troubled to ask me I would happily break my own two arms for her . . .' a significant pause followed, 'or anybody else's,' a further pause, 'for that matter.'

Dewi took a small step backwards, down into the gutter, and nodded his head curtly, as if in parting. He half-turned. But then he thought better of it, stuck out his square chin and moved back up close again.

'I trust,' he intoned gently, his eyes still not meeting Hooch's but focussing approximately a foot above his head, 'I *hope* that you will refrain from pestering my Katherine. Or maligning her. Or troubling her. Because there has been far too much of that already. And I am very, very tired of it . . .

'But if you do,' he continued, his voice barely audible now (just a cool gust, an icy imprint), 'then trust me when I say that I will hunt you down, that I will find you, that I will take you, that I will hold you, that I will squeeze you, that I will *smash* you. Because it would be no bother to me. It would be no trouble. It would be . . . it would be like plucking a stray feather from a duck-down pillow . . . see?'

Dewi held his dusty hands aloft. Huge hands. His index finger and thumb pinched lightly together. He blew an invisible feather into the air. Sawdust lifted from his lips and the tip of his nose. It was a beautiful gesture. Excessive. Baroque. Infinitely tender.

Hooch's wise eyes followed those capable fingers, keenly, moistly, from behind their thick but clear bifocal lenses. He swallowed hard. He said nothing.

Only Josephine – who was slightly more observant than the others – saw that Dewi's huge hands were shaking. Not with fear. Nor passion. *Anger*? No. And not rage, either . . . It was something else. Something softer. Restraint, maybe? No. Not restraint. Not exactly . . . Her eyes widened, suddenly. Could it be? Could it be sympathy?

Sympathy?

'*Oi*. What's that, then?'

Josephine started, surprised by the sudden, unexpected proximity of the small boy, Patty, who had silently materialised at her shoulder. And while she could barely stand to drag her eyes away from Dewi – his sandy brows, his smooth voice, his magnificent fingers – Patty seemed hardly to have noticed the intense altercation between the two other men.

'What's that?' he repeated. 'Is it food?'

Jo looked down. In her right hand she still held the grease-stained paper bag from the bakery. 'It's a doughnut,' she stammered.

'Hand it over,' the boy ordered.

She passed it to him, silently. Patty snatched the bag and rammed his fist inside of it. He was hungry.

Dewi, meanwhile, in that slightest – that shortest – that *briefest* of interludes, had swiftly taken his leave of them. Jo turned and stared after him, her whole heart scythed. Beautiful, *beautiful* Dewi, she murmured, her chin lifting, her pupils dilating; beautiful, *beautiful* Dewi, standing right there, just in front of me, and as the cruel winter sky above is my witness, he didn't even *know*.

'If you love to sew so much, why are you working as an estate agent?'

'*What?*' Ted did a double-take.

They were crossing the road together, strolling directly towards the four people on the opposite pavement.

A fifth was just joining them. Another man, grossly overweight and wearing thin, green, tie-dyed trousers with a black and red striped mohair *Dennis the Menace* jumper. His name was Shoes. Wesley knew him well, but as he approached, his face showed no inkling of recognition. Not for Shoes. Not for Doc. Not for any of them.

His eyes hiccoughed slightly, however, at the sight of Hooch's hat; the incongruously cuddly logo, then they focussed straight in on the girl.

He stepped up onto the kerb.

'Who said anything about sewing?' Ted asked quietly.

Wesley didn't answer. He was standing directly in front of Josephine.

'Someone must be paying you,' he murmured silkily, inspecting her face which was plain – like he'd imagined – but with something about the mouth, the chin, that seemed oddly exceptional. A firmness. A roundness. She was a Jersey Royal, he decided. Not your average potato. She was small and smooth and seasonal. Her hazel eyes were liquid, like a glass of good cask whisky mixed with water.

'Pardon?' She looked quite astonished to see him. So close.

'Someone must be paying you. You don't look like the others. You aren't like them.'

'I'm Jo from Southend,' Jo found herself saying.

'I don't care where you live,' Wesley said, 'you're wasting your time here. You won't find what you're looking for. Go back to Southend . . .' his voice dropped, unexpectedly, 'while you still can. D'you hear?'

He turned – not even waiting for an answer – then he paused, 'You have jam,' he said, 'on your sweatshirt.'

Jo looked down. 'I was eating a doughnut,' she muttered, trying to lift off the worst of it with her thumb.

Wesley was already walking.

'How did you know?' Ted asked, quickly catching up, 'about the sewing?'

'Ah,' Wesley touched the tip of his nose mysteriously with his glossy stump.

'You *smelled* it?'

'When I picked up your jacket,' Wesley demurred, 'I noticed the handmade label. Beautifully finished. Just like the original. And you were comforting yourself,' he continued, 'earlier, when we were walking, by rattling that bunch of keys. It reminded me of the sound of a machine . . .' he paused, 'and I couldn't help noticing how you felt the curtain fabric in Katherine's house. Almost without thinking. And the material on the cushion covers. Plus you have two strange calluses on your index fingers. It all seemed pretty . . . well, pretty conclusive, really.'

'Nobody knows that I sew,' Ted whispered, at once amazed and conspiratorial, 'except my Great Aunt who taught me. You're the first. You must promise not to tell.'

'Tell?' Wesley chuckled. 'Who would I tell? More to the point, *why* would I tell them?'

Ted held on tight to his briefcase, saying nothing, but with his knuckles showing white, his lips silently enunciating, his nose gently shining. He was panicked, for some reason.

Wesley glanced sideways at him and felt a sudden, fierce glow of satisfaction – as if a blow torch had just been lit inside of him. This is how I become powerful, he thought, turning, casually, and glancing back at the girl again.

She had her jammy thumb in her mouth and she was sucking on it. But she wasn't – as he'd anticipated – staring after him. Instead she was looking behind her, towards a small, scruffy, ivy-covered bungalow with an inappropriately large wooden verandah to the front of it.

On the verandah stood a huge, square man, staring straight back at him – eyes like arrows, poison tipped – with the kind of crazy intensity which implied not only dislike – or pique – or bile – or irritation, even, but hatred.

Hate. Pure. Clear. 100% proof. Strong as poteen.

Perhaps it was a mistake to return here, Wesley mused idly. He glanced over at Ted whose lips were still working feverishly.

He smiled. What shall I give this man, he pondered, his mood instantly lightening; and what, I wonder, shall I extract from him?

He chuckled to himself, cruelly, then pulled his two hands from his trouser pockets, wiggled his four remaining fingers – it was cold, it was too *damn* cold – puckered his lips, swung out his arms and walked boldly onwards, expertly whistling the chorus to *When the Saints Go Marching In*, while gradually – almost imperceptibly – speeding up his pace, so that he might stride along jauntily, in time.

Six

She was cycling on the pavement. At worst, Arthur mused tightly, an illegal act, at best, wholly irresponsible. And that, in fact, was the only reason he'd troubled to notice her. He was not, by nature, an observant man when it came to women. In all other respects his observational faculties were keen, although in general, if he looked for things, then it was mainly for the stuff that interested him: roadsigns, landmarks, industrial centres, museums, farm machinery, traditional breeds. He had an inexplicable soft spot for Shetland Ponies.

She jinked past him. He'd been walking – strongly, cleanly – since sunrise. Her sweet perfume assaulted his olfactory organs as she clattered by. It tickled his nostrils, but crudely. She smelled of cigarettes and dog violets.

Twenty minutes later he caught up with her again. It was a long road, the A127, north of Basildon. She was on her knees, cursing. The traffic whizzed past them. Its speed and its volume were mentally trying. But he was a veteran.

'Something wrong?' he asked, his voice (he couldn't help it) fringed with a facetious edge.

'Nothing earth-shattering,' she grunted, as if instantly gauging the true nature of his gallantry. 'Flat tyre.'

Her voice was so low that he almost started. Husky didn't do it justice. His mind struggled to think of another canine breed – even more tough, even more northerly – to try and express it with greater accuracy. He could think of none.

'You have a pump?'

She looked up, took her littlest finger, stuck it into her ear and shook it around vigorously.

He watched her, frowning, unsure whether this was an insulting gesture of some kind which he – because of his age, perhaps, or his sheltered upbringing – had hitherto yet to encounter. She stared back at him, quizzically. He was all sinew. Grizzled. He reminded her of a dog chew. Tough and yellow and lean and twisted.

'Sorry,' she said, removing her finger, 'I've got water in my ear.'

'So you *do* have a pump,' he pointed at the pavement to the right of her. She raised her eyebrows, picked up the pump and gave it a thrust. The air blew out of it like the tail-end of a weak sneeze.

'Yes I do have a pump, but I also have . . .' she paused and then spoke with exaggerated emphasis, 'a *fast puncture.*'

He pushed his baseball cap back on his head.

'*Cute,*' she said, pointing at the little, squidgy koala-like creature smiling out from the front of it.

He stared at her, blankly. Then something registered.

'I lost my . . .' he scowled, defensively. 'It's new.'

She half-shrugged.

As her shoulder shifted he noticed – and it was difficult not to – that instead of a dress she seemed to be wearing some kind of long, antique undergarment. Not see-through. But fragile. An apricot colour. Over that, two pastel-coloured silky pearl buttoned cardigans, half-fastened, and over these, a thin brown coat featuring a tiny but anatomically complete fox-fur collar.

As he watched, she shoved her hand into the pocket of her flimsy coat and withdrew some Marlboros. She offered him the packet.

'Smoke?'

Arthur shook his head. She shrugged, knocked one out and stuck it between her lips, feeling around deep inside her other pocket for a light. She withdrew a large box of kitchen matches, opened the box and carefully removed one. It was at least three inches in length. She struck it and applied its bold flame to her cigarette, inhaling gratefully, then blew it out while still keeping the cigarette in place. A complex manoeuvre.

Arthur continued to gaze at her. For some reason he found the blowing pleasurable. He watched closely as she replaced the remainder of the match back inside the box again.

She was possibly the palest woman he had ever seen. Her hair was bright white. Shoulder-length. Thin. Straight. Most of it shoved under a small, round hat fashioned from what looked like dark raffia. With cherries. The kind of hat old women wore in fairytales.

But she was still young, if jaded; crinkling gently at her corners, like a random, well-worn page of an ancient love letter. She had disconcertingly pale blue eyes. Eyes the colour of the exact spot where the winter sky brushed the sea. Eyes the colour of the horizon, he supposed. Trimmed with white lashes, and topped by two haughty brows. A phantasm's brows; cold and high and light and spectral. Barely there. Just a suggestion of hair.

Puffy underneath . . . the eyes. He thinly smiled his recognition. Oh yes. A drinker. He knew the signs. And he warmed to her, then, but it was a warmth imbued with a profound contempt.

'It's portable,' he noted.

She nodded, and spoke with the cigarette still dangling, 'Yes. An absolute bloody miracle of engineering.'

Her tone troubled him. 'How far?' he asked.

'What?'

Smoke trickled ineluctably into her right eye. The eye filled with water. She blinked it away.

'I said how far?' he repeated, pointing ahead of them.

'Canvey.'

'Oh. Far enough.'

He nodded sympathetically, looking down the road again, then he checked his watch. It was only eleven-fifty.

'Second hand?' she asked curtly.

'Pardon?'

'Do you have a second hand?'

'Uh . . .' he finally caught up with her, 'yes . . .' he blinked, 'yes I do.'

'Give me the exact time.'

He checked his watch again then paused for a moment. 'It's now eleven fifty-one,' he said, 'precisely.'

'Right.' She began to fold up the bike. Her hands flew from wheel to seat to crossbar, inverting, twisting, unscrewing. She knew what she was doing. Her hands were small and bony and chalky, but she was impressively adroit. It was quickly done.

'*Finished*,' she exclaimed, slamming the seat down and tapping it smugly, 'and the time now?'

He inspected his watch. 'Eleven fifty-one and twelve seconds,' he said.

She smiled, then stopped smiling. 'Dammit,' she cursed, 'I forgot the sodding pump.'

She grabbed the pump and clipped it into position.

'The manufacturers say it should take twenty seconds,' she explained, standing up and dusting off her knees, 'but I can halve it.'

'Right. Good. I'm actually heading towards Canvey myself,' Arthur informed her, deigning not to comment further on the fold-up phenomenon but staring down the road fixedly. He loved the road. He loved *roads*.

'On foot? Are you crazy?' she scowled over at him. Smoke in her eye again. 'It's a piss-ugly walk. Nothing to see.'

'I like to walk,' he said, 'I like the *fact* of walking.'

He found the pale flash of her lashes fascinating.

'It's miles.'

'I know exactly how far it is.'

She spat on her hands and rubbed them together. Then she thought of something and stopped what she was doing.

'I get it,' she said, a teasing tone suddenly hijacking her low voice as she removed the cigarette from her mouth and held it, half-concealed, inside her moist, milky palm, 'you're one of those . . .' she scrabbled for the word, 'those following people. A *Back-ender*. You walk places.'

'Behindling,' Arthur corrected her, looking disgruntled, but nonetheless refraining from either denying or affirming her assumptions.

She chuckled dryly (sounding, Arthur couldn't help thinking, like a territorial squirrel: a base, clicking, gurgling), then she focussed in on him again, 'It's been all over the local papers because of the clue mentioning Canvey in that stupid, chocolate bar treasure-hunt thingummy.'

'The Loiter,' Arthur interjected impassively.

She nodded. 'Clue three, I believe. Daniel Defoe once called it *Candy* Island,' she grimaced, 'whoever the fuck *he* is.'

'Robinson Crusoe,' Arthur's eyebrow rose disdainfully, 'he wrote it.'

'Oh . . .' she shrugged, 'and what with that poor man dying, obviously.'

'Don't hike across beaches if you can't understand the tides,' Arthur counselled, somewhat unsympathetically, 'especially in Anglesey. The water's always been treacherous there. Everybody knows it.'

'Good point,' she concurred, 'you heartless bastard.' Then she smiled, casually up-ended her cigarette, softly blew onto the smoking tip of it and carefully inspected the glowing embers below, her knuckles peppered with flecks of ash.

Several long seconds passed before she replaced the cigarette between her lips, grabbed hold of the bike, carried it to the edge of the pavement and stuck out her pale thumb. Now she was hitching. Now she was done with him.

Heartless. Yes. *Bastard*. Yes. Arthur took these two words on board – not even flinching – and packed them neatly into his mental rucksack. 'Good luck,' he said, yanking up his actual rucksack, settling it comfortably between his two lean shoulders and walking on again.

Katherine Turpin turned and stared after him, her chin high, her lips skewed, her characteristically disdainful expression seeming, for once, oddly ruminative.

He was raddled. Yes. Emaciated. Yes. A rope. A bad thumb. An oar. An *old* oar. But even she had to admit that he walked, well, *beautifully*. An oiled machine; his legs snapping in and out with all the smooth, practical precision of a trusty pair of ancient, large-handled kitchen scissors.

There goes a man, she thought idly – cocking her hitching thumb a couple of times like she was striking a flint or popping a cork – there goes a man who should always keep moving.

'He'll head straight for the library.'

Doc threw out this apparently random observation towards Jo so pointedly, and with such clear intent, that had his words transmogrified into a volleyball they'd have hit her square between the eyes. They'd have fractured her nose. It was a fine nose.

'I said the *library*,' he reiterated, 'and that's an absolute bloody certainty.'

Jo glanced around her, just to double-check she wasn't simply imagining. No. It was beyond question: he had purposefully singled her out. She drew a deep, preparatory breath. 'But how do you know?' she asked cautiously, her voice wavering slightly at the prospect of a rebuff.

'He always goes to the library when he first arrives somewhere,' Doc elucidated matter-of-factly, as if there was nothing at all remarkable in his sudden decision to include her, 'he considers the library the best place to gather local information.'

He paused for a moment then added, 'And while I suppose to an outsider Wesley might seem a little old-fashioned in this respect, in reality the whole process is much more complicated, much more . . .' he pondered for a moment, 'much more *social* than . . .'

'Oh yes.'

This unexpected interruption from Hooch's direction was followed by a big wink, a small burp and then a succulent chuckle as he rubbed a gloved hand over his heart and lungs, his ribs and nipples, 'It's all *very social indeed*, eh, Doc?'

Doc stiffened, visibly, at Hooch's intervention. He plainly did not appreciate it. In fact and in principle he was far too sober a creature to involve himself in suggestive banter. He tried to play a higher game. His entire approach to the Art of Following was underpinned by a profound sense of ceremony. It was an intensely serious business; at least, he wanted it to be.

He *needed* it to be. For how else might he – a weak old man, no funds, no education, no family to speak of – sustain his tacit position of undisputed pre-eminence in matters concerning Wesley, if not by strictly eschewing casualness and irreverence and pointless tomfoolery?

How else, precisely?

After a few seconds' strained hiatus, Doc turned from Hooch and back towards Jo again, a slight frown still pinching the loose skin between his eyes.

Hooch, however – not in the least bit subdued by Doc's subtle rebuff – jinked in rapidly, grabbed Doc's communicative baton, and ran swiftly on with it. 'What he *actually* does,' Hooch expanded ebulliently, 'is he strolls in there, casual as anything, and quietly asks the first person he comes across serving behind the counter if she's the *Head* Librarian. I've seen him do it . . .' he threw up his hands, 'must be a *hundred* times . . .'

In his excitement, Hooch's generous lower lip grew shiny with spit, flecks of which settled on Jo's cheek and neck after every emphatic *s* and *t*. She tried not to flinch, but didn't succeed entirely.

'And although chances are that she probably won't be . . .' Hooch bowled on, perfectly oblivious, 'Head Librarian, I mean; he'll still find her captivating. And he'll gradually get her talking. He has this ridiculous theory about the universal language of mammals . . .'

Jo frowned. Hooch shrugged, 'It's just a pile of *bollocks*, basically. But he'll invite her out for a drink, eventually. He's charming. He's got no scruples. He'll ask out virtually anybody; even saggy old dears in their fifties.' He grimaced (plainly appalled by the notion).

Doc rolled his eyes at this.

Hooch noticed. 'I only mean,' he quickly modified, 'that his motivation isn't *entirely* sexual.'

'Not entirely?' Jo echoed, slightly alarmed.

For a second nobody said anything, then Patty sneezed three times in quick succession. When he'd finished, a drip of moisture clung tenaciously to the tip of his nose. He flipped it off with a sudden, violent jerk of his head.

'Sawdust,' he exclaimed, '*bah!*'

'Bless you,' Hooch murmured, quickly withdrawing a paper tissue from his pocket, patting his mouth with it and then carefully inspecting his pristine anorak for any stray remnants of damp residue.

Doc, meanwhile – after swiftly yanking a meandering Dennis to heel – formally introduced Jo to the rest of the party. 'This is Jo, everybody,' he said, 'and I'm Doc obviously, he's Hooch, that's Patty, and this here is Shoes.'

Jo nodded at Shoes, then instinctively glanced down at his feet.

They were bare – filthy – his toenails the approximate length and shade of ten rooks' beaks. Dennis, for one, seemed absolutely riveted by them.

'Shoes here is very clever with his feet,' Doc explained, following the direction of Jo's gaze, 'he can use them like hands if he chooses. He can even hold a pen with them.'

'I can eat a meal with them,' Shoes volunteered, 'I have double-jointed knees.'

Shoes was a fat Geordie hippie in his forties.

'That'd be a great bonus,' Jo smiled, 'if for some reason you needed to write a letter and eat a meal, concurrently.'

'I must confess, I never yet tried it,' Shoes replied, blinking uneasily, 'but I suppose it's always an option.'

'*Concurrently*,' Hooch parroted, under his breath, feeling blindly again for the pad in his pocket.

'He *can't* write,' Patty interrupted scornfully, 'even with his . . .'

'If you wouldn't mind,' Doc spoke simultaneously, moving in a few steps closer to Jo and pulling out his pager, 'perhaps you might go over the details of what just went on back there – between you and Wesley – for the benefit of the rest of the group.'

The rest of the group?

Jo glanced around, unsure whether to be delighted or disturbed by her sudden inclusion. She scratched her head, nervously, 'I can't recall . . . I mean not *exactly* – not word for word . . . but he seemed . . . Wesley seemed to have acquired the impression from somewhere that I was being . . . that I was actually being paid to follow him.'

'And are you?' Hooch asked, his pad open, his pen raised.

Jo looked startled, 'Paid? Who would pay me to follow Wesley?'

'The same person, probably,' Patty speculated mischievously, 'as pays Doc to follow him.'

'Shut up,' Doc spoke softly.

Patty wasn't quelled, though. 'I've seen Wesley in the library,' he expanded nonchalantly, 'and he doesn't do nothing special with maps or globes or computers . . . Mostly all he ever does is sleep or read stupid cowboy books with bloody great letters . . .'

'Large type,' Hooch corrected, 'he's a lazy reader, but his vision is infallible.'

'How can you tell?' Jo asked.

'By watching. He favours . . .' Hooch licked his thumb and quickly paged back through his jotter, 'he likes J.T. Edson and Louis L'Amour. He finds them relaxing. But he reads plenty of other stuff. Only last week it was . . .' he inspected the jotter again, '*The World Encyclopedia of Twentieth Century Murder* by J.R. Nash, and some big old tome by Thomas Paine – the philosopher – and then . . .' he flipped the page over, '. . . something called *Orientalism* by . . .' he coughed, '. . . by a Mr Edward W. Said.'

'Louis *L'Amour*?' Jo echoed, apparently bewildered by this sudden barrage of information.

'You didn't actually say yet,' Doc continued tenaciously, 'whether you are being paid to follow him.'

'She did say she came from Southend,' Patty interrupted, 'I heard that much.'

'Do you come from Southend?' Hooch asked, already writing.

'No . . . *Yes* . . .' she struggled with her answer for a moment, 'I was from Canvey itself, originally.'

'Almost local,' Shoes sucked on his tongue, 'you messed up, man. You messed up *badly*.'

'Messed up?' Jo frowned. 'You think I messed up?'

Shoes turned to Doc, 'I'd've played the local card, Doc. I'd've merged into the background – like the estate agent – and got taken into his confidence that way.'

'You think I messed up?' Jo repeated, rather more emphatically.

'Of *course* you messed up,' Patty snorted, jumping off the pavement, into the road, then back onto the pavement again.

'Why?'

'Because he hates being Followed,' Doc interjected, smiling (as if the thought of Jo messing up was somehow completely irresistible to him), 'and he never speaks to the people Following. That's the whole point. It's the rule. We are the *Behindlings*. Wesley actually coined our name as a kind of swearword, as an insult, but we don't treat it that way; we quite like it. It unites us. It . . .'

'It *legitimises* us,' Hooch interrupted.

The others all nodded in unison at this, but Jo was still frowning, so Doc expanded further, 'Wesley thinks you have to be backward to follow things. I'm talking organised religion, football teams,

61

brand names. Anything at all. He's a free spirit. People call him an anarchist – in the papers and so forth – but he despises labels; even that one . . .'

'*Especially* that one,' Shoes butted in, before instinctively tipping his head towards Doc and drawing a couple of steps back again.

'The funny part about it,' Doc continued, 'is that people are *drawn* to him. They can't help themselves. They like what he stands for – although he constantly bangs on about not standing for anything. And he has this strange way about him – a kind of simple charm – an innocence. Add to that all the pranks, the trickery, the mischief-making . . . and not forgetting the confectionery Loiter . . .' Doc paused, 'Wesley's an angry man, make no mistake about it. We've all felt the brunt of it in one way or another.'

Hooch grunted, gently, under his breath, as if this comment had an especial significance for him, personally. Shoes just sighed, tellingly.

'He's high-minded and he's unpredictable, and most important of all: he's a trouble-maker, and trouble-makers value their privacy. So he resents our eyes. We irritate him. In point of fact,' Doc grinned widely, 'he *loathes* the watching.'

'Poor Wesley's hiding from the truth,' Shoes interrupted.

The others all looked askance at this.

'What truth?' Jo indulged him.

'The truth that he needs Following. Because – let's face it – he *is* the very thing he's so set upon despising. At root *he's* the contradiction. *He's* the puzzle. That's what nobody understands. But we do . . .' Shoes looked around him, detecting scant support in the others' faces. 'Well *I* do,' he qualified.

'Shoes is very philosophical,' Doc sighed, 'but no good at deciphering things. And terrible with maps. So we all try and help him out, time allowing.'

'I do tend to go my own way, intellectually,' Shoes averred.

Patty – who'd finished his doughnut several minutes previously – now made a meal out of scrunching up the paper bag and drop-kicking it towards the hippie. It hit Shoes squarely on the thigh. Shoes' wide face rippled piously, then he stretched out his left foot, picked up the bag with his toes and tossed it straight back to him. 'Put it in a bin, lad,' he said.

'*Aw*, fuck it man!' Patty exclaimed, full of bravado, but he took the bag and shoved it hard into his jacket pocket.

'Wesley also said,' Hooch told Doc, inspecting his notebook again, 'that *she wouldn't find what she was looking for here.*'

There was a pause. Hooch eyed Jo closely, 'What *are* you looking for, exactly?'

Jo did not answer this question immediately. She was still gazing at Shoes' feet. Then her focus shifted gradually onto Patty's coat pocket. Her mind was working differently. It was working lengthways, *horizontally*.

'Love.'

Her face brightened. '*Love*,' she repeated.

'Love?' Doc echoed querulously.

'Yes,' Jo grinned. '*Love*. I was just thinking . . .' she counted off the words, one by one, onto her fingers, 'Wesley . . . the library . . . Louis L'Amour . . . *love*.'

They all stared at her, blankly. 'Clue One,' she said, 'remember? Look for *love*.'

'Okay . . . Okay . . .' Hooch laboriously drawled out his vowels as he wrote down the letters, 'Looking for love, you say? *L* . . . *o* . . . *v* . . . *e*. And your full name is?'

He glanced up. Four backs, one tail. All emphatically retreating.

Seven

'If you *must* know,' Ted whispered furtively, his nimble fingers
fiddling with the small gold buckle on his lizard-skin watch strap,
'I was with him less than fifteen . . .'

He stopped speaking, turned abruptly and craned his neck
anxiously towards what seemed – at first glance – to be a thoroughly
unobtrusive door, standing slightly ajar to the rear of the office.

'. . . but when we finally parted company,' he eventually continued (having lost his drift but plainly having found – to his
satisfaction – that the coast was now marginally clearer), 'it was
in the general, and I mean the *very* general vicinity of the local
library.'

While Ted spoke, his spine remained corkscrewed, yet his words
– for all their undisputed softness – were propelled from the corner
of his mouth and over his shoulder with astonishing accuracy and
fidelity; as if he were delivering a tricky golf shot across a sloping
green, but using only the gentlest putt of breath.

Under the circumstances, Ted's extraordinary wariness was not
only prudent, it was positively necessary, for beyond that inoffen-
sive door stood no less a man than Leo Pathfinder, his boss; a bluff
and exuberant creature, a mischievous imp, often fondly referred
to locally as 'the little pitcher with big ears.'

The unerring accuracy of this description (although, in truth,
Leo was no jug-head) had necessitated – during the years Ted
had been employed under Leo's tutelage in the dark world of
estate agenting (now numbering almost six) – his gradual adoption of certain basic ruses and stratagems, all cultivated with
the fundamental aim of trying to maintain – in his life and in

his affairs – some paltry semblance of inner peace and personal privacy.

Ted's skill as a whisperer, the occasional retreat of even his most expressive features into the protective shelter of The Deadpan, his timely adoption of a slightly forced *naiveté*; each of these little mannerisms and humble quirks regularly assisted him in his heroic struggle to maintain some tiny semblance of emotional independence in the ravening face of Leo's all-consuming curiosity.

It was, without doubt, a supremely humble and irksome existence, yet Ted had always been made most painfully aware (by none other, in fact, than Mr Leo Pathfinder himself), that it could never be deemed proper or fair-minded or *sporting* for a grown man to overstate the magnitude of his work-a-day woes.

While life with Leo could be tough, humiliating, sometimes even physically dangerous (an unfortunate incident involving Ted's left sinus and a badly directed veterinary thermometer being a case in point), Ted was hardly – and this truth was undeniable – a prisoner of *war*.

Leo was a blow-hard. He was gregarious. He was sociable to the point of immoderation (able to call, at any time, on the active support and keen participation – in his convoluted Ted-related devilry – of numerous visiting Estate Agenting Executives, the man who ran the sandwich round, the cleaner, certain suggestible clients, the local bookmaker, the bingo caller . . .) and while it would be erroneous to label him a consistent man, he was, nevertheless, quite revoltingly methodical.

Fortunately there were sometimes small hiatuses, brief pauses, little breathing spaces from the relentless pressure of Leo's obsessively systematic observations – there *had* to be – and these Ted celebrated with all the blissful fervour which a ninety-year-old man might exhibit on discovering – after many years of drought – a small but sweetly intrepid erection floating daintily in the tired suds of a hot bath.

As part and parcel of their daily lives, both Ted and Leo spent certain portions of their working day taking out clients to view vacant properties. For Ted these were periods of inconceivable joy and quietude.

Leo was also an atrocious timekeeper – generally preferring

to start his day some considerable time after the early hour clearly specified in his contract of employment – and this represented yet another small but nonetheless significant boon in the microscopically-observed drama of Ted's exquisitely benighted existence.

Last, but by no means least, there was Leo's moustache; his wild whiskers – his soup-strainer – his bold and brave and beautiful barbel.

To employ the commonplace lingo and designate the moustache as merely 'a Handle-Bar' would be to do it a deep injustice. Leo's moustache was a hugely ornate and flamboyant structure, almost burgundy in colour, which stretched voluptuously from the deep channel separating his nostrils, dipped like a sumptuous summer swallow over each cheek and concluded its dramatic journey in a saucy, curling, upward flourish (the kind of gesture a haughty waiter might employ on lifting the finely embossed silver lid from a succulent tureen of baked lambs' livers) only a whisper from the dainty lobe of either ear.

Leo's moustache was so grand and so mesmerising in its scope and its audacity that it could always be depended upon to make friends squint, strangers gawp, dogs growl and babies squeal. Unfortunately (as with all this world's artifacts of peerless pulchritude: The Golden Gate Bridge, The Cistine Chapel), Leo's barbel was confoundedly difficult to preserve in all its hirsute glory.

And so it was – on that relentlessly icy winter morning – that while Ted surreptitiously struggled to accurately describe the general whereabouts of Wesley to his mysterious interlocutor, Leo was quietly holed-up inside the office's tiny back cloakroom, deeply engrossed in the brief but complex daily ritual of combing out and re waxing his moustache.

Fortunately this process always necessitated – Ted knew not why – the boiling of a kettle, and above its steamy whining he calculated that Leo could probably detect little from the office area beyond the repetitive mutter of distant voices sparring. Even so, as he finally turned to apprehend his fact-seeking friend across the clean, smooth span of his low-quality, high-glossed MDF desk, his gentle face remained cruelly bleached by a pale fog of unease.

'Oh I know perfectly well where Wesley is, *locationally*, it's more his state of mind that interests me.'

The man who spoke was known as Bo because his surname was Mackenzie, and the calf-length gaberdine mac was his main sartorial preference (even during climatic conditions generally thought inappropriate to the wearing of protective garb).

In all other respects though – excluding the mackintosh and the nickname – he bore absolutely no resemblance to *Columbo* the TV detective. He was not an ingenious sleuth. He had little grasp of irony. He was an improbably tall ex-tennis pro with perfectly straight eyes, badly receding black hair (which he grew long to the rear, hoisting it up neatly into a glossy ponytail) and a pathological inability to dither: the kind of inability, in fact, only ever possessed by the successful gambler (who'll always call a spade a spade, except, of course, when he doesn't), the pulpiteer and the bully.

He and Ted went way back. They'd attended school together. And after, when Bo's legendary backhand had buckled (during a much-publicised Canvey-based charity mixed-doubles match with a popular local lady councillor, a post-menopausal pop singer and a lesser-known royal biographer) he'd funnelled his considerable energies into the fertile field of major and minor-league sports journalism.

Unfortunately, Bo's imagination in print (and, alas, also out of it) had always been rather cruelly curtailed by the rudimentary stylistic limitations of serve and return. But Bo was not now, nor ever had been, the kind of man to allow a scandalous want of talent to impede his indomitable physical encapsulation of spunk and grit and zeal.

'But *how* do you know where he is?' Ted asked (diligently ignoring the question about Wesley's state of mind). 'How could you possibly know he was in the library?'

Bo scowled, 'Internet, stupid.'

He waggled his right foot. On the floor just next to it stood a small, rectangular, fabric-coated bag containing his laptop and a choice combination of other high-tech journalistic gadgetry.

'Really?' Ted's innocent eyes widened. 'You're saying it actually records where Wesley is, from moment to moment, right there, on your portable computer?'

'Yes,' Bo growled, 'how the heck would I know otherwise?'

'You're saying he's . . .' Ted paused as the true horror of the situation descended upon him, 'he's *bugged*?'

Bo snorted, 'Don't be ridiculous. It's nothing like that. People keep tabs. *His* people. They watch him. They ring in. They help each other. It's a voluntary thing.'

'Good Lord,' Ted mulled this over for a minute, 'that's terrifying.'

'How?' Bo was uncomprehending.

'How what?'

He took a deep breath, 'How is it terrifying that Wesley's on the internet? Everything's on the fucking internet. That's precisely what it's there for.'

Ted smiled sagaciously, 'Remember *1984*?'

'All too clearly. The year I lost my virginity.'

Ted stopped smiling, 'You lost your virginity at *ten years* of age?'

Bo looked unremorseful. 'I was two years younger,' he expanded nonchalantly, 'than your dear friend Katy Turpin, who kindly plucked my cherry from me.'

Ted's colour rose slightly. 'Anyhow,' he rapidly continued, 'I didn't mean the year, I meant the novel. *1984*. We read it at school. The film starred John Hurt.'

Bo shrugged.

'John *Hurt*,' Ted reiterated. 'He was in *The Elephant Man*. He was nominated for an Oscar.'

Bo stared at Ted in scornful bemusement, '*The Elephant Man*? What the *fuck* does a film have to do with anything?'

Ted picked up a bendy ruler from his desktop and manipulated it between his two hands, carefully. 'A *book*,' he murmured gently, 'it was a book, originally.'

Bo looked up coolly so that he might make a meal out of inspecting the ceiling fan, but instead found himself blinking into a rather uninspiring strip light. After a couple of seconds he focussed in on Ted again. Ted had suddenly acquired a fluorescent white stripe across his nose.

'*God*, Rivers,' in his pique Bo returned temporarily to the reassuring cruelty of formal class lingo, 'why I ever even gave you the time of day at school still remains a monumental fucking mystery to me.'

Ted said nothing. Bo, he mused, had clearly forgotten the exact nature of their scholastic interactions. Maybe this blip indicated some deep psychological problem involving malfunctioning synapses? Or perhaps – and more probably – the simple act of forgetting helped him to sleep a little sounder during the long, bleak hours of the early morning (although, frankly, Bo did not – he had to admit – look in any way like a man who had ever suffered from a shortage of shut-eye. He was devastatingly vital; spruce as a fine Swiss pine).

On considering Bo's spruceness – and its implications in terms of any illusions he may've clung to relating to the existence of a fair and vengeful deity – Ted's throat involuntarily contracted and his mind turned briefly to Wesley's story about the supposed cruelty of ancient Roman pigeon farming. He wondered whether Bo might jump for this scrap – did it qualify as newsworthy? – but before he could speak, Bo spoke himself.

'So does *he* think it's frightening that he's on the internet?'

Uh . . .' Ted's brain fizzed. He put down the ruler and fingered his tie, 'I don't know. I didn't ask him. How could I? I only just this second found out about it.'

'Oh come *on*, Rivers,' Bo hissed impatiently, 'after spending well over an hour in his company, even a cretin like you must've unearthed *something* printworthy.'

Ted tried to think for a moment, 'I found out . . .'

He paused, then spoke, all at once, in a guilty rush, 'I found out that he lost his hand after he fed it to an owl. But I don't think you should write about that. It seemed very personal.'

Bo grimaced, 'Old news. Everybody already *knows* about the sodding hand.'

'They do?' Ted felt inexplicably disappointed.

'What planet are you living on, Rivers? How could you have missed out on all that fuss in the papers early last year about his long-term evasion of Child Support payments?'

'He has a child?'

'A girl. Nine years old. Lives in Norfolk on a kind of crazy Fen zoo. Keeps reindeer. A total freak.'

'And the owl?'

'That's where the fucking owl lived, you moron.'

'Oh.' Ted mulled this over, then stared up at Bo again, a newly-burnished respectfulness shining in his brass-brown eyes, 'So what other stuff have you unearthed about him during your investigation?'

Bo shoved his hand into his mac pocket and withdrew a crumpled roll of paper. He tossed it down onto Ted's desk. Ted reached out, picked it up and unfurled it. The sheet was a computer print-out containing a huge list of biographical facts about Wesley, as well as a selection of articles amassed and reprinted from a variety of sources.

1994, Ted read randomly, *Wesley (at this juncture operating under the pseudonym Parker Swells – for further information see www.parkerswells.co.uk) completes a B-Tec in Business Studies with honours at the (as then was) North London Polytechnic (for student reports, course details, interviews with significant lecturers etc. see section entitled wes:b-tec/northlondon). He applies for several jobs in the field of banking. It is during this time that he meets a woman called Bethan Ray, becomes sexually involved with her and then steals a priceless antique pond from her garden. He is subsequently charged with theft and mental cruelty.*

Ted stopped reading. He frowned then firmly folded the sheet over. 'But how can you be sure it's all true?'

'Of *course* it's true,' Bo snatched the sheet back again, 'and if it isn't, who gives a fuck? I'm not here,' he spoke loudly, initially, then lowered his voice slightly as the kettle clicked off in the cloakroom, 'to tell you about Wesley, or to discuss some pathetic book you might've read at school, or to chat about the nature of truth or the underlying problems of technology . . .'

He drew a deep breath, 'I *am* here, however, to find out, to accrue, to *glean* information. And you are here to give it to me. Unless, that is . . .' Bo's eyebrows rose suggestively. His silence spoke volumes. Ted squirmed a little under the weighty pressure of all this quiet insinuation, but still he said nothing.

'I mean that *is* the understanding between the two of us, currently?'

'Yes,' Ted finally murmured, breaking eye contact to inspect his desktop, 'it's just that . . . in *retrospect* . . .' he picked up the ruler and bent it virtually double, 'in retrospect it seems like I wasn't very well primed. Perhaps I should've been more aware of certain things – special areas of interest – to do with the competition. That kind of stuff.'

'The Loiter.'

'What?'

'The *Loiter*. So where did you take him?'

'Pardon?'

Ted looked up, guiltily. Bo was pressing his hands down hard onto his desk. He had knuckles like horse chestnuts.

'I said *where* did you take him?'

'It didn't mention,' Ted asked, swallowing nervously, his shoulders hunching, 'on the internet?'

'No. It listed the Furtherwick Road – this address, presumably – but that was all. The information's always fairly sketchy. Everybody has stuff they want to keep to themselves. Even the informants. That's the . . .' he thought for a while, '. . . I guess that's the *irony*.'

'Well, we just . . .' Ted paused, 'we just walked down the road a way . . . we had a look around . . . took in the sights . . . uh . . .' he cleared his throat, 'looked at the school and stuff . . .'

'You didn't view any houses?'

'*Houses?*' Ted almost squawked. 'No. Absolutely not. Absolutely no way did we view any houses. No,' he crossed his legs, then his fingers, under the table, 'it was all just . . . well, just simple lay of the land stuff, really . . . he needed to find his bearings . . . he said he wanted to . . . to *mooch* around . . . he said he was interested in geography . . . and pigeons . . . and birds' feet, generally . . .'

As Ted laboriously belched up these unedifying informational gobbets (he had evasion written all over him. He was too genuine by a mile. Honest as a humble bunny. *More* honest), Mr Leo Pathfinder, in all his neat and tidy well-groomed glory, could be observed – a new moth, glistening, fresh from its pupa – silently emerging from the cloakroom behind them.

He pushed the door wide and posed dramatically in its sweep, his hair preposterously bouffant, his moustache quivering, his index finger raised and pressed firmly to his smiling lips in gentle warning.

Bo – who was facing him – saw Leo immediately, yet gave Ted no intimation of his silent re-entry. His eyes barely flickered from their minute inspection of Ted's benign physiognomy.

'I don't know . . .' Ted continued, now utterly immersed in what he was saying, 'I mean I'm not *certain* if it'll help you, but early on, when we were still in the office, Wesley told me some fascinating stuff about pigeon farming. He said that people prefer to cling to the idea that factory farming is a very modern thing, but in actual fact the Romans used to keep pigeons – and I mean literally thousands of them – inside these huge, nasty, airless . . .'

Bo said nothing, just continued to stare at him, focussing on his nose, especially. Ted took his silence as a sign of encouragement and so kept on talking.

Behind him, meanwhile, Pathfinder was on the move. He began to tiptoe, exaggeratedly (holding up his hands, as if scalded, lifting his feet in a crazy goose-step, like a deviant Lipizzaner), very quietly, very deliberately, over from the far wall.

'Sometimes they'd clip their wings and break their legs so that the birds couldn't move around too much. I mean if you can only *imagine* . . .'

Four foot away. Three foot. Two.

Then all at once, like an industrial rubberized, burgundy-bewhiskered Zebedee, Leo sprang – emitting an ear-splittingly wild yet eerily pitch-perfect yodel – and landed, seconds later, with both his hands, stiffened into a terrifying, claw-like rictus, clamped down hard onto poor Ted's shoulders.

Ted jolted, he bucked, his eyes popped.

'*WAH!*'

He kicked himself backwards – his swivel chair pivoting – and as he spun, his jaw jerked insanely like a low-budget skeleton on a funfair ghost-train. The wheels continued rolling and twisting. Twice he almost toppled, nearly taking Pathfinder with him. Leo was agile though, and sprang out, sideways.

'*YES!*' he bellowed.

The chair finally stalled – it stopped spinning – but Ted's jowls continued juddering, his usually sallow complexion now the exact same hue as a sweet potato skin.

'Oh fuck me, Ted, your *face*,' Bo cackled, bending forwards and placing both his hands flat onto the desk again.

'Was it good?' Leo panted, scurrying around to Bo's side to get a better look. 'Did I *kill* him?'

Ted's breath came in nasty gasps as his hands, white knuckled and shaking, clung onto his knees. His cheeks were hollow, his tie skewed. The material on his trousers, several inches below his right thigh, had mysteriously darkened. Moisture. A tiny patch of it.

Ted gulped, flattened his hand, covered the stain, pushed himself up, turned and ran – scalded, staggering – into the close, steamy privacy of the tiny back cloakroom. He slammed the door behind him.

Outside they continued laughing. Leo laughed so hard that his mouth grew gummy.

'I need *water*,' he yelled joyously, 'right *now* Teddy.'

Ted heard Leo shouting, but he didn't move immediately. What a small room this is, he found himself thinking. His back was still jammed firmly against the door; his head, his hands, his heels, his buttocks, all hard up against it.

It was solid behind him. And reassuring.

His breath returned gradually. His palms stopped sweating. His eyes moved down slowly from their temporary refuge in the uncontentious angles of the ceiling, and turned, ineluctably, to catch the pitiful half-formed blur of his reflection in the mirror.

He gulped several times – his trembling lower lip curling down clownishly – then he reached out his hand – inhaling deeply, pushing his chin up, sticking his chest out – and hooked his shaking fingers around the smooth metal of the sink's cold tap.

'*Water*,' he whispered quietly, resting his hand limply on the faucet for a moment, his damp, brown eyes scanning the room for a suitable receptacle to hold it in.

But then he froze. Because suddenly – out of nowhere – he was beset by a vision. And it was a queer vision. It was plush. It was singular; as strange and unexpected as it was outlandish.

Water. Yes. *Water*. A vision of a pond. A small pond. With a bayonet-toting regiment of green reeds on its periphery, white lilies the size of soup bowls floating effortlessly on its surface, exotic carp – in bright golds and oranges – twisting sinuously just underneath.

A pond. A *beautiful* pond. An image of infinite calm. A picture of pure serenity, of boundless peace, of wonderful – of endless – of *exceptional* tranquillity. An astonishingly complex biosphere, just . . . just *hanging in mid-air.*

He closed his eyes for a while, felt a warm breeze on his skin carrying the scent of wild jasmine, heard the infernal gnats buzzing . . . So how on *God's Earth*, he found himself thinking, do you set about stealing a pond? A *garden* pond?

His mind struggled to embrace the viability of such an under-taking – the logistical problems, the practical details, the horrible technicalities – and while it battled to do so, his fingers began cohering; his palm contracted (like a woodlouse, furling up, at the first sign of danger), his hand tightened, then squeezed, then twisted . . .

His eyes flew open as the tap began gushing; he smiled broadly, bent over, splashed his face in cool water, straightened up again, felt it drip off his chin, down his neck, onto his collar. He thought about Wesley –

Him

To steal a pond.

To steal an *antique* pond.

Now that was truly something.

Eight

There's lamb and lynx and lion,
Yet no fowl and no fish, either,
Left on my terra firma.
So wait awhile –
Malinger
And if you stay a loser,
Then plant your feet firmly on Daniel's Candy
To find a pill that's sweeter still,
A sugar far more bitter

Suddenly . . .
Huh-huh
HAH!
. . . having a little trouble . . .
Huh-huh
HAH!
. . . inhaling . . .
Huh-huh
  Tired.
HAH!
Huh-huh
  He was tiring. Had to regulate his . . .
HAH!
. . . breathing . . .
Huh-huh
  Slow things down . . .

HAH!
. . . a little . . .
   Almost always happened . . .
Huh-huh
. . . five hours . . .
Huh-huh
. . . in . . .
HAH!
   Arthur checked his watch. Four and three . . .
Huh-huh
. . . quarters . . .
HAH!
   Approximately.
Huh-huh
   He checked it again. Four . . .
Huh-huh
. . . hours fifty . . .
HAH!
   Precisely. There you go. Just as he'd predicted. Five hours. Only
ten . . .
Huh-huh
. . . minutes . . .
Huh-huh
. . . under. Not bad going. Simply had to regulate . . .
Huh-huh
   Had to focus. Had to stop pushing. Just . . .
HAH!
. . . cruise . . .
Huh-huh
. . . awhile. Just cruise. Just . . .
   Okay.
Okay
   Yes.
HAH!
   And . . .
Phew!
. . . better.
   Candy Island? *Jeeee*sus! (*Pulse was racing. Chest pumping.*

Heart banging like ... heart throbbing like ... fragile-pink-shuddering-hairless-newborn-rodent ... Stop! ... rat ... Stop! ... fieldmouse ... Stop HAH! – thinking!)
Huh-huh

Candy? What the heck was that all about, anyway? Yes he *knew* it was a nod to Defoe (Arthur hawked, then expertly spat the dense yet compact globule over his shoulder) but the actual *meaning* of the reference ...
Huh-huh
... as Defoe used it, originally?

Of course – and this was the worst part – Wesley himself probably didn't have the first ...
HAH!
... idea about the phrase's basic etymology. He was so damn slap-happy, so relentlessly superficial. A cunning magpie. A stinking plagiariser. And so *determinedly* cheerful about it. Such a blissful bloody ...
HAH!
... philistine.

Arthur bent down abruptly to tighten one of his shoelaces – so abruptly, in fact, that the weight of his rucksack almost toppled him. He quickly stiffened his legs, his thighs, stretched out his arms; palms pushed forward – grumbling furiously – rapidly re-located his centre of gravity, tapped the ground lightly with his fingertips – just to make certain – then yanked hard at the lace and firmly re-tied it.

Wasn't the poor – Huh-huh – lace's fault, was it!

Defoe? A preposterous seventeenth century opportunist, a loose cannon, an incorrigible hypocrite. And that – let's face it – was putting it politely.

Candy.
Candy ...

Arthur stood up. His face glistening. He grimaced. He re-adjusted his back-pack. He walked on again.

Presumably there was some vague historical connection with the sugar industry, but in truth he was pretty uncertain as to the finer details. I mean wasn't *everybody*? He *was* fairly sure, though, that Defoe hadn't ever been explicit about the origin of this phrase in his copious writings, or its actual . . .

Phew! Deep breaths. Deep, deep . . . One-two. One-two. Yes. That was better. That was . . .

. . . meaning. And if it had another source – Shakespeare? Chaucer? *Dick* bloody *Francis*? – Arthur was buggered if he knew what it might be. He was a specialist, *dammit*. A *Specialist*. He was the first to admit it, and proudly. Not for him the comprehensive route, the broad-based background in everything from the novels of Jane Austen to the origins of world debt to the nesting habits of the black-headed gull (Arthur Young, a *Generalist*? Never!).

Arthur Young was *partial*, he was a pundit, a boffin, a connoisseur. He was – and there was nothing wrong in it, either – he was . . . he was *particular*.

There

(But hang on a second. Hang on a minute. Because . . . because wasn't this his area? The seventeenth century? Farming methods. Livestock quotas. The consequences of enclosure. All the rest of that miserable, desiccated, dry-as-a-bone malarkey? Wasn't this his speciality? Wasn't . . . ? Ah, fuck it. Fuck . . .)

Something was very wrong here.

One-two. One-two.

Shetland ponies
Hah!
  Industrial landmarks
Hah!
  Machinery dating back to the industrial revolution
Hah!
  Walking. Walking. *Walking.*
HAH!

Just the same (*so put this in your ruddy pipe and smoke it*), he'd painstakingly re-scrutinized the relevant chapters of the book in question the previous evening (Defoe's excessively lauded *A Tour Through the Whole Island of Great Britain*) for any other direct reference to Canvey, just in case something tiny might've slipped his mind. But it hadn't.

HAH!

It hadn't. Thankfully. So he took the phrase to be a topical seventeenth century reference, something throw-away, incidental, insignificant . . .

Left knee was creaking a little. There was a lesson in that, wasn't there? Yup. Shouldn't have bent over so violently.

He did know, though, from what little he'd retained from his own long distant researches – and not forgetting those of his esteemed relative; his great, great, great . . . how many greats was it? Six? Seven? Sod it – that they'd farmed sheep on the island, originally. The fat-tailed variety.

And they'd made special, extremely strong, exceedingly coarse, border-line-loathsome cheeses. From goat's milk. Sent them, post-haste, to the London slums. Corroded their mean and impoverished palates with them.

Anything else? He struggled to remember. He'd last walked this route way back – way, way back – in 1973. A long time ago now. He calculated the numbers. Good God. As long ago as *that*? His thin lips tightened. His shoulders hunched-up, dispiritedly.

1973. A world away. They'd still had a swing bridge then – to gain access . . .

The swing bridge!

Ah yes. He remembered it. And he also remembered – that very same instant – a rather scraggy, slightly worthy, ludicrously keen, ridiculously independent, squeaky-clean, still, still, *still* just-teenage Arthur (*remember?*), precocious as a kitten. Square as . . . well, *square*. Eyes like a leveret. Wide. Round. Credulous.

He'd been a *babe in bloody arms!* Fresh as a peach. Prickling with idealism. Literally prickling . . .

Left turn now. Left turn. Shoulders back. Head up. Keep deep . . .
Keep breathing

Before then – the 1930s, was it? When the bridge was built? (This date stuck in his mind for some inexplicable reason) – they'd used rowing boats. And you could walk over, if you were careful, at low tide. There were stepping stones (and casualties).

What was the name of the silly boy who drowned in Anglesey?
Warren, was it? Warren Summer? Warren Sum-n-er. Yes. Warren
Sumner . . . That was him. Yes. Good.

No

Colin.
It was Colin Sumner.
It was Colin.

Arthur still retained most of his short-term memory.

Okay, not all of it, by any means, but at least some things remained
intact. No matter what the . . . No matter. Some important . . . it was
still working, still ticking over, still turning, despite everything.

Canvey. The bridge. The swing bridge.

Hmnnn. Air suddenly feels cooler. Brisker. Moister

Local people – as he remembered – had been almost unnaturally fond of this fine but patently rather antiquated construction.

The swing bridge.

He couldn't properly recall what they'd called the damn thing . . . It did have a name . . . Now that *was* a challenge. He knew – or at least he *felt*, instinctively – that it'd had a person's appellation. A man's name. Something like Peter. The Peter Bridge. No. No, *Colin*. The Colin Bridge. What?

You're thinking about the dead kid. You're confusing . . .

How about Cannon?

Cannon – heavy armament – brand of camera – TV detective – bridge?

No. Arthur paused for a moment, placed his two hands onto his skinny hips and racked his brains . . . Cannon . . . Calvin . . . Colvin . . . The *Colvin* bridge. Of course. Of *course*.

And it was quite like Colin . . .

The Colvin Bridge; demolished the very same year he visited (it was flooding back, suddenly. Memory worked that way; damming up, the pressure building, *building* . . . then something giving; the wall – the buffer – the block – the *nothing* . . . then information – the news – the facts – the evidence – the data . . . a mass of it – an *agony* – gushing right past him in relentless torrents. Useless stuff, mostly. Rubbish – guff – padding).

In February. 1973. That was when it finally fell. So it must've been approximately this time of year when he'd visited, originally, because the bridge was still there, but no longer swinging. No longer working. January . . .
Weird.

Arthur shook himself out of his reverie and walked onwards. He glanced around him. The fields were crammed with geese and peewits . . .

He re-analysed his route, carefully recollecting each and every single *individual* part of it: The road. The A road. Shouldered by potato fields. The water tower. The Pizza-Hut. The Texaco. The KFC . . .

Chickens. Yes. He'd seen some. And buntings. Bungalows. Big sheds. Old pubs a-plenty but with brand new faces. All tucked and lifted. Freshly painted.

And the pylons – *hundreds* of them – stretching out their metal fingers, deftly knitting the obliging winter white into a brazenly scratchy patchwork of wire and whizz and buzz. Marching towards the coast. A relentless army. In thundering formation.

Then –

Ah yes . . .

– the gradual flattening. The browning out, the bleaching. The stubby trees hunched up like pinched and twisted spinsters against the relentless slow-rolling lashes of sea breeze. The bushes, up on their toes, flaring, hissing, like angry yellow cats: lichen-ridden, feral, stray, bony, stricken. The landscape, sour and dry-grassed and mean and sulky. Low. Yanked back from the sea. Nearly dry, still resentful. Still *sucking*.

More roads. More mud. Tarmac. Roundabouts. More tarmac . . . *A-ha! Golf.* There had to be, didn't there? (Nothing grand. Just putting.)

The cuts, the banks, the creeks . . .

Then finally, the refineries. Balanced on the coastline like a clutch of steel reptiles. Like iguanas, nodding complacently – perhaps in friendship, possibly in challenge – towards the hoary, pewter, slate-smashed sea. Dry-clawed, shining, harsh, bulbous, slithering, *contained*, pristine.

Heavenly cities. Silver-streaked. Honed, funnelled, tanked-up, stripped-back, chiming and whistling (what was this? Home time? Lunch time? Some terrible emergency?). Like Dorothy's Oz – once, twice, three times over – cursed and wizarded by crazy, metallic, sky-high titfers, neat smoke billowing in strictly circumscribed plumes (a celebratory cigar, smoked gingerly at a birth or a wedding), the odd, random bellow of industrial cantanker.

Arthur paused a while and looked about him. He was here, now, wasn't he? He had arrived. This was Canvey. No. This was Benfleet. He was in neither one place nor the other. He was on the outer perimeters of both. One foot in either.

He pulled a map from his pocket. A piece of paper had been attached to it by a small silver clip (with another, rougher, less detailed map on top penned in thick black felt-tip). He glanced over towards the half-floating, mud-ridden clutter of the main marina. Low tide. Or low-ish –

Hmmn

Benfleet station, just behind him –

Check

The new bridge. Brick built in '73 –

Check

No name. Or none to be seen (did they never bother naming bridges any more, once the hopeful sixties were over?).

He set off again, crossed this unexceptional edifice – swamped in day-glo banners, for some reason; high tides? Tall ships? – took a sharp right beyond the main body of the marina, then abandoned the big road and trip-trapped back across a lesser tributary (if you wanted to string your fingers around the slim waist of the torrent, then this brief, thin segment was plainly the place to do it) over a perilous-seeming, tiny, hand-built wooden walkway, through an empty field full of broken bottles – aluminium cans, rotting paper, empty plastic canisters – and up onto the seriously-raised, neatly-grassed bank of Benfleet Creek ... Curling like an adder. Man-made. Well-maintained. Quite deliciously – *quite deliciously* – prescriptive.

Arthur followed the creek, striding good-naturedly along its slithery ribbon. He side-winded. There were herons here, and things – if possible – were even plainer. *Quieter*
Sssssshhhh!

Scrub-land. Mudland. Sodden pasture. Everything just as it should be, by his reckoning –
Right.

He inspected his map again. He glanced up. Meadow pipits And slime. Plenty of it. The tide still out, but dribbles of brown liquid trickling in like strong ground coffee through a cheescloth filter. The earth still soggy. His boots – he grimaced – growing increasingly muddy. He walked on, heavily.

Sometimes there were horses; shaggy-maned, winter-coated, tethered by old rope to broken fences (holding nothing out, holding nothing in), exhaling fierce jets of steam at his silent passing. Head-tossing. Foot-stamping. Whinnying. Lip-smacking. Wanting attention. Wanting words, signs, whispers, kisses, anything. Just a *sign*. Or release, maybe. But Arthur walked on, determinedly, tightly bound as an Egyptian mummy.

Things grew wilder. He slipped and tripped through a sudden abundance of teazel and bramble, but kept his garments pristine all the while, never snagging. He ducked under the flyover ...

Ah yes. The flyover. This was definitely . . .
Uh . . .
An innovation

Wasn't it? *Wasn't* it?

He passed beneath it, bent double, his back-pack troubling him. The soil underfoot, he noted, still recoiling from the shock of the thunderous cacophony above. Sheep-stepped, hoof-pocked, shit-splattered. Groaning.

Out the other side. He straightened –
Ouch!

He creaked a little. Over a small stile. Onwards. And on, and on, river-winding, cold-cutting, cheeks smarting, until finally, *finally*, he paused again. He peered about him. He stamped his feet.

He took in the vista. He had not seen another soul in well over an hour (he'd seen the cars, whizzing past him, but that counted for nothing).

Below where he stood lay a scruffy, mud-splattered wharf-like construction. A pier. A mean, wooden finger, pointing rudely towards nowhere. One boat attached to it, but not *floating*. A permanent craft, of some ungodly denomination. A stilted canal-boat. A hutch.

His hands were blue with the cold. He'd removed his gloves earlier, when he'd met up with . . .

Pale eye. Snowy owl. Ivory woman.

His mind flipped rapidly through a curious assortment of disparate images.

Cruella de Ville. Coconut macaroons. French poodles. Bambi.

Cold. It was bloody *cold* Goddammit. And misty now. He blew on his fingers. He inspected the stricken-seeming craft from a distance. He put his hand into his coat pocket. He pulled out a key (a small key attached to a piece of string, attached, in turn, to an old-fashioned luggage label with spidery black writing on it.

He did not read the writing.).

The air was damp now; quiet yet weighty: full-bellied with the snarl of speeding cars in the distance. He found the combination pleasing. Silence. Humming. A goose flew past him. Eye-level.

Wha?!

He jumped. *Canadian.* He heard its wings pumping. A clean sound. Its round eye appraised him. He shrugged to himself, almost embarrassedly.

Then, carefully – as was his way, invariably – placing one foot gingerly next to the other, walking sideways; hunched-over, knees bent; he made his way gradually down the bank (the Sea Wall, he supposed they'd call it, locally, but not concreted here, like on the coast-line proper), through the grass and the slime, without slipping – never slipping – towards this moon-craft. This wreck. This strange, scruffy, humble, chipped and creaking, something-and-nothing berth-dock-anchor. This mooring.

The mist will grow thicker, he reasoned – once he'd finally reached the boat; seeing the door hanging loose on its hinges, a window, cracked, smelling gas from somewhere, leaking, possibly – the mist will grow thicker –
It must
– and gently soft-focus this stricken craft for me . . .
How ridiculous these thoughts are. How utterly out of character.
But he'd always loved the fog. He loved what it represented, what it *implied,* what it stood for

So what does it stand for, exactly?

Arthur shrugged off these thoughts just as quickly and efficiently as he shrugged off his rucksack (the latter with possibly a fraction more difficulty – his shoulders were killing him) and then smiled up benignly at the sodden, cloud-smitten sky. These were sweet fancies. They were not typical –
What the hell is this curious light-headedness about, anyway? Excitement? Depression? Overbreathing?

87

In general Arthur was not a man particularly prone to random feelings of arbitrary optimism (well if not *never*, then at least *rarely*. He was a solitary creature. And glum, habitually). Heck. He was just tired. That was it. Definitely. And he needed his medication.

Or a stiff, stiff brandy

Good *Lord*. How easily, how *smoothly* that'd slipped out of him. Five long years, dry as the Sahara. A stiff *brandy?* With *his* liver? What a curiously reckless, what a crazily inappropriate, what a stupid, what a stupid, what a stupid . . .
A stiff brandy?
Arthur Young took a tremulous half-step out onto the truncated pier. It groaned under him, but it did not give. It was secure. Not so the handrail which crumbled like ripe stilton under his fingertips. *Woodworm.* He placed both his feet together. He pushed back his shoulders. And then, in a single, smooth motion, he reached out his arm and threw the key – the string – the tag – up, up up into the foggy air.

There!

He diligently supervised its multiple adventures – its brief spiral-ling rise, its determined fall (like a sycamore seed, a helicopter blade, an injured grouse on the wing), its eventual splash-landing, its half-hearted floating, its gradual submerging – with a strong, with a wicked, with a *powerful* sense of satisfaction.

There

It did not matter a damn. He smiled blearily, his lips numbed by the cold, his cheeks damp and stinging. It did not *matter* one iota. He took a deep, steady breath and stared firmly ahead of him. No key. No *keys*.
Because this was a door already open.

Nine

'It *has* to be the start,' Wesley declaimed passionately, his two elbows practically indenting the soft pine counter-top, 'it just *has* to be the beginning of a whole, new, *completely* comprehensive language of mammals.'

He was holding forth in Canvey's rather small but surprisingly high-ceilinged, semi-pre-fabricated library, to a charming and comely woman who wore a pale blue nylon twinset – effortlessly exuding the kind of easy stylishness rarely attributed to artificial fibre – some ludicrously playful kitten heels – not the heels, surely, of a dedicated librarian? – a heavy, calf-length beige skirt – sharply pleated to the front *and* the rear – a coral necklace – her ten wildly impractical false nails painted the exact-same peachy-coral colour – and a mop of blonde hair set in solid tribute to Angela Dickinson circa 1964. A woman in her late fifties.

This lucky female was standing on the opposite side of the waist-high, well-buffed library counter, over which her hypnotically pointed mamillae asserted their powerful dominion with such thrust and determination that it was as much as Wesley could do not to push his flattened palm onto them (simply to ascertain whether they'd cave or resist . . . Oh let them resist . . . But let them *cave* . . . *Lord*, why was sex always so fucking *contrary?*).

She was almost certainly the chief librarian, although she wore no formal indication to this effect about her person. No tag, no badge, no pin or anything. Just had an aura of inexplicably *kindly* authority.

'And you honestly think coughing is central to this new language?' she asked playfully, her lavender eyes twinkling behind

89

a large pair of expensively cumbersome, baby-blue-framed glasses. She was charmed by Wesley's conversation. But she was incredulous. Both responses in equal measure. Wesley always found this combination to be a *happy* mixture. He provoked it knowingly.

His ravaged olive-paste eyes twinkled straight back at her (was she a *real* pointy woman – like the wonderful, huge-hearted, exquisitely-well-starched kind who starred in all the best films of the 1950s – or was this riveting display purely the result of a lower back problem and an ill-fitting brassiere?).

Wesley tried not to stare. But it was a struggle. The breasts reared up at him like angry cobras, they pointed like cheeky schoolgirls without any manners. *Oh.*

'What else?' Wesley smiled, struggling to keep atuned to the flirty meander of their conversation, 'I mean I'm no linguist or anything – this is purely an instinctive reaction – but what else unifies all creatures quite so absolutely as a sharp, hard *cough*, when you really come to think about it?'

He paused, then added, his voice dropping, but still showing a certain flash of *sangfroid*, 'Apart, I suppose from those other three great unifiers: the fart, the burp, the sneeze.'

The chief librarian snorted, then covered her neatly-painted lips with her neatly-painted hand to try and mask it, pushed her glasses straight and shrugged, somewhat coquettishly. Her name was Eileen, and at root, at heart, she was incorrigibly Otherwise. (*Otherwise?* She was a mish-mash, a mosaic, a *medley*.)

Eileen was Otherwise (plainly and simply): she was the bird in the hand worth two on the bush, she was the silk purse from a sow's ear, she was the stitch in time who saved nine – she was all of these things and more in her Littlewood's underwear and skin-tone support stockings (only the merest *hint* of French eau de Cologne, but with industrial quantities of Harmony, for good measure, enveloping and supporting her bright, blonde hair).

Eileen.

An English rose, but with solid, Irish foundations. A refined and elegant lady – undisputedly – but with an accent steeped to its well-turned shins in the coarse, muddy burr of the Estuary. Blissfully miserable. Softly tough. Strictly gentle. Horribly lovely.

Irish parents: Siobhan and Flannery. Walthamstow born and

bred. A north-east Londoner, an east-seventeen-teen, then twenty-something, then faltering, gingerly, on that awful ravine of thirty (*thirty!*) when in 1975 her whole damn family – aunts and uncles, nephews, nieces – upped and shifted, *en masse*, to Canvey.

She'd already served a full ten year sentence inside the Love Penitentiary: *marriage* – maximum security – to a wretch called Patrick, who smoked Silk Cut and worked as a plasterer (a *devoutly* Catholic union. Messily divorcing. They'd had no children. Eileen, it turned out, was hopelessly barren).

Poor Eileen: a planner, a dreamer, a lover, a traveller, yet still somehow – but *how?* How the heck had she managed it? – still living bumper-to-bumper with the people who'd raised her. Same house, same job, same prospects as her mother. 1975. Everything just as she'd dreaded it.

Needed a change of direction – but nothing too violent, or challenging – so when the whole street migrated (staggering, as one, to this tried but untested gumboot territory), Eileen packed her bags, hitched up her skirts and *clambered* (broke a nail, bruised a knee) onto the back of the bandwagon. Joined the exodus. Started a brand new life for herself, next to the Estuary.

I mean there were new houses here, weren't there? And jobs promised. There were plans and stratagems, designs and sophistry. Multiple incentives for the poor, the keen, the needy. A social experiment, they called it, to shore up the demoralised Canvey community after the chronic floods of '53. To re-populate, re-invigorate, rejuvenate. New schools, new shops, new industry, new bridge, new . . . new *library*.

'But where did it come from?' Eileen asked, placing her own two elbows onto the counter in a perfect duplication of Wesley's (their funny bones now very nearly touching. Her 24-carat gold charm bracelet sliding down her arm a-way – Wesley liked charms, and he liked Eileen; she was cute and obliging as a baby wallaby – her breasts pushed together, the underwire creaking like the straining bow on an ancient, sea-tossed, strong-timbered lobster smack).

She stood so close she could smell his breath, sweetly flavoured, as it was, with rum and raisin. With toffee (he'd offered her one. She'd refused. It'd looked slightly soggy and was frosted with lint. And there was a No Eating policy in the library. No Food. No Dogs.

No Noise. No Running. Standard library requirements. Eileen – while soft-centred – was a terrible stickler).

Wesley ate the toffee anyway and grinned at Eileen, passing the sweet from one cheek to the other. He knew just what it meant to duplicate body language. It was always a good sign. He glanced at her left hand – wedding band – then snapped back to attention.

'I was actually in Cornwall,' he explained, 'in the middle of nowhere, out walking, when this sheep coughed from behind a nearby hedge. I almost jumped out of my skin. I thought it was a person – the cough was so . . . so *human*. It was creepy. But once I realised . . . well, an absolute *revelation* . . .'

While Wesley was speaking, the library's swing doors swung wide behind him. He felt a gust of cold air but did not turn to face it, merely watched all the action gradually unfolding inside the high-polished reflection of Eileen's two, wide lenses.

Doc . . . The girl (the *new* girl – Miss Whisky-Eyes, Miss Sticky-Finger) . . . Patty . . . Shoes . . . then Hooch, five seconds later . . . Another person; a woman with a baby (in a pushchair); Hooch held the door open for her. Wesley automatically counted her among them (he'd had mothers and babies Following before, but only very briefly. It wasn't especially workable, or *healthy*, for that matter).

The woman paused as the door slammed behind her, then peeled off to the right, splitting from the others –
Good. That was better.

The rest slowly filtered past him, one by one, glancing nervously around them, nobody speaking, feet shuffling, weatherproof jackets squeaking, noses streaming . . .

Then he heard the girl. 'Fiction,' she whispered. 'Over there, I reckon.'

Shortly after, Hooch (a muffled boom – like heavy-artillery practice at a firing range, five-plus miles away) murmured, 'I *told* you so,' then sniggered obnoxiously.

The girl led the rest of them into the far left-hand corner (she's been here before, Wesley surmised, slotting this fact away for later). They all followed her, except for Patty, who slid the flat of his grubby hand along the counter-top – savouring the high-polished gloss and the squeak of his palm on it – then stopped and waited.

Wesley's lips tightened. He found the boy irritating. Children never understood the way of things. Following especially. The rules. The protocol. Didn't have the subtlety.

Eileen was still talking –

Bugger

– he tuned in again, but too tardily to catch the gist of it.

'. . . unless it's a two way thing,' she finished, ringingly, her bright eyes engaging his, demanding a quick response from him.

Bollocks

Wesley immediately threw all his eggs into one, small basket.

'*Cat* person,' he exclaimed trenchantly, pointing the middle and index fingers on his good hand at her (like he was aiming a friendly gun – the kind that fired out a flag emblazoned with the word *Bang* or *Gotcha*). He acted as if the need to recognise this simple truth – this unifying attribute, this cat-fact – surpassed virtually everything.

Eileen frowned, thrown slightly off kilter, 'Uh . . . no. No. I'm allergic, actually.' She shrugged. She was not impressed. But she was briefly distracted.

'Ah.'

(*Fuck.* That was clumsy.)

Wesley glanced down. Dennis was sitting on his right foot.

'Hello there Dennis.'

Wesley smiled at him. Dennis yawned. Eileen stood on tiptoe and peeked over the counter.

Dog

'We actually have a No Dog policy in the library,' she explained.

Dennis stared up at her, impassively. His stumpy tail ticked.

Left, right, left, left, left.

'Dennis here,' Wesley explained, ignoring the policy (he was no fan of policies), 'has diabetes.'

No palpable reaction.

'And he cannot bark. He is dumb, which is rare for a terrier. But he barks in his dreams. Dennis is a *dream* barker.'

Eileen stopped frowning. Her eyebrows (hard plucked as a good turkey dinner) rose a full half-centimetre.

He barks in his dreams

She let this beguiling thought slowly penetrate her. *Oh.* That was just so . . . so right, so pretty . . . so . . . just so *darling.*

93

He barks in his dreams

Wesley had selected his ammunition masterfully. Because Eileen
– as it so happened – was an absolute *glutton* for dreamers. She was
a pushover, a mug, a *fool* for dreaming. She was a cinch, a patsy,
a stooge, a greenhorn . . . Forget librarian – chief librarian, even –
because in the real world, in the harsh – too harsh – light of daytime,
day *dreaming* was her actual – her *bona-fide* – profession.

She was a dreamer by instinct, by nature, by inclination; a *de
facto* dreamer. Always had been. Dreamed so much sometimes
she hardly noticed the day's closing or the season's passing (wore
light summer dresses in winter, until the cold made her shiver).
Forgot birthdays, mealtimes, hair appointments, anniversaries, all
in a miasma of other-worldly hankering.

Lived in the eternal summer of dreams. A long, slow, blue-
skied, green-grassed, yellow-hued, daisy-kissed, wheat-smelling,
poppy-bleeding, bee-buzzing, stonechat-smacking pastureland of
dreaming.

Hardly knew what she was doing – point of fact – hour by hour.
Did a whole week's shopping without even noticing, made the
bed, brushed her teeth, put on her face every morning, all in a
deep, sweet, haze of not-thinking. Saw real life through a mirror,
covered in condensation. Blurred at its edges. Wore a cobweb
coat to dinner. Sipped on nectar. Broke the worldwide record
for dandelion blowing. Flew on little wings. Shared the mossy
bed of the badger. Fought with the weasel. Darned and seamed
her daytimes with fine-stitched patchworks of light and downy,
feather-bellied imaginings.

Nothing too spectacular. Nothing wrong or weird or dirty or
anything. Just all things familiar and rosy and comforting. Her
dreams were as soft and clean as she was. There was nothing in
them to be ashamed of. I mean there was no *law* against the *yearn*,
the *keen*, the *wish*, was there? *Was* there?

Wesley made a sharp mental note of Eileen's reaction. *Dreamer*
(almost lost her back there with that cat person clap-trap. But now
she was hooked. Now he could play her).

A mere four feet away, the small boy, Patty, was still carefully
inspecting the constellation of spit and snot he'd just recently
downloaded onto the counter-top. He was too short to lean on the

counter properly. Instead he stretched himself up and over. Stood on tippy-toes, fingers grappling, coat riding up, trousers slipping down to reveal the top half of the lean cheeks of his flat-boy-buttocks. Tummy, hips, belly-button, all perkily protruding.

He was thin. Pale skinned. Unhealthy looking. He hawked expertly then swallowed noisily. He was a boy with a minor sinus problem.

Eileen peered over at him, then back at Wesley again. There was a piece of paper – just to the left of their elbows – lying on the counter: Wesley's *Library Membership Application Form*. It was only partially filled in. Eileen reached out her hand for it. 'We'll be needing your current address,' she said, 'and your date of birth, obviously.'

Wesley grabbed the form and the pen he'd been using previously.

'Do you like music?' he asked, scribbling away diligently.

'Music? *Hmmn.* Yes, I suppose I do,' Eileen answered, idly watching the small group in the corner: the man with no shoes whom she'd seen in there earlier, and the girl, the girl with short hair.

'I play the banjo. You should come and listen. I use the *Clawhammer* technique, due to my, uh . . .'

He lifted his right hand. Eileen's eyes widened.

'I'll be playing later, about three-ish, once I've hiked around the Island's perimeter. On the private fishing pier near the Gas Storage Terminal . . .'

He glanced up, 'I'd love to see you there.'

He pushed the slip of paper towards her.

Under DATE OF BIRTH (Eileen focussed in on it, with a slight start), Wesley had written:
It is only with the heart that one can see rightly
Then an inch or so lower, in the margin,
What is essential is invisible to the eye.

Eileen glanced up at him, perplexedly. But he was staring over towards the fiction section, at the small crowd pulling books from the shelves there. Then suddenly he was bending down to stroke the dog, then stepping back, then smiling, nodding, turning, walking, opening the door. Quick as anything. Quick as . . . Without even . . . without . . .

Eileen's gaze flew to the section marked ADDRESS and it was then that her half-quizzical-smile froze; *c/o*, it said, *c/o Ms Katherine Turpin*, followed by a horribly familiar Furtherwick Road number.

Ms Katherine . . .

What?

The smile remained stuck; stiff at its corners.

Patty cleared his throat. Then he cleared it again, even louder. Eileen put down the form, her expression smeared with joy and fear, hope and hunger.

'I want to join this library,' the small boy said (he was a simple boy and Eileen's Otherwiseness meant nothing to him), 'but I'm rubbish at writing things.'

It is only with the heart that one can see rightly,

What is essential is invisible to the eye

The Little Prince. Antoine De Saint-Exupéry. Her favourite book, her favourite writer, her favourite person in the whole wide world, ever ever *ever*.

Eileen deftly slid Wesley's slip under the counter – her face still a casualty ward of mixed emotions – then turned towards the child and asked if she could help him. As she listened dutifully to his answer, she dazedly twisted her wedding band on her neatly-painted finger; her soft, sweet, lavender eyes slowly clouding over.

Ten

Hmmmmn

Dewi chewed solemnly on a heavily-salted tomato sandwich as he peered through his living room window, his dust-iced skin zebraed by the sharp stripes of winter light which gushed, unapologetically – like hordes of white-frocked debutantes flashing their foaming silk petticoats in eager curtsies – between the regimented slats of his hand-built shutters.

He chewed methodically, his muscular jowls working – deliberately, repetitively – his dark eyes staring out, unblinking. He was waiting for Katherine. But he was thinking about Wesley.
Wesley.

Wesley 'the joker'. Isn't that what they called him? Or Wesley 'the wild card'. Or Wesley . . . Wesley 'the *maverick'* (that was a popular one, just currently). But there were others, too, and plenty of them: 'The Scholarly Beadle' (a pretty pitiful soubriquet, all things considered), 'The Post-Millennial Prankster' (and people actually got *paid* to write this crap?).

Wesley.

Dewi stopped chewing. He swallowed, slightly prematurely, experiencing some difficulty; gulping. He sniffed. He swallowed again, then picked a tomato pip from his molar with his finger. The pip was dislodged. He bit down hard upon it. He crushed it.

But weren't these people – these mild-mannered commentators, these hacks, these pen-pushers, these thoroughly indulgent, head-shaking, lip-biting, gently tutting people, these *mollycoddlers* to a man – weren't they all forgetting something? Something important?

Weren't they forgetting – I mean he didn't want to *piss* on their fucking *chips* or anything – but weren't they forgetting the damage? Yes. As blunt as that. Plain as that. *Boring* as that: The damage – The devastation – The pain – The *destruction*.

(Tedious truths, Dewi was the first to acknowledge – truths invariably were, weren't they? – but truths just the same. Indubitably.)

Caught up – as they obviously were – in all the fun of it (the waggishness, the roguery), couldn't they at least show a pretence of concern over the possibility that they might, in some small way, be in serious danger of overlooking the crucial, the more salient, the rather *less* salubrious issues?

Wesley the *Heartless*. That was more like it. Just the kind of monicker he was really crying out for (didn't it at least mean something?), or Wesley the Careless. Wesley the *Killer* (so much more fitting than the Beadle thing). Or Wesley the *Bastard* (Hell yes. Even better).

Good *Gracious*. Dewi's hands were suddenly shaking. He tried to relax them, forming tight fists one moment, flexing them the next. He glanced down, anxiously. As his head dipped he was momentarily blinded by a gush of light. He flinched. He blinked. He straightened up, immediately. His eyes scanned the road again. To the left of him. To the right.

Could it really have been Wesley? He frowned. But *seriously* . . . Could it really? Back in Canvey again? The *actual* Wesley? Here? Large as life? In the flesh?

But how was that possible? More to the point, how would he *dare*? And what on earth might his reasons be? (To gloat? To crow? To strut? To swagger?)

Wesley *back*? No. Never. The more he thought about it the more . . . the more crazy it seemed, the more . . . well, ridiculous. Ludicrous. *Inconceivable.*

Dewi's frantic eyes briefly desisted from their anxious scanning of the roadway, relaxed, refocussed, then suddenly – quite unintentionally – caught an oddly disquieting glimpse of their own violent expression in the window's clear reflection. He flinched, then looked sideways, almost shiftily.

This was not like him.

This is not . . . This is not *like* me, he told himself, This is . . . this is . . .

Inconceivable? But was it? Was it really? His right shoulder jerked upwards, in a tiny spasm, towards his dust-slicked ear-lobe. Yes. *Yes.* Absolutely. It *had* to be. Because over the past two years Wesley – or the idea, the concept, the very *notion* of Wesley – had somehow acquired a marvellous, a fabulous, an almost . . . yes, an almost *mythological* significance for him.

The way he saw it, Wesley was an absolute one-off. He was the genuine article. He was out there, on a limb (teetering, maybe, but clinging on, determinedly). He was unique. He was unparalleled. He was completely and totally and utterly unprecedented.

Even so, this phenomenal – no – this *extraordinary* singularity as Dewi (perhaps somewhat naively) perceived it, was patently not apprehended by him as any kind of virtue. Quite the contrary. For when Dewi actually imagined Wesley – when he conjured up an image of him, inside his mind – Wesley was not configurated, not defined, not *delineated* quite as your average, ordinary, every-day mortal should be.

Within the deliciously wholesome confines of Dewi's imaginings, Wesley took on the form of something infinitely less, and yet – quite paradoxically – something immeasurably *more* than your average, commonplace, rough-hewn homosapien. Because for Dewi, Wesley was actually an absolute, undisputed, honest-to-goodness *monster.* A monster in all the traditional senses: small-brained, big-jawed, heaving, sweating, baying, howling, gesticulating, clawing, gnashing . . .

The vilest, the cruellest, the most unapologetically lawless, coarse, despicable and licentious creature. A horned demon. Fork-tailed. Fanged. Cloven.

But that wasn't . . . that couldn't . . . even *that* didn't encompass . . . it didn't . . .

Because when Dewi tried to visualise Wesley, the initial image he generated rarely remained constant. It switched. It varied. It altered. It disintegrated. It *morphed* (morphed? Was that the proper, modern word for it?).

Inside Dewi's agitated imaginings, Wesley was not merely *bestial,* he was more . . . so much more complicated than that. More

99

terrible. And infinitely less predictable. He saw many forms. He was a Shape-Shifter. He was a Changeling. He was a Centaur, or possibly a Gorgon, or maybe even a Satyr. Yes . . .

Yes. That was it. A *satyr*. With hooves. With muscular thighs. Curling hair. A pan-pipe . . .

A pan-pipe?

No . . . No. The image was changing. It was disintegrating again. It was vacillating, reconfigurating . . .

Either way, Wesley was something decidedly foul but strangely intangible, something thoroughly ancient but heinously ungodly. He was the anti-everything. He was the unthinkable.

For Dewi – and he was hardly a man alone in this particular respect – life held many uncertainties (could he afford this month's rent? Did his saw need greasing? Was he allergic to walnuts? Were his plug-holes blocked up again?), yet among all of these manifold uncertainties there remained one thing – and one thing only – of which he was profoundly certain. No – tell a lie – there were two things, but the first of these was simply a given: that he loved Katherine Turpin; that he loved her truly, unselfishly, and to distraction – that she was a Queen to him.

And the second thing? It was related to the former, inextricably. The second thing Dewi knew for certain was that even if – by a very large stretch of the imagination – he was able to grasp the notion of Wesley's actual physical *being* – his mortality – he was still totally incapable of comprehending the idea of Wesley as a moral *entity* – incapable, in effect, of believing in Wesley's *humanity*.

Because Wesley was not like other men. He lacked something. He missed an essential quality (gentleness? benevolence? *decency?*). He was not a proper person. He was a pitiful creature. He was lost. He was damned. He was hollow. He was empty.

To all intents and purposes, Wesley did not really exist. Not morally-speaking, anyway. He was a vacuum. He was struck-out. Deleted. He was nothing.

Dewi shoved a thick strand of hair from his eyes, noticing, idly (as he pulled his hand away), how the film of dust on his fist had been severed by a thick slick of tomato juice; his four knuckles split into two. Neatly riven. Dissected. He paused for a moment, breathing deeply.

And yet . . . And yet if it really had been Wesley he'd seen – all things taken into account and everything – if it really *had* been him, then what could he seriously expect to *gain* from this strange and unexpected Second Coming? What more could he take from them – realistically? Hadn't he taken enough the first time around? Hadn't he stripped them bare? Hadn't he humbled and humiliated them *then* sufficiently?

What more could he take, damn him?

Dewi placed the remainder of his sandwich down onto the window ledge. His stomach was churning. And time was passing. He shifted his weight. He wiped his mouth. He glanced at his watch. Twelve twen . . . Twelve *twenty-one*?

What?

Two whole minutes later than she ever was, normally?

Sweet Katherine

Not that he kept tabs or anything.

Twelve . . . twelve . . . twelve *twenty-two* already?

By twelve twenty-three Dewi had already run several times through every conceivable option:

A delay at work

A random conversation

A breakdown

An accident

Or was it something more insidious? Something to do with the Estate Agent? With Ted? Sharp-suited, sandy-coloured Ted. Or with the kid in her garden? Or the boy-girl? Or the ruined old fellow with the little dog? Or the notebook-clutching fool in the plastic hat? The Followers. The Behindlings.

He clenched his teeth in frustration. He'd guessed they'd be back. He'd predicted it. After the book initially came out – almost two years ago now – they'd come then (not in hordes, not in their hundreds, but in dribs and in drabs, in gangs, in clutches. Just enough of them, basically, to bug, to chafe, to niggle him).

And they'd continued to come. Predictable as bad weather. Twice as persistent. Men, mostly. Sad cases. Trouble-makers. Wolves in sheep's clothing. Saintly sinners yearning to share something (experience? Pity? *Semen*?).

And the locals joked about it, to start off with. Then the

101

neighbours started complaining. But Katherine? She didn't seem to notice, or if she did (and she must've) then she never spoke out about it, never let on to anyone, just pretended she didn't care, just lived her life, same as ever, quietly, firmly, impassively.

That was Katherine.

Oh *God*, he'd wanted to hurt Wesley, then. To damage him. Because he couldn't comprehend it. He couldn't understand how a stranger could be so cruel. So cavalier. So careless. It was more – so much more – than just the fact of the matter, it was the basic, fundamental bloody principle of the thing.

The *principle*.

And then ... And then finally – ah yes, *finally*; the sheer, raw *pain* of this spuriously conclusive word made him almost catch his breath – just when it seemed like all the fuss and the misery might actually be in danger of diminishing a little – two whole years of trouble, two whole crazy *years* – the icing on the cake, the culmination of everything: that stupid fucking *pointless* competition. The treasure hunt.

The *Loiter*.

And clue three? Daniel's *Candy*.

The woman serving in the chippie had explained the connection to the man in the queue standing two customers ahead of him. Daniel Defoe, she said (*Robinson Crusoe*, ironically, had been his favourite book as a boy) once called Canvey by that curious name in a book about Great Britain. A travel journal or something.

Candy Island. And Dewi knew – he *knew* – right there and right then, that these five sweet letters spelled an infinity of trouble; for him, for Katherine. Pretty much the same stuff as before, only more of it this time. Much more. Because of the treasure, obviously. And because of that poor man dying so tragically. The publicity.

Oh *Lord*. Today was just the beginning. It wouldn't end here. Dewi kicked one hefty, steel-toe-capped boot against the other. Where the leather stretched thinly over the worn crest of the toe, a sleek shimmer of metal was visible, peeking through. When it struck the second boot it clanged sonorously, like an old, dented gong, upended in a cellar. He did it again. He did it a third time.

Wesley. *Wesley*. Dewi shook himself. He was still dusty. He inspected his forearms. Dusty. His palms. Dusty. Surely it *couldn't* be simply a coincidence? He'd seen his photo on the book cover. And he'd seen the same picture, by sheer chance, on the late night news. Last year. Springtime. A stupid scandal over paternity. And then, when that poor man drowned on Guy Fawkes Night, in Anglesey, in the midst of all that terrible *tragedy*: Wesley's foul and unrepentant grin, plastered everywhere, staring out at him from magazine racks, from the tabloid papers, from the broadsheets (even the *broadsheets* couldn't seem to get enough of him).

And the pay-off?

'Colin Sumner won. That's the important thing. Colin Sumner's a winner.'

No thought of an apology. No remorse. No pity.

What kind of a thing was that to say? *Colin Sumner won? He's a winner?* A man *dead*. What kind of a stupid, smart-arse, senseless, thoughtless, pointless . . . ?

Good *God*. Twelve twenty-five, already? A delay at work. Had to be. Or a conversation? But who would Katherine speak to? And why? Katherine didn't speak much. Not in general. The locals found her difficult – different, *inexplicable* – even though she was one of them.

A local. She *was* local, wasn't she? Born in Canvey. But never fitted. Always too large, too brave, too bold for her surroundings. Always too bright, too fierce for a place like this. Too grand for this fucked-up, washed out, anaemic little town.

She was different. That was all. With her fine, low voice . . . her too-light eyes . . . her small hands . . . tiny hands. Fingers like pieces of stripped willow.

She frightened people. She frightened him, too, sometimes (he made no bold claims to be braver than the rest of them). Yet he loved every inch of her. Every hair, every dimple. The good parts, the bad parts. She was strong meat. She had *vision*.

Ever since she was a girl she'd had it. Her father a headmaster. Her mother a minister. Tricky combination. Methodists, to the core, imbued with that ancient, powerful, crazy-Dutch puritanism. Devout people. Hard-edged. But not her. Not Katherine.

Twelve *thirty*? So perhaps she'd returned early, without him seeing. Perhaps she'd secreted her sweet self and her bright red bike clean away while he was still in his kitchen. Home early.

Perhaps she'd received prior word about Wesley? Advance warning.

But who would warn her? Nobody *trusted* her. Only him. Only Dewi. And she despised him for it. She didn't *want* to be trusted. Didn't need it. Had no use for it. She laughed at his loyalty. She teased him for it. She found it hilarious.

But that was just Katherine. That was her way.

Twelve thirty-*three?*

So who might she speak to, realistically? The newsagent? The butcher? The girl in the bakery? No. Never. Even shopkeepers kept their distance, exchanging only nods and grunts, refusing to allow any transaction – no matter how plain or small or innocent – to be incriminated by syllables. She terrified them. Men especially. And wives, obviously. And mothers. And children. Little children, even.

She preferred it that way.

Twelve thirty-five.

Oh God. Oh *God* should he go over there a second time? Could he chance it? Could he?

Dewi turned on his heels and marched towards the door. But no. What if . . . He froze. Three seconds passed. He doubled back on himself. He paused. He put his hands to his head. He gazed over at the telephone, helplessly.

Perhaps he should ring her. Would he ring? Could he? His right hand twitched. No.

No. He returned – shoulders slumping – to the window, to the reassuring white and shade of his hand-built shutters. He camouflaged himself again (the minutes still tip-toeing past him like a troop of well-marshalled fieldmice in feather slippers), the tension in his huge torso gradually subsiding into a slow-burning, acid-churning, belly-numbing resignation.

A big bull. A soft *heifer.* Dewi exhaled two great gusts of air – once, *twice* – through his dust encrusted nostrils, then dutifully, diligently, tenderly, *fearfully,* he continued his patient vigil for dear, sweet Katherine.

Eleven

They all grabbed what they could. Jo got there first – so did marginally better than the rest of them – claiming *Utah Blaine, Catlow* and *The Man from Broken Hills*. Doc snaffled an early hardback edition of *Hondo*, which she suspected was one of L'Amour's earliest. But *Utah Blaine* was his most successful, wasn't it? His most famous novel?

Oh come on . . .

Who am I kidding?

She didn't have the first idea about cowboy fiction.

Even so, she quickly squirrelled off her booty to a small table in the children's section where she sat down on a tiny chair – somewhat conspicuously, her elbows pressing pale dimples into the lean flesh of her thighs – and carefully removed a bunch of crumpled sweet wrappers from her coat pocket (six in total), slowly sorted through them and finally located . . .

Okay. Clue 3

She partially re-read it. She struggled to assimilate it

Uh . . .

– Look for love –

Fine. She'd got that already: love – L'Amour . . .

– Where liquid is solid –

Hmmn . . .

Somewhere cold? Somewhere icy?

– Where 62 fell,

46 still . . .

There were too many numbers – what the hell did they all

mean – page references, maybe? She pushed the clue aside for a moment, pondered.

So . . . look for love somewhere *icy*. Or look for L'Amour somewhere cold. Somewhere chilly. Hang on . . . hang *on*. Utah – *Salt Lake City*. Not ice . . . not ice, but *salt*. Had to be.

Jo grabbed a hold of *Utah Blaine* and turned to the back cover where she inspected the synopsis, keenly. (*Nah*. This was just too easy. This was just . . . this was *silly*.)

Okay. Set in a town called Red Creek where some poor bastard called Joe Neal had been lynched by a nasty bunch of land-grabbers . . . then . . . Utah Blaine, a stranger, rolls into town objecting to the misuse of vigilante law . . . Bad guys, locals mainly, are led by some greedy, low-down, cowboy killer called Clell –

Clell?

– Clell Miller . . .

Blah, blah, blah

– Nothing particularly riveting. All standard, hard-knuckled Western fare, basically.

Jo frowned, turning the book over. Inside flap?

Nope. Paperback. So where would L'Amour's biographical details be? First page? Preface?

She inspected the first page. Another brief plot summary . . . No biographical details to speak of . . . Only –

Uh . . .

– second page in, next to the copyright, some vague reference to how L'Amour first published under the pseudonym Jim Mayo –

Jim Mayo?

Jo casually perused the front preface again. *Hmmn*. Some pretty average writing interspersed by the occasional striking description of – say – an angry cowboy with a face 'red as a piece of raw beef' –

Yik

– making threats against Blaine . . .

Blah, blah . . .

– more stuff about Joe Neal's ranch; the *46 Range* . . .

The . . . ?

Oh Fuck

She glanced up, guiltily. Did anyone . . . ? Did . . . ?

Bollocks. Hooch

– Hooch was staring at her.

Had he . . . ?

Jo closed the book and rapidly turned to the next one. She picked it up, inspected it, thumbed through it, began reading, randomly, smiling to herself, goofily, as if she got some real *thrill* out of all this cowboy twaddle.

Glanced up again –

Bugger

– Hooch was coming over. He was clutching his own paperback which he'd already flipped through, twice, in a desultory manner. Jo rested her right elbow on the front cover of *Utah Blaine*. She began talking, even as he approached her.

'I notice L'Amour initially published under the pseudonym Jim Mayo,' she said (as if keen to exchange everything, like a real team player).

Hooch wasn't taken in. He scowled as he pulled out a chair at the tiny table but then thought twice about sitting down on it.

'Mayo? You think that means something too?'

Jo shrugged, 'Who's to say?'

'Well I'm not getting anywhere with this.'

Hooch showed Jo his own paperback: *Showdown at Yellow Butte.*

Jo half-smiled, '*Yellow Butte*? That's some *purdy* title you got yourself there, Hooch.'

Used his name

Hooch was neither disarmed nor amused. 'I think you probably pronounce it *boot*. It's a geographical location.'

'Nah . . .' Jo took the book from him and flipped through it, casually, '. . . it'd be like the butt of a gun, surely?'

'That doesn't have an e.'

'Are you certain?'

He was certain. 'In actual fact,' he continued (she grinned, internally), 'the word probably has its earliest application in the form of a large Roman cask, or *butt* – as in water butt – then subsequently in the guise of the mound or hill behind a target – another common usage – which, presumably, leads on to the notion of a person *being* the butt – of a joke, or whatever. In other words, they are the thing *behind* the target. The mound.

The hillock. Or in that particular instance, the object *behind* the joke . . .'

'. . . The fool, the pillock . . .'

Jo smiled, winningly. Hooch frowned, snatching the book back again, 'In terms of etymology, pillock'd probably have its origin in *pillory*. But that's an entirely spontaneous guess. Don't quote me on it.'

She pursed her lips. This man was hard work.

'So, did you find anything of further interest in your . . .'

Hooch craned his neck to try and inspect the scope of Jo's L'Amour bounty.

Jo removed her elbow from *Utah Blaine*, turned it onto its back, and read out brief sections from the synopsis in suitably disengaged tones . . . 'Man called Joe Neal is lynched by land-grabbers in a town called Red Creek . . . uh . . .'

She quickly moved on to the other two books and did the same again.

'What we need,' she continued – on finishing – and slightly more emphatically, 'is some kind of biographical insight into L'Amour's life. But does such a thing even exist, I wonder?'

'You reckon?'

Hooch's enthusiasm was already waning.

'Doc, I noticed,' Jo continued, 'has a copy of L'Amour's first book, *Hondo*, and it's in hardback, which means it'll probably have more biographical stuff on the back jacket flap. Then there's always the internet, obviously . . .'

'I guess so.' Hooch shrugged, boredly, turning to stare at Doc – who was perched on a stool, in the corner – then at Wesley, who was, that very moment, throwing down a pen, pushing a slip of paper over the counter-top towards the librarian, bending down to stroke the dog, then turning, waving, leaving.

Jo watched too. She watched the librarian. The librarian seemed rather agitated. She was reading whatever it was that Wesley had written onto the slip. She seemed surprised. Involved. Taken aback. Jo wished she might take a peek at the message herself. The librarian's hands were shaking slightly as she quickly shoved it under the counter. It was plainly something fairly electrifying.

What could it be?

'See how much that dog dotes on him?' Hooch murmured, not focussing on the librarian but on Wesley – always on Wesley.

'Pardon?' Jo turned back to face him again.

'Straight behind him – see? – out of the library. Always does it. Worships him. Terriers have no loyalty. I hate that. I loathe dogs, actually . . .' Hooch paused, then slowly pronounced the word *canine*, under his breath, his lips pulled back from his teeth like an anxious chimpanzee. It was exceptionally unappealing.

Jo frowned, then peered after Wesley. Sure enough, the dog had followed him, stuck tight to his heels through the swing doors and disappeared without even a cursory backward glance towards his master.

Doc was still busy reading *Hondo*, but he'd noticed. He closed the book, pushed it away, waved at Hooch, then did a finger walking motion with his left hand. He seemed unperturbed by Dennis's inconstancy. Hooch nodded, throwing his own book down onto the table and strolling off to grab his coat from the back of his chair.

Jo was watching Eileen, as she carefully assisted Patty in filling out his form. She glanced furtively around her, grabbed *Utah Blaine*, stood up – the book still in her hand – and slid it slowly – almost distractedly – down the fabric above her pocket. Good . . . good . . . The book was sliding in. It was slipping in, it was almost . . . it was very nearly . . .

Damn

She was just about home-free, when something stopped her. Or someone –

Shoes

– the bloody Geordie, of all people – had suddenly materialised behind her, his plump, dirty hand had slipped around her wrist and firmly wrested the book from her fingers.

'That's no way to go about things,' he whispered softly, (his breath on her neck, the scratch of damp mohair on her wrist), 'not in a small community like this. The Behindlings have a code of . . . well . . .'

He spoke louder, 'I'm getting a couple of these out on loan. You can always borrow one later if you feel the need.'

He was already holding the hardback *Hondo* Doc'd been inspecting. He reached down and picked up Hooch's paperback too. With *Utah Blaine* that made three books altogether.

Jo gave the paperback up without argument. She yanked a blue, knitted hat out of her pocket (as if this was actually all that she'd been intending to do in the first place) and pulled it over her head. 'You know what?' she asked, adjusting it around her ears. Shoes simply grinned at her.

'I'd love a peek at *Hondo* when you've finished with it.'

'Of course you would,' Shoes continued to grin, stupidly (was he stupid? He *seemed* stupid) as he carried the three books with him up to the counter.

Eileen was still busy with the boy and his form, but she turned, very obligingly, to help him with them.

'It's me again, remember?' Shoes beamed, handing three brand new library cards over. Pushing the books towards her.

'So *that's* what he was doing first thing,' Doc muttered, pulling on his jacket as he strode past, 'the canny bugger.'

Eileen took the books and reached over to grab her stamp. Her back was turned for the briefest of instants, but that was all it took Patty, up on his toes, his arm swinging over the counter, his fingers feeling, blindly, then clutching, then . . . then . . .

He scrabbled.

Jesus. Eileen was obviously going to . . .

Jo kicked her chair. Very quickly. The small chair. Turned it over. Made a huge clattering racket. Attracted everyone's attention. Pulled an agonised expression. Mimed *sorry*. Shrugged. Bent over. Righted the tiny chair again. Shoved it under the table with a firm, four-footed, rubber-padded *squeak*. Collected her six clues from the table-top, shoved them into her pocket, clamped her hands together. Strode towards the door; following Doc, following Hooch.

Just as she was pushing the door open, Patty jinked in speedily ahead of her, shooting through, chuckling, making her gasp at his guile, at his bare-faced . . .

She caught the door as it slammed back towards her, peered over her shoulder, saw Shoes following behind – the three books held securely – and paused, judiciously, still holding it there, until he

too was out and through and charging off – full blast, bare-toed –
up the well-shod, densely-populated High Street ahead of her.

Twelve

The house was a mess – it was *always* so – but Katherine Turpin knew exactly the scope of it; the subtle calibrations of disorder, the various proportions of clutter. In this respect – as in many others – she verged – hell, she *staggered* – on the systematically sluttish (only her bedroom was the exception. Her *boudoir* was pristine. But this room was her secret anomaly, her perverse aberration).

Katherine was *diligently* chaotic, *consistently* scruffy, *discerningly* squalid, because nothing – not any small thing – in that tiny, filthy, miserable little bungalow escaped the fine tooth-comb of her careful attentions.

She'd been blessed (but was it a blessing?) with the hunter's round eye; the eyes of a merlin (could see a vole skulking at fifty metres) – the keen nose of the shrew (the shrill voice too, if ever she needed it, although crueller in content than tone, by a margin) fine, feline ears (could actually *move* them – like a cat does – but only if she concentrated, hard, at a party – to illustrate her versatility – although she was rarely, if ever, socially busy), and the *sharpest* incisors for killing and chewing.

'Fuck and *double-fuck*.'

Katherine slammed the front door behind her, growling like an old scooter-motor, and threw down the bike – still folded – her arms aching horribly. It was *twelve* fucking *fifty-three*. She'd had to walk the best part of it after the Southend turn-off (so a lorry carrying baby food or yoghurt or UHT – or something suitably *sloppy* – finally took pity on her after forty long minutes standing by the roadside, absolutely freezing her bloody arse off, and did her the

113

great honour of carrying her that far. But no further. And after? *Nothing*).

There'd been fog. It'd been *icy*. And the bike was portable but *bugger me*, it was heavy. Had little wheels to the rear – like the kind you got on a supermarket trolley; just as stiff and stupid and clumsy – and a strap you were intended to pull it by, but to pull it meant stooping at a ridiculous angle, ricking your back, straining your knees, so she'd picked it up and carried it instead, all the long, hard trog back into bloodless Canvey.

Saw that twat who worked in the Lambeth Café. The miserable shit. Drove straight past her. She'd been at school with him. And the local sports injury chappie in his pathetic little van. And Mr and Mrs Sullivan from two doors down. *Two doors*. The snivelling . . .

She sniffed the air. The air smelled *hmmmn*. The air smelled . . . Good stilton. Old hay. Something queer and . . . queer. Something *mouldering*. She glanced around her. Peach schnapps bottles. In the hallway. They'd been moved. Shoved up against the wall. One bag had tipped over, leaving schnapps remnants on the parquet.

She sidled through like a ghost at the feast: like a vengeful spectre whose bones had been disturbed in an ancient cemetery . . . The living room. *Aha!* Her cushions on the sofa. They'd been adjusted. And the embroidered throw on the chair'd been straightened. And dear Mr Tiger's fur (how *could* they?) had been smoothed down, smoothed *back*, all neat and straight and shiny and tidy. *Urgh*. He was de-scruffy. He was slick and tame and glossy as a pussy. Not dear, emery-board-furred Mr Angry Tiger. Not lovely, familiar, *dear* Mr . . .

Katherine scuffed the tiger's spine with the heel of her hand, delicately, like she was tenderly rubbing a big kitten's belly. Okay. What else? The net curtains (she'd noticed while walking up the path – no, before then, even; all the way over from the other side of the stupid *street*, Goddammit) had been yanked out of kilter. They were skewwhiff. Not at all as she liked them. Not at *all* as she arranged them herself, in general.

Oh *yes*. And the inevitable trail of sawdust. She'd seen that too. Had glared at it, briefly, before finding her key and unlocking the front door.

The distinctive angle of the hydrangea . . .

Katherine's grey-blue eyes glimmered. She pushed her aching shoulders back, ominously. She had been *invaded*. Indubitably. And by the look of the cushions – set straight, puffed out, propped up – Gentle Teddy had been here; with his pale ginger hair, his fiddling fingers, his throat-clearing, his stooped back, his nervousness, his *neatness*.

The sawdust? She grimaced. *Dewi*. Dewi outside, peering in furtively at this pale-hearted invader.

Yes. A picture formed in her head. She scowled (still not entirely content with the shape of it), her calcimine eyes casually resting on the well-packed shelf behind the TV.

Hang on. Something distinctly amiss there . . . A vacancy. She focussed. Two mango-stone creatures staring straight back at her; clay-nosed, wire-legged, beady-eyed, unblinking. Gap between them. The middle one. Where was he? Where could the *middle* mango one be?

Katherine stalked over and gazed down behind the TV, just in case there'd been a faller. Nope. Retrieved a dried azalea – dust-splattered – a small dice she'd been looking for, an old two pence coin and a copy of the special *TV Times* edition of *The Tomorrow People*'s children's adventure series ('Based on the exciting Thames Television programme . . .'), its spine broken, its pages bent over. She kissed the cover. '*Starring Mr Nick Young as John . . .*'

And there was his picture. *Ahhh.*

She tossed the book and the azalea onto the sofa, slipped the dice and the coin into her jacket pocket, turned, no longer smiling, her eyes scouring the room.

It was then that she saw it.

Huh?

She quickly circumnavigated the sofa and padded towards it. This *thing* on her work table. This *thing* unfamiliar. She drew closer. Her eyes nicked off to the left, instinctively (her sand, the neat heap, depleted. Pressed flat. Something . . .)

Lamb's tail.

Wuh?

Good *God* – out of nowhere – and then there, in the sand (the two things interrelating, corresponding, unifying, *merging*, with a brainstorming rapidity), the word, the *scribbling* . . .

Now what . . . ?

The word . . . *a . . . n* . . .

No (She adjusted her angle, squinting) . . .

. . . *a* . . .

No . . .

c . . . u . . .

Uh . . .

c . . . u . . . n . . .

C-u-n-t? In a strange joined-up style of writing.

Cunt? Could it be?

In *sand*?

A *lamb's* tail?

Katherine Turpin grabbed the tail, marched smartly through the bungalow and into the rear lean-to to check up on her chinchilla –

Phew

– she breathed a sharp sigh of relief. Bron was *fine*. He was asleep in the corner, nose twitching. Apparently none the worse for anything. She picked up the cage, anyway (not without some difficulty – it was as wide as it was heavy), lugged it through to the kitchen and placed it squarely onto the free-standing butcher's block – for *security* – stepped back and inspected it (was as satisfied as she could be), then went and ransacked one of the cupboards in search of liquor.

Ah yes,

The comfort of the . . .

She located a Special Edition litre bottle (*perfect* for this kind of emergency), twisted her hands around it, shuddered. Unscrewed the top and took a huge, deep *glug* (tossing the lid with furious aplomb over her shoulder so that it hit the wall and landed – rotating, maddeningly – on the counter), then stalked back towards the front door, swishing the tail rhythmically in her right hand like a cheerleader's baton (or a magician's wand, or a duellist's sword, or a long cheese finger at a tediously second-rate social occasion), the schnapps bottle still in her other, the wave of warm air in her wake creaking with profanities as she slammed the heavy door emphatically shut – *whack!* – behind her.

Poor Dewi, clumping heavily down his verandah steps, toolbag in hand, head in the clouds, planning the quickest and most efficient route for his upcoming journey (he'd missed one job already – he was late for another – but she was *home* now, wasn't she?) glancing up, distractedly, to observe Katherine Turpin – the focus of all his concern, the core of his being, the centre of everything – quietly *incandescent* with . . . with . . . (was it rage? Could it possibly be?) standing in his pathway. She was blocking him. She was *tiny*.

'You have been in my garden again,' she murmured, her deep voice purring like a lawn-mower. Dewi considered responding (but how? To deny? To affirm?) then didn't bother. Katherine was plainly not in the mood for listening (was she ever, honestly? Did she *ever* listen?). She was waving something at him. Something white and yielding.

He focussed in on it, frowning slightly. Then she swatted him with it, savagely. She hit his chin. It didn't hurt. It was woolly.

'Just *leave*,' she spoke slowly and quietly, enunciating cleanly, 'my damn hydrangea *alone* Dewi Edwards. Do you hear me? You *mad*, you *monolithic*, you fucking crazy *wooden-hearted* fool? You *dust* creature. You *maniac*. Do you hear? *Stay out of my garden!* Do you understand? *Stay out* of it you stupid, lumpen, snail-trail-leaving piece of crap, *damn you*. You pest. You *silly* . . . you soft-brained, huge-handed, imbecilic, interfering, tomato-munching simple-minded clod of a man . . .'

She paused. '. . . *damn you*,' she repeated, slightly losing her thrust, in conclusion, but not caring.

She took a step back, took another swig of schnapps, swallowed, blew hard on the tail (dust floated off, and up, and away into the ether) then turned, still harrumphing, and sped out of the garden.

Dewi gazed after her.

Lamb's tail, he meditated, scratching his huge chin with his big fingers, softly, gently, perturbedly. *A tail of lamb.*

She caught Ted on the trot. He'd just pulled his jacket on, was primed to go, standing – for a second – behind the door, and refilling some perspex property-detail holders with a bunch of brand new, freshly-printed photocopies. He'd only just that minute finished producing them – his final job of the morning.

He was almost out of there – for lunch – it was almost *lunchtime* – it was very nearly – he had . . .

Bugger

Pathfinder – thankfully – was busy on the phone arranging a viewing when Katherine burst in, smacking the door purposefully – *forcefully* – into Ted's pliant and unassuming buttocks. He yelped. He was living on his nerves and his nerves were still jangling.

'*You!*' Katherine growled warningly through the glass door, leaving a hot puff of condensation on the glass (obscuring her angry mouth, momentarily), brandishing the bottle at him. Then she side-stepped and let go – allowing the door to close with its own momentum – and stood before him, breathing heavily.

Ted turned to face her, still managing to retain the air of a man behind glass – a specimen – pinned-flat, stiff, dumb. He was frightened. Katherine hung like a white moth before him; tiny, fragile, sheeny, but ineluctably befanged. A *biter*.

'It's just . . . it's only . . .' he began limply.

'Oh no you *don't*,' Katherine grabbed his lapel and menaced him with the bottle again, 'not with *Dumbo* sitting over there like a big, fat fart at a fucking wedding. *Outside.*'

She yanked him through the door with her, then pushed him hard against the window.

'Where the *hell*,' she asked coolly (her breath steaming in the cold again), 'is my middle mango animal? What have you done with him? And why did you stroke Mr Angry Tiger? I *told* you never to stroke him, didn't I? Didn't I tell you never to stroke him?'

'You told me,' Ted managed, nodding, 'you *did* tell me, yes, on more than one occasion, Katherine.'

'Don't use my name in that patronising way, *Ted*,' she snapped, 'and another thing,' she held up the lamb's tail, menacingly. She waggled it at him, almost comically. But she wasn't smiling.

'Lamb's *fucking* tail.'

'You've been drinking,' Ted said.

'So do you really think I'm a cunt, Teddy? Is that *honestly* what you think of me?'

Ted's eyes widened. 'A drunk?' he asked, horrified, honestly mis-hearing, 'do I really think you're a *drunk*?'

'Read my lips, Ted. Do you really think *I-am-a-cunt*? Do you honestly think *I-am-a-whore*?'

Ted stared at Katherine, open-mouthed. 'A *cunt*?'

He whispered the word, plainly appalled by it. 'I don't think I . . . I don't . . .'

Katherine's pale eyes tightened. She grew thoughtful for a moment.

'No. No it's not really *you*, is it? It's not Ted. The cunt thing. It's not a *Ted* thing. You're right. So it was somebody else? Then who *was* it? Who was in my house? Who did you take there? Was it the journalist? Was it him again? Was it the tennis champion? Has he been bugging you? Has he been threatening you? Did he force you to take him over? Has he been up to his mischief in my house? Did *he* stroke Mr Angry Tiger? Was it him?'

'Uh', Ted didn't quite know which question to answer first. They all seemed equally unappealing. Katherine scowled at his silence. She had no *time* for silences. She growled at him.

'You're *confusing* me,' Ted whimpered plaintively, 'with all these . . . these questions. The point is . . .'

'*Tell* me the point.'

Katherine took a swig of schnapps, then stamped her foot like a small, short-tempered white pony as she swallowed.

'*Yargh.*'

Too strong.

'I thought you'd given up drinking.'

'And I thought you were my friend, Teddy. But you stole my mango creature. And you think I'm a cunt. Although in point of fact *cunt* isn't really your thing, is it? Cushion covers are your thing. And property details. And suits. And bits of . . . bits of lint, and no fucking sex and *Deep Heat* . . .' She shrugged, resignedly, '. . . so be it.'

'You have a new tenant,' Ted interrupted her, 'I got someone in for you. But not . . . but not . . . It's just . . . well they got . . . they . . . they looked around this morning.'

'Fuck off.' Katherine flipped Ted's tie out from under his waist-coat and blew a boozy raspberry at the cat on it. She didn't like cats. *Sylvester* particularly.

'No. I'm serious. I got you a lodger. But the problem is . . .'

'Who is she?'

Katherine yanked at the tie, pulling Ted forward slightly.

Ted put up a hand to straighten the tie. Katherine slapped it away.

'That's partly . . .' he started.

'I need a fag. Hold this.'

Katherine passed Ted the schnapps bottle, stuck the tail between her teeth and felt around inside her jacket pocket.

'The problem is, it isn't . . .'

Ted watched her, anxiously. Her mouth was full. That had to be a good thing.

'It was Wesley. It was *him*. Wesley. It was all a little con . . . confusing.'

'Who?' Katherine spoke through the tail, not concentrating properly, her teeth showing prettily. 'Who's Wesley?'

Ted swallowed, nervously, 'The one who wrote . . . the one with . . .'

'*Wesley*?' Katherine looked up, sharply, her spectral eyebrows rising dramatically. She stopped fiddling. She removed the tail from her mouth. 'You jest, surely?'

'Uh. No. No, I'm not joking. I wouldn't . . . *uh* . . .'

'Shit.'

Katherine frowned. She sounded nonplussed. Her eyes slid furtively down the High Street. She glanced at the people as if she'd only just . . .

There were plenty of them. People she knew, mostly, doing their shopping. Coming out of the chippy. The Wimpy. The Post Office. The Wine Bar. The pub. Some she didn't know.

She glanced at the traffic, on the road. She wiped her mouth with the back of her hand. She straightened her hat and her silky cardigans. Then she looked up at Ted again, noticed the schnapps bottle still clutched between his fingers, grabbed it back from him, cleaned the lip with her palm, fastidiously (as if he'd been drinking from it, surreptitiously), took a quick swig, then stuck her thumb inside like a fleshy cork and held the bottle dangling loosely from her hand that way.

Ted watched on, anxiously. She swallowed and swung her hand a little. The bottle swung too. He thought she might drop it – make a mess on the pavement, outside the agency – or disconnect her thumb at the joint with the sheer weight of the bottle, maybe; pull it out of its socket.

Sure enough – four seconds later – the thumb came loose with a familiar clicking. Ted cringed. *Urgh.* He *hated* the way she did that. Her strange double-jointedness. It was just *so* . . .

'When do I meet up with him?' she asked.

'Well he said he'd come to the house at around three, but I told him I'd have to . . .'

'*Yeeeuch.*' She flapped her hand at him – cutting him dead – turned on her heel and walked off. Five steps later, however, she paused, spun around, pointed the tail at him, 'And *you* . . .' she told him ominously, before snatching the tail back and marching off at top speed, that sour half-sentence still hanging in the cold midday air, still ringing in his head like a small pebble in a milk bottle, rolling and bouncing down a steep, cobbled hill.

Ted gently expelled a modest, acid-based burp as he tucked in his tie again and stared helplessly after her, his face a detailed study in forlorn disquietude.

One thing at least, he thought, was absolutely for certain: nobody could exit better than Miss Katherine Turpin.

Thirteen

It was a fourteen mile round trip, all told; a slog, a solid four hours' worth, if he was lucky. And the weather was shitty (the sky sheeted up and promising, if not snow, then sleet), and his waterproof mac was in his back-pack, and his back-pack was hidden inside the small thicket where he'd been sleeping – a cramped, hollow, shallow indentation, but *dry*, and trimmed with spiky blackthorn, the lower branches still drooping (inexplicably, for so late in the season) with hard, slightly-shrunken, damson-coloured berries.

Sloes

Their fierce juice had stained his hands, his elbows, the nylon fabric of his sleeping bag. It'd seeped practically everywhere. He'd scrubbed it off, at dawn, in the river, stopping himself from gasping by cursing until his tongue was cut, finally, by his gappy teeth chattering –

Cold

Wesley glanced behind him.

In actual fact he was pretty keen to investigate the blackthorn's holistic and nutritional potential. The sloes were edible but disgusting (he knew they flavoured gin – and wonderfully – but this didn't say much about their dietary capabilities). He needed to consult a good herbal dictionary (in the library, perhaps – next time, maybe). He made a quick mental note of it. Slotted it away.

Fourteen miles. A *solid* four hours. But he still didn't start immediately. At first he simply meandered awhile; planned ahead a little; strolled part-way down the High Street, past the Post Office, the estate agency (no one of note inside except for a short, squat, ruddy-faced creature who was sitting squarely at a desk

123

and devouring the contents of a large jar of stuffed green olives with his stubby white fingers while appearing not in the least bit discomforted by the awful fact of having some kind of foul, ginger-skinned rodent clambering across his bleary-seeming but greed-enlivened physiognomy. This miserable creature – Wesley deduced – was none other than the fabulously bewhiskered Path-finder).

He wandered on further, past the haberdasher's and the grocer's, the chip shop and the Wimpy until he stood – just fleetingly – outside Saks; a small, unpretentious, slightly dilapidated wine bar.

Inside Wesley was able to discern only two people, in total (two men, more precisely, sitting on stools in the gloom by the counter, sharing a quiet yet amicable beer together), both of whom – he stared even harder – were wearing customised shirts and caps, so probably worked there.

But he appreciated the look of this place – its scruffy, subterranean, almost saloon-like aura – and on a blackboard outside, in badly-formed lettering, he read a list of attractions including *pool and darts and satellite and pub grub and music.*

Wesley paused, weighed up these enticements, looked for a lunch board (couldn't see one), carefully considered their refuse disposal procedure, frowned, cracked his knuckles, then slowly walked on again.

He instinctively strolled seawards (it was a knack he had. His Dad had been a marine. The sea was in his blood – in his bones – in his spleen. He had a salt water compass concealed deep inside of him), heading back up the Furtherwick, past Mango-stone Katherine's, past the pale-green bungalow with the ungainly verandah (no one about currently, no man-moose, his nose glued to the shutters, no perceptible stirrings inside whatsoever).

Wesley paused for a second. What did it *mean*, this curiously huge verandah? What did it say? Was this a practical individual? Was this an exceptionally public person? Or a private man living – uneasily, perhaps – in the public arena?

Or was the verandah symptomatic of some kind of internal burden: whacked up, thrown together, *externalised*, to some degree? A carbuncle? A weight? A trial? A problem?

Was it something additional? Something tacked on?

Hmmn

Did it represent a man with an overriding, an inflated, a *disproportionate* interest in some particular issue? Some particular *person*, maybe? A sad man? A silly man? A nosy man?

Ah screw it anyway.

Wesley strolled on past a brand new hotel; a conversion, but smart looking. (*Fancy.* Things had certainly started looking up in this Godforsaken armpit of a town lately. Although when the Great Floods came, it'd be the first damn place to go under – sea defences or no sea defences – fuck the whole sodding *lot* of them.)

Other houses, in plenty (Not enough trees though, not nearly enough proper trees. Oh God he missed the trees. He *missed* them. The sky so fucking huge – like an empty, grey soup-bowl – a vast china meat platter. *Horrible*) then past the car showroom and onwards.

Hang on. Hang *on.* Wesley stopped abruptly –

Yukka

– in a pot, across the road, in the entrance to a small house with a stone clad frontage; just to the right of the driveway.

He immediately crossed over. *Two yukkas.* Even better. A big one – planted directly into the soil next to the neat, gravel driveway (suffering from a little frost damage by the look of it; these plants demanded sheltered conditions, a greenhouse or a length of fleece – at the very least – during this time of year), and a smaller one – a cutting of the bigger, presumably – just behind it, in a large, dark-green, ornamental pot.

Right. Wesley glanced around –

Damn

– the bloody *dog.* Where did he come from, all of a sudden? Had he trailed him, unseen, all the way from the library? (God knows, he was slipping. Was he losing it completely? Was he going *blind* or was it only hunger? Had to eat something. This was getting crazy . . .)

But . . . ah, yes. *Yes.* That was good, actually. The dog was . . . he was *handy.* Grand as a diversion. If only he could just . . .

Uh . . .

Wesley called Dennis over. Dennis did his bidding, quite obligingly

– he admired Wesley enormously. Wesley possessed all those attributes – in abundance – which terriers found irresistible: low standards of personal hygiene, high self-esteem, a flagrant disregard for social niceties . . .

'Sit, Dennis. Right there. *Sit*. Now *stay*.'

Dennis sat.

Okey-dokey

Quick as he could, and partially obscured by the dog, Wesley pulled a sharp hunting knife from his trouser pocket, unsheathed it, squatted, cut two long, pointed leaves from the smaller yukka, tossed them down next to him, turned to the larger plant, delved into the soil at its base, found a root, took his knife, applied it with force to the thickest part, cut, yanked it free, then pressed the soil carefully back into place again.

He glanced around him as he shook the soil from his hands, grabbed the spines, the root, slid his knife away and hot-footed it (but not running. *Never* running; anything beyond a lope was an admission of guilt).

Okay

He strode onwards (dog still sitting, waiting patiently for the release word) –

Bollocks to the dog

Let the Old Man release him

– towards a seductively wide expanse of green up ahead.

Open plan. Parky. But just grass. No shrubs or trees (the fucking *trees*, where were they?). Muddy underfoot. Clumpy. Used for parking, chiefly, or for travelling fairs in the summer, or circuses, or car-booters . . .

Up ahead, the sea wall (a huge, concrete bastard, like something from Alcatraz or Colditz), and balanced on top of that, or virtually, a large, slightly perplexing, art deco cafeteria (newly refurbished) with LABWORTH CAFE written in large, black lettering around its circular perimeter.

He squinted at this awhile, struggling to remember it from his last visit to Canvey –

Space craft

Oil drum

Water tower . . .

Yeah

– he remembered. It'd been virtually derelict then, but he remembered.

Wesley rapidly orbited the children's play park – nobody there: too bloody cold – still foggy out to sea (and the wind howling and screaming the other side of that wall like a nine-month-old baby in the midst of some kind of chronic teething catastrophe).

Wesley glanced behind him.

Balls

Hooch. Way off in the distance, casually inspecting the price tag on a large, metallic blue-green Volvo Estate (Hooch drove a beat up white Escort van. Wesley knew it intimately: the tyre tread, the number plate, the small indentation on the door – passenger side. Knew that damn van like the back of his hand. Cursed that damn van with ludicrous regularity).

Doc was just behind him. Then the rest of them. Shoes. The girl, walking with the kid. They were talking. The girl made him uneasy. He was almost certain she was working for the Company. She was sneaky. But she had a marvellously open face for a snitch, and that bare-arsed cheek, that gall, that quisling-like quality appealed to him tremendously. Fraudulence of such magnitude – so neatly *packaged* – was always admirable.

Why shouldn't it be?

Wesley turned and quickened his pace. To his left: *The Carousel*; a huge, crouching, plastic construction. Shed-like. Orange-brown. Bricked. Cheap. Open in the summer for gaming, for bingo, for indoor bowling, possibly.

Left of that, over a small road: *The Majestic*. A large hotel. Art deco. So must've withstood the floods back in '53 – in *some* shape or form – still to be here today. And so resolutely. Although – come to think of it – the sea wall was actually breached –

Uh . . .

Where?

– to the East a way? By the jetty? The marshes? The very direction, in fact, that he was currently heading –

But not . . .

Wesley jinked left –

Not quite yet

He upped his pace; around the hotel's voluptuous curvings, then slinked quickly – seamlessly – through an unobtrusive side-passage – *Ah*

Rubbish

Black refuse bags a-plenty. He kicked a couple, squatted down, carefully placed his yukka stash next to him on the floor, then pulled one open and delved inside . . .

Tin foil, used napkins –

Ouch

– cocktail stick.

Back in again –

Yes . . . ?

Yes!

Lemons. Exactly what he was looking for – God he was *hot* today – and a cherry or two (he tossed the cherries into his mouth, chewed, swallowed ravenously, kept the lemons – six slices – still plump – *fantastic*. Ripped off a bit of the tin foil, wrapped them up in it, shoved this package firmly into his jacket pocket).

Bag of peanuts –

Waaah!

– just past their sell-by. Amazing. Stuck them into his pocket, alongside the lemon.

Another packet –

Bingo!

– opened, though. He removed a stray match from inside the lip and tossed it over his shoulder then emptied the contents onto his tongue in one go, chewed with prodigious enjoyment, swallowed.

Anything else? Nope. Old tissues. Crushed cans. Cigarette butts –

Oooh

– half-smoked cigarette – pink-lipstick-tipped. He tapped out the used and blackened tobacco until the weed grew browner, then sealed the open end, neatly, and pushed it, carefully, inside the left cuff of his jumper.

Right. That was that. He tied the bag up again, grabbed the yukka, stood up, glanced around him, furtively. No rear exit –

Bugger

– back out the way he came in, then.

He headed grimly for the street – the soup-plate sky – the wind – those painfully familiar shapes on the horizon . . .

Oh Lord

Oh bloody, bloody Jesus Christ

– sometimes he longed so hard for that lonely feeling that his stomach contracted and his temples began throbbing –

Fucking Hell

STOP all this GRIPING

Sharp left. Over the road. Sea wall – concrete – lowering above him. Twelve short steps to climb it. No chance – no damn *time* – for pointless bellyaching –

One

Two

Three

Four . . .

– up to the top –

Yaaargh!

The foul cold air hit him, without relenting –

Fr-fr-fr-fucking-fr-fr-freezing!

– wind slicing into his cheek-flesh like a razor-fish – making his ears hum, his eyes water, his teeth tingle . . .

But he turned straight into it, his lips smeared into a grin, his hair flying back (a thousand tiny hands, a million lost souls, wailing, pushing, *pummelling* against him). He *threw* himself – recklessly, belligerently – into the skin-chapping *blare* of oceanic pandemonium. (Okay. The English Channel. But still mean as fuck for all of that.)

Wesley smiled to himself, derisively, pulling the collar up on his jacket.

One foot, then the other

One foot, then the other

And so – in this trifling way, and in this violence – began The Walking proper.

Fourteen

No electricity. That couldn't be just a coincidence. And no phone line, either –

Ditto

Had to *try* not to get paranoid, but sometimes the people who . . . the people . . .

Damn!

Arthur was struggling to get the Calor Gas heater going. He'd already checked the weight of it. Heavy. Full of butane. But something wasn't quite right with the nozzle. He'd found it on its side, kicked over – by the intruder, presumably. (The *Intruder?* Or was it something a little less informal, a little more . . . hmmn . . . *choreographed*, maybe?)

What did it matter?

It wasn't a bad boat. High-ceilinged. No need to stoop in the galley. Painted a kind of nautical lime throughout – quite recently, by the look of things. Jaunty. Running water (drinkable but metallic-tasting). Bedroom in the bow. Hard bunk, old mattress – skinny and stained and rather dirty. Four books on the tiny bedside table. Arthur'd picked them up, one by one . . .

Dickens' *Bleak House*, *Origami 3; The Art of Paper Folding* (by celebrated 'Master of the Paper Arts', Robert Harbin), *How to Survive in the Desert* (written by some nutty American lone wolf in the early 1970s), and finally, some crazy autobiographical thing called *Making an Exhibition of Myself*, by a man named Jonathan Routh – a legendary practical joker from the 1960s.

Arthur flipped through the last book, frowning, read the opening two pages, then tossed it down onto the bunk, dismissively.

There was a cupboard, though, under the bunk. He'd slid back the door. Inside were a pile of clean sheets, folded with a military precision and a pile of *National Geographics* (ah, those familiar yellow ribs; like meeting a dear old friend at a funeral wearing a bright daffodil buttonhole).

He'd checked the dates: 1976–1983. And pretty much all entirely there (must be worth something). Then two stray editions – right at the bottom – dated 1999. March and February. He pulled these out for perusing later, his own long-term subscription (he'd been collecting these magazines since he came of age) having finished a full seven years previously: round about the time he started saving up seriously – the time he gave up drinking – smoking – the time he gave up a whole load of . . . the time he gave up everything. Everything except spite and bile and shite and walking and walking and . . .

Enough.

Arthur clenched the canister between his knees and applied more pressure to the nozzle area. A short hiss, then nothing. Needed more light. Back was hurting again. And he was hungry. He glanced through the galley window. What was the weather doing? Still quite foggy. But he was dressed in his outdoors gear, felt warm.

He grabbed an apple from the sideboard, a quarter of soda bread, a chicken leg, then headed outside with them. Turned back at the threshold – remembering the nozzle – debated whether he could manage his lunch and the canister in his other hand. Decided he could. Went back for it. Grabbed the canister. Remembered the *National Geographics*. Saw them on the drainingboard. Put down the canister (*gracious*, that was heavy), picked them up, rolled them, stuck them firmly into either pocket. Shoved the chicken leg and the other stuff – where to put it – yes, in the hood of his jacket. Canny. Bent down to retrieve the canister again – felt the food rolling around so kept his shoulders straight to avoid a catastrophe – grabbed it again, lifted . . .

Left hand *Geographic* slipped out of his pocket and onto the floor. Slid part-way under the refrigerator (not working).

Bugger

He staggered forward, anyway.

The canister was incredibly heavy. He'd rick his neck if he wasn't careful. So he was careful. Bent from the knee.

Crossed the creaking walkway and headed up the embankment. Made it to the top without too much difficulty (had set his heart on this lunching location – sheer perversity, really – but there was the view up here and everything) relinquished the canister, took the magazine out of his pocket . . .

Where the *heck* was his lunch? What on earth had he . . . ? Couldn't for the life of him . . . couldn't . . .

Arthur sat down, looked at his hand – all scrunched red-white from the pressure of the canister, his fingers temporarily locked into plump, pink talons – then opencd the magazine and began working his way through it.

So . . . February edition. Licked his thumb. Held the pages up close to his eyes. Needed his glasses for small type but had left them . . . had . . .

God . . . *awful* letter on the Cossacks and one – now this was interesting – about how civets wcren't really cats. They were actually the biggest and most canine of the *viv* . . . the *viver* . . . the *viverridae*. A genus which included mongooses and genets.

Mongooses! Mongeese!

Then finally, a whole, damn *ream* of information about biodi . . .

'Excuse me.'

How much time had escaped him!

It was still bright. Still foggy. His arse was numb.

'Excuse me.'

A man was standing almost directly behind him.

How the . . . ! How on earth did he . . . !

Arthur corkscrewed his top half, nearly dropping the magazine.

'I think you'll find,' the man courteously informed him, taking a final, languorous drag on the cigarette he was smoking and then tossing the end away, 'that you're sitting on an ants' nest.'

'What?'

'An ants' nest.'

'Are you *kidding*?' Arthur threw down the magazine and leapt to his feet. As he swung around something dealt him a light blow on the back of his neck. It startled him. For a moment he thought the

133

stranger had hit him, but that same instant realised he was being irrational. The man was at totally the wrong angle, logistically.

'Uh . . .' the man spoke again, 'a piece of chicken . . .' He was bending over, retrieving something, 'and an apple just fell out of your . . .'

The apple was rolling gaily down the embankment. Arthur went after it. Skidded twice, but caught it decisively once it'd reached bottom. He glanced up towards the man again. He had the winter sun behind him, like a halo. His face was an eye-burning blur of dissolving skin.

'Is this your craft?' the man asked.

'No,' Arthur answered instinctively, blinking suspiciously, then, '*Yes*. Yes it is, actually.'

The stranger quietly processed this answer, seeming to find no contradiction in it.

'I set some of my traps around here,' he told Arthur, 'in case you sensed anything awry. I've been knocking about since Wednesday.'

'No I didn't,' Arthur answered, looking gingerly about him, 'no I didn't sense . . .'

Awry?

'Just string,' the man continued, 'string traps. Nothing to worry about . . .' he paused, 'for humans,' he added, as an afterthought. Then he paused again, tangled, 'Not *for* humans. The traps are for *rodents* is what I mean.' His voice was smiling.

Arthur headed back up the embankment. When he reached the top, the man was bending down, picking up the magazine.

'I bought this edition myself,' he said, dusting some mud off it, 'when it first came out. I remember it very clearly.'

He checked the date, 'February '99. That's the one. I got so infuriated by it I nearly wrote them a letter . . .'

'You did?'

'Yup. There's this whole fucking tirade about the ecology of biodiversity – did you read it yet?'

Arthur nodded.

'Yeah, well the main story,' the man continued, almost as if Arthur hadn't nodded, as if he hadn't read it, 'involves some excruciatingly fat-headed scientific *twat* making his way through a rainforest and spraying the trees, willy-nilly, to gauge the number and variety of insects in that particular jurisdiction. Spraying with fucking *pesticide*. In the name of research. In the name of *biodiversity*. A million dead insects, just like that. And what about the birds who feed upon the insects? What about them? And what about the animals who catch the birds? Jesus *wept*, it bugged me.'

The man glanced up.

Oh my God. It was him. It was him. It was him. It was Wesley.

'Chicken leg,' Wesley said, slicing through the sudden silence between them with the cold and succulent hen's limb; proffering it to Arthur, cordially.

'Thanks.' Arthur took it from him. Saw the hand. *The hand.* Fingers missing. This sight so familiar in his imagination it was like a poem or a favourite song or . . .

A poem?!

His eyes filled with liquid. He thought he might sneeze (what a painfully *ineffectual* reaction. Was he Man or Mouse? Was he trapper or trapee? What was *wrong* with him?).

'Couple of ants on it,' Wesley said, gazing – with a half-frown – at the cuddly creature on the baseball cap Arthur was wearing.

Arthur looked closer at the chicken leg.

'Turn around,' Wesley continued, 'and I'll try and get the rest off the back of your jacket.'

Arthur turned around, hesitantly, almost not believing in the ants. Perhaps the ants were imaginary. Perhaps Wesley was imaginary. But when Wesley drew near him and swatted at his back a few times, iron-handedly, there really was no disputing his status as a solid entity.

'*A-ha*,' he expostulated, 'it's no bloody wonder they're crawling all over. You still have a hunk of bread stashed in there.'

He removed the bread from Arthur's hood. Passed it to him.

Went back to rigorously swatting him again.

'Couldn't believe that thing about civets not being a part of the cat genus . . .' he muttered.

'Actually,' Arthur suddenly intervened, stepping forward – and downward – out of harm's way, 'I'll take the coat off and do it myself, if you don't mind.'

He thrust the food he was holding into Wesley's hands, 'Have this if you want it. I haven't touched it.'

'Are you serious?'

Wesley was delighted.

'Yes.'

Arthur was embarrassed.

He yanked his jacket off. He couldn't think straight. He felt . . . he felt, well, *ridiculous*. Must've stood up too suddenly, he told himself, knowing it was bogus as soon as he'd thought it.

Wesley took a few steps back, crouched down onto his haunches – one knee in front of the other, solid as a rock, like a Navaho – and began devouring the chicken.

'I've been eating gull since Friday,' he said. '*Loathe* all that plucking. My thumbs are still raw with it.'

Arthur flapped his hand – rather ineffectually – against the jacket. He said nothing. Couldn't see any ants there. Couldn't see anything.

'But I've grown very adept at catching them lately. I'm in the gull-*zone*.'

'Catching what?' Arthur glanced over at him.

'Seagulls. At the dump. The lorries all come thundering in around one-ish. That's the best time to nab 'em.'

'I suppose . . .' Arthur said –

Don't let him draw you in, Arthur,

Don't let him reel you in

– 'I suppose they must taste rather like chicken.'

'No. They taste like seabird. But this . . .'

Wesley brandished the drumstick, 'this tastes rather like chicken.'

Arthur grimaced. Walked straight into that one.

Wesley indicated towards the heater with the chicken leg, then took another big bite of it, 'That thing empty or what?'

Mouth crammed as he spoke.

'It's full. But the nozzle's dented. It got knocked over.'

'I can fix it for you. I'm good with nozzles.'

'No. I'm . . . that's fine. I'll be fine.'

Wesley studiously ignored Arthur's protestations. He stood up and went over to the canister. He circled his way around it a couple of times – as if stalking it – then stuck the chicken leg between his teeth, placed the bread and apple onto the ground, removed a knife from his trouser pocket and crouched down. After continuing to gaze at the canister for a while, he carefully inserted the knife and painstakingly dug around inside the mechanism.

Arthur slowly put his coat back on again.

Before he'd fastened the zip, the canister was hissing. Wesley turned it off, then on, then off.

'There.'

'Thanks.'

He put the knife away and delicately ripped the last strands of flesh from the chicken leg with his teeth. His eyes were unfocussed as he chewed on it. He was considering something. When he'd swallowed, he stood up and tossed the bone over the river. It hit the opposite bank. Disappeared inside the long grass there. He had an impressive arm.

'Do you have any drinking water on board?'

Wesley wiped his hands on his trousers.

'Yes.'

'Great. I'm gonna show you something amazing. Just hold on a minute.'

He grabbed the bread and apple and headed off towards a nearby thicket. In twenty seconds he was back again, a large rucksack slung over one shoulder and a plastic bottle (its neck roughly severed) held firmly in his good hand.

He slung the pack onto the floor and offered Arthur the bottle, 'Go inside and fill it.' Arthur didn't move. He didn't appreciate Wesley's *tone*. It was peremptory.

'Almost to the top,' he added.

Arthur took the bottle and carried it inside –

Why am I doing this?

– he filled it at the sink and then returned outside with it.

Wesley was kicking at the ridge on top of the embankment, then scuffling his trainer into the fine soil he'd loosened. After a while he kneeled down and began scooping gently at the soil with both hands.

Arthur drew closer, breathing heavily as he crested the slope again.

Ants. Thousands of them.

He recoiled.

Wesley noticed, even from his kneeling position, 'It's only ants,' he said, grabbing hold of the water bottle and quickly tipping several dark handfuls inside; some soil, but ants, mostly. The ants swam around in the liquid. Wesley shook off his hands expertly, then put his palm over the bottleneck and violently shook the whole.

'In my rucksack, the side pocket, on the right, you'll find a thermos. Bring it to me.' Arthur went for the thermos. Side pocket. On the right. There it was. Red-topped. Tartan patterned. He pulled it out. *Wesley's* thermos. Had one quite like it himself, actually. In green.

'Okay,' Wesley said, standing up – his bad hand still blocking the neck of the bottle – 'let's move over here a-way, before the rest of these insects get their heads together and come after us for a revenge attack.'

They walked several yards along the bank, then Wesley sat down. 'Take this,' he proffered Arthur the bottle, 'and try and keep it still so that the sediment can settle.'

Arthur took the bottle.

'Sit down.'

Arthur didn't want to sit down. But after five seconds he sat down anyway.

Wesley was digging around inside his pockets. From the right one he removed something small, wrapped up in tin foil. He unfurled the foil carefully and revealed some dehydrated-looking lemon slices. Next he unscrewed the plastic cup and lid from the top of his thermos, placed the lemon slices inside it, then delved back into his pocket again. This time he removed what Arthur could only characterise as a home-spun toy. Made from a big, hairy *pip* of some kind. Wire legged. Pearl eyed.

'Mango-stone creature,' Wesley calmly enlightened him, pulling an old handkerchief out of his pocket and a crumpled packet of Wimpy coffee sugar, then replacing the toy gently back inside again.

'Bottle.'

Arthur passed him the bottle. Wesley neatly wrapped the handkerchief over the lip of it then slowly tipped it up and began pouring the ant-liquid, nicely sieved, from the first container, into his thermos.

When this was done, he tore open the sugar, poured it in, screwed the lid back onto the thermos and shook it for a while, smiling over at Arthur like a roguish barman preparing something incendiary.

After a minute or so he stopped shaking, opened it up, grabbed the plastic cup, poured a portion of this foul-seeming concoction into it and handed it across.

'There you go.'

Arthur stared into the cup, worriedly. He was not a happy bunny.

'Cheers,' Wesley said. 'You won't regret it.'

Arthur took a sip. Wesley was wrong. He regretted it immediately. He squirmed and then swallowed, grimacing.

'Ant lemonade. The stings give it *bite*.'

Arthur took a second sip out of sheer perversity, swallowed. It certainly had . . . *uh* . . . piquancy.

'Clever, eh?'

Arthur half-nodded.

'Can I try?'

Arthur passed the cup back again. Wesley took a sip himself.

'Hmmmn,' he sucked his teeth, 'but is it sweet enough for a lady?'

Arthur scowled, 'A lady?'

'A librarian.'

'Ah,' Arthur's lean face slipped effortlessly into a knowing smile. 'Of course,' he said, then he abruptly stopped smiling –

Can't give anything away

Wesley gave him a straight look. He took another sip, squinting – distractedly – towards the houseboat.

'Let me ask you a question . . . *uh* . . . ?'

He stared at Arthur enquiringly. Arthur stared back at him, blankly.

'Your *name*?' Wesley asked.

139

Arthur continued to stare at Wesley, still blankly, but his mind was racing.

'Art,' he said finally. It was uninspired. But he'd suddenly remembered a boy at school with the same name as him, yet smarter than he was, and better liked. The other kids'd called him Art.

'Art?'

'Yes.'

'The point is, *Art,* I want to use this address,' Wesley indicated towards the boat. 'In actual fact, if you're cooperative, I'd quite like to use you, too.'

Arthur's back straightened – perceptibly – with sheer hostility.

Wesley grinned, seeming either to notice or not to notice (it was impossible to tell), and offered Arthur his good hand. 'My name is Wesley,' he said, 'and some time soon – if I'm not very much mistaken – a man will come calling at your houseboat to ask you some questions about me. When this happens I want you to negotiate a deal on my behalf. Tell him I asked you to. Tell him that you are my broker. If he questions your authority, tell him – and this'll be the main thing – tell him,' Wesley spoke with special emphasis, 'that *I never speak to the people Following*, that you are the negotiator, the go-between. He'll know what you mean.'

Arthur was confused. He felt almost . . . what was it? *Nauseous?* To be . . . to be *implicated* in this whole thing. And so quickly, so *readily.*

'But what . . .' Arthur paused for a second, 'what would I be negotiating exactly?'

Wesley shrugged. 'That's entirely up to you. All I know is that this man will come – trust me – and he'll want to make a deal. I want you to broker it however you see fit . . .' he paused. 'I like you, Art,' he continued, 'you shared my lemonade with me. I fixed your canister. You gave me some chicken. We exchanged some thoughts on biodiversity. I think we have an understanding.'

Arthur was silent for a moment, then he said, 'And what do *I* get out of it? What do I get out of this so-called, this *proposed* deal?'

Wesley grinned again. Heavy teeth. Gappy. Like a pony.

'That's for you to decide. You take exactly what you want. Take everything, if needs be. It's entirely your . . .' he considered what he wanted to say. 'It's your call.'

Arthur sat quietly, pondering what Wesley had asked of him, still confounded and yet curiously . . . curiously *affected* by this offer he'd been made –

Oh come on

This is his gift

This is how he ensnares them

Be strong

Be strong

'Want any more, Art?'

Wesley offered Arthur the cup again. Arthur shook his head. Wesley poured the remaining liquid back into the thermos, sealed it, slowly gathered all his possessions together, stood up, grabbed his rucksack and stashed everything neatly into it.

Arthur watched him – observed the guitar neck protruding. No. Banjo. Wesley played a banjo.

'You have a phone?' Wesley asked, once he'd finished.

'Inside the vessel? No.'

'I mean a mobile.'

'No,' Arthur lied, then . . . then, 'Yes. Yes I do, actually.'

'So give me the number and I'll phone you later. See how things are progressing.'

Wesley withdrew a pencil from one of the side pockets in his rucksack. It was barely a couple of inches long – smaller, by far, than Arthur's littlest finger – an old black and red-striped HB. Sharpened by blade, scalloped to a square tip. It reminded Arthur –

Out of the blue

– of those lovely old pencils his grandfather had used –

Smell of soft lead

Smell of new wood

– to fill in the crossword. To play noughts and crosses. To write out planting lists at the start of the gardening season.

That kind of pencil.

Arthur took it and wrote his number down on the back of an old receipt he'd discovered in his pocket. He found himself shuddering slightly as he handed it over.

'Cold out, isn't it Art?'

Arthur nodded. His hands felt cold. He suppressed another shiver.

Wesley stuck the pencil and the receipt into his trouser pocket and pulled his rucksack onto his shoulders.

'Fuck me it's *heavy*,' he groaned, and started walking. Five steps on and he spun around, as if he'd suddenly thought of something. 'You know,' he spoke quietly, even at this distance, but perfectly audibly, 'these burdens never get any lighter, do they?'

Then he smiled and turned and walked on again.

Jesus. Was that it? Was that everything?

Arthur stood up himself, almost panicking, discovering his voice already inhabiting his mouth, already speaking.

'*Wesley*,' his voice shouted. Then again, '*WESLEY*.'

Wesley broke his stride for the final time, turned.

'What if I say no?' Arthur's voice yelled . . .

Calm down Arthur

Don't go and blow it

Don't go and fuck it up without even . . .

'What if . . . what if I want nothing to do with it? Nothing to do with the deal? What happens then?'

Wesley threw his hands into the air. For a moment Arthur thought he hadn't heard him and steadied himself to shout again. But then Wesley spoke, 'Nothing happens. It's your choice *entirely* . . .' his voice faded, before coming back again, stronger. 'Like I already said; it's your *call*, Arthur.'

Then he waved his fingerless hand in a half-salute, turned with an air of absolute finality, and continued on his way.

Fifteen

Ted always asked for Leo's permission before he used the computer – asked him repeatedly, every half-hour, with an almost military rigour – even when Pathfinder was out of the agency; attending to a client, at lunch, or just plain wagging (in the winebar or at Bingo or having his regular 'massage' with 'Terry' for an old 'hamstring-related fencing injury'). Under these circumstances Ted would simply write him a note, in longhand – neatly signed, neatly dated – saying something like:

> *Leo, it is ten-thirty a.m. and I need to use the computer again.*
> *Thankyou,*
> *Ted*

And because on some days Ted used the computer continually – almost without interruption (except, of course, to get Leo's permission) – to the outside observer this established procedure, this formalised *ritual* between the two of them, might've seemed at best, laborious, at worst, quite ridiculous.

The computer wasn't even a strange or new or novel innovation. It had been there – on the desk, in the office – from the very beginning, and had always formed a vital component of Ted's basic job description.

In actual fact, his Computer Studies O level had been the absolute making of him, employment-wise (what the hell else could he do? Who the hell else would have him?) and had looked wonderfully contemporary on his *curriculum vitae*, way back at the onset of what he now – and very modestly – called his 'Agenting Career'.

(Previous to that there were six 'lost' years in the British Navy. The catering corps. His late father's idea:

'You start off frying the eggs, Ted, you end up running the ship . . .'

Not an experience he looked back upon with anything remotely approaching equilibrium: it took upwards of six months to scrub the sheen of grease from his skin – he was like a body-builder, but without the body – without the tan, without the thong. A pale and ineffectual jar of jellied petroleum.)

Ted was a paid-up participant in the digital age, but (and there was always a *but* with Ted, or a *yet* or a *despite* or a *notwithstanding*) even *this* part of his life had hardly been plain sailing.

In the mid-eighties – the pinnacle, the peak, the *prime* of his schooldays – they'd had a technological shortfall (a Word Processing *paucity*) at Furtherwick Park, so he'd started out with a keyboard, drawn in felt-tip, on cardboard, and a veritable *slew* of hypothetical scenarios:

(a) Pascal clicked on 'font' before saving her document. What happened next? Did she lose that difficult maths problem she'd been working so hard upon?
(b) William has just written an 80 line, free verse epic poem about 'Esme' straight onto his desktop. In your opinion, was that a misguided or a sensible thing for him to have done?

And due to this 'Temporary Word Processing Deficiency', Ted had spent half his time doing secretarial stuff in Elementary Typing with the meanest crew of girls you could possibly imagine; devilish harpies who spent a large proportion of their thrice-weekly lessons ripping the piss *unmercifully* out of this poor, long-limbed, tight-arsed, blushing, clumsy, ginger-topped *pansy* who laboured (and not without difficulty) under the cuddly pseudonym of *Mister Teddy* . . .

(Hang on there. Hang *on*: he *was* that pansy. But he'd *show* them – he'd shown them, hadn't he? – when they all left school with their shorthands and their words-per-minute, unable to get a *job* because they were computer illiterate. Secretary? A ridiculous sodding *anathema* in the 1990s.)

Yes. He'd shown them alright.

Well, in actual fact he hadn't really shown *anybody*. Not computer-wise, anyway. Because Leo had played this little joke on him (when he was still too fresh and too raw in those sweet and silly early days), and while Ted had *known* that it was a joke, initially, he was soon, nevertheless, persuaded by it, *subconsciously*.

It was a simple ruse. It was elementary. Leo had painstakingly altered the screensaver, in his spare time, late one evening, so that when Ted turned it on the following morning, it'd told him – in no uncertain terms – and in the most offensively jagged script imaginable, that

LeO iS deeP inSide oF Me. He INhabits My eVerY nerVe, My veRy cOrE, mY evERy fibRe!! Yes! YeS! *YES* He Is riGht, *DEEp* INSIde OF mE – witH hiS big HAndS and His kEEn tonGuE aND HIs BOLD anD sTRonG aND INSIStaNT cOCk. Yes! yES! YeS!! hE is rISEn and he is COme! He iS COMe! HE is comE aND coMe and COme aLL ovER me!! AHHHHHHHHhhhHHHHHH!

Do Not PLAy wiTH my KeyS So TEDDy. It is TicklinG. It is HA HA ha fucKINg Ha Ha HA!

I am LEO's whORE. So have CleaN hanDs whEN yOU touCH me, okAy? And alwAYS asK NICeLy wheN you – uH! uH! *UH!* USE ME.

(Insist*a*nt? Someone had forgotten to use *spellcheck*, apparently.)

It was childish and it was puerile – it was sheer, pointless bloody *folly* – so Ted pretended that it didn't bother him, but it did. It bothered him enormously.

Because he was a prude, but a gentle prude, with wit and discrimination and sensibility. A kindly prude, with a soft core.

Leo depended upon this softness as he gradually transformed that computer into a purely hardcore entity. He did it slyly and cynically, with small interventions, little nudges and ticks and touches. He made that machine his own. He colonised it. He monopolised it. He squatted like a mating toad inside its deepest inner recesses – clinging on, clutching, *squeezing* – until its disarmed and prostrated eighty-digit keyboard quite literally *groaned* when his plump and clumsy pale male finger deigned to press on it and slowly enter.

He downloaded porn (predictably) – stuff with hairy women and shaved women (God*damn* he wasn't fussy), stuff with old women with falsies, lasses with big asses, girls in their nighties taking pisses in bushes, stuff with horses and collies. He downloaded tit-shots and beaver-shots, shit-shots and tot-shots, shots with women in such curious positions that it was hard to tell which end was which and what exactly . . . *uh* . . . was what. This confusion aroused him.

And the upshot, finally? Ted grew to mistrust the computer. He touched it with trepidation. He kept things to a minimum. He didn't chat, he didn't shop, he didn't surf. He was furtive. He kept all his interaction strictly professional and clean and neat and minimal.

The computer was such a *girl*, after all (a lady? *Never*). The computer was, in actual fact, one of those awful schoolgirl secretaries who'd tormented him so much as a teenager, but she was older now, and wiser: with her sharp tongue and her big breasts, her high heels and her bright lips, her painted nails and her mini. But a *virtual* secretary. An *almost* bully.

And she was temperamental – like all girls could be – and very demanding: questions popping up, with relentless alacrity. Shall I do this? Do you want that? Always needing answers. Always wanting them immediately.

She could be a cow. Refuse him things if he was clumsy, and for no good reason, either. She was extremely unreliable, entirely unpredictable; she was . . . she was cheap and mean and *nasty*.

Ted treated her cautiously. Couldn't ever turn her on – *turn her on?* (Where had all this *gender* stuff sprung from?) without the powerful suspicion – all too often validated – that Leo might've set him up with something suitably revolting – a sound, a picture, a short film, a message – as a joke (but not so funny with clients waiting, peeking over his shoulder every time he pressed a button, hanging out for a phone number, or an address, or an asking price, or a surveyor's report, or a written contract from a tardy solicitor).

It had speakers. Leo had wired them in. Speakers which made noises like that implement at the dentist which sucks spittle from the patient's mouth during a polishing with the hygienist: messy, sexy, *dirty* noises.

And he *hated* them. He hated the noises. He hated the pictures, the porn, the obscenity. He hated that bloody computer. And he hated Leo, especially. But above everything and everybody else, he hated himself. Because he was weak and hunched and soft and silly. Because if it wasn't for him, he wouldn't be here: with Bo and Katherine and – God knows who else – after him. With everybody depending and yet *not* depending. And with Wesley knowing about the sewing and everything. With *Wesley* . . .

Two-thirty p.m. Ted glanced about him, then sat down at the computer (Leo was completing his *Spot The Ball* coupon: he made twenty choices, daily, and soon he'd be sloping off to deliver them . . . *Yup*. Sure enough, he was up and he was out of there . . .).

Ted checked his watch. He now had fifteen minutes leeway – if he was lucky.

He quickly kicked the switch on the plug with his foot, pressed *power* (the computer fizzed into life, hiccuped quietly, like she'd had too many Snowballs in the pub at lunch, then ran through some setting-up data, with an officious buzzing) . . . Right . . . *uh* . . . hang on a minute . . .

Ted hunted around on his desk for a scrap of paper, found one, scribbled down the time. Two-thirty-one. Wrote;

Leo, I'm using the computer for a short while . . .

Thought for a few moments, hand poised in the air, added, *Thanks*, signed his name and dated it.

He turned towards the screen again. The computer blinked back at him, flirtatiously. He firmed his resolve.

'I'm gonna go . . .' he muttered to himself, gingerly, 'I'm gonna go . . . *online* . . .'

He grabbed the mouse and clicked it, cautiously –

Oops

– the computer refused him – point-blank – on his first attempt –

Damn

Forgot to connect the phone-line

Ted scrabbled with the wires for a moment, unplugged the phone, plugged up the . . .

Okay

. . . tried the same manoeuvre a second time.

The computer churlishly demanded the password. Wouldn't do a single damn thing without it, Buster. Ted tapped it in, then listened, slightly worriedly, as she processed his request, sent out feelers, made a muffled ringing sound, purred awhile, *boinked* . . .

The screen went blank then lit up again.

Okay, okay . . .

Ted looked for the right box then silently typed in . . . *uh* . . . now what was the address he was after? *Uh* . . . www – *uh* . . . *yes* . . . www.behindlings.co.uk.

He'd noticed it on Bo's print-out, earlier. He'd memorised it, surreptitiously – not that he'd intended . . . Not that . . . It was only . . .

Survival? Realism? Morbid bloody curiosity?

Ted sniffed, self-consciously. He wasn't proud of himself. There was something . . . not wrong, no, and not unnatural, either . . . something . . . well, kind of . . . *invasive?* Was that it?

But this was for Katherine (he told himself). Yes. It was for Katherine and it was . . . he had to be honest, it was for the pond thing. *Pond.* That great pond story. Two unconnected matters, somehow – inexplicably – connecting here, with him.

I mean, to steal a *pond* and everything . . . That had to be worth . . .

The computer buzzed. He jumped, then shuddered, guiltily . . .

That had to be worth . . . *uh* . . .

Fantastic. He'd made contact with the site already – the graphics began downloading . . . (This was a Wesley-specific site. The main one – the real caboodle – and impressively professional-looking, too, all things considered . . . which in itself was, he supposed, slightly . . . *hmmn*, well, slightly *creepy* . . .) and – *yes* – things were going fine – hadn't seen the pond stuff yet, but there was information on Wesley's general whereabouts over the last seven days and a hotline . . . *uh* . . .

Click

A tiny click. That was it. Nothing bigger or louder or stronger or fiercer.

Just a click. Like an old-fashioned camera taking a picture. Like the sound of a handset placed down onto a receiver –

Click

Then the whole thing just went . . . just went . . . just . . . wrong . . . no . . . just went . . .

Ted reached out his hand.

Just went . . . *Christ* . . .

Just went . . .

HAYWIRE!!

Screen filled up with a strange, red lettering, repeating and repeating and repeating and repeating. Computer made a kind of strangled squeak (a *yelp?*) like it was being suffocated, slowly. Or rapidly. Or kind of . . . kind of . . . kind of *curdled* . . .

Ted frowned. He released the mouse and moved a hesitant index finger towards the keypad, pressed the space-bar, nervously. Nothing happened. He got more emphatic. Slammed the keypad. Nothing. Just chaos – continuing – and more red – and more chaos.

He tried not to panic. Was this a crazy happening of Leo's devising? But it didn't *seem* like Leo's kind of . . . didn't . . . Ted continued tapping, ever more frantically.

Now even the mouse wasn't working. It'd quit. It'd been swallowed. It'd been mauled . . . *devoured* by . . . by . . . what *was* this thing? Was it *his* fault? Was it outside? Was it contagious? Was . . .

Fuck. Everything just jamming and then this spew of information, awful red, then jamming again. Then that terrible last gasp, that choke, that horrible sinking feeling that you sometimes got at the cinema when there was a problem with the projector and the film reel started . . . started *melting* . . . and then . . . and then . . . and then . . .

Virus.

Oh shit. Oh *shit.*

Ted yanked out the plug at the wall – saw the computer die literally split *seconds* before he killed its power (he pretended he didn't see it) like that machine in a hospital which monitors your heart and goes, and goes . . . *blip, blip, blip, blip, blip, blip, blip* . . . then . . . *zeeeeeeeeeeeeeeeeeeeeeeeeeeeeeeeeeeeeeeee*.

Ted grabbed the permission slip he'd written out earlier, crumpled it and binned it. He felt sick. He was frantic. Kept looking about him. Over his shoulder.

Oh shit. His face was wet with sweat. Armpits soaked. Hands like . . .

Oh shit oh *shit* –

Now he was really, really . . .

Oh *Mary Mother of bloody Jesus* –

Now he was *really* . . .

He crossed himself, instinctively. It was a bred-in-the-bone habit – completely automatic – yet to the casual, pagan observer (from the street, from the pavement, through those huge plate glass windows), Ted might've looked like he was actually tying a *noose* for some kind of imaginary hanging – for a lynching – for a Necktie Party. With himself – gentle, kindly, brown-eyed Mr Teddy – as the honourable, the very honourable, Necktie-*ee*.

Sixteen

Suddenly every-*damn*-body wanted a piece of thc boy. He was ultra-magnetic. His allure was irresistible. He was the prizc draw – the golden goose – the plum pudding. They all craved a slice of him.

Absolutely bloody *typical*, Jo ruminated (gazing up ahead towards his small but lean and fast-loping torm, hcr ncat features hard-etched with unashamed yearning, but her tidy mouth half-smiling, as if – somehow, some*where* – she was perfcctly well-apprised of her own hypocrisy).

So from being the *least* interesting individual on this whole bloody island, she mused, testily (and not entirely unreasonably), he's now the most wanted, the most fascinating, the most . . . Hcr eyes rapidly jinked left a-way and scoured the horizon – giving the lie, immediately, to all her fine hypothesising.

'I'll be depending on you . . .' Shoes observed furtively, as they eclipsed the Wimpy at a fast trot.

'Pardon?' Jo had almost forgotten that she was walking with him, that they were talking, that they were already in the middle of something. She was still hare-brained from her early start –

Exhausted

Had been working too . . . Had grown too . . . Had become too . . . Now what had they called it? Those people from the Hospital – those smug, useless, worthless Health Administration brown-noses? Too intent? Assiduous? Violent? *Earnest*?

Ah . . .

Earnest

But was that reasonable? Was that . . . was that . . . was that *just*?

151

Jo blinked –

Yes

And then there'd been the meeting with Dewi. To be so . . .
so . . .

Invisible

– it'd brought stuff back which she'd all but forgotten about.
Teenage stuff. The . . . the *pull*. God. Then to top it all off, the
added stress of her unexpected discovery – with the Loiter – I mean
wasn't that just . . . just *crazy*? Really? Wasn't it?

Far too much complication for one . . . what had they called her?
Earnest? Far too much complication for one plain, clean, *earnest*
female to endure, let alone . . . let alone process.

Why am I here?

'Oh *you* know . . .' Shoes chided, gently, 'to tell me what's going
on with that slip of paper. For some stupid reason the boy has taken
against me lately. He keeps stuff back. And he rips the piss a bit,
too, when he thinks he can get away with it.'

'Really?' Jo shot Shoes a sympathetic sideways glance. From close
up his profile was magnificently unbeguiling. He was corpulent (his
chin a shuddering cacophony of roughly pleated flesh, a scrum of
melted beef lard in a furious blue-white, an unguent waterfall;
each dribbling tallow-cascade part-solidifying upon a former, fatter,
thicker layer. His chin was like something you might see in a
cavern – underground, spot-lit – inside a *gorge*. Something pale
and dimpled that dangled from the ceiling. Something petrified).

The bottom half of Shoes' face was decidedly unshaven, but at
the top end, his dirty blond hair receded, unforgivingly, and the
hairline was dark with ancient dirt. Black-ingrained.

But no. She looked closer. Not dirt. *Ink*. A coarse navy stain. A
spider's web spanning his skull, and a mess of other crazy stuff,
curling, in sensuous tendrils, along his nape, behind his ear.

Her eyes settled, finally, upon the three books he was clutching.
Had to keep him sweet. For the books. Needed the books. Couldn't
risk him . . . although didn't the boy say earlier that the Geordie
wasn't much of a reader (wasn't that what the boy had said)? That
he *couldn't* read? Which was actually – when she thought about it –
rather . . . well, rather . . . what was the word she wanted? Strange?
Ironic?

Funny?

Nope. Jo tempered herself, sharply. That was cheap. That was a bad way to be thinking. Even idly.

'I'll do what I can, Shoes,' Jo replied (using the name again. Had to keep using the names), struggling to keep her breath at the pace they were moving.

The boy – several yards ahead of them – was deep in conversation with Hooch. Hooch was smoking a roll-up (the tiny cigarette bound in a curious dark brown paper). He offered it to the boy (Jo's every medical instinct rebelled against this gesture) but the boy declined.

No.

She saw his lips shape it.

No.

Patty had one small fist pushed inside his green Parka pocket, his four knuckles, visible, pushing out, hard, against the cheap jacket fabric. The slip of paper – she presumed – still hidden within. He plainly wasn't giving anything away. Not yet. Or at least she didn't . . .

Hooch suddenly dropped back. 'Little shit won't give it up,' he grumbled, flicking his half-finished fag over his shoulder. He was limping slightly. 'Although if I know Wesley it'll just be a few rhymes about birdsong and lavender. That's generally the line he takes with librarians. Goes all sentimental on them. Gets their sad old juices flowing with this namby-pamby schmaltzy stuff. Poetry's *always* been a brilliant hook for his whoring.'

Jo grimaced. Even during their brief acquaintance she'd already begun to develop a sizeable sheath of misgivings about Hooch's take on things (at least with Doc there was some suggestion of integrity. Although what that meant – morally – in relation to the actual practice of Following – a questionable occupation at the best of times – she wasn't sure exactly). She disliked Hooch's tactlessness, though. His cynicism. His subtle but constant overstepping.

Hooch noticed Jo's tick. He was struck by it. 'So what's *your* problem all of a sudden?'

She shrugged.

'No. Go on,' he was emphatic, 'spill it.'

'It's only . . .' Jo smiled brightly at him with her neat lips and straight teeth – a beaming smile (but her cork-coloured irises were so tightly fixed into their glassy whites that when she blinked they very nearly *squeaked* with suppressed hostility), 'it's just a matter of . . . well,' she shrugged, 'of accuracy, really. In riddles, precision is everything, don't you reckon?'

Nobody agreed. Nobody disagreed. In fact nobody said anything. So she continued on, determinedly, 'And you just said, "If I *know* Wesley." But surely the whole point is that you *don't* know Wesley . . .'

Hooch interrupted, but Shoes got in first.

'Oh he *does*,' Shoes defended him, patently horrified by the tack Jo was taking, 'he *does* know Wesley. Hooch knows everything. He's . . .'

'But I *do* know everything,' Hooch spoke up himself, echoing the Geordie crossly, and talking him down, eventually, 'I know all there *is* to know about Wesley. I'm an authority. I've watched him for over twenty-two months now, and I'll tell you this for nothing: there's not much you can't learn about a person during twenty-two months' serious observation. That's almost two *years*. It's probably difficult for an outsider to even conceive . . .'

'I'm hardly the outsider here, Hooch,' Jo's tone was unexpectedly cutting.

'And bearing in mind, Hooch, the days you took off, every now and then . . .' Shoes hastily intervened, trying – and rather nobly, Jo felt, under the circumstances – to distract Hooch slightly.

'What of it?' Hooch snarled (ignoring Jo's comments, ignoring her). 'My mother's *funeral*? When the van broke down in *Morecambe*? What of it? That hardly amounts to . . .'

'Yes. No.' Shoes was already regretting his intervention, but still he kept on at it, 'And . . . well . . . then there's . . .' he winced, nervously, 'then there's . . . then there's the problem with your . . . your foot and everything . . .'

'The *spur*? Big bloody *deal*. So I had a minor operation on my spur. That's hardly the stuff of major television *drama*, is it now?'

Shoes kept quiet this time. They walked on. Eventually, though, he muttered, 'Doc's always said how important it is to appreciate the fact that Following, while an apparently intimate act, is not, in itself, an *act of intimacy* . . .'

His voice petered out.

Hooch harrumphed. 'The thing about Doc,' he spoke loudly, at first, then quietened down, on reflection (although Doc was now a good way ahead of them, striding on, resolutely), 'is that sometimes he talks a whole load of *palaver* that he can't even make head-or-tail of himself. Because he thinks it makes him look clever. And he wants to create the same kind of *mystique* around himself that our dear friend Wesley has. But the whole thing's just *moonshine*. Just humbug.'

This time, Jo intervened. 'If Wesley refuses to speak to the people who follow,' she said, 'surely that means he doesn't much *appreciate* the Following, and that, in turn, means that even while there's a real comradeship between you all, and a real *physical* closeness to Wesley, still there's no proper . . . no proper . . .' Jo lost her thread, but it didn't matter. She'd made her point . . . 'So isn't that what Doc's getting at? Isn't *that* what he meant?'

Hooch flashed Jo a glance several stages beyond withering. But she didn't wither. In fact, if anything, she rallied, 'I mean how many times have you actually *spoken* to Wesley? Face to face? How many *proper* conversations have you ever been involved in with him? Fair enough, you might know what his favourite food is or his date of birth, you might know facts about him, but . . .'

(And Jo could see, by Hooch's expression, that even withholding *this* much information was very nearly killing him)

'. . . but do you know *why* he likes, say . . .' she grasped something from thin air – they were passing a seafood stall – 'why he likes whelks one day better than eels, or whether he drinks tea because he enjoys it or because he suffers an allergic reaction to instant coffee?'

'Here's a funny thing . . .' Shoes quickly interjected, 'and it's fairly incredible, Jo, but I actually have . . .'

He paused, delicately, 'I actually have . . .' his voice dropped to a whisper, 'I actually have your name *tattooed onto my arse*.'

Jo blinked. Twice. This was not quite the kind of input she'd been anticipating.

'Pardon?'

'I said it's a funny thing,' Shoes repeated, 'but I actually have . . .'

'She heard you the first time,' Hooch growled, then quickened his pace, pre-emptively, to catch up with the boy again.

'But how,' Jo was frowning now, 'how do you even know what my full name is?'

Shoes didn't respond immediately. Only once Hooch was completely out of earshot did he silently beckon her to move in a little closer to him. Jo drew nearer, but hesitantly, her stomach twingeing.

'The thing is,' he whispered (his breath smelled of processed pork and Stimerol), 'you don't want to wind him up too much. Hooch is very . . .'

'You think I wound him up?'

Jo drew back, instinctively, looking suitably delighted at this possibility.

'No. *No*,' Shoes shushed her nervously, 'I can see I've got my work cut out with you, Josephine. *No*. What you need to understand is that Hooch is actually very . . .' Shoes quietly pondered what he needed to say, 'I don't know. He's very . . . very powerful. Important. To everything. And you'd do well to remember that fact if you're really *serious* about the Following.'

Jo was fazed by Shoes's jitteriness. It was plainly deeply-felt.

'Are you intimidated by him, Shoes?'

'Am I what?' Shoes was suddenly no longer concentrating. In a flash he'd moved off. He'd *switched* off. He was elsewhere.

'I said are you . . .'

Shoes stuck up his hand to silence her. 'Hold on a minute, hold on . . .' he was chuckling now, '*look* . . . the dog. Dennis. The little terrier. Up ahead. See him?'

Jo squinted.

'Doc's calling him. Oh yes. *Ha*. Oh yes just . . . just *look* at . . .'

That was it. Shoes broke into a quick trot to catch up with the others. Jo resisted doing the same. But she quickened up, marginally, when Hooch finally left the side of the boy, joined Shoes, and jogged on himself.

Shoes was still audible – way ahead – talking to whoever'd listen to him, 'Next to the *yukka*. Would you believe that? Next to the bloody *yukka*.'

Jo finally drew level with the boy. His pace had remained

constant. She slowed down to his speed, with relief, watching the others pull away, confusedly.

Patty seemed impassive now, had calmed down noticeably since his earlier euphoria in the library. Jo struggled to catch her breath, 'What the *hell* is all this . . .' she inhaled for a second, '. . . *phew*. I said what the hell is all this yukka business about, anyway? Can you fathom it?'

The boy shrugged.

'Does the yukka have some kind of . . . ?'

She coughed with the exertion.

'I'll tell you what I *don't* know,' the boy's tone was sarcastic, 'I *don't* know what they're all getting so worked up about. He only uses it for laces. The stringy bit. And he makes foam – like soap foam – out of the roots. He's always done it.'

'Really?'

'To keep clean.'

'And he makes laces?'

'Yeah.'

'Wow.'

The boy gave her a scathing look then focussed his eyes way beyond the others – who were all now standing with the dog, and the yukka, in a huddle, outside the small hotel – and over towards Wesley. On the horizon.

'Do *you* know where he's going?' Jo asked softly.

Patty stopped in his tracks. Jo stopped shortly after him.

'Of *course* I know where he's going. He's walking the island. He's done it every day since he was here. Don't you know anything?'

'Course I do,' she defended herself, staunchly, slightly hurt by his savagery, 'it's just that I know different things, that's all.'

The boy shrugged, 'If you want my opinion, I think he's losing it. Doing the same stupid walk every day. He's taking the piss out of everybody.'

Jo cut to the chase.

'If I give you a fiver will you let me take a peek at that piece of paper you took earlier?'

The boy sneered. 'Are you *kidding* me?' He was grossly self-righteous, 'I don't want your fucking money.'

His jaw, she noticed, was sharp as cut tin. His eyes were a

157

cold grey. The colour of black ice on a fast road. He really was too thin.

'I already turned down that other bugger, and he offered me a hell of a lot more than five.' He pointed up ahead of him.

'Doc, you mean?'

'Sod *off*.'

He actually seemed to find this funny.

'Hooch, then?'

The boy grinned then took a step closer to Jo, 'You see that's not what I'm in it for. Not short change. That won't satisfy me.'

'You're in it for the competition, then, is that it?'

The boy shrugged.

'Or for the Following?'

He didn't even credit Jo's second guess with a reaction.

'I'm not *clever* or nothing,' he told her, fiddling around inside his pockets as he spoke, 'but I do like puzzles. I've always been good with them. Crosswords in the papers and in books, and wordsearch. And I like working out stuff. And I *watch* stuff. And I keep my ears open . . .' he smiled at Jo, 'in actual fact I saw you in the library . . .'

'What do you mean?' Jo stiffened.

'I saw you read something in that book you had. Your cheeks went all red. I saw that. And then you kicked over the chair just after. On purpose.'

'To help you,' Jo interjected.

The boy snorted, derisively, 'To help *yourself* more like it.'

He withdrew the piece of paper from his pocket. White. Neatly folded. He dangled it in front of her, taunting her with it. Then he screwed it up, smirking, and threw it at her feet, his slate grey eyes mocking her, almost *goading* her to scrabble for it.

The three others, Jo noticed, were now all looking their way.

'What you need,' the boy spoke softly, 'isn't written on there. What you need is in here,' he tapped the side of his head, 'and if you want some of it, then I suggest you leave the others, leave *him*,' he tipped his head towards Wesley, in the far distance, rapidly disappearing, 'and follow me.'

'Where are you going?' Jo asked – Wesley was moving left, tight left, out of vision – she felt almost (was it *panic*?) at the thought of losing sight of him. But this was a challenge from the boy, wasn't it? It might prove foolish to deny him. And she was thirsty, *dammit*, and her feet were aching.

The others were silently heading back, like three strange birds, like vultures, fully intent upon feasting on the boy's dropped bounty.

And Jo wanted it. She *wanted* it.

(What had he written to the librarian? Was it rubbish? Was it poetry? Was it a clue? Would it incriminate him? Would it exonerate him? Why did she care? *Why* did she?)

'I'm going for a Coke, Josephine,' the boy half-turned and spoke cheekily over his bony shoulder, 'and for a very quick *wee-wee*. Do you think you might possibly be coming along with me?'

Seventeen

What was it with this walk? It was definitely sneaky. Initially unremarkable – everything muddied-right-up or wrung-right-out, or plain and grey and horizontal – but then it gradually snuck up on you (furtively, stealthily), tapped you softly on the shoulder (made you twist, made you stagger) stared you full in the face (without tact, without graciousness, without the slightest modicum of bloody courtesy) and blew the world's fattest, wettest and most unrepentant raspberry.

It was aberrant. It was . . . it was deviant. And worst of all – worst, worst, *worst* of all – it was time-warped. *Seriously.*

The hours just melted. That, or they simply elongated. They kicked out their legs, picked their noses and yawned, rudely, like a clutch of hearty schoolboys in double chemistry.

The minutes? Like sneezes. Or tiny kisses on the nape. Or flea bites. Or buzzing black midges. Urgent, sometimes, like the industrial snarl of the greenfinch, or the shamelessly arable, silver-muddied, plough-bladed *tssweee!* of the tiny warbler, hiding-and-seeking it in the blonde reeds of summer.

Ah, *summer.*

Wesley shuddered. Three-thirty and the sky was already nagging its way peevishly towards a tight and grey and implacable evening. Icy cold. Danker, now. The fog still gliding in and out – like a suspicious moorhen treading water with its prodigious pale toes on a busy river. Now you see him . . .
Gone.

The seconds drowned at high tide; grabbing for him; lunging at him, *gasping*, or they shivered disconsolately at low tide, barely acknowledging him before turning tail and slinking off, sullenly. Or both. Or *either*. They lapped reassuringly. Close upon him – far away. They were full of sense and inclination, but utterly devoid of weight or meaning.

This was surely the best kind of walking. He'd done it several times now – the span of the whole damn island – it was his *job* to keep circling (claws held tight, tucked in, like a vulture, a hawk, a raven; riding the ill-tuned, honk and parp of those choppy church-organ thermals – up, up, up, up . . .

down

– looking for weakness, stretching his wings, being irrepressibly keen, endlessly curious, revoltingly *beady*).

There was still plenty here to preoccupy him. Familiarity breeding (not contempt. No. He was never contemptuous. Contempt was just another kind of weakness) *more* familiarity.

There was the dump – which he loved – the Stonehenge of slag and scrap, the Babylon of debris. The smell, even in winter, was really quite heady. Rich and sweet with both form *and* integrity. In fact if stink were audible (Wesley conceptualised, idly) then it would be a lactating vixen, its foot caught and tearing in a steel-sprung trap. It would be a howl, but keening. A scream, only rounder.

He'd taken too long, but he'd indulged himself a little. Couldn't help it. Pretended he was hiking in the American Delta (he'd never been to America, but he felt its expanses locked up inside of him – wrapped-up tight with string and paper, bruised by a plethora of airmail stickers – in a thousand different illusory sense-memories.

He'd smelled it. He'd read it. He'd felt the parch and the gust of it. He'd eaten key-lime pie, drunk bourbon and communed with the bison. He'd headed Westward, crossing frontiers, smashing stuff up willy-nilly, scything, apportioning, opening, *appropriating*, but in his belly, in his crop; internally, mentally, *bacterially*).

When the sea wall finally toughened up and became concrete, he'd sprung up onto it, like an acrobat alighting – following a sprint, a bounce, a minutely-timed flick-flack – on the back of a cantering pony. He liked to indulge his childish whims. He liked to reel and totter on walls, precariously.

162

One step, two steps, taking it slow, taking it easy, finding his buzzing brain briefly – and blissfully – sedated by the careful regularity of one foot then the other, one foot then . . . He paused for a second, looked up, just quickly, to locate his wider bearings, and then –

WOW!

– he started (wobbled) and clutched at the air with his hands . . . Because suddenly he was wantonly jolted, he was upper-cut, he was hijacked by a huge, brash, bulbous *shimmering* edifice. Lights starting to blink and twinkle as the sun finally ducked and staggered – pissed and bloodshot – behind the sea.

The Oil Refinery. *Ahhh.* Wesley stood straight on the wall, shoulders dragged back by his rucksack, appraising it thoughtfully. He was bewitched by its humming and its clatter – all that convoluted metal glittering back at him, so . . . so *imperturbably.* All that *industry.*

His glance lowered. He admired the muted swathe of seabirds on the remaining patches of mudflat, paddling, contentedly – winter-throated and dozy – between him and this . . . this kinky, tortile, flexular . . . this . . . this big, sexy silver thing. This swirling, Byzantine monstrosity. This *beauty.*

Hmmn. Wesley bent his knees. Then stretched. The joints ached. He was tiring.

But he continued to stare, wondering. I mean would there be anything in it? For *him*? Could there be? He clenched his hands into balls and remained in place a little longer (just like he had yesterday, and the day before the day before). These industrial people *needed* to see him. They had to be cognisant. They had to be heedful. They had to be prudent and careful and wary. Or at least – as a matter of pride, a matter of *principle*, really – they had to *think* that they had to be.

He walked on. The sea wall was thinner now, several feet off the ground on one side, the other a deep drop into the wide tidal outlet between him and the monster. But soon the monster diminished, its headland wore to nothing, it shrank into a grumbling, monochrome muffle behind him. Now there was just sea. Everything had grown flat and quiet again. Wesley watched his feet.

The foxes liked this wall well enough. They shat on it. It was their boundary. Old, purple faeces, crammed with blackberry and elder and bits of insects. He bounded over these purple markers, conscientiously. He kept his eyes peeled.

Shivering rabbits sat up and appraised him, dwarfed by the harsh, sharp, linear shading of oil-black bridges. Disused. Rusting. Ancient, iron-elbowed rollercoasters, (industrial lemon rind, arcing and looping from nowhere to the sea), black towers, piers, angry dead promontories.

He smiled at them all, gently.

This was the shattered, hacked-up back-bone of a once hard-worked industrial legacy. This was the ancient trash of modernity. These were the scribbles in the margin. This was the graffiti.

But my *God* – Wesley stopped smiling – all that effort, all that toil and stink and shit and *drudgery*. And why? And for *what*? For this? Only the proud, mouldering bones remaining for the wildflowers to strangle, for the thistle to scratch, for the rain to tap upon in hollow melody?

Wesley stared at his feet, with increased attention, but then glanced up again, furtively, and saw a fantastic spidery mast – a spire – just standing right there, in the middle of nowhere – practically whited-out with council warnings – an impossible temptation for any adventurer.

It was getting dark, though, and the concrete of the wall was getting higher and fuzzier against the deepening blue around him. The water was blackening. The gulls were setting off intently, in ranks, towards the freezing pale and darkening grey.

By the time he'd reached the place he needed to be, the sea, the wall and everything remaining were submerged inside a warning blue-black grimace of octopus ink. No stars. The moon low, behind cloud, calling gently to the tide in chilly whispers.

Would she still be there?

Wesley suddenly considered the librarian. Eileen. It was unlikely. It was too cold for one thing. And the fishing pier was closed off by a gate (white-painted, gleaming crudely like false teeth under ultra-violet) with a sign prohibiting entry. How would she have clambered over in those delicate little shoes she'd been wearing earlier? He remembered the shoes, clearly. What had he been thinking, setting up this stupid meeting? And why *here*?

Wesley pulled his rucksack from his shoulders and threw it over the gate. The gate creaked when he leaned against it. He whistled. Nothing. He pushed at it, tentatively –

Yes.

It opened. There were bushes to the near end – a mass of brambles desperately scrabbling to drag this straying edifice back into the close, warm palm of dry land again. He moved past them. He walked tentatively, the pier creaking. And then . . .

He saw her.

She was frozen, halfway along, standing in a sudden pool of toothy yellow (the moon's grin flickering, uncertainly, like a burned-down candle in a gusty stairwell). She was half-turned towards him, her arm outstretched, her fingers beckoning. She was struck dumb. He could see her lips moving.

She pointed.

He looked.

Heron. Right there, on the drop of the pier. Five foot away. Or six. Statuesque in the darkness – the night fog picking him out in a muted tapestry of black and grey. Gaunt but wilting.

Wesley drew closer. The bird shifted but it did not fly. He felt Eileen's hand reaching out for his. Her fingers so cold she must have been waiting just about forever. Her breath in mist. Her hair like candyfloss. She touched his hand – the cold nose of a kitten – then set it free again.

He was two hours late, and she had waited.

'We've been here,' she whispered, 'a long, long while, just listening to the night falling and the moon rising and the sea lapping. It's been . . .' she struggled, 'it's been . . .'

'It's late,' Wesley whispered back to her, 'I'm sorry.'

'It's been . . .' she continued, not even countenancing his apology, 'it's been *heavenly.*' She paused and drew breath, 'When I first arrived and it was still light, he tried to fly, but he couldn't make it. Too weak. He's an old one. I think this might be . . . I mean, I think he might be . . .'

She didn't dare say it.

They were quiet. The bird shifted. Bone creaking audibly against quill; his last will and testament etching itself, with gradual inevitability, into nature's cruel registry.

'Will we save him?' Wesley asked the sky.

Eileen turned to appraise him fully, '*Could* we?'

Her eyes were bright with childish expectation; prised wide by dolls' houses and tin drums and teddies. Trussed up with gilt-edged ribbons. Wesley was suddenly all her Christmases. He was her beardless Santa, bringing flesh and bone and lust and hope, all jumbled up together and slung into the duck-down-trimmed sack thrown over his shoulder.

He smiled. She was so silly. In that moment he thought that he had never seen anyone so full of honest expectation, so sincere, so *clean*.

He took her hand and raised it to his face (that *hand*. Cold as a side of refrigerated pork, and softer still. It smelled of apricots). He touched it gently to his cheek.

How he wished he could live in this enchanted place – this hopeful world she inhabited so effortlessly – but it was a strange land – they spoke a different language, had different customs – and its borders were patrolled too closely. It was inaccessible to him; it was cooped and cloistered, trapped deep inside of her. It pumped in her blood: a sweet, scented garden, blooming and shining inside the seven smooth layers of her brilliant skin.

'But first we must catch him,' Wesley spoke, 'and he's bound to resist us. Are you game, Eileen?'

(Used her name. Used it easily.)

'Are you ready?'

Eileen drew a deep breath and then carefully adjusted the small velvet collar on her coat. She stood straight and determinedly in her kinky heels. She was primed, at a word, to do his bidding.

Wesley slowly unbuttoned his corduroy jacket, 'You must move to the left of him, hold his attention. I'll come from the rear. Perhaps you should be singing something, but only very softly . . .'

'But what should I sing?' she interrupted him, keenly.

Wesley paused. He grinned to himself.

'Something by . . .' he stared at her in the darkness. He could smell the roses on her. Their bruised petals tickled his sinuses. 'Something by *The Carpenters*. But hum it.'

Eileen was quiet for a second. It was a beautiful hiatus. Then she drew breath and softly began humming. After three seconds, though, she stopped.

'*We've Only Just Begun* . . .' she whispered, 'do you think he'll like it?'

'It's . . .' Wesley felt the sudden urge to pinch and kiss the translucent flesh on the inside of her elbow. He imagined the mauve intensity of those turquoise and lilac veins and his cruel fingers plucking at them, '. . . it's perfect,' he told her.

Eileen began humming again. Her voice was low, but the song was lower, the bottom notes collapsing like a confident ballerina into the powerful arms of her partner.

Wesley stood and listened. He closed his eyes for a second. Oh, he told himself, this is one of those moments . . . He tingled. He shuddered. Then he opened his eyes, removed his jacket, took something else – was it the knife? The *hunting* knife? – from his trouser pocket, hid it behind him with one hand, while holding the coat up – high and close in front of him – with the other.

Eighteen

Rabbit-duck?
Duck-rabbit!
Ludwig? Ludwag!
Catch me out, honey,
And I'll catch you at it

He hadn't made it easy for her. But why the hell should he? He was just a boy. She was just a girl. It was biologically determined that things would be complicated.

She'd bought him a cold drink (wouldn't he prefer something warmer? A cocoa or a *Horlicks*? Did they even do *Horlicks* here? No.

No, he wanted a cold drink. He didn't like his drinks warmed. He liked them bubbly. He liked them icy. He liked them cheap and sharp and sweet).

Jo ordered herself a milky tea – she was absolutely ruddy *freezing* – cupped her hands around it, held her chin over the steam, felt her nose running, and sniffed, under her breath, repeatedly.

At least he'd let her buy him something to eat (a sacrifice of some considerable magnitude on his part, apparently). His needs were very particular – she noted – as he guardedly selected a serving of coleslaw in its own polystyrene tub, a packet of fries – French, puckered, browning – and a seeded burger bun, with gherkins and extra onions (cubed, minutely, in the characteristic Wimpy way), but without the meat (without the *patty*. Now that was . . . that was *funny*), followed, climactically, by a large and sticky Brown

169

Derby (ice cream in winter? Was the boy deranged?) with all the nutty and saucy trimmings.

Patty – it soon transpired – had absolutely no table manners to speak of (or not to speak of, as the case may be, except with his mouth full, his eyes rolling and his two sharp elbows tent-pegging the table). Yet this lack wasn't just a casual deficit; he seemed cheerfully and positively opposed to all forms of etiquette. He reminded Jo of a feral canine. A scavenger. One of those lean mutts who patrolled the dusty suburban streets in Tenerife or Tunisia. In packs. One of those mean beasts. Tick-infested – too thin – hungry – snarly – *hungry*.

Then to top it all off – and adding insult to injury – instead of calmly unburdening while he was grabbing and prodding, fingering and scoffing (he did promise to unburden, didn't he?), the boy proceeded to try his level best to interrogate Jo instead. He needed to get his head around her. He needed to *fit* her, somewhere – to parcel her up, to slot her in, to neaten her. It was, she presumed, a ten-year-old boy thing.

'You grew up in this shithole, then?'

His first question. He had a droplet of salad cream in the gap between his mouth and his nose. Jo stared at it, resignedly.

'What's your problem with Canvey?' she countered. She was a local girl. She had local pride.

'Wesley has written,' the boy told her, straightening his backbone as he quoted the master, 'that the Estuary Islands – and Canvey in particular – remind him, geographically, of the American Delta.'

Jo was unimpressed, 'Lots of people say that. I think it's basically just . . .' she considered her choice of words carefully, 'just *crap*, really.'

'Why?'

The boy opened his bun and arranged some french fries on it. He laid them straight – in a carbo-raft – then painstakingly tipped the coleslaw over.

'Has Wesley ever been to America?'

The boy shrugged, 'Dunno. But his dad did. His dad was a marine in the British Navy.'

'Really?'

'I believe so,' the boy nodded his small head, gravely.

Jo smiled. Against her better judgement, she found herself warming to this prickly creature. This tyke. This urchin.

'I didn't know that,' she told him, 'but it certainly explains a lot.'

The boy stared at Josephine across the table, his Cola suspended halfway between its soggy red paper coaster and his lips. He was deeply unimpressed by her cheery veneer. He detected more than a whiff of grown-up condescension in it. He was a wise child. And sensitive.

'You don't know *squat*, then,' he barked out, 'do ya?'

He took a swig of his drink, wincing, grotesquely, as it hit his fillings. Jo rapidly revised her good opinion.

'Anyway,' he persisted, 'you can't've liked it that much around here if you were in such a bloody hurry to leave.'

'Don't be ridiculous,' her voice was sterner than it might've been (why on *earth* had she gone and mentioned the Canvey connection? It was obviously going to plague her), 'Southend's just a spit up the road. It's visible from the headland. It's no distance at all.'

The boy raised his brows at her.

'Sensitive,' he said, taking an ice cube from his drink, and biting down hard upon it, 'aren't we?'

'No,' Jo paused for a moment. 'No. Not sensitive. Just . . .' *God.* His crunching on that ice was making her spine quiver, 'just . . . just a stickler.'

(Oh she was sensitive alright. The wounds were still there. Still raw. Even after all this time. This boy was much cleverer than he looked. This boy was . . .
Was he a danger?)

'Let's talk about Clue Five,' Patty said, getting down to business, wiping his hands and lips on a napkin (now that was a concession, wasn't it? To the stilted and gibbering God of Etiquette?) before removing a sheath of papers from the inside pocket of his bomber jacket.

The salad cream beneath his nose had survived the napkin's absorbent swipe undiminished. Jo took a sip of tea, still staring at it, blankly . . . Now what was he up to? Was this malevolent little shit avoiding something?

Or was she?

The boy found the clue he required among his small stack of papers which were all tied up – and very neatly, at that – with a blue rubber band, then divided into sections by multi-coloured clips. One paper, she couldn't help noticing, was a photocopied photograph – colour printed – of a woman and a baby. From the late 1970s.

Jo reached out her hand and spun it around, 'Who's that?'

'None of your bloody business.'

He snatched the picture back.

'Sorry.'

Jo withdrew, offended.

'My mother and my big sister,' he suddenly blurted.

'Really?' She inspected his face, sympathetically, 'I bet they worry.'

'Why should they?' the boy snapped.

Jo dumbly shrugged her injured acquiescence.

'I don't live with them, anyway,' he told her, 'I have a foster family in Derby.'

'I see.' Jo nodded, staring at his mean lips, thoughtfully. This boy *caves*, she ruminated, if you withdraw after questioning – if you simply back down – if you ignore his parry.

'Why Clue Five then, Patty?'

(Had to use the name. Had to test her theory.)

'No bloody reason,' the boy growled.

'Fine,' she conceded.

'Just because . . .' the boy spat out – he couldn't help himself – 'just because I know a lot about it, but no one ever explains it to me. The stuff I know. They think it's all a big joke when . . .' he thought hard, 'when I don't,' he scowled, '. . . they think I don't *comprehend* nothing properly. Too *raw*, Hooch says.'

'That's tough,' Jo tried to seem sympathetic – she *was* sympathetic. 'You can always show me what you've got, if you like, and I'll see what I can make of it.'

Patty carefully considered this offer – munching like a rodent on a mouthful of coleslaw – then grudgingly pushed Clue Five towards

172

her. Jo looked down at it, casually. It was perfectly familiar. She had her own well-thumbed copy snuggled up neatly inside her front coat pocket.

'Right. *Clue Five* . . .'

She read the clue out loud, expressionlessly . . .

'*Rabbit-duck . . . Duck-rabbit . . . Ludwig . . . Ludwag . . . Catch me out, honey . . . And I'll catch you at it.*'

She looked up, 'So tell me everything you know.'

The boy cackled through his mouthful of food, 'You really think I'm *that* stupid?'

'Not at all.'

Jo was silent.

The boy finished chewing. He took the clue back and pointed to it.

'Everybody says,' he told her, lowering his voice, swallowing, glancing over his shoulder, 'that it's all about cricket . . .'

'That much I realised,' Jo intervened.

Patty didn't appreciate her intervention. He clamped his mouth shut like a snapping turtle and stared up at the ceiling.

'I was . . .' Jo paused, trying to make things better (why this ridiculous urge to ingratiate herself with the boy? Why should his good opinion matter a damn to her?), 'I was brought up in a family of three brothers, which means I'm pretty good at most games involving either a bat or a racquet . . .'

'Okay, so the way *I'm* seeing it,' the boy continued, ignoring her pointedly, 'is that a Rabbit is when the batter doesn't score any points . . .'

'Nope,' she couldn't stop herself, 'that's a Duck. A Duck is when a batsman doesn't score any runs. In cricket they don't call them points, they call them runs.'

The boy winced, enraged at being corrected in a sports-related matter by any creature of – however approximate – feminine gender, but then he rallied, 'Okay . . . so a Rabbit is what they call you when you're rubbish at cricket, and a Duck . . .'

'No,' Jo shifted in her chair, 'well, yes, *kind* of. Rabbit is a term of abuse. Someone might say, for example, that so and so *isn't a complete Rabbit* – which means, in effect, that they aren't completely useless.'

The boy frowned, 'So a Rabbit *isn't* completely useless?'

'No. No, a Rabbit *is* useless. I was just . . .'

Jo fell silent. The boy was scowling, furiously.

'In fact you were right,' she tried to bolster him, 'because a Duck *is* nothing and a Rabbit *is* useless. And that's all pretty much in keeping, thematically . . .' (Oh God. Now she'd really gone and lost him.) 'I mean it fits in. With the other five. With the general *tone* of the other five clues. Kind of downbeat, and very . . . very evasive . . . *uh* . . . In actual fact I was wondering . . .'

She struggled to yank herself out of the hole she'd just landed in. 'I was actually thinking about maybe looking at some kind of map of the night sky. I wasn't sure whether there might be a constellation of stars named after either of these two creatures. I'm sure there could be a hare up there or something. Or a goose . . . Well maybe not a goose, but a fowl of some kind . . .'

While Jo rambled on, Patty eyed her, sardonically, as if it had only just dawned on him that she was clean out of her tree.

'My surname is Bean,' she continued, struggling to fill the silence between them, and worsening matters, considerably, 'which is a breed of goose. An ancient breed. Brown feathered, with a bright orange bill and feet. Black tipped – the bill. Doesn't come to Britain very often. Its habitat is much more . . .' she paused, 'well . . . *Central* European.'

The boy continued to scowl at Jo (it was an expression he patently had a long-term investment in), and only when he was absolutely certain that she'd been suitably diminished by his potent disapprobation, did he turn and scowl – methodically – into his bowl of melting dairy dessert, instead. He took a few sarcastic mouthfuls, chewed bitterly, swallowed scornfully, but after a minute or so – and against all his worse inclinations – the infallible Brown Derby seemed to sweeten him.

'Point is,' he said, resting his spoon on the table, 'the clue isn't about cricket at all, really. Hooch says it's about the other bloke. It's about that Ludwig fella.'

The boy pronounced the name with a soft w.

'Beethoven?' Jo jumped in, 'He was a Lud . . .' she took care to soften her own w accordingly, 'he was a Ludwig, wasn't he?'

'Yep. But that's just a cover,' Patty tapped the side of his nose, 'and we know better.'

'Do we?'

'Hooch says it's much more likely to be about philosophy.'

He stared at Jo intently. 'Philosophy,' he confided, 'is like history but without any dates. And like geography but without any places.'

'That's very . . .' Jo's eyes were dancing, 'that's very profound, Patty.'

Patty shrugged, disdainfully, 'It's only what Shoes told me. Here . . .' He rifled through his papers again, 'I grabbed this from Hooch ages ago when he wasn't looking.'

'You stole this from Hooch?'

The boy nodded, unperturbedly, and showed her a scruffy drawing etched in black biro – just an outline.

Jo picked it up. 'What is it?'

'Guess.'

Jo stared at it. 'I suppose it looks a little like . . .' she paused, 'well, a rabbit.'

'Ha.'

The boy was delighted.

'What?'

'Nothing. Turn it up the other way.'

'How?'

The boy showed her.

'Now what does it look like?'

'Uh . . .' Jo rubbed one of her eyes and squinted. 'A goat. It looks like a goat without legs. Or a llama '

'Give over.'

Jo stared harder.

'Then maybe a d . . .'

'Duck,' the boy bellowed. 'Yes. A duck.'

Jo had been intending to say donkey (it was a terrible drawing), but she bit the ass back on her tongue and simply nodded, smiling.

Patty dropped down in his seat, kicked out his legs, yanked up his shirt and drummed on his tight stomach.

'So there you go.'

His grin was all Cheshire.

'Do I?' Jo was perplexed.

'Rabbit-*duck*, duck-*rabbit*, you stupid idiot. It's philosophy. There's more on the back. Turn it. Take a look.'

Jo flipped it over. There she read:

From Ludwig Wittgenstein's Blue Book. The duck/rabbit is Wittgenstein's answer to the Problem of Universals (Plato) ie Does something have an intrinsic essence? W. says no. He says one thing can be two things at once, and that this disproves the fundamental Platonic notion of 'ideals'.

'Good God.' Jo was impressed.

'Clever, huh?'

Patty was delighted by the intensity of Josephine's reaction.

'Yes. I mean I . . . And you say you got this from *Hooch*?'

He pulled himself straight again, covered his belly and leaned forward, conspiratorially, 'He's not as dumb as he seems, that one.' He touched the side of his nose and winked. But before she could push him further on the matter he burped then said, 'So go on and explain it.'

'*Uh* . . .' Jo frowned. 'Well it's . . . it's pretty *complicated*, Patty.'

Patty harrumphed as she flipped the paper over and looked at the illustration again, turning it first one way, then the other. 'So does . . .' she finally murmured, 'does Hooch know you stole this from him?'

'Dunno,' Patty was supremely indifferent to Hooch's feelings, 'what's it all about, then?'

Jo frowned. 'I'm not . . .' she re-read the information on the back, one last time, 'in all honesty, Patty, I don't really know. But in terms of the general *thrust* of the thing,' she took another sip of her tea, 'what I'm actually feeling here is more . . . it's much more of an . . . an *atmosphere* than anything.'

She glanced over at him. Patty's expression was uncomprehending. He was fast losing patience. 'I don't give a shit about atmospheres,' he growled, 'I only want to know its *mean-ing*.' He split his syllables, menacingly.

'But that *is* what it means, because . . .' Jo battled to explain it, 'because, well, in effect, what Wesley's saying here is that the great philosopher – *uh* . . . Ludwig Witt . . . Wittgen . . .' she struggled, briefly, with her pronunciation, 'Wittgen*stein* was actually a bit of a wag – see? Ludwig-Ludwag – and a wag means a joker. Now that's relevant to Wesley because he's a famous practical joker himself – or that's how people *see* him – but he's sort of saying . . .' she peered up at the ceiling to try and gather her thoughts together, 'he's kind of implying that in exactly the same way that a great thinker can also be a great joker, a great joker can also be a great thinker . . . He's sort of poking fun at himself but also kind of defending his . . . *uh* . . .' Jo chuckled to herself, quietly, 'He's such an unrepentant fat-head. You just have to . . . I mean you just have to stand back and *admire* it, really.'

She leaned over, liberated the clue from Patty again and quickly re-read it.

'The way I see it,' she told him, 'this whole Rabbit-Duck Duck-Rabbit thing actually has a *double* meaning. It refers to *both* cricket *and* philosophy, because . . .'

'But *how*?' Patty butted in. '*How* can something mean two things at once?'

The boy shoved his Brown Derby to one side, grabbed hold of the straw from his drink and twisted it, violently, around his middle finger. Splashes of cola arced through the air. Some hit the window – his shirt – the back of his chair.

Jo didn't notice, though. She was seduced by the clue, caught up, completely, in its simple complexity.

'But *how*?' Patty reiterated, even more loudly.

'Well that's . . .' Jo shrugged her shoulders, 'that's sort of the whole point, Patty,' she spoke distractedly, 'that's precisely what grown-up people do when they're being especially . . . well, especially grown-up.'

Patty was nonplussed. He still wasn't getting it. He leaned across the table, snatched back Clue Five and the *duck-rabbit*, then slapped them down, hard, onto the plastic table-top. The china and the cutlery rattled rather ominously. A member of staff looked up from the counter.

'But what I *need* you to do . . .' he told her, the tops of his

177

cheekbones jerking furiously, 'is to tell me the *answer*. To *explain* it all to me so that I can get to . . . so I can . . . so I can understand the *riddle* part of it, see?'

Jo was un-fazed by Patty's raging. She took another sip of her tea (it was cooling down. It was lukewarm now) scratched her neat nose and then peered around the room, calmly. 'Give me a pen,' she instructed him, 'and a spare piece of paper.'

Patty took a sip of his own drink (he wouldn't jump to her command. He was master of his own destiny), hiccuped loudly (to indicate the strength of his passing contempt), then leaned back and pulled a biro out of his pocket and something to write upon – a small, white sheet, which he unfolded, flipped over (little fingers delicately raised, his eyes holding hers, confidently, his mouth half-smiling – like some kind of amateur magician).

Jo snatched the paper (ignoring all his cocky ostentation. Bloody *hell* this child was heavy-going), laid it flat, smoothed it flatter still, grabbed the biro and carefully wrote: *Clue Five* at the top of the page, underlined it, then neatly continued, in her small, well-formed hand:

1) Wesley thinks that the famous philosopher Ludwig Wittgenstein was a bit of a joker. Wag means joke.

She glanced up, 'Okay?'

The boy rolled his eyes.

Next she wrote:

2) Ludwig invented the duck/rabbit idea as a way of saying that one thing can also be something else at the same time. For example . . .

Josephine thought hard for a minute,

. . . a friend can also be an enemy. A crate is a crate, but if you turned it up the other way it could also be a chair (if you sat on it), or a table, even, if you rested a cup of tea on it . . .

She looked up, 'Alright?'

178

The boy shrugged. He was unfocussed.

'It's pretty complicated,' she attempted to clarify things, 'but it's only a question of applying a little bit of . . . well . . . lateral . . .' She re-thought her vocabulary, '*practical* thinking.'

Next she wrote:

3) By using the words 'duck', 'rabbit' and 'catch me out', Wesley is saying that the Loiter is a kind of game – like cricket – but he is also indicating . . .

Jo crossed out this word.

. . . SAYING that whatever it is that we are all looking for – the prize – isn't actually WHAT IT SEEMS. That's the important part.

The last four words Jo underlined three times. On the third underlining she broke through the paper, but then tidied up the small hole she'd created, as best she could, with her index finger.

'Okay?'

Patty was still staring at her, blankly, his feet banging out a tap-dance under the table. Jo sucked on her tongue (this boy was revoltingly hyper-something. He was crying out for a handful of Ritalin), and then continued writing:

4) In this clue, as in many of the others, Wesley employs . . .

She crossed out 'employs'.

. . . USES a word that makes the reader think of sweetness. Or confectionery. In this case, 'honey'. He uses it sarcastically. In Clue One, for example, he uses the word 'sucker' – as in lolly – but remember: a sucker is also a word that refers to someone being taken for a fool. Is Wesley warning us of something here?

DOES WESLEY THINK WE ARE ALL . . .

At this point the pen ran out. Jo shook it a few times.

. . . FOOLS?!!

She finished with less of a flourish than she would've liked, but once she'd taken the time to re-read her handiwork she seemed moderately pleased with it.

'There.'

She shoved the piece of paper back over to Patty.

'Thank you.'

He took it – a smug little grin dimpling the corner of his thin lips – and held it up in front of him, squinting disdainfully at what she'd written (not really reading, only pretending), then peering up and over, every so often, to try and gauge her reaction.

Jo stared back at him, tiredly. She was lost. He had lost her. She couldn't begin to understand what he was about, what he wanted, what he was after. During his dumb show, her eyes focussed, passively, on that tiny point where her pen's sharp nib had broken the paper's thin ply, minutes earlier. The light was now filtering through this hole, like a sparking Pluto, or a pin-prick Jupiter.

1–2–3 . . .

She suddenly crackerjacked out of her reverie.

'*Oh my* . . .'

She bounced forward, 'You horrible *little* . . .'

'What?' Patty darted back, snatching away the paper, his grey eyes sparkling.

'*What?*'

(It was one of those flawless ten-year-old boy questions, so complete and facetious, it demanded no answer.)

Jo leaned forward, urgently, 'You *kept* it, you *bugger*.'

Was she furious? Was she delirious?

Patty clucked his tongue at her, faux-sympathetically, '*Aw*. You honestly thought I'd dropped it back there?'

He proceeded to gently flap the scrap of paper back and forth in front of her, as if inciting her to try for a grab at it. A lunge. A snatch.

Jo didn't move. She was not to be provoked. She eyed the fluttering form, inscrutably, until it slowed down, until it almost stopped.

'So what *did* you drop?' she asked, still eyeing it determinedly, her voice sounding brittle as nutty toffee.

Patty sucked in his cheeks, '*My* application form, you fucking bloody *mare*.'

'Did you really.'

Not so much a question, as a dehydrated whip-crack.

'Huh?'

Jo took a sip of her tea. Cold. Pushed her cup away. Swallowed. Shuddered.

'What?' he asked her, and then a second time, '*What?*'

Still no answer.

Finally he turned the paper over and focussed in on it himself. His sneer froze.

His eyes rolled.

Then he threw his small head back, hit the thin wall of the cubby with it, expostulated, kicked his knees up, automatically, hit the table with them, expostulated again, tossed himself forward like a small boy-comet, covering the table-top with a hail of flesh and limb and howl and debris. There he rested, breathing heavily.

Why are ten-year-olds, Jo wondered, mildly, (picking up a gherkin and his slightly battered disposable plastic Cola cup) always so unremittingly bloody *dramatic*?

When Patty finally rose, he did so rather moistly but with a tremulous dignity.

'I don't suppose,' Jo chanced her arm, 'you might possibly recollect . . . *uh* . . . ?'

No.

Patty lifted his left hand to silence her – as though swearing an oath of allegiance to his own stupidity – while their four eyes met in a superbly well-defined architectural arc of mutual consternation across that dirty plastic table-top.

Nineteen

The first of many strangers arrived with the darkness, and it was almost – Arthur thought – well, *poetic*, really, under the circumstances, that the first should be the darkest, and quite positively the strangest. Of Middle-Eastern – maybe Iranian – extraction. Spoke no English. They communicated in French, but what little conversation they did have was inconclusive. Arthur wasn't fluent enough to establish anything definitive: like why he was there exactly, or who he was, or what he wanted.

(Was this man – oh *Lord*, what a prospect – part of some kind of vaguely shonky, distinctly shady, potentially lunatic *international* conspiracy? Was this whole scenario much bigger – much more complicated – than he'd ever imagined it might be? He'd always believed the whole Wesley thing to be a peculiarly British phenomenon. A Labour of Sisyphus, but strictly parochial. Warped – pointless – faddish.)

Arthur didn't want – how to put this, exactly – he didn't want to feel like this strange man had alarmed him (*startled*. Yes. That was more like it. The man had surprised him, had ... had *startled* ...) but when he subsequently considered the intense and – in all honesty – rather curious interlude that had taken place between them – straight after, and only briefly, because events then rapidly took on their own ... their own *momentum* – Arthur decided (he rationalised?) that it was mainly the stranger's ... his ... his impertinence that had left him feeling ...

Impertinence?

Was that it? Or was it something marginally less aggressive,

183

something marginally more . . . Not impertinence. Audacity? Yes. Yes? No.

No, it was his disconnectedness. It was his . . . his aura of detached *familiarity*. Was that coherent? Did it make any kind of . . . ?

Arthur had been standing in the kitchen (back to the door, just a couple of feet along from the small window which afforded him a view of all-comers from the Benfleet direction), messing around with his mobile phone (was totally embroiled in what he was doing. Hadn't seen the man approaching. Hadn't even the slightest *notion* . . .) when this swarthy, medium height, medium build, medium everything kind of person walked on board (the door had been closed. He'd shown some . . . well . . . some *affinity* with the broken door mechanism. Arthur had experimented – several times, in fact – to find a way to open and close it without needing to shove himself against it, bodily. It was warped. It was rather prone to jamming).

This man had entered the boat (casually tipping his head so as to avoid knocking it into the door frame – indicating, Arthur surmised, that he was about 5'8" or over. Was that . . . Could that be *construed* as medium?), shut the door calmly and firmly behind him, then just stood there, rubbing his two gloved hands together (because of the cold, Arthur presumed. It was minus three on the thermometer), staring jovially across the galley at him, smiling.

Full teeth, gums, even a tip of tongue.
Flirty.

'Can I help you?' Arthur was startled.

The man paused a while before replying, his eyes glancing around the boat, as if hunting out something in particular. They focussed, briefly, on the gas canister (currently burning), then alighted on Arthur's laptop computer. The computer (on the sideboard) was open and operational. He was working on a document entitled *Agreement of Sale*. Underneath this heading Arthur had written; *I've had a change of heart. Let's proceed . . .*

The mobile phone Arthur held was connected to it by a wire. Arthur was either sending this document somewhere, or possibly receiving something.

The stranger casually inspected the computer's *'batteries running down – save your document and switch to your mains supply'* notice, which was temporarily flashing, and also took in (his head tipped, like a bird's) a tiny, unobtrusive beeping; the audio-warning it was also issuing. His eyes finally tightrope-walked the wire, to the small black phone in Arthur's hand.

'The batteries . . .' Arthur murmured, balancing the phone carefully onto the windowsill, walking over towards the computer and abruptly banging the lid down. The computer squawked, enraged.

'*Uh* . . . Can I *help* you?' he repeated.

The man put all his fingertips to his lips. Both hands. An impulsive movement (like he'd just tasted something exceptional and wished to congratulate the cook on it: *Ah delicious!* In that European way – that gesture the French had. The Italians – or like he was a tiny mouse, gnawing, determinedly, on a juicy wild strawberry).

Seconds later, he moved his hands away. 'I have no English language,' he spoke softly, his voice higher than Arthur had expected it to be – almost fluting, almost feminine – but his accent so heavy that his words were pretty much indecipherable.

French, was he?

'Have you come about Wesley? Is that it?' Arthur asked, cautiously.

This man speaks no English, Arthur, so why are you still talking in it?

'Ah . . .' the man considered this question for a moment (as if it was entirely frivolous, utterly irrelevant, totally inexplicable).

'*Wesley?*' Arthur repeated. 'Is it about *him?*'

(To be saying the *name*. To be so *embroiled*. It just felt . . . it was just . . . it was madness.)

The stranger widened his eyes, then nodded, '*Ah, oui,*' he smiled, '*Oui. Precis, monsieur.*'

He seemed at ease with French, but by no means fluent in it.

He was still looking about him.

'*Puis-je . . . uh . . . Puis-je, peut-être . . . uh . . . vous aider?*' Arthur asked, haltingly.

The man ignored this question and instead pointed genially towards the computer, '*Wah! Pas d'electrique, huh?*'

185

('Wah'?!)

'Uh . . .' Arthur shook his head, slowly, 'Uh . . . non. Non.'

But before he'd quite finished speaking, the man was on the hoof again, was walking over to the window (increasing their proximity by a considerable margin. Arthur did not *flinch* as he brushed past him, no, not flinch so much as move, very quickly, very efficiently, into the furthest recesses of the bright green galley).

The man stood squarely in front of the window, staring through it intently, his gloved hand resting on the glass.

He'd moved over there so suddenly – Arthur surmised, from his sanctuary behind the cooker – with such unexpected speed, such determination, such *energy*, that it was almost as if this manoeuvre represented some kind of . . . some kind of resolution; as if it prefaced some sort of . . . some sort of notable . . . no . . . *fundamental* plan of action. Like he was all fired up and ready for something.

Or was it – Arthur swallowed, nervously – was it just a sound? A movement? Had he been alerted – *frighted* – by something external, maybe?

Arthur struggled to hear this something. But he heard nothing. Just the river outside, gurgling. The heater. The computer. Of all his senses, his hearing was the weakest.

Much to the stranger's obvious irritation, his cautious instincts had proven entirely founded. '*Merde*,' he muttered. '*Quel qu'un arrive.*'

He rapidly withdrew, moving backwards, slipping effortlessly – without even looking – towards the door, grabbing the handle behind him, twisting it, opening it – *damn* him – moving back and beyond it. A cine-reel, rewinding.

On his way through, though, he suddenly remembered . . . He suddenly recollected . . . Ah, yes. Arthur.
Him.

He held the door open for a second longer, shrugged apologetically (*Was there really an apology in it?*), grimaced, closed the door quietly and strode off down the walkway (Arthur listened. Couldn't hear a sound), turned a sharp right (not clambering up the embankment, but opting to walk along the bottom of it – a rather perilous route: the mud was still slippy, the tide was gushing in), turned a swift left into the river bending, and disappeared.

The sky was getting dark and still darker. Arthur craned his head, watching the final movements of his visitor through the broken glass in the door. He'd been intending to fix it earlier – had tried to, ham-fistedly – but the cardboard he'd tacked up there had already fallen off and onto the floor. He pushed at the door (*bugger*. It stuck. Hadn't quite acquired the knack yet. Tried it again. *That* was it) and moved cautiously out onto the walkway. It remained foggy in his section of backwater. Couldn't see far.

Was it *always* foggy here?

Quel qu'un arrive

In the distance . . . An old . . . *The* Old Man. Arthur drew a sharp breath, ducked his head, turned abruptly, walked back inside the boat, closed the door, gently, and crouched down behind it. His heart was pounding.

Jesus. The Old . . . Hadn't . . .
But was there any question of him having . . . ?
    No.
But was . . . But . . . ?
    No.
Keep your wits, Arthur. Keep your wits. Wesley never speaks to the people following. Not even the Old Man. Not even him.

After a couple of minutes, Arthur slowly arose and peeped out through the broken pane. The other side of it –
Fuck
– stood a dreadful looking hippie and another man with white irises. A blind man. They made a maverick pair.

'Sorry to disturb you, but we saw the light,' the hippie spoke first, stepping – rather nervously – onto the walkway, then reconsidering and stepping off again, all the while trying (and failing) to disguise his surprise at Arthur emerging so very eccentrically from his crouching position.
Fat Hippie
Gracious me
Look at the damn state of him

187

Arthur finally materialised – in all his entirety – from behind the door, and stood straight and tall at his end of the walkway.

Just pretend you were doing DIY or something

He felt his stomach fluttering, but forced himself to grow bold again.

Don't even think about the old fella

Don't even . . .

'Sorry to disturb you,' the Hippie repeated, 'but did you happen to see another man pass this way? Brown hair? In his thirties?'

Right.

'D'you mean the Arabic gentleman?' Arthur asked, placing his palm onto what remained of the handrail, tentatively.

The Hippie frowned at this description, 'Arabic?'

'Or Iranian. The Iranian gentleman. He just left here.'

'An *Arabic* gentleman?'

'Or Iranian.'

'*Two* gentlemen? *Both* Middle Eastern?'

'No. No, there was . . . No. There was only one person. Arabic. *Or* Iranian. Only one. They just this minute . . .'

'I see.'

The Hippie nodded and then turned confidingly towards the blind man, as if in some doubt of his having heard the exchange between them, 'He's now saying that it was only *one* gentleman, Herbie, and that he just this minute left here.'

The blind man tossed his head – like a newly-harnessed pony – thereby implying that either he'd heard the conversation himself (and needed no interpreter – he was only *blind*, after all) or that he didn't – for some unspecified reason – feel like Arthur's testimony was entirely trustworthy.

Arthur frowned. He had the distinct feeling that the piss was being taken out of him. Either that or the Hippie was an absolute fool.

The Hippie paused – thinking deeply for a moment – then half-turned to consult the blind man again, 'An *Arabic* gentleman, Herbie. Would you describe Wesley as looking – in any way – like a person of Arabic extraction?'

'I'm *blind*, you damn Hippie imbecile . . .'

Arthur smirked to himself.

Exactly

'And anyway,' the blind man continued, 'if somebody *had* just left this vessel, we almost certainly would've seen him . . .'

He lowered his voice slightly, 'Bear in mind, Shoes, that the stranger may well be lying.'

'I have no reason,' Arthur sharply interrupted, 'to lie about a man having just left this craft. He left along the bottom path. You mightn't've seen him from where you were. It's foggy . . .'

You're blind

'and it's already getting dark out. I have no idea which direction he originally came from. It may well've been Canvey.'

'Good point,' the Hippie conceded, perhaps just a touch too easily (Shoes did not enjoy conflict. He was a hippie. It was more than a fashion. It was a philosophy). Arthur growled to himself, under his breath, then half-turned, as if intending to retreat into the cabin.

'Just by-the-by,' the Hippie stopped him, before he could escape them, 'it might be helpful for you to know that Herbie here got slightly peed-off clambering down your embankment. He's blind. It's steep and very slippery. I had trouble with it myself, although obviously I'm . . .' he smiled, humbly, 'I'm lucky enough to be fully sighted.'

While he spoke, Arthur was staring –

Discreet

Be discreet

– at the Hippie's bare toes, but once he'd gleaned the basic gist of what he was saying (and the casual censure implicit in it), he glanced back up at his heavy, pale face, deeply affronted.

'It would certainly be rather *foolish* . . .' he spoke, somewhat harshly (as was his way), 'to somehow imagine that this particular piece of rural wilderness was now, or ever would be, in any way adapted to the special needs of the mentally or . . . or *vi . . . vi . . . visually* impaired.'

Jesus Christ what a swine I'm being.

Jesus Christ his feet must be freezing.

'I think it would be fair to say that the man we are looking for is of *Caucasian* stock . . .' the Hippie elucidated, preferring – under the circumstances – to show the cruel wit of Arthur Young a Christian cold-shoulder.

The blind man nudged the Hippie, 'Ask the little turd how long he's been staying here. Ask him if he knows who owns this craft.'

Arthur – stiffening visibly – heard the blind man's comments first hand but even so, the Hippie took it upon himself to repeat them again, but slightly modified, for the sake of diplomacy. 'I don't know if you've been staying here long,' he began tentatively, 'or what your *connection* to this craft might be exactly, but the man we are looking for had a camp – or at least, he did do, yesterday – in that clutch of bushes, over there . . .'

The hippie pointed.

'Yes,' Arthur's lofty gaze returned – irresistibly – to the hippie's toes. The nails were so long that they were almost curly. And the width, the thickness, the *dirt*. Arthur didn't consider himself to be – not at heart, anyway – a fastidious person, but even *he* . . .

'*Yes?*' The Hippie looked slightly confused, 'You *did* see him?'

Arthur nodded, composedly.

Hah

'And when would that've been?'

'Well . . .' Arthur considered this question, at his leisure, 'let me see . . . he started camping here on Wednesday, and I've seen him around just about every day since then. But today? I guess approximately half an hour ago – or an hour. I can't be totally sure.'

The hippie turned to consult the blind man, 'How long ago do *you* reckon it must've been, Herb?'

'Half an hour, max,' the blind man assured him. Then he crossed his arms – not a little aggressively – and fixed Arthur firmly with his fluttering white stare, 'You weren't here yesterday,' he stated baldly.

Are you calling me a damn liar?

'I suppose you must be a couple of those . . .' Arthur chose his words disdainfully, 'those *Following* types.'

'Yes we are, mate,' the blind man answered.

Mate?

'And as it happens,' Arthur continued, 'I *was* here yesterday. This is my boat. I've had permanent tenure of it since January 1970.'

So screw you.

The blind man snorted. He was having none of it.

'Let me see . . .' Arthur pondered, provocatively, '*yesterday* . . .

190

uh . . . Wesley was setting some traps. I believe he ate gull for lunch – caught at the dump. We had a rather interesting discussion about bio-diversity . . . and later . . .' Arthur paused, haughtily, 'I think he said that later today he would be . . .' The Hippie seemed mesmerised. The blind man was still glaring (but foiled, disgruntled), 'breaking up camp and meeting with a librarian. Drinking lemonade. *That* was it. We made lemonade, earlier.'

'Lemon slices from The Hotel,' the Hippie spoke excitedly to the blind man, 'I *told* Hooch he was mucking about finding lemons in the trash back there.'

Arthur's expression was briefly a picture –

The trash?

The blind man suddenly raised his right hand. He was holding a white stick in it. The stick was splattered with mud. The hippie ducked slightly to avoid being swiped by it.

'Somebody's coming.'

The blind man seemed certain.

Arthur glanced up behind the two of them and along the embankment. In the middle distance (wading through the fog like it was a palpable entity) he saw another man approaching. Another stranger. Tall. Suited. Holding a briefcase.

The Hippie twisted around to try and look himself, but because of the acuteness of his angle at the base of the embankment, he was obliged to wait a little longer to get a proper sighting. When the man finally came into focus, however, the Hippie appraised him but didn't show – or not so far as Arthur could tell – any sign of recognition.

He turned back around to face the blind man. '*Suit*,' he muttered disparagingly (Arthur saw the blind man baulk at this description. He was wearing a suit himself, and a heavy grey crombie).

'Let's get out of here,' he added, 'before Doc gets away from us completely.'

He took the blind man's hand, turned him, then slowly began guiding him back up the bank again. They were whispering as they clambered. Sharing confidences. But Arthur wasn't interested. He couldn't hear them, anyway, and he wasn't bothered. He was already distracted by the approach of the fourth stranger. The fourth arrival to this icy, darkening, godforsaken hole in under an hour.

'Wesley *chose* him,' the Hippie whispered, 'for the negotiation. He lives here. A little frosty, admittedly. But definitely not a Follower. He doesn't have the Following . . . the Following *odour* . . .'

'You've got it all wrong, Shoes,' Herbie shook his head, 'he said he'd been here since 1970, yeah? Well that's absolute rubbish for starters. And then there's the computer . . .'

'The computer?'

'Didn't you hear it bleeping?'

The Hippie gave this some thought, 'I suppose I did. But what about it?'

'There's no bloody *electricity*.'

'Are you sure?'

'Can you see any wires?'

'*Uh*?'

'Overhead. There aren't any. I'd've heard them buzzing. I'm not hearing anything at the moment except the clink of the Power Station, and that's still a couple of miles away.'

The Hippie peered up into the sky.

'If you want my opinion . . .'

'I do,' the Hippie interjected.

'I think this guy's a plant. He's from the company, probably. Or a pressure group. Or the papers. Shall I tell you how I know, Shoes? Shall I tell you why?'

The hippie licked his lips, like an oversized cat, waiting fatly for a delicious portion of free cream. The blind man rarely disappointed him. The blind man was keen. The blind man was a blade – his sharpness was legendary.

'You don't mention this to Hooch, okay? You don't mention this to Doc.'

'I wouldn't think of it,' the Hippie sighed, ecstatically.

'Okay,' the blind man took a deep breath, in preparation, 'that craft belonged to Wesley's father. Has done for years. Since 1973, to be exact, when he was working for the petroleum industry. And if that skinny little *fuck* back there doesn't know that, then he doesn't know *squat*.'

'Jesus *bollocks*, Herbs,' the Hippie was blown away, 'where the heck are you getting this from? It's legendary. Is it police stuff? Is it inside information?'

'Nope. Just basic detective work,' the blind man smirked. 'I went to the Town Hall and they turned up trumps, for once. Most obliging. I put my Temporary Careworker on the case this morning. Poor blighter's fingers were bleeding by the time I'd finished with him.'

The blind man mimed someone struggling against the cruel advances of a copious filing system, chuckling to himself, gleefully. Then he poked the Hippie – twice – very sharply, very playfully, very *exactly* in the centre of his ribs. Perfectly certain, as he was, of their precise location.

Twenty

Katherine Turpin yanked her front door open and stared out at Wesley, her pale face – considering how late it was (inexcusably so), and *who* he was (more particularly) – set into a cool mask of quite commendable equanimity.

'Congratulations,' she told him, after an extravagantly lengthy span of keen-eyed scrutiny (during which time, Wesley supposed, she'd discovered virtually everything she needed to know about him: –

Handsome
Wounded
Infernal
Filthy)

'You are three hours late.'

One hundred and eighty minutes. Fuck. That was forever.

'Well, *hello* there,' Wesley pushed straight past her and into the hallway. 'Would you mind closing the door? Are you Katherine? Is Ted about? Did he wait for me?'

He spun around, as an afterthought, holding out his hand to her, 'I'm Wesley, by the way.'

'And any illusions you may've clung to . . .' she calmly continued, closing the door (but not because he'd asked her to. She'd have closed the damn thing anyway. It was *her* door. It was *icy* out there), 'about creating a favourable . . .'

She paused and then inspected the proffered hand more closely. It was the damaged one (just a thumb) and it was tremendously gory.

'*Blood.*'

The enlivened tone of her husky voice denoted fascination (perhaps even *glee*, Wesley observed, delightedly) rather than any of the more customary emotions.

Katherine's keen eyes glanced down further. 'Oh *man*,' she expostulated crossly (her frisky ebullience instantly terminating), 'it's dripping all over my clean floor.'

Clean floor?

Wesley raised one quizzical eyebrow, but didn't take this opportunity to inspect (or curtail) the mess he was generating. Instead he stuck his puggish snout high into the air, and sniffed around, like a hound. 'This place still reeks of hamster,' he informed her with just a hint of flirtation, 'which is absolutely fine by me.'

(We need compromise, he was implying, on *both* sides, here.)

Katherine frowned over at him, bemusedly. He was quite a card, this Wesley. And unabashedly *chippy*.

She readjusted her former evaluation of him accordingly:

Mongrel

Card

Chippy

Filthy

Yup. That was pretty much the sum of it.

Wesley stood straight and unblinking (if somewhat uncomfortably) throughout Katherine's brief critical reassessment of him, his second arm – his *good* arm – tucked up inside his coat (the sleeve dangling limply, the tip shoved, Napoleonically, into the pocket). Something large, something bulky, was also concealed under there. These two factors weren't liable – Katherine decided – to be entirely unconnected.

Wesley smiled cryptically at Katherine's expression of quizzical perturbation, his cheeks still part-frozen from the cold outside, his two mucky eyes glowing sulphurically.

Odour – malodour – *in*odour; it suddenly didn't matter. Of far greater significance (at that particular juncture) was how *bony* she looked; how proud, how loud, how delightfully faded; how fucked-up, how worn-out, how sexy – jaded – drained – *sculpted*.

She was a beauty.

And the crucial part of it (the best part) was this wonderful sense of *contrariness* which seemed rooted at the heart of her: she was sharp and yet lovely, pallid and yet blooming, succulent yet rotten, skinny yet . . . yet curvy; her breasts –

Ah yes, her breasts

– pendulous as two over-ripe figs on a fragile switch; pulling it down into a tender curtsey, flirting with gravity, drooping softly and slackly and gently and carelessly.

Hmmn. He could hear . . . He . . .

Wesley closed his eyes.

He could hear the flies buzzing. The flesh, the sugar, the sweet . . . the luscious infestation of tiny black pips. Yes. He was in Eden. But after the fall. With Eve – in the Orchard – once things finally got interesting.

Katherine cleared her throat. Wesley opened his eyes again, still swaying slightly, his nostrils twitching, delinquently.

She smelled of booze – he could scent it on her; that sickly, high, sweaty aroma – but she seemed basically sober (had a sober personality, he could tell; was a rigorous whore with a Methodist core), although her eyes – blue-grey like the fragile eggs of the Glossy Ibis: slightly bawdy, distinctly goatish – appeared in some danger of glazing over. In her left hand she held an empty whisky tumbler.

'Chinchilla,' she finally corrected him, 'you *monkey.*'

He had no idea what she was referring to. He'd forgotten almost everything in his sensuous miasma.

While they both stalled for a moment (to digest, re-appraise, re-arm and – in Katherine's case: he'd called her a cunt, the *bastard* – take aim), the estate agent – Ted – silently emerged from Katherine's sitting room (he had waited. He was scrupulous to the point of lunacy), padded down the corridor in his stockinged feet and gently tapped Wesley on the shoulder.

'So you finally made it,' he started off, genially, (no hint of a rebuke), and then, 'but what on earth have you . . .'

He didn't finish.

Wesley dumped his rucksack, turned around, and – by way of explanation – unzipped his mac. Ted promptly delivered a neatly circumscribed little shriek (like the scream of a small girl on a hot beach after stepping on a washed-up jellyfish).

The bird Wesley clutched to him was long and limp and very

dead; its throat almost severed in one brutal cut. It was wrapped up, tightly, in his jacket, and the coarse brown fabric – like the bird itself – was saturated with blood.

Katherine Turpin circled tightly around him (space – in this small hallway – was at a premium), intent upon securing herself a better look.

'What *is* that?' she asked, already knowing the answer, battling back her incredulity, almost succeeding, 'and why are you hiding it?'

'Heron. Protected Species,' Wesley cordially informed her.

'Not from *you*, apparently.'

Wesley gave this comment a moment's consideration. 'I don't honestly believe, Katherine,' he smiled at her, intently, staring raptly but gently, into both of her eyes, 'that *anything* is absolutely safe from me.'

Was he making fun of her?

Ted unleashed a nervous giggle, then blushed as he gulped it down like a youthful lover clumsily swallowing his gum before a sticky kiss.

'May I just say,' Katherine turned her back on the pair of them, disdainfully, 'that if you're seriously proposing to *stay* here,' her voice – thoroughly cool, typically casual – sailed like a paper plane over her shoulder, 'then you should get that cadaver *out* of my corridor.'

She swept off regally – all a-flutter in her antique apricot, her feet slapping the tiles, flat and bare – towards the kitchen (needed another drink. Really needed it), carrying with her (and it was not an entirely welcome burden) the uncomfortable sensation of having been trumped, or topped, or *bettered* in some way.

Wesley quietly considered Katherine's recommendation, folded over its corner (for easier identification) and summarily shelved it. The heron was here now, and it was definitely staying.

Ted – regaining a tad of his former composure – moved in closer to inspect the bird. He drew near enough to brush his fingertips against its soft neck-feathers, then peered at the flesh below, as if inspecting the skin for seams or tucks or stitches. He found none. God was many things, Ted mused, but he was no master tailor.

'Did you kill it?' he eventually asked.

198

'Yes,' Wesley nodded, 'it was old and starving.'

'How did you catch it?'

'A librarian helped me. It was her idea.'

'A librarian?'

Ted stopped his close inspection and looked up sharply.

'A woman called Eileen.'

'*Eileen*?'

'You know her?' Wesley paused for a second, then clucked his tongue, tartly. 'But of *course* you know her. You know everybody.'

Ted was astonished, 'You're telling me *Eileen* asked you to slaughter this creature?'

'Oh no no no *no*,' Wesley shook his head, 'Eileen's far too tender. She believed we were saving it.'

'So she must've been . . . it must've been . . . *awful* . . .'

'When I cut its throat? Nope. She didn't see. I was quick. It was dark. I wanted to spare her. Next time I see her I'll tell her it died . . .' he paused, employing his two dark eyebrows rather wickedly, 'at night, in its sleep.'

He grinned – his smile rapidly slithering beyond the bounds of the cynical, trespassing onto the heartless, annexing the insensible – then he adjusted the bird slightly. It was heavy.

Ted was still unable to picture these furtive happenings – as Wesley had described them – with any kind of clarity. He needed precision. He demanded transparency.

'And so you were . . . You . . .'

'What?' Wesley was bored, was moving on already. He peered down the corridor, after Katherine. He could hear a glass jingling in what he presumed to be the kitchen; the metallic rasp of a screw-top lid.

'And where did this all happen?'

'Pardon?'

'With Eileen.'

'Where? On a private fishing pier. And we didn't *fuck*,' Wesley grimaced, 'if that's what you're getting at. She's much too sweet. I'd give it at least – at the very least – two dates before I even touched her.'

Wesley paused, then added – for the sake of accuracy, 'By that I mean sexually.'

Ted was so appalled by what Wesley was telling him (I mean Eileen was an *angel*. Eileen was a goddess. She was Gaia. A Madonna. A mother figure. And . . . And *married*. Irretrievably. He really couldn't . . . he simply . . .) that even Wesley found his brave – if unobtrusive – show of old-fashioned moral outrage difficult to ignore. He tipped his head to one side, flipping a stray lock of hair from his eye.

'I have a reputation,' he explained boredly, 'for sleeping with librarians. But *so* bloody *what*?' he self-justified. 'It's just a rumour. It's a fucking *crock*. I'm gonna put this bird in the kitchen. Are you any good at plucking? Might you be staying on for something to eat later?'

'I don't . . .' Ted frowned, conflictedly, 'I still want . . .' he followed Wesley a few steps down the corridor, reaching out his arm to him, resting his hand on his shoulder, 'I'm just not entirely sure that this arrangement . . . I'm not confident that Katherine . . .'

'I can handle her,' Wesley grinned roguishly, purposefully misinterpreting the locus of his agitation, 'and I'm touched by your concern, Ted,' he hitched up his shoulder and pushed down his cheek towards Ted's hand. Touched Ted's fingers with it, 'you soft-hearted creature . . .'

Then he quickly withdrew the cheek, scowling, 'What *is* that?'

'Sorry,' Ted moved his hand, touching the offending fingers together, feeling them adhere, 'rubber glue. Katherine had a puncture.'

'Nowhere painful, I hope.'

Ted didn't get the joke.

'It's just that . . .' he returned brazenly – fearlessly – to his former subject, 'it's . . . What you might not realise is that Katherine tends to express everything she feels through . . .'

'Let me guess,' Wesley interrupted, pursing his thick lips, 'through . . .' he glanced around him, 'through dirt? Through *chaos*? Is that it? No. No, she expresses stuff *sculpturally*, with mango pips and wire. What better way? Am I right? Or is it beansprouts? Or booze? Or the *heat*? Or is it . . . perhaps . . . could it . . . could it *possibly* be . . .' Wesley mugged a parody of astonishment at him, 'could it be *sex*, Ted?'

Ted regretfully abandoned this line of conversation, but he still couldn't let Wesley get away from him entirely. He grabbed the loose sleeve of his mac. 'Just while we're alone, Wesley, you wouldn't happen to know anything . . .' he dropped his voice, guiltily, 'about *computers*, would you? It's . . . I have this rather pressing . . .'

'Nope. Not a damn thing,' Wesley lied guilelessly, 'but . . .' he thought for a moment – picturing Arthur in his mind's eye, very solidly, for some reason – 'but I think I might know somebody . . .' His thoughts suddenly drifted, 'Guess what?'

'What?' Ted frowned, confounded.

'I *like* her brutality.'

Ted frowned deeper, still not following.

'Katherine's. Her brutality. I like it. I find it . . . I find her endearing.'

'The thing is, Wesley,' Ted tried again, 'it's all much more . . . more *complicated* than you're actually . . .'

'What is?'

'This situation. With Katherine. And Canvey. There's a local journalist – a man called Bo, who used to play tennis, professionally – and he wants to know . . . and he doesn't . . . well, he might make things a little tricky for her if I don't . . . he sort of *implied* . . . he . . .'

Ted tried his damnedest to clarify things. It wasn't easy.

'And then there's Dewi . . .'

'Ted, Ted, *Ted*,' Wesley crooned, brushing his delicately insistent fingers away, 'let's talk about all this stuff later, shall we? Would you have a *heart*? My arms are breaking.'

He started walking.

Ted gulped, 'But at least . . . Could you . . .'

Mary Mother of Bloody . . .

Wesley spun around, scowling, 'What?'

Ted flinched at the scowl, 'I just . . . I only wondered whether . . .'

'What?'

'Well, whether it was true about the pond. All that stuff about . . . all those stories about . . . about the pond.'

If it was true, then at least that would be . . .

That would mean . . .

201

At least that might make everything . . .

Wesley paused for a split second. He plainly didn't like this question. He tried not to . . . had it been anybody else he would've – as a matter of course – he would've refused an answer. All this *stuff* from the past . . . the way it *haunted* him . . . the *boredom* . . . but Ted was . . .

The poor sod.

'It's all true, Ted,' he told him gently, 'every stupid detail. Only not quite so pretty, and a little bit more – as life invariably is – a little bit more . . . more *messy.*'

'Just so long as . . .'

Ted leaned against the wall, exhausted. Closing his eyes. Weak with relief.

Wesley frowned at him for a moment, then shrugged, turned, and strolled off down the corridor, still clutching the bird to him, his tired mind (God, the way . . . the way that poor bird *fought* . . . the way it *buckled* when . . .) slowly switching tracks, like a heavy goods train, redirecting itself, gradually, to sternly focus on the rather more pivotal issue of dinner.

Twenty-one

Doc sat heavily on the pavement, his shoulders slumped forward, his knees pulled up tightly, sweating copiously, breathing emphatically; fagged out, knocked up, *spent*, entirely.

His old, overworked joints popped and creaked, like a distant fireworks party (hosted several miles away in a quiet, black valley). In fact, when he turned his head at one point, the snap, the *click* – like a rifle cocking – made Hooch, who stood to his right, politely holding out a plastic mug of tea, start back suddenly and slop the scalding liquid onto the tender skin between his right thumb and his index finger. He cursed, but silently, not wishing to distract – even for a second – from the sheer panorama of Doc's exhaustion; its drama. Its pathos. Its out and out majesty.

Doc had already yanked off his mud-encrusted boots – tossing them hastily onto the grass verge behind him – and was now struggling to remove his chunky thermal socks from his heavily callused feet; slowly drawing the thick fibre clear of the fragile skin, paying special attention to the delicate areas where old blisters – and new – leaked sticky plasma into the thick woollen knit and formed a kind of glutinous bond there.

When the first sock finally came away completely – *victory!* – Dennis trotted over and ploughed his keen nose into it. Doc knocked him back, expostulating gruffly, then tucked the sock firmly into a battered boot. He did the same – moments later – with the second sock, then gently wiggled his ten pulverised toes, quietly conducting a grim inspection of them.

It was a dark, dark night. But Doc was not dark. He was radiant. His mundane labours were being grandly illuminated by an old-fashioned streetlight. He sat under it, dwarfed by the lofty grandeur of its wrought-iron spine, its generous yellow areola; like a pixie perched squatly under a supernatural buttercup; his breath vaporising around him into a soft golden floss, his generous figure compacted into bright, abstract blocks: sentimental as a Hogarth, stark as a Hopper.

He was whacked. He'd had *enough*. Even Dennis was showing signs of trauma (after his recent tragic cuffing), dramatically collapsing onto his side in the gutter, then jumping up, with a growl, as a large jeep rumbled past them.

Police.

A whirling flash of sapphire suddenly rotated – in a delirious foxtrot – with Doc's own dizzy nimbus of gilded amber.

Hooch flinched at the sight of it, glowering owlishly from behind his glasses (as if momentarily whiplashed by this unexpected convergence), then craned his neck nervously after the whirling blue globe as it gradually retreated.

He had every reason to feel anxiety: his white van was parked on a double yellow (just a few feet along from them), half up on the pavement, half off, the back door swung open to reveal a small stove (unlit), two camp-beds, an unzipped sleeping bag, an ice-box, a pair of Wellingtons, two back-packs (his and Doc's: Doc's much the larger) a rolled up tent and a clean shirt on a peg.

Only once the jeep had passed into the distance did he turn back towards Doc again and commiserate softly with him, 'You'll kill yourself this way, Old Man.'

He spoke fondly.

He offered Doc the mug of tea. Doc half-turned, reaching out his arm for it.

'Too true. Too true.'

He didn't sound regretful. Or chastened, even. He embraced his destiny willingly. Tragic or otherwise. He wasn't particular.

His hand eventually made contact with the cup. But Hooch held on to it, a second longer, as if fearful Doc might drop it. His fingers seemed stiff and hot – paradoxically so, in all of this iciness – burning with a scarlet, puffy-jointed arthritic buzz (early morning and late evening. Extremes of temperature. Always a trial for him.).

'I saw The Blind Man,' Doc muttered, nodding towards the retreating jeep to indicate his train of thought, taking the cup, finally, gripping at it tightly and ducking his head in thanks for it, 'I believe you said he'd turn up.'

This comment seemed to wash over Hooch, initially.

'You must've done twenty-odd miles today,' Hooch ruminated, 'or thereabouts.'

'Yup,' Doc confirmed. 'Seventeen for the perimeter and then the rest. Probably eight or more this morning.'

The Old Man sighed once he'd finished speaking, still not breathing easily – getting no pleasure from his calculating (if anything, all the more exhausted by it) – then took a sip of his drink. He sighed again, gratefully, after swallowing.

'I sometimes wonder,' Hooch couldn't resist pushing his luck a little, 'whether he doesn't do these ridiculous distances just to take the mick. I mean the island's perimeter every fucking *day*? What's the *point* of it? Why's he doing it?'

Doc chuckled, indulgently, 'I've thought it myself, Hooch, I have. When my toes start their throbbing and my chest starts its heaving. It's not his usual style – to retrace like this ...' he paused, as if unable – or unwilling – to consider the deeper ramifications of Wesley's behaviour, 'but he's younger than we are and a genuine ... well, *adventurer*. He takes real joy in it. And he has all that boundless energy. All that anger. He walks them off. He observes stuff. He – I was only just thinking this, an hour or so ago, to fight off the tiredness while I was Following – he kind of ... he integrates himself. He becomes a part of things. And that's a gift. There's nothing untoward in it. Absolutely not.'

'I had a kip in the van,' Hooch justified his absence on the perimeter walk, with a slight vocal tightness. 'The spur's been playing me up a bit lately.'

'No explanations necessary, Hooch,' Doc reached out a heavy hand and tenderly caressed Dennis's chin with it, 'least of all to me.'

His rebuttal wasn't entirely sincere. Following was a job, after all, like any other. No margin here for skivers or wasters or half-cocked loafers. Hooch knew it. The corner of his mouth twisted slightly. His eyes narrowed a fraction behind his glasses. He turned and peered suspiciously after the police jeep again, thereby re-accessing Doc's earlier allusion, 'You were saying The Pig turned up this afternoon, then?'

Doc winced, not appreciating the coarseness of Hooch's language. He took another sip of his drink – to indicate his displeasure – then answered, after swallowing, 'He did. Joined us just before two-thirty. On his own, he was. Shoes passed the time with him.'

'What a ridiculous sodding *liability* that man is,' Hooch sniped, 'and what an unrepentant bloody *flea*. I told you he'd show his face at some point, didn't I?'

'You were right, Hooch,' Doc affirmed, tiredly.

'The South East is his manor. The Estuary. He always turns up here, regular as clockwork.'

'He was affiliated to the docks in Shoeburyness for twelve years, he was telling me. Then close to Purfleet for five. Customs-related stuff, I'd expect. Then a spate at Grain, when his eyesight started going. It's his patch alright.'

'His *beat*,' Hooch spat, 'and I bet the sightless little tit already grassed us up with that bloody lot.' Hooch thumbed, grimacing, after the police jeep.

'Give the poor sod a break, will you?' Doc put his mug of tea down, grimacing exasperatedly. 'Herb's an *ex*-cop and he's *blind*. How the hell could he be expected to know you were parked illegally?'

'He'd sense it,' Hooch pretended to be joking, but he wasn't entirely, 'he's like a damn bat. He has a bat's radar.'

Doc merely snorted, choosing not to fuel Hooch's psychotic imaginings any further.

'Wesley hates him. I know that much,' Hooch muttered, resenting Doc's flagrant lack of involvement, determined to provoke him further.

'You *don't* know that.'

Doc was immediately engaged again.

'I do. He can smell a pig at fifty paces. *Loathes* them.'

'*Ex*-pig,' Doc corrected, 'and a loyal Behindling.'

In the distance the police jeep's brake lights were sparking. It stopped. It indicated. It began a slow but inexorable three-point turn.

Damn

'So whereabouts exactly did he catch up, then?' Hooch asked, a touch of real tension entering his voice.

'Just after you left us. Just beyond the hotel.'

'And how did he know where we were?'

'Now *there's* a question . . .' Doc was tense now, too. 'Probably used his . . .' He tipped his head towards the blue light.

'I *knew* it. The swine. And did he tell you anything?'

'Nope,' Doc lifted his tea out of the way and then slowly began pulling his socks on again, 'I already said Shoes kept company with him. They were a distance behind me. The going was heavy. And the fog . . .'

He impatiently mopped some cold sweat off his forehead, 'I lost Wes at the putting course. He put on a spurt. Got away from me there.'

'Did you see the new girl afterwards?'

'I did. Not fifteen minutes since. On the High Street. With the boy. Outside the pub. Climbing into an old brown Mini. Thick as thieves they were.'

'I still can't get over Wes talking to her like that,' Hooch grumbled (as if this simple act had been a terrible offence to him, personally).

'It was certainly a little . . .' Doc paused, '*odd*.' He shrugged. 'They'll both be up here in a minute, I shouldn't wonder.'

'Not if the little rapscallion sees . . .' Hooch tipped his head, morosely, towards the approaching police vehicle.

Doc finished yanking on his boots then set about rapidly re-tying his laces, 'You're on the bloody money there.'

Hooch nodded sagely to himself, gazing over the road towards Katherine's bungalow (the lights were on but the curtains were drawn. The stained glass in the front door was glowing brightly).

'And now Wesley's back here again, you reckon?'

'Yup,' Doc affirmed, 'I lost him on the fourteenth mile or thereabouts, so I don't know for certain. But it's what I'm assuming . . .'

'Perhaps he's considering renting from her,' Hooch said, almost joking, but with a slight edge of anxiety.

'Never. Not our Wes. And why the silly tart'd give him house-room – even overnight – after what he did to her . . .'

Doc had removed his pager from his inside pocket and was frowning at it, bemusedly, as he spoke. He gave it a shake. 'Something's definitely up with this thing today.'

'It's not just that,' Hooch told him, 'I tried the info-line earlier. Didn't get any answer. No updates, anyway. And the last message deleted. Which'll go some way to explaining why the weekend crowd haven't made an appearance yet.'

'I've had dozens of text messages,' Doc half-smiled, 'but I haven't responded. I like it quiet. Makes a nice change, eh?'

'*Snap*,' Hooch concurred.

'It's never happened before,' Doc opined, 'at least not in my memory.'

'Then your memory's getting shaky, Old Man,' Hooch seemed delighted to set Doc straight on the matter, 'because it happened the February before last. In Skeggy. Skegness. Went down for two days then, remember? We were freezing our arses off in that three man tent with Martin Hopsmith, just before he got cancer.'

'Good old Mart.' Doc turned off his pager again and stuck it into his pocket, scowling as the police jeep pulled to a standstill in front of them.

'Estate agent at two o'clock,' Hooch spoke – barely moving his lips – over the sound of the engine, 'check it out.'

Doc glanced over. Sure enough: the estate agent, pushing aside Katherine's living room curtains, then the nets, spotting the police car, frowning, letting them swish gently back together again.

The jeep was driven by a young officer. He was accompanied by a diminutive female wearing casual gear. The officer unwound his window, opened his mouth, but before he could say anything, Hooch had bounded forward onto the roadway. 'I'm *right* on the case, lad,' he shouted, indicating with his thumb towards the van, 'just picking up my old pal here . . .'

He bent his knees slightly to try and confirm eye-contact with the un-uniformed female, 'If you're from the Social, love, and it's the boy you're after, he's just down the road a-way, outside the pub. We saw him there not ten minutes since . . .'

The woman frowned back at him, blankly –
Love?

The police officer, meanwhile, had turned off the ignition, unfastened his seat belt and jumped out of the car. He glanced over his shoulder for any sign of traffic, then strolled over.

'I'm not here about the van, sir,' he told Hooch curtly, 'but I'm sure you can appreciate that this is a busy road and as such . . .' he paused, closely inspecting the still-seated Doc, momentarily losing his thread, then promptly relocating it, 'it's always our priority to keep it clear.'

While he was speaking his right hand made the slow but ineluctable journey from his side to his front pocket, 'In all good conscience,' he smiled (an edge of steel in the artificial glow of the streetlight sparking off his fillings), 'I should be writing you out a ticket.'

Hooch hopped back onto the pavement, plainly appalled by this possibility. 'I'm right onto it, officer,' he told him, needing no second warning. 'Coming Old Man?'

The officer's head snapped around at the sound of Doc's familiar nomenclature. Doc was grumbling to himself under his breath as he untangled the dog's lead with his uncooperative fingers. Once it had been neatly unwound, then applied, he tried to stand up, unleashing an almighty grunt, staggering slightly.

The officer put out a firm hand to steady him. Doc contrived to ignore it.

'Doc,' the officer said.

'Don't wear it out,' Doc mumbled, making brief but furtive eye-contact, then looking down again, sullenly (he always pushed his luck with the local constabularies. He noticed himself doing it, disliked himself for it. But irascibility was one of the few real advantages old age afforded him. Seniority was his trump card; he played it, unstintingly.

And anyway . . . Anyway, Behindlings were no lovers of authority. Behindlings were harassed by the forces of the law, traditionally . . . Although they were so good when . . . The Welsh lads . . . so sympathetic when . . .)

No

'Might I trouble you with a few questions, sir?'

As if on cue – but for no explicit reason – Dennis suddenly bounded forward towards the officer (bowing cheekily, bottom in the air, his small stump wagging provocatively). This unexpected manoeuvre very nearly toppled the Old Man over. He tripped two short steps after the animal, cursing him furiously.

'Are you alright there, sir?'

Doc crossly yanked Dennis to heel again, swiping his stiff fingers through the air, 'I'm perfectly fine,' he snapped, 'and stop "sir-ing" me. I was a scaffolder for thirty-five years. A working man and proud of it. Destroyed my bloody hands at it. And my knees.'

He resentfully showed his free hand to the young officer, as if its heinously arthritic state was somehow his personal responsibility.

'And anyway, like Hooch just said,' he rumbled, his voice unexpectedly deepened by a heavy bubble of phlegm rising, 'if she's with social services . . .' he indicated, contemptuously, towards the un-uniformed female (clearing his throat, noisily – the persistence of his catarrh making even Hooch flinch a little), 'and it's the young lad – Patty – you're after, then he's down by the pub. He . . .'

Doc turned his head sideways and expelled a dark globule onto the pavement, brusquely apologised for it, then glanced sharply off to the far right, alerted by an unexpected movement on the edge of the roadway.

It was the girl, Josephine, walking quickly towards them, her coat overlaid by a pair of red and yellow braces – nauseatingly reflective – like the kind of protective garb cautious cyclists wore, at night, in out of the way places.

'In actual fact,' his voice brightened, 'you should have a quick word with this young lady,' he pointed, 'she was keeping company with the little bugger a short while earlier.'

Josephine was walking in the gutter, her arms folded tightly, the hood on her duffel coat up, her chin down, her nose glowing coldly.

'*Josephine,*' Doc boomed. 'Where'd Patty get to?'

Jo jumped (as if having had no expectation of seeing anyone on the path ahead) then stopped, confusedly, before starting up again and walking rapidly towards them, 'I just drove him to Benfleet, to the train station . . .'

She paused, mid-flow, noticing the police car on the other side of the road with its lights off and the officer standing – perhaps a little uncomfortably – alongside the others.

'*Uh* . . . It's a fair old trip home for him,' she bundled on, clumsily. 'Bolton or Derby or somewhere . . .'

'Just tell me you didn't give him the fare,' Hooch demanded.

Josephine stopped dead, a couple of feet from them, 'Why?'

Doc rolled his eyes, despairingly.

'She gave him the money, Doc,' Hooch's harsh voice was leavened with both boredom and resignation.

Jo frowned, pushing her hood back, 'Is he . . . is Patty needed by the Police for something?'

The constable – who'd been quietly scrutinising Jo as she approached, but had said nothing – suddenly opened his mouth to speak, but before he'd uttered a syllable, his un-uniformed colleague was clambering out of their jeep, swinging herself up lithely onto the running board, pressing her two elbows into the roof for support, and bellowing, 'Josephine bloody *Bean*.'

Jo glanced sharply over the road, her own mouth opening slightly (the way a snake's mouth opens in panic or in the heat). She stared at the woman for several moments. Then something registered.

'Anna *Wright*,' she spoke slowly (and rather less enthusiastically. *Bollocks* to Canvey. There was no hiding here.).

The male officer did a double take. 'Good God,' he muttered, 'Josephine *Bean*. I heard you on the radio the other day, talking about . . .'

He ground to an abrupt halt, as if suddenly reconsidering the delicate social implications of Jo's sanitary campaign. Jo appreciated his dilemma, fully. 'The *environment*,' she filled in softly – seeing Doc and Hooch exchange curious glances – then adding, 'Edward *Cole*, right?'

'Right,' he grinned. 'Maths, physics, geography.'

'We . . . uh . . .' Jo turned towards Doc, uneasily, 'we were all at school here together – in Canvey . . .'

'*God* you look different,' the female officer shouted (making absolutely no effort to leave the confines of the car), 'it took me a moment to recognise you without your hair. Remember her *hair*, Eddie?'

She waved to the uniformed officer. 'Blonde. Gorgeous. Right down to . . .' she touched her waist, 'like *Alice in Wonderland*.'

Jo smiled at this description, but seemed correspondingly pained by it.

'And you've been doing *sterling* work at Southend General, I hear,' she yelled, 'all credit to you there.'

'Yes. Well. *Thank you*,' Jo shouted back. (Doc cringed at the volume. Jo noticed. Her shoulders lifted with the stress.)

'We should meet up for a drink later. How about it? My shift finishes in . . .' the officer inspected her watch, 'just under an hour.'

Jo paused, uncomfortably, 'I would love to, Anna . . .'

'*What?*' The officer put her hand to her ear. Jo glanced towards Doc, then raised her voice, fractionally, 'I said I would *really* love to, Anna, but . . .' She floundered.

'But you should,' Doc suddenly interrupted – his expression supremely benign, his voice utterly phlegmatic – 'you *should* meet up. That would be very . . . very *lovely* for you. To . . .' he eyed the male officer, slyly, 'to catch up with your old school *pal*,' he smiled with an almost mesmerising insincerity, 'after all this time.'

He continued to smile.

Jo's eyes widened (Doc seemed about as trustworthy as a ravenous cat in an aviary) –

It goes way beyond that . . .

Way beyond hunger

Jo blinked –

I am being slowly ingested

Here, in Canvey

Devoured again

Just like before.

She paused for a second, drew an extremely deep breath, then turned back to face the un-uniformed officer. 'You're *right*,' she shouted, 'that would be . . . it would be . . .' she grasped for the appropriate word, '*fun*,' she rounded off, lamely.

Fun was not a word generally found to the forefront of her vocabulary –

Fun.

'Great.'

The un-uniformed officer beat a jovial little percussive solo onto the jeep's roof with her fingers, 'You know Saks, Josie? Just down the road? Directly opposite the Bingo?'

Two cars flashed between them. Jo waited until they'd passed, then nodded, mutely.

Nobody calls me Josie
Nobody ever called me Josie here
Saks? Oh my Sweet Lord

'Just after eight, then. Okay?'

'Yes,' Jo nodded, 'that's . . . that'll be . . .'

The jeep's radio – having previously purred along in a thoroughly unobjectionable monotone – now began crackling at a prodigious volume. The female officer clambered back inside to deal with it.

'That'll be fantastic,' Jo spoke into thin air.

Doc scowled at her. This girl was so . . . so gawky. So *blundering*. Useless at deceiving. Not a dyed-in-the-wool Behindling. Not a born sleuth by any stretch of the imagination.

'Before we all get *completely* carried away here,' the male officer strove – semi-jovially – to regain the assembled company's attention, 'your white van still needs moving, sir. And if I could possibly have a quick word . . .' he switched his focus to Doc, 'about . . .' he paused for a second, as if considering how best to frame his enquiry.

'She's already told you,' Doc grumbled impatiently, nodding his head towards Jo, 'the boy's in Benfleet, at the station, probably heading back here on foot, even as we speak.'

'It's not a *boy* I'm looking for,' the officer butted in (he was thoroughly sick of this boy, and bemused by every mention of him), 'I'm actually trying to track down Wesley. I've been informed that you're the one person most likely . . .'

'He's over there,' Hooch interjected (patently infuriated by the widespread perception of Doc's Following seniority), pointing across the road towards Katherine's bungalow, 'in *that* house.'

The officer's gaze followed the line of Hooch's index finger. He scowled, 'But that's . . .' He stopped himself, just in time, his eyes meeting Josephine's, almost apologetically.

'The whore's house,' Hooch completed his sentence for him.

The officer stiffened.

'Are you able to confirm this, sir?' He turned back to Doc who was staring over at Hooch, infuriatedly.

'Is it a summons?' Hooch brazenly enquired, apparently oblivious to Doc's finer feelings, 'because of all the trouble with those seagulls in Rye?'

This was one intervention too far for the officer, 'If you really want a ticket, *sir* . . .' he snapped.

Hooch looked to his laurels, swooping down – with a defiant snort – to grab Doc's half-finished mug of tea, tossing the remainder into the gutter, throwing the cup into the back of the van and slamming the doors shut with a bang.

The officer returned his full attention to the Old Man, 'I believe your people track Wesley by phone and the internet? We tried to do the same, but the lines are down. There were rumours of a virus on the site. Would you happen to know anything about that?'

'Should I?' Doc asked, unhelpfully.

'The lines are down?' Jo interjected, 'and a *virus*?'

This was plainly news to her.

The police officer nodded, 'Since earlier this afternoon, apparently.'

'But has that ever happened before, Doc?' Jo turned to the Old Man.

'Skegness. About eighteen months back.'

Not Doc, but Hooch again, peeking out from behind the protective shield of his van's front passenger door, 'That site's really losing its *focus*. Needs shaking up a bit if you ask me.'

The officer threw Hooch a look of such coruscating disparagement that had he been even remotely morally suggestible his cranial cortex would've withered and then disintegrated. Instead he simply cleared his throat, scratched his head and climbed back on board.

'So *are* you filing a summons, then?' Doc asked. The officer turned to face him again, shaking his head slightly, 'That's a private matter, sir.'

'So you're not filing anything?'

The officer raised his eyebrows, smiling warningly.

'So it's a family matter, then?' Doc persisted, fully intent on maintaining the pressure. The police officer stepped back a few inches. 'It's a matter of some . . .' he considered his words, carefully, 'some *sensitivity*, shall we say.'

'Ah.' Doc rubbed his hands together, drawing another breath to continue his interrogation, but the officer was having none of it.

'I'm afraid that's the best I can do for you, sir.'

He bent down – as a final gesture – to stroke behind Dennis's ears, but the terrier (in an arbitrary change of heart) curled his head sideways and out of the officer's way.

The officer chuckled under his breath, smiled up at Jo, gave Doc a smart, half-salute and crossed back over the road again, tapping his hand onto the car bonnet as he circled his way around it to alert the woman officer – still on the radio – to follow him. This she duly did.

'Find out exactly what it is that they want.' Doc was handing out curt instructions before the pair had even made it through the front gate.

'We weren't even friends,' Jo murmured (perhaps a little accusingly), 'she was always really . . . well, *bossy*.'

Doc didn't react to this. 'We'll be down at The Lobster Smack from here-on-in. We're camping nearby. And remember,' he warned, 'they're probably just as interested in us as we are in them, so be wary.'

'Interested in us?' Jo echoed blankly.

'The Behindlings. They like to know what we're doing, where we're staying. Things about the competition. Contacts and stuff. Whatever we know about Wesley, obviously. His activities. Trespass, blackmail, the bribery, especially. Don't even . . .'

'Sorry – the . . . *sorry?*'

But before Jo could question Doc any further he'd slapped his thigh (calling Dennis to heel), and was heading briskly for the van. Hooch started up the engine. Doc picked up Dennis then paused, just for a second, before throwing him on board.

'If you come into the pub later and there's a blind man hanging around, don't breathe a word of anything in front of him. He's one of . . .' Doc pointed towards the jeep. 'Ex-special branch. Play it by ear . . .' Doc swiped his hand through the air, '*you* know.'

Do I?

Jo nodded, bemusedly, then opened her mouth.

'Know what I found especially interesting?' Doc quickly cut in. Jo shut her mouth again.

'The way he said, "It's not about a *boy*." With a special emphasis. Did you notice? That emphasis? Not about a *boy*.'

Doc gave Jo a significant look, tapped the side of his nose, then threw the dog on board and climbed in stiffly after him.

Hooch didn't drive away immediately. He waited until the officers were standing at Katherine's door and knocking, until their knock had been answered – by a flustered-seeming Ted – until they'd invited themselves in and the door was shutting.

Then he let rip; accelerating sharply from a standing start, his tyres squealing, his suspension crashing as he came down off the pavement, his exhaust rattling a coarse tattoo onto the tarmac. In a gesture of defiance, Jo supposed.

She stood and stared after the fast-retreating van, frowning at the prodigious volume of its exhaust emissions, and observing – quite dispassionately – how the back doors hadn't been shut properly. The right one flew open. A rucksack (Doc's) tumbled out and almost collided with a red Ford Corsa travelling – more sedately – in the opposite direction.

The Corsa sounded its horn, swerving. The van stopped. Its hazards went on. Hooch jumped out and ran around to retrieve Doc's possessions, looking – as far as Jo could tell in the half-darkness – not even remotely concerned by the chaos he'd unleashed. Two further cars ground to a halt behind him. Then a third. One flashed its lights to speed him up. But he smiled and took his time.

Jo shook her head, appalled –

And these people are my allies?

God have Mercy.

Hooch climbed back on board, with a swagger (how did he manage it?) but this time pulled off quietly (Doc's calming influence, presumably).

Once the van had gone, Jo turned her attentive brown eyes back towards the neat white bungalow and stared at it for a while, inspecting every external detail, as if thoroughly engrossed by its neatness, its symmetry. After a while, gentle drizzle began falling. Jo continued standing. She continued staring.

Tiny droplets of rain soon formed a diaphanous cloche over her close-shaven head. But only when the water achieved sufficient density (once slightly larger droplets began dribbling down her forehead, the back of her neck) did Jo emerge from her reverie and shake it – twice, most expertly – like a small, damp, brown vole on the edge of a riverbank.

Then she pulled up her hood, as far as it would go, and gazed helplessly up the road. 'But *why* won't it go away?'

This querulous question emerged so quietly from the dreamy darkness where her face had once been, was framed so sadly, so meekly, that had – by sheer chance – a tiny muntjak been passing, it would've paused, lifted high its pale, soft muzzle and huffed a benign but inquisitive blast of sweet, straw-scented breath into the cold night air.

It would've shown no fear.

Jo's hood swivelled around (a tiny Horsewoman of the Apocalypse, momentarily steedless), towards Dewi's green bungalow (the lights were off. He was working late, presumably).

'I'm so *sorry*,' she murmured woefully, hunching up her shoulders, expelling a small, dry cough, adjusting her luminous plastic braces, wiping her ghostly nose on her harsh, woollen cuff and stepping – with a self-loathing *splash* – back (always back) into the gutter's spurtling trough.

Twenty-two

Ten minutes later, they were arguing like lovers.

'It's a gift, you *dolt*. Where the fuck are your manners?' Wesley was sitting at the kitchen table, surrounded by feathers.

'Oh it's a *gift* now, is it? D'you hear that, Bron? D'you hear that?' Katherine raised her husky voice (and her pale hand, correspondingly; holding it high in the air, palm turned ceiling wards, like an alabaster juggler) to include an – as yet – invisible caged animal in their conversation. 'He calls me a *cunt*, Bron, he leaves a lamb's tail behind him with *no* explanation, he steals my mango-stone creature, he messes with my hydrangea. And now this: a magnificent wild water-bird *slaughtered* for supper.'

'Cunt?' Wesley frowned, bemusedly (falling at the first fence – refusing all the others). 'You've lost me there.'

Katherine paused for a moment, caught slightly off balance.

'Was Dick an ancestor, then?' Wesley queried, returning dutifully to his plucking (the only trace of implicit innuendo in this question evinced by the slight arching of his left eyebrow).

'Dick who?' Katherine scowled.

'Turpin. I saw that huge pub named after him up on the motorway.'

'*A* road,' she demurred, 'and there's no real connection. Our ancestors were Dutch. The name was . . . was bastardised.'

'From what?'

Katherine paused, wavering.

'Brouwer.'

She pronounced it softly but with faultless inflections.

'Oh yes,' Wesley nodded, 'yes, the phonetic link's *very* explicit.'

219

Katherine poked out her tongue at him. Her tongue was long and deliciously pink.

'*Ouch,*' Wesley suddenly shoved his thumb into his mouth (as if her spiteful tongue had pricked him there), 'this thing's a tough old pluck . . .' he sucked at it, thoughtfully, 'although you'd think I'd be used to it; I've been living on seabirds since late November.' He drew the reddened thumb from his lips and studied the pad, critically. 'I was camping down in Camber,' he looked up. 'Ever been there?'

'Never.'

Katherine shrugged her shoulders and lifted her jaw (projecting a steadfast impression of mulish obduracy). But there was a twinkle – he could sense it – lost in the ivory lamina of her skin, somewhere; the base of her throat, the tiny, fleshy pleats in the crook of her arm, or wedged tightly under a dirty finger nail, maybe (she had capable hands – the finger-pads criminally printed with thick slicks of black bike oil, the cuticles ragged and cygnet-grey).

When Wesley pulled his thumb free, a small piece of down remained just above his lip.

'The Dutch have . . .' he returned to his former subject, readjusting the heron expertly on his knee, 'an extremely . . .' he felt the tickle under his nose and scratched at it; the feather shifted a couple of millimetres, 'a very troubled history in this area, don't they?'

'Do they?'

Katherine focussed in on the feather, pointedly. He caught a side-long glimpse of her face, 'Brought over to save this joyless crap-hole from the ravages of the sea – to build dykes – seventeenth century, or thereabouts. But were *slightly* too good at it, so – in the true spirit of British Hospitality – got treated like absolute *shit* ever after . . .'

He gave her a significant look, 'I can only guess it must be he . . . hered . . .' he sneezed, '. . . *itary.*'

He shook his head, snorting brazenly.

Katherine merely scowled (the Dutch stuff held no interest for her. Why should it? She was the mistress of her own destiny) and picked up her glass of liquor. But before she could sip at it, she sniffed (a lean white rabbit cordially inspecting a juicy sprig of peppery chard), put the glass down, pulled an old tissue from the cuff of her sleeve, and dabbed softly at her nose with it.

Wesley observed this apparently commonplace act with a quiet but still palpable satisfaction. *Ah yes.* She was duplicating. He was inveigling.

Katherine quickly shoved the tissue away and then defiantly topped up her drink. She took a large mouthful of it, tossed it back and swallowed, her ash-smoke eyes watering as she straightened her head again.

In the furthest reaches of the kitchen, meanwhile, a subterranean rustling – prompted, perhaps, by the glass and the bottle's tinkling – made Wesley abandon his plucking for a moment and twist around on his stool.

Where did that spring from, exactly?

In a roomy cage balanced precariously on a butcher's block in the far corner, he saw a large grey rodent lazily emerging from a pile of loose wood shavings, peering around him (eyes like immaculate cobs of smokeless coal), blinking, then yawning (one of those long, unimaginably thin-mouthed rodent yawns). Scratching his ear. Grooming.

Bron. Katherine's chinchilla.

Wesley inspected this creature with the cool, level gaze of an experienced butcher. Plump, but mainly fur. Large eared. Betailed. Exquisitely bewhiskered; stark, white antenna, straight as power lines, centred on his nose, dynamically oscillating.

He chuckled, picked up the heron's slack neck, supported its head in his bad hand and waggled it provocatively at the sleepy rodent. The chinchilla stared back at the heron, blankly, its two front legs held delicately poised in the air.

'Would a heron predate on him out in the wild d'you reckon?' Wesley queried, mischievously.

'There's only one merciless predator in this kitchen,' Katherine countered sharply, 'and it certainly isn't lying dead across your knee.'

Wesley stopped his idle waggling to inspect the rodent more closely. The rodent, in turn, inspected Wesley.

'Is that a male rodent you have there?'

'Why?'

'Because he seems to be . . .'

The rodent was masturbating.

221

'Bron likes to touch himself,' Katherine interrupted defensively, 'it's no big deal. He finds it comforting.'

'Not an unusual predilection,' Wesley concurred, 'but Good *God* woman,' he pointed at the creature accusingly, 'in the fucking *kitchen*?'

The chinchilla (as though chastened by Wesley's finger) released his genitalia and bounded over to a small plastic tray in the corner of his enclosure. There he began digging – sand flew violently in every direction – and finally, rolling.

'Now what's he doing?'

'He's digging, you fool. He has a sand tray. He's South American.'

'And you think South Americans *like* to dig, as a broad generalisation?'

'The Aztecs:' Katherine didn't falter, 'legendary excavators.'

'Infamous,' Wesley conceded.

The rodent shook himself clean and then dutifully recommenced his self-abusing.

'Bron,' Wesley muttered, mulling the name over, trying but failing to make a connection.

Katherine began hunting around for her cigarettes. She eventually located a packet in the cutlery drawer. She tore it open and drew one out.

'Smoke?'

'Thanks.'

She stuck two cigarettes into her mouth, strolled over to the gas oven, pressed the ignition button, fiddled with a knob on the hob and bent over.

Wesley watched her, with interest, plucking on, blindly; two thirds of the heron's chest area now all but bare. Katherine lit both cigarettes, took one out of her mouth, padded over and placed it between Wesley's lips.

'You have . . .' she leaned in close to him –

Violets

'. . . a little piece of fluff . . .'

She plucked it off.

'There.'

She returned to her place by the kitchen cupboards and lounged against the worksurface. Wesley dangled the cigarette loosely on his lip, barely inhaling on it. He glanced over towards the cage again. 'Did you think to light one up for the little fella?' he enquired, 'I think he'll be needing one shortly.'

'I am . . .' Katherine spoke with an especial languor, banging her rump sharply against the cutlery drawer,' I am *killed* by your wit.' She thought quietly for a while, then added, '. . . and I'm certain there's something Biblical about not eating predators. In Leviticus or somewhere . . .'

Wesley refused to rise to her.

'Flesh is flesh,' he pronounced flatly, 'there can be no moral hierarchy when it comes to murder. But if you insist on such a thing – if there *has* to be – then this lovely creature would surely be at the top of it.'

'You reckon?'

'Of course: ancient, almost starving, very nearly dead from the cold already . . .' He fingered the puny bare flesh on the chest, 'no meat here to speak of.'

'Had I only known . . .' Katherine drew deeply on her cigarette, 'I could've killed us a robin or a goldfinch or a rare species of *wood*pecker – fried it up in batter, for a tasty little starter . . .'

Wesley lifted the heron's wing, took out his knife and cut firmly into it. He sawed for a few seconds until it came free (the cruel sound of bone shattering), then he opened it out, like a fan. 'Goldfinches migrate in the winter,' he informed her. 'What do you think?'

Even Katherine found it difficult not to be impressed by the wing's unfolding; by its bright and flawless close-knit construction. Wesley attacked the second one. He removed it – after a brief struggle – then placed them both, side-by-side, on the table-top.

He looked around him. On the floor close to his feet – stuffed into an old half tea-crate – were a pile of shells, some mouldering sheafs of wheat (semi-weaved into a dolly) and two coils of wire; one brass, and thin, the other steel and thicker.

He grabbed the steel wire, cut off a long segment with his knife and rapidly threaded one end – in and out, in and out – through the top strut of the left wing.

Katherine watched him intently, her mouth slightly open.

'Don't just *gape*,' Wesley reprimanded, 'loosen your clothing and come on over.'

She didn't move initially. She continued inspecting him for any casual indication of cursory derision –

Nothing

– so she took a last puff on her cigarette, balanced it, carefully, facing inwards, between the two taps on her stainless steel sink and slowly walked over.

'Katherine Turpin,' she muttered (her reputation preceding her, like a series of bright ripples in a shallow puddle of dirty water), 'game for anything.'

'Kneel down for me.'

She frowned. She rested her hands on her hips, briefly. Then she knelt – her face glowing – before him.

'Good.'

Wesley carefully inspected Katherine's apricot layers. He removed the first two (they came away easily; the silky wools massed, slithered, formed warm piles on the floor) then paused ruminatively when he reached the third and fourth (the first two'd had sleeves, the others had been casually doctored – the sleeves torn away, and the collars – so that the frayed edges which remained tickled lightly at her throat and shoulders).

Underneath these half-altered items she wore – he smiled when he saw it – an old-fashioned 1930s peach bodice. Loose-ish. Under that, an old, ill-fitting, heavy-fabric, cream-coloured bra.

'I'll try not to scratch you,' he told her, as he slowly threaded the wire across her collar bones, under each of her double straps, over and around the back of her. When he'd finished, the first wing hung limply at her shoulder. Almost apologetically.

He threaded in the second wing – this one with more difficulty because of his missing fingers – the cigarette still hanging slackly between his lips, his hands still bloody and feathery, then adjusted them both gently, touching her throat, her neck, her nape, her hair.

The whole process took many minutes. Katherine knelt – blissfully mute – goosebumps forming intermittently.

(He was very dark. Very handsome. Like the bad character in a children's story. Shadowy, temporary, incomplete.
She liked that. She . . .)

224

He finally drew back, removed the cigarette from between his lips, and held it away, conducting a thorough – and rather lordly – inspection of his achievements.

'Katherine Turpin,' he told her, 'you are . . .'

Angelic wasn't cutting it.

'A little fairy. Playing on the compost heap. Kicking up the turnip heads. Trampling the cabbage leaves. Full of spite. Full of . . . full of *air* . . .'

'*Tinkerbell*,' he suddenly remembered – as if he'd only just met up with her after almost an eternity, 'once she'd got all disillusioned,' he pushed back Katherine's hair – light as thistle-down against the broken skin of his ruined hand, 'all pissed-up and fucked-off and bitter.'

Katherine remained kneeling. She hunched her shoulders and smiled at him. She seemed to find this nasty fairy evocation particularly pleasing. Her wing's reach was five foot at least. The wire pulled across – and pinkened – her breastplate. Her bra-straps creaked under the pressure of it. The wings shuddered mothily as she breathed in. Wesley breathed in too. He leaned forward and *inhaled* her. Her eyelids dropped. Her lips parted. She thought he might . . .

Ted walked in.

'Oh Jesus bloody *Christ*,' he stuttered, barely missing a wing with the door.

'Hi Ted,' Wesley was unmoved, 'what do you reckon?'

'She . . .' Ted gawped at her. Smears of blood on her neck. Wings. He could see her . . . her bra. Bad fitting. One breast half-slipping out beneath it. Like . . . like . . .

Tripe.

Ted didn't understand women. Not at all.

Katherine reached out her pale arm, took the cigarette from between Wesley's fingers and smoked on it herself. She stared deeply into his vile, sage eyes. The wings fell lop-sided.

Wesley liked this even better.

'You are fallen,' he announced.

'Don't I know it,' Katherine countered.

Ted cleared his throat

I'm such a . . . such a lump

'I'd hate to spoil the . . .'

I'm such a . . .

'but I think there might be . . .'

The heron's torso lay across the kitchen table, a bloodied embankment, between himself and Wesley. Wesley was sitting on a stool, remarkably self-contained, plucking away again, vigorously –

Remember the pond.

Katherine clambered to her feet, looking around – slightly dazed – for her glass on the counter, finding it, drinking from it, her wings slipping further.

'Spit it out,' Wesley said.

She turned – alarmed – almost ready –

Oh my God

– to oblige him. Then she realised.

'Trouble,' Ted continued, and pointed, somewhat ineffectually, back down the corridor. 'Is it Dewi?' Katherine's voice was hardened by self-disgust and the liquor.

Wesley glanced up, sharply.

'I think . . .' Ted interrupted again, 'I think it might be . . .'

'Behindling,' Wesley flapped his bad hand, 'just ignore them.'

'No, but . . .' Ted floundered, 'well, there *are* Behindlings; the old guy we saw in the Wimpy earlier, and another man in a white van . . .'

'Hooch,' Wesley grimaced, adjusting the bird again.

'But it's the Police, too. They just pulled up outside. In a jeep.'

'Looking for the boy,' Wesley shrugged. 'He's under some kind of care order. It happens all the time. It's nothing, believe me.'

Before he'd finished speaking, however, there came an authoritative rap on the front door, followed, seconds later, by the lifting of the postal flap, a short hiatus, then its *snap*.

'Will I answer it?' Ted asked, breathing slightly faster. Katherine lifted her shoulders (as if suddenly feeling the chill) then bent stiffly over to pick up her pool of cardigans from the floor. 'It's my door,' she said, her voice, as she crouched down, sounding – and for the first time – a little slurred.

The doorbell rang. Just a second too long to be entirely friendly. 'Let Ted go,' Wesley told her, 'those wings'll make it difficult to manoeuvre properly.'

He stood, placing his hand, as he rose – the *slightest* pressure – onto her shoulder. This weight pressed through her body and into her heels. They glued her to the floor.

Ted had gone already. Wesley followed, just a few steps behind him.

'Don't mention the bird, Ted,' he instructed him, his voice hollowed by the close walls of the corridor. 'If it is the police and they notice the blood, tell them it was a rabbit . . .'

The floor was . . . was *warm*. Katherine sat down on it, like a child in a sandpit – hands spreading flat behind her, knees falling open. The wings were heavy. She collapsed onto her back and stared up at the ceiling; bird-bones creaking, feathers skidaddling. The *ceiling* . . . right above her. So profoundly reassuring. So flat. So white. So very familiar.

'I have some rather bad news for you, sir,' the male officer spoke first, earnestly clasping his two hands together and glancing over anxiously towards his female accomplice. She nodded back at him, curtly.

Ted was there. Wesley had insisted. He needed a witness, he'd said – always did with the Law – and, much more importantly, an intermediary, because he tried not to speak to the people Following. The police were no exception.

'Do you want me to . . .' At the mention of bad news, Ted indicated modestly towards the living room door, 'I'm happy to make myself . . .'

'Ask them if it's about the boy,' Wesley instructed brusquely, 'ask them if it's about Patty.' Ted shrugged, half-apologetically, at the handsome male officer (Ed Cole. He'd found him a lovely semi in Ellesmere Road, only last year).

'I have no information *whatsoever*,' the officer spoke to Wesley directly (ignoring Ted completely. Ted crumpled, involuntarily), 'about any situation involving a boy. We're here to discuss a *girl*. We're here to talk about Sasha . . .' he paused, uncertainly, 'your daughter.'

Wesley was standing over by the window. He'd tugged the

curtains aside and was gazing out through the nets. It was raining. Only lightly. Under the streetlight opposite he could see a lone figure.

The figure – the girl – the informer – the double-face . . . It *had* to be – was staring (shoulders slumped forward, rather poignantly) towards the small green house with the prodigious balcony. She muttered something – he saw a puff of steam, a tiny cloud condensing in the dark night air – then stepped down heavily into the gutter and slowly began walking.

The gutter . . .

Ah

Wesley turned, abruptly.

'What did you just say?'

Ted could tell that he wasn't concentrating.

'Sasha,' the male officer repeated, 'your daughter. She appears to have gone . . . gone . . .' he struggled to find a word in his vocabulary less frightening than *missing*, 'walkabout,' he said, finally.

Ted had a vision of the Duchess of Kent, in Eltham, opening a Conference Centre.

'Sasha.'

Wesley repeated the name. It seemed alien to him. He paused, mulling it over.

'Hang on,' he suddenly butted in – although nobody else was actually speaking – 'has something happened to her?'

Still – Ted noticed – he seemed more irritated than concerned.

'We hope not,' the male officer spoke, 'but her grandparents have reason to believe that she's intent on making her way down here to Canvey. She disappeared first thing this morning. She took twenty pounds and left a note saying . . .'

'But where's her mother?' Wesley asked.

'Her mother . . .' at last the woman officer felt able to contribute something, 'is on the Island of Madeira. On Honey . . .' she corrected herself, 'on holiday. Her parents thought it best not to worry her – not at this early stage, anyway. As you probably already know, they currently enjoy full parental rights over the child – have done since she was a baby . . .'

'Bloody Iris,' Wesley muttered, 'but the kid won't get too far on twenty quid . . .'

'I think you underestimate her,' the female officer smiled, sarcastically, 'apparently she's very tenacious. Takes after her father.'

Wesley stiffened. He didn't like this at all.

'She's been gone since first thing this morning . . .'

The male officer quickly took over. 'She left for school, as normal, but didn't arrive. In the light of your . . .' he paused, '*celebrity*, the force became involved a little earlier . . .'

He looked over at Wesley as if expecting some kind of commendation for the promptness of their reaction.

Wesley stared back blankly at him. Giving nothing.

'We know she caught a . . . got on a *train*,' the officer stumbled, as if spooked by Wesley's blankness, 'to London. But we don't know if she actually got there. She left a note saying . . .'

'Was she alone?'

'I was just getting to that part, sir. She took . . .' the male officer faltered, 'it sounds slightly . . .' he grimaced, 'she took a . . . a *reindeer* with her.'

'She took a *what*?'

Ted couldn't help himself. The male officer turned towards him, almost smiling his relief. Ted's cheeks reddened.

Wesley glanced over. 'The grandparents farm them,' he explained, tightly, 'they run a Christmas-themed Garden Centre in Norfolk. They keep,' he held up his bad hand, smiling darkly, 'beautiful exotic owls there.'

Ted shivered.

'May I . . .' the female officer spoke again. She was staring at Wesley's shirt, his hands.

'What?'

'It's just that you seem to be very . . . very *bloody* this evening, sir.'

Wesley shrugged, 'I killed a rabbit earlier.'

'Well it certainly must've put up quite a *struggle*, sir.'

She was mocking him.

'I *skinned* it,' Wesley growled, 'and we're having it for dinner.'

The female officer turned to the agent, her eyebrows raised, 'Is that right, then, Ted?'

Ted opened his mouth. He shut it. He glanced over at Wesley

229

whose jumper was – no point denying it – literally *coated* in bird down. He nodded his head.

'How . . .' to distract attention from the lie he addressed Wesley directly, 'how old is she?'

'Who?'

Ted swallowed, 'Your . . . your missing daughter.'

Wesley shrugged, 'Six . . . maybe seven.'

'*Ten.*'

The female officer shot Wesley a potent look.

Wesley didn't buckle. 'I've never met the girl,' he shrugged, 'and the truth is that I have no interest in her. I had none when she *wasn't* missing, so I might be in danger of seeming a little . . .' he pondered, '*hypocritical* if I suddenly began caring about her now that she is.'

The female officer considered his answer for a moment. 'Do you ever actually think about *any*body except yourself, sir?'

Wesley laughed out loud. A bark.

'Of course not,' he said, 'what a silly question.'

'That's as may be . . .' the male officer quickly stepped in (struggling to keep the atmosphere down to a simmer), his right hand clutching at the collar of his stiff white shirt –

So damn hot

– 'But I'm sure you must still feel some . . . some *concern* over this situation, sir. She's only young. It's freezing outside. She's coming down to see you. She left a note behind saying . . .'

'In actual fact,' Wesley interjected, 'I'm *not* especially concerned. The girl has never been fed any illusions about my intentions towards her. I have none. I'd call myself the *anti*-father, but I'm too indifferent to be anti-anything. I am the *non*-dad. Is that . . .' he paused, 'does that explain my feelings with sufficient candour?'

'She's a ten-year-old *child*,' the female officer's voice was harsh, 'and it's the middle of *winter* . . .'

'If you're so *concerned*, madam,' Wesley interrupted, 'then perhaps you should be out in the cold looking for her instead of standing here and harassing me.'

'She's a ten-year-old child, in the *pitch* dark, alone . . .'

'With a reindeer,' Wesley corrected her. 'I find it's always a good ruse,' he continued facetiously, 'to take a deer along to increase your sense of anonymity. The force must be literally at their wits' *end* trying to hunt her down. Talk about merging into the background . . .'

The female officer's fists tightened. Wesley – observing as much – put his own hand to his cheek. His bad hand. Rested it there for a moment.

The male officer quickly interjected again, 'Do you have any reason to believe that she'll know where to find you in Canvey, sir? Is she aware that you're staying at this address currently?'

'She may know,' Ted piped up, struggling to be helpful, to improve the atmosphere, 'if she has access to the net.'

'It's down,' the female officer snarled, still glaring at Wesley – his cheek, his bad hand – 'since first thing this afternoon.'

The male officer glanced over at Ted, supportively. 'Her grandparents do have a computer, though. So she may well have looked at the site last night. From what we've been told she was certainly aware of it.'

'Down?' Wesley frowned, dropping his hand to his side again.

'Yes,' the officer nodded, 'some kind of virus.'

Wesley stared at him, as if in doubt of his sanity.

'That's ridiculous,' he said.

'Why?' the female officer snapped.

Wesley shrugged, his face closing, 'It just is.'

He turned to Ted, 'Give me your phone.'

Ted scrabbled around in his jacket. He pulled out his mobile. Wesley took it and stuck it into his trouser pocket, 'I'm getting back to dinner. Will you see the officers out for me, Ted?' He left.

Ted stared – round-eyed – at the two officers. He swallowed. He took a deep breath –

The Pond . . .
Frogspawn throbbing and bubbling in the shallows . . .
The sweet, yeasty stink of thick, green pond-weed . . .

Then he indicated – summoning all the intrinsic authority of real, quality agenting (a straight arm pointing, a smile of untold promise and efficiency) – towards the wide-yawning doorway and its heavy muscle of straight, black-tiled tongue beyond.

Twenty-three

The infamous Saks was just about as smoked-up, packed-out and crazy as she'd ever imagined it might be. Friday Night. The town's outer periphery. Depths of winter. *Canvey.*

Jo steeled herself, then pushed her way in, pulling back her hood as she staggered through the door, mopping her cheeks and lifting her chin – her eyes two wide saucers of anxious misanthropy – before forging a determined but unsteady (was that really *her* feet squelching so audibly?) route to the bar.

After five minutes of standing around in a thick scrum of drink-seekers (each part of her duly poked, nudged and trodden on by a dozen oblivious elbows, rumps and feet; fivers and tenners scything through the air like tiny, paper jack-hammers) she found herself a stool (walked straight into it, banged her thigh, nicked her calf), felt its seat with her palms, blindly, and then gratefully straddled it, holding her legs high off the floor (bent hard at the knee) like a tenacious spider riding out a flash flood on a bobbing wine cork.

Ten minutes later and she'd somehow connived to grab – wonder of wonders – a second stool. She yanked off her coat, slung it over, rested her sodden feet on its highest rung and linked her arms around her knees, struggling – and almost managing – to create a small, shoulder-high sanctum amidst the heinously convivial Friday night commonality.

During a brief lull she stood up and ordered herself a beer, then quickly sat down again, clasping her hands around the bottle and shuddering with an ill-concealed social anxiety. Cold. *Cold –*
And way too busy in here

She was still very wet; dripping, in fact. But when she glanced around (bending her head at the neck, like a tortoise blinking up from the shelter of its shell into the mean spring sun) it felt like she was the only one. Everybody else seemed as crisp, high-baked and cheerfully compacted as a creaking oak barrel of quality ship's biscuits. *Dry.* Dry as Oscar Wilde in mordant humour. Dry as an actor's mouth before the first twitch of the curtain. Dry as a maiden Aunt's favourite pale sherry . . .

Roasted, seared, dehydrated.

Dry

She felt disgustingly conspicuous. And she was certain that when she'd first arrived she'd caught a glimpse of that nosy girl from the bakery over by the door. The one who . . .

Jo whimpered miserably under her breath –

Losing it.

Didn't want to seem . . . to seem . . . *paranoid* but there were almost certainly several others . . . from the . . . the . . .

Past

– A man with a ponytail standing by the cigarette machine. A pal of one of her brothers, maybe?

From the basketball team? Athletics?

Tennis

Oh God, yes.

Jo swigged hard on her drink and gazed at him, almost stupefied by those characteristics which rendered him familiar. He suddenly disengaged himself from the conversation he was having (with another man; ludicrously tall, in a football shirt) shifted position slightly and returned her stare. Cold. Very bold. Slightly stroppy.

Jo panicked, shifting her eyes sharply sideways as she rapidly detached the bottle from her lips. It immediately repaid her clumsy manoeuvrings by bubbling up and then foaming over –

Shit

He was laughing at her

Look at him laughing

No –

Don't look

Her coat slipped off the stool as she shook her fingers clean, assisted – in part – by a woman squeezing past her to get to the *Ladies*. A man close by stood on the hood, then apologised.

'Sorry,' he said, 'you okay down there?'

He bent down to retrieve it the same moment she did. Their heads collided.

'That's . . . *Yes*, I'm . . .' she retrieved the coat and held it tightly on her knee, blushing furiously. She sucked her tongue. She chewed on her thumb nail. She glanced over towards the door, repeatedly.

Only two more people entered in the course of this brief but torturous duration; a woman in heels with burnished auburn hair who was afforded a wild welcome from a group in an alcove to the left of the bar (was there some kind of loathsome Texan-themed eaterie through there?), and a very thin man.

The thin man wore a baseball cap (his cursory nod to modernity) and an incongruously ancient brown leather waistcoat. He seemed, if anything, slightly older than the majority of Saks' Friday night revellers and – this single detail distinguished him, more so, even, than his greying temples – he was absolutely *sopping*.

He peered around the bar intently as he kicked the door shut behind him (Jo held only a partial view from her stool, but – as luck would have it – all major obstructions between them were sentient, prodigiously convivial and in perpetual transition).

Jo noted that he was carrying a heavy rucksack on his back, that his baseball cap was khaki and featured a logo she vaguely recognised (not one of the major sports corporations, something a little more specialised, more . . . more *niche*-y; she gave it a sharp but sneaky double-look), that his boots were cleanish (from the rain) but that his ankles and his calves were exceedingly muddy.

A walker, she decided.

A stalker, potentially –

Behindling

Must be

Instinct drew him from the crowds by the door to the crowds by the bar. He bumped into several people inadvertently, struggling to move forward with his bulky load, finding it difficult – at first – to focus properly in the bright light, the smoke.

The bag was obviously very heavy.

Jo watched him dispassionately for a while. Then it grew too painful. She reached out her hand –
Oh the legacy of working in a caring profession
– and touched his arm.

He swung around at her touch, hitting a man carrying two beers, who slopped them, cursing, onto the wooden floor. He didn't think to apologise. Instead he squinted down at Jo, his mouth a lean line of almost geometric disapproval.

'There's a spare stool here if you want it,' she said, then added, a little embarrassedly, 'I mean for your rucksack.'

He wasn't half as grateful as she might've expected him to be (if she'd had expectations, but she didn't, really). He gazed at her, frowning. She moved her coat from the stool, her skin goose-pimpling at his hostility, 'Take it.'

She tried to sharpen her tone.

He nodded and pulled off his rucksack. He placed it onto the stool, yanked off his jacket and slung it over, finally his cap, then rapidly pushed his way – side-stepping the painful duty of thanking her – to the bar.

It was a tight squeeze. He soon facilitated his easier access (his foot – she later observed, after some poor soul had tripped over it – still carefully looped around the leg of the stool), by unleashing a gigantic sneeze. This cunning expedient cleared the decks impressively.

He leaned across the counter, caught the barman's eye and ordered himself a tomato juice with a squeeze of lemon, a pinch of salt and tiny dash of Worcester Sauce in it –
Alcoholic
Nurse's instinct
He was very meticulous about the exact proportions –
Confirmation
If any were needed
This exactitude would not – Jo idly calculated – particularly endear him to the barman.

She stared fixedly at her beer bottle, peeling the corner off the main label with her clean nail and listening distractedly as the thin man endeavoured to engage the now-truculent barhand in conversation –

The cheek of it

'Keep the change.'

'Thanks,' the barman responded. By the dryness of his tone Jo deduced that the amount proffered was by no means excessive.

'In fact if you wouldn't mind . . .' the thin man continued, then paused, before adding, 'I'm looking for somebody . . .' he paused again, 'hang on . . .'

He removed something from his waistcoat pocket. A palm or a phone, inspected it for a moment (by which stage the barman was almost stamping with frustration – a furious queue rapidly forming behind him) but the man continued, unperturbedly, 'I'm actually looking for a woman called . . . called Katherine. Katherine *Turpin*. I believe she's well known around here, has a . . . how to express it? A *reputation*.'

Jo looked up –

Is he crazy?

Doesn't he . . . ?

Doesn't . . . ?

'Never heard of her,' the barman interrupted coldly.

Did the thin man notice? That coldness? Josephine gazed at him pointedly through her down-turned lashes.

Rehindling. No doubt about it.

The man returned to his stool, grumbling under his breath. He held his drink – she noticed – with a certain show of awkwardness, the way you might hold a large cockroach, a used syringe or a disgustingly ripe nappy.

'Excuse me . . .'

He'd placed his rucksack onto the floor and was perched on the stool now, inches from her (his knees turned politely in the opposite direction to forestall her getting – God *forbid* – the wrong impression).

'Do you happen to live locally by any chance?'

From his tone – how embarrassing – he seemed to be presuming that she'd been listening in on his previous conversation –

Military training?

Jo glanced up. Her face must've registered some kind of surprise, because he apologised. Very formally. He was . . . He was . . .

Older

'I'm sorry. I was just wondering if you might be . . . well, *local*,' he repeated.

Jo gave this question a moment's consideration. She was about to answer. ('No, I'm from Southend,'), but before she could, his thin face broke into a disarming smile, 'I'm soaking.' He shook off his arm, droplets of moisture splashing down onto the wooden floor, 'and I can't help feeling a little . . .'

Jo put a clumsy hand to her forehead where a tiny pool of liquid still balanced invisibly across the thin line of her brow. Her fingers released it.

'. . . self conscious,' he finished humbly.

The human face
Just a facade

'Yes. I was . . . I was walking myself,' she mumbled, shaking a fresh concatenation of rivulets from her cheeks, her colour rising.

'Pardon?'

Slightly hard of hearing

'I was . . . walking,' she repeated, 'and got a little . . . Well, I mean I got very . . .'

'It's a filthy night,' he smiled again, this time rather more creakily. 'My feet are absolutely . . .'

His phone rang. Volume turned high. He almost spilled his drink.

Jo dropped her coat again. He scooped down to pick it up, then looked around for somewhere to rest his glass. The bar was too far – bodies already crushing in and around the counter. Jo put out her hand and took her coat, then removed the drink from him, grimacing submissively.

'I'll just hold . . .' she said.

'Thank you. Sorry.' He clutched at his waistcoat –

That waistcoat
Worn as the skin of a Chinese pensioner

In the pocket she noticed . . .

Can't be

. . . an old, well-thumbed copy of Louis L'Amour's . . .

Fuck me

. . . *Silver* . . .

Huh?

. . . Silver C . . .

Huh?

. . . Sil . . .

What the . . . ?

The thin man drew the phone from his pocket. He pressed a button and placed it to his ear. Jo turned modestly towards the bar, ending up with an eyeful of a woman's cigarette (held – ever so politely – behind her back) and the top of her companion's bedenimed rear.

Silver Canyon

Good God

'Yes?' Arthur spat, irritably.

Jo looked up at the ceiling –

Silver Canyon

– then down at the floor again.

'No,' his tone sweetened dramatically, once he'd identified his interlocutor, 'no, I'm in town, I'm . . .'

But he had a harsh accent just the same. Not a local accent. Not Kentish. Maybe a Londoner. A Cockney. But posh. And a strange voice, too; like a shallow wave washing over shingle.

'I left the craft . . . No . . . I walked back under the flyover. I had . . .'

His voice suddenly grew softer, 'Several people came. One of them an Ombudsman. Two others. Someone from – well I think it was English Nature or the National Trust – something charitable at any rate. They didn't discuss . . .' he placed a careful hand over both his mouth and the receiver, 'they didn't discuss exact *amounts*, but I got the impression that you could pretty much *dictate* . . .' he was quiet for a moment, 'but that doesn't . . . It can't *be* my decision. They're offering money to *you*, for services ren . . . ren . . . rendered . . .'

A very long silence. 'But that's ridiculous. You expect me to negotiate and then to . . . to . . . to *keep* . . . ? That's . . .'

Now he sounded furious, 'I'm not interested in playing a *moral game*. I'm not interested in *implicating* myself. I'm simply doing you a . . .'

Short pause, 'Do you *always* do this?'

Shorter pause, 'So you actually never . . .'

Stunned silence.

'Yes . . . Yes. But they were very . . . terribly hush-hush. Another guy who . . . No. No. The ombudsman seemed extremely keen to . . .'

He paused, 'I realise they have no actual restraining powers as . . . as . . . as *such*, but he was . . .'

The thin man stopped sharp, mid-sentence and cleared his throat. When next he spoke his voice was italicised by indignance, 'Of *course* he didn't shit me up. I merely thought . . .'

He paused.

'I'm in a bar. No. No, *not* the Lobster Smack. That's too . . . I came the other way, I already said, under the flyover. This place . . . It's on the High Street. It's called . . .'

Arthur positioned his thin fingers over the phone's mouthpiece and turned to Jo, 'Excuse me . . .'

He tapped her on the shoulder.

'Excuse me.'

She jumped out of her reverie and spun around to look at him.

'Sorry,' he smiled, 'do you happen to know the name of this bar by any chance?'

'Saks,' Jo said.

'Thanks.'

He returned to his conversation, 'It's called Saks. It's very full. We'd be much better off . . . Well . . . I . . . Yes. Well that's . . . that's entirely up to you, but . . .'

Jo wiped her nose –

Silver Canyon

She found herself looking down at his bag and his hat. The hat. It had a special logo on it. A squidgy bear-like . . . no *koala*-like creature. Above it the word *Gumble*.

He was still talking. 'No. I . . . If it's a standard type I might have some idea, Wesley, but I'm hardly . . . I can't . . .'

Jo froze.

1 . . . 2 . . . 3 . . . 4 . . .

Ten-second delay.

'Josie. *Josie.* Hey!'

Jo turned around, still almost oblivious.

Huh?

Anna.

Anna.

Anna *Wright*, literally ten inches away, fish-eye lensed by her unexpected proximity.

'Packed or *what*?' she bellowed.

Jo tried to stand up, shocked. No room.

'Need another?'

Anna pointed at her beer.

Jo inspected her bottle, panicking –

Get away from here

'No. Hello. That would be . . . *Yes*. That would be fantastic.'

'Back in a minute.' Anna moved off to the right, pulling a wallet from her pocket. The thin man had . . . he'd stashed his phone away already. And he was looking at her. He was pointing –

What?

'Oh *right*,' she gabbled, her nose tingling sharply, 'of course. There you go . . .'

She passed him his drink back, dabbing her nose – self-consciously – on her sleeve.

'Thanks.' He grabbed his coat, 'Your friend's just arrived. I should probably . . .'

Stop . . . Stop . . . Stop shaking your head, Jo,

It's a statement of fact

He stood up, balancing his drink, his coat and his rucksack unevenly in his arms, pushing the stool closer to her with his knee and staggering to a small gap next to the bar.

'That's very . . .' she said –

Gentlemanly

He was facing away from her but he was still – she observed anxiously – just within spitting distance. She shoved her beer between her knees and smoothed a hand over her short hair. Anna was fighting her way back already. She hailed several people and kissed two cheeks (twice, in the air) on her brief walk over. Seemed to know everybody –

Dry as a bone,

Goddamn her

Jo had no chance – and no room, either – to manoeuvre before Anna'd handed her a second bottle, grabbed the stool and plonked herself down on it. She was drinking red wine. Burgundy.

'Jesus you're *soaking*.'

Jo looked down at herself, 'I know. I . . .'

'I have had the worst fucking day,' Anna interrupted, 'you simply would not *believe* . . .'

She scrabbled around in her pockets and pulled out her cigarettes and a lighter, 'Smoke?'

'No. No I . . .'

'*Nurse*. Of course you bloody don't. Do you mind?'

'Not at all. And thanks for . . .'

Jo raised the second bottle.

Anna lit up. She inhaled, she exhaled.

'So,' she smiled, slipping the packet and her lighter back into her pocket, 'what's the story?'

'Pardon?'

Did she know about the hospital?

The trouble?

How could she?

'With Wesley. What's the story there? I almost shat my *pants* when I saw it was you walking along that road tonight. I couldn't . . .'

Jo peeked surreptitiously towards the thin man by the bar. Anna was such a foghorn – such a *squawker* – he must be . . .

She shifted on her stool. Her coat fell from her lap –

Damn

'You okay there, Josie?'

She retrieved the coat.

'No I'm . . . That's fine.'

She bundled it up again, trying not to spill her beers. She'd barely touched the first one. She sucked on it to gain time. Drank down about half, inhaled, hiccuped, apologised, then wiped off her mouth with her hand.

But Anna had focus. She had zeal.

'So what's the story with Wesley? Eddie said you actually *knew* those two old men out there this evening. The grumpy one's called Doc. He's the leader, apparently. His son Followed, but only very briefly. Drowned in Anglesey a couple of months back. Got caught up in that whole chocolate-wrapper-challenge thing. It was all over the papers.'

'The Loiter.'

'Pardon?

'That's . . . That's what they . . .'

Anna's eyes tightened fractionally, 'So you *are* involved with them to some degree?'

'Well, no . . . I mean . . .' Jo nodded (Anna's powers of deduction were plainly not all they might be), 'only by sheer coincidence . . . I wasn't . . . I just happened to bump into them earlier.'

Anna was nodding too now, encouraging her.

'I didn't really . . .'

'And you also know, I presume,' she interjected, 'the kind of man you're dealing with here?'

Jo's eyes widened, uncertainly. She slowly shook her head.

'He's a pig.'

Jo swallowed, with difficulty.

'Killed his only brother,' Anna continued, stony-faced, 'trapped him in an abandoned fridge and then left him there to die. Totally cold-blooded.'

Jo struggled to hide her dismay, 'But he was only . . .'

'Seven. That's *way* too old for accidents. He was the kind of child who'd pull the wings off butterflies. Probably broke into churches and stole the collection with his mates. Played on the organ. Pissed in the vestry. That kind of thing.'

Jo wriggled on her seat. She peered over at Arthur, agonisedly – *Nothing*

Anna sipped on her drink, 'His father was a seaman. Always away at sea. Mother didn't clamp down on him *nearly* hard enough if you ask me . . .'

Jo inspected her beer bottle. She didn't want an argument.

'And obviously – from the Force's point of view – if people didn't feel the need to Follow,' Anna rolled her eyes expressively, 'then there wouldn't be . . .'

She sucked on her cigarette, disapproval oozing from every orifice.

Jo stared back at her, bright with embarrassment.

'When he arrived on Wednesday,' she continued, 'they contacted us straight away . . .'

'Sorry?' Jo butted in.

'Pardon?'

'*They* contacted the force?'

'Meaning?'

'You said *they* contacted the force?'

'Yeah,' Anna nodded, missing the point (on purpose, was it?), 'but he was clever. He stayed over on the far side – Northwick, Westwick, Salting. No roads. I mean we're happy to go out on surveillance, but we draw the line at hanging around in the middle of a freezing field all day just to watch some arse-wipe catching a rabbit and taking a shit in a ditch . . .'

Jo winced, sympathetically.

'He was spotted on the rubbish dump at one point. Somebody reported him. He was catching seabirds apparently. We thought we might be able to detain him on it for a while, but he got out of there too quick and always went for the unprotected species. He's a cunning little twat. Survived out of jail for this long, let's face it.'

'Apart from . . .'

'The first two convictions. Of course. But that's what made him. The publicity. Eddie says he walks the perimeter every day,' Anna continued, then she paused, speculatively, 'although I guess you must know that already if you've been . . .'

'*No,*' Jo jumped in. 'No I don't know anything. I was only in town this morning and I came across . . . *uh* . . .'

Patty

'. . . This . . . This *boy* asked me for a handout for his train fare home. I took him for something to eat . . . the Wimpy. That was . . .'

'Oh the *boy,*' Anna nodded. 'Yeah. Eddie said everybody kept going on about some boy . . .'

'He Follows. He lives in Derby. I think he has an outstanding care order, so . . .'

'Eddie said he thought you might be involved from some kind of weird, environmental standpoint. Wesley likes to project that whole . . . *you* know. The Green thing. But we couldn't figure out . . .'

'Oh God no,' Jo demurred, 'I . . .'

'Well that's something at least. Because he's honestly – and I have first-hand experience of this – he's a *total* bastard. Very messed up. Very nasty.'

Jo was staring at Anna with a kind of wild unfocussedness. Anna frowned at her, impatiently, 'Are you . . . ?'

Jo blinked, 'So how come . . . what was . . . why did you have to speak to him this evening, then?'

Anna shrugged, coldly. 'Just police business,' she drained her glass, 'but he'd better watch his back. He steps out of line and we're gonna take real delight in nabbing him. I'm not kidding . . .'

Jo nodded, mutely. Not approving. Not disapproving.

'He was down in Camber before coming here. Did you know that?'

Jo shook her head, 'No I . . .'

'The *hypocrisy* of the man. He went to Rye. The town. They have a port there. And they know for a *fact* that he changed the signs on the river. They have signs near the port stating that members of the public shouldn't feed the gulls – the gulls mess on the boats and some of them are feral. This gull apparently attacked a child and nearly severed its finger . . .'

Jo frowned, gently, 'I hardly think that a gull would . . .'

'Oh *yeah*. I forgot,' Anna laughed, 'you're into all that natural history crap. Well anyhow, he changed the signs. Replaced them. And nobody could tell for a while because he'd done them *exactly* the same, and everyone who used the port regularly was taken in. You know?'

'So what did they . . . ?'

'Oh stuff about how tourists were at liberty to feed the birds if they wanted and that the people who thought they could dictate on this matter because they owned a boat or sat on a council were deluded. That animals possessed universal rights. The sky is free. *You* know . . . Just the same bollocks as always. Really *petty*. He's such an unreservedly small-minded little fucker. I think that's actually what I hate most about him.'

Josephine nodded. She sipped on her beer again.

'He's mentally deranged. And that *hand* of his. When I spoke to him earlier he lifted that hand and put it on his cheek . . .' Anna re-enacted this gesture, her nose wrinkling up in distaste, 'I know it doesn't sound like much but it was actually really . . . It was disgusting. He fed that hand to a bird apparently. I don't believe a word of it. It's just part of the myth.'

Jo shrugged.

'I mean, sure, he stole that woman's pond in 1989. Some deluded little tart he was shagging. That was true.'

'*Shit.*'

They both turned around. The thin man had spilled his drink. A glutinous, bloody-coloured mess was rapidly spreading over the counter. The barman was scowling. Jo blinked. Anna paused for just a second and then continued talking, 'She was a recruitment officer for a major bank. He applied for a job there but didn't get it because of his . . .'

She lifted her hand.

'So then he tracked her down and had sex with her. She asked him if he'd help her fix her pond – install a new water purifier. But he objected – for some fucked-up reason – and the next thing she knew, he'd stolen the damn thing. An antique pond. No trace of it left. All the fish just left on the verandah swimming around in glass bowls. A lawn laid over where the hole had been. Really, *really* psycho stuff. I read the police notes. *Scary.*'

'I think the theft was intended to be . . . to be *symbolic*,' Jo muttered.

Anna gave Jo a warning look. 'Afterwards he released some *eels* – can you believe it? From a pie and mash shop in the East End. Bow . . . In actual fact that might've been before. I forget the proper *order* of things . . . But they tried to prosecute. Couldn't find him for about eighteen months after. He was walking to the coast, alongside the river. There was much less access then. He's obsessed by the Estuary, although he hails from Gloucester, originally.'

Jo nodded.

'All tiny misdemeanours,' Anna persisted, 'petty felonies. But – and now get *this*, Josie – he won't pay child support for his own kid. Has to be hauled up in front of a court. Claims he's penniless. Even after the book and all that other stuff. Cash off the internet. Sponsors and what-not. And let's not forget the deal he must've struck with those confectionery people. No *money*, he says. He is *warped*. He is seriously messed up.'

Anna paused for a long drag on her fag. Jo tried to fill in the gap, 'Yes. But I don't suppose it's . . .'

'They know for a *fact*, for example,' Anna continued, 'that he broke into the Soane's Museum in London, *repeatedly*. I was reading this today on my print-out, just before the machine went down . . . And that's another thing. Apparently there's some kind of . . .'

'The . . . Sorry . . . The Soames Museum?' Jo interrupted.

'Oh God, yes. It's in High Holborn. London. Some strange architectural Museum. They had a real problem with pigeons soiling the sandstone building so they got a trap set up inside this atrium thingy – I dunno. It's complicated. All totally above board, though. They had one bird as bait, to lure the others. It was *nothing* . . .'

Anna waved her hand around in the air to dissipate the cloud of smoke hanging in front of Josephine's face, 'But Wesley decided to break in and set the birds free. Literally *three* bloody birds maximum. *Pigeons*. And he really messed the joint up. Not just the once, either. He did it several times. And this place was virtually *impossible* to access, which I suppose he deserves credit for – oh *Christ*, just listen to me. They had to hire a full-time guard. And he *still* broke in again. He definitely wasn't working alone in that instance. They don't think he was working alone . . .'

Anna threw her cigarette onto the floor, stubbed it out with her heel and glanced around the bar, catching the eye of the tall, dark-haired man Jo had part-recognised earlier. The man with the ponytail. Slick-looking. Big. Raincoated.

'Fucking *Bo*,' Anna muttered. 'Tennis Ace. Dyslexic. Premature ejaculator. Oh *bollocks*. He's coming over. Don't mention a word of what we've been discussing. He's become a journalist since we were all at . . .'

'Anna, Anna, *Anna*.'

The ponytailed man kissed Anna on her neck, pushing his hands around her waist, from the back. But even as he was caressing her he was staring – tight-eyed – at Josephine across her shoulder. He had an agenda. It was manifest.

'Fuck off, Bo,' Anna chided, elbowing him in the chest when he didn't instantly relinquish his grip on her.

Bo took this in his stride, letting go, crouching down and sliding his broad hand across her leg instead. He unleashed a flirtatious part-smile part-sneer in Jo's direction (he thought he was Gary Numan with bigger muscles and a little more hair – or Brian

Ferry circa *Love Is The Drug*), 'I don't know if you realise this,' he stage-whispered, 'but anything you say to Anna here, even in casual conversation, may well be taken down as evidence and used against you, later.'

Jo's expression did not change. Her face remained as smooth and uncomplicated as the pale shell on a hen's egg.

'Hang on . . .' he paused for a second, 'weren't we at school together?'

He was still staring at her intently.

'And didn't I actually see you *Following* earlier?'

'Jo's working at Southend General,' Anna curtly intervened, knocking his hand from her knee, 'where she's making great strides in the gynaecological department. She's heading an environmental sanitary product campaign. You may've read about her in the local press.'

'No *way*,' Bo was smirking, 'you're fucking with me.'

Anna shrugged at Jo, apologetically, 'He's not terribly clever, and he doesn't *read* much, either. Only the sport, which he writes, very badly. And sometimes, I suspect, not even that.'

Bo swigged on his beer. 'Anna and I dated for a while,' he told Jo, burping, 'but I dumped her. She's still smarting.'

'His penis is the size of my little finger,' Anna continued, unabashedly, 'same thickness, same length. His biggest muscle is his tongue. And he never put *that* to much good use, as I recollect.'

Bo smirked on, defiantly, while Anna inspected her smallest digit. 'I'm actually being *ludicrously* overgenerous,' she sighed, 'that's so typical of me.'

Bo honed in on Jo again, totally unconcerned by Anna's assault on him, 'I *did* see you Following. You were in the Library earlier.'

Jo said nothing.

'Playing with the big boys now, are we, Bo?' Anna snorted, 'trying to grub yourself up a piddling exclusive for your pathetic little Canvey rag? Oh *Diddums* . . .' she chucked him under his prodigiously square chin, 'that's so *sweet*.'

'You wished you knew what I know, Officer,' Bo snapped, draining his bottle with a swagger, every inch the cool hack-sleuth.

'Meaning?' Anna gazed down at him, sympathetically.

'Just what I say,' he placed the empty bottle next to Jo's stool, almost touching her ankle with his hand before slowly drawing it away, 'I have a contact.'

'Who?'

'You'll need to *beat* that information out of me.'

He winked at her.

'Ted. The estate agent,' Anna sighed. 'No beating necessary.'

Bo rocked back on his heels.

'How the . . . ?'

'Oh come *on*. You've been breaking his balls since all that graffiti rubbish with the Turpin girl. And I saw him tonight with Wesley. He's right up to his puny, ginger neck in it.'

Jo suddenly stood up. Her coat fell to the floor. 'I need . . .' she put her hand to her face, her cheek, 'I must . . . I need the toilet . . . *Here* . . .'

She thrust the untouched beer at Bo and launched herself off – like an ill-constructed canoe hurtling down a particularly treacherous stretch of white-water – towards the *Ladies*.

'Was it something I said?' Bo murmured, grabbing Jo's coat and lounging against her stool to swig on her beer. He looked around him, cleared his throat, then casually slipped his hand into one of her front pockets, withdrawing some car keys and a couple of sweet wrappers.

'I didn't see you do that,' Anna warned him, lighting up another cigarette and tossing the empty packet onto the floor.

Bo pushed his hand in again.

'Tell me,' Anna asked him, exhaling a little self-consciously and then turning her face into the light, 'do you see anything . . . anything out of the ordinary . . . just . . .'

She touched her cheek, where Jo had touched hers only a minute before, and where a good hour earlier, Wesley had touched his.

'Just *there*?'

Bo frowned, drew slightly closer, adjusted his angle so as not to cast her in shadow, and stared.

Twenty-four

All he needed was a pen and some paper to prove his point to her.

Ms Katherine Turpin (the female in question) was wedged tightly (and inexplicably – and no one dared ask why, exactly) between her fridge and her kitchen cabinets; bottle in hand, fag on her lip, flat on her arse and maintaining the constant – if physically unfeasible angle of 63 degrees.

She'd consumed the best part of a litre of apricot brandy and she hadn't even peed yet (or expressed the slightest urge – Wesley couldn't for the life of him work out how she'd managed it; her bladder must've been fashioned from industrialised rubber) but she was still successfully projecting (due, in the main, to her scabrous barrage of vocal comebacks) a perfectly passable simulation of trenchant clear-headedness –

Trenchant

– Wesley smiled –

That was her

That was Katherine

One wing had fallen off (the wire emerging from beneath her bra-strap, concluding in a lethal point ten inches behind her, etching random diagrams into the cupboard's pale melamine) and she was sitting squarely and heavily on what remained of the other.

Ted had picked up the fallen wing and was holding it on his lap – sometimes tucking and straightening, sometimes just stroking. Wesley was flitting around between them like a lunatic gnat; hypothesising – self-justifying – scheming – cooking.

The heron's cadaver was now plucked and cut, the breasts

(and every other passably edible scrap) seared in fat, thrown into a stewing pot with thyme, bayleaf – Wesley carried his own fire-dried supply in his rucksack – a spoonful of Marmite and a litre of water.

In her fridge – when he'd chanced to look, hoping for something healthy or hearty as (he erroneously believed) would befit a part-time sprout cultivator – he found only her extensive collection of high quality organic chocolate (plain, some flavoured with lavender, cardamom, chilli and juniper).

'Fairtrade,' Katherine told him, raising a single, imperious finger above the door which eclipsed her, 'I get it posted.'

Wesley casually scrutinised a finely-embossed wrapper. '*Whizz-o,*' he murmured.

'*Huh?*'

She squinted up at him (looking like a Greek marble sculpture after a very major earth tremor), 'Seventy fucking *percent* pure cocoa solids. *Organic.*'

Wesley gave the chilli bar a tentative sniff. He withdrew, grimacing.

'Beat *that.*'

He just smiled.

'*Give* it here.'

Katherine put down her brandy, took the cigarette out of her mouth, looked around for an ashtray, couldn't find one so pushed it clumsily through the bottle's lip. Its burning tip fizzed out quietly inside the two remaining inches of liquor. She reached out her hand, then suddenly changed her mind.

'Is there a cup?' she asked. 'Or a mug? Teddy?'

Ted looked up. A blue mug of water sat on the table at his elbow. He drained it and passed it to her.

'Thanks.' She tipped the last few remaining drops out onto the floor, conducted a fastidious inspection of the mug's interior and then vomited cleanly into it. She filled it to the rim, stopped, to order, then passed the mug back to Ted again, wiping her mouth on the pale curve of flesh inside her right arm.

'Chocolate,' she instructed loftily.

Wesley held out the bar. She took it, unwrapped a corner and nibbled on it, daintily.

'I'm the man who became a social outcast for sleeping inside the body of a horse,' Wesley told her, 'and even *I* could teach you a thing or two about the social graces.'

Ted felt the mug's enamel warming, inexorably, beneath his finger-pads. His gorge rose.

'Where's . . . where's Saks, Ted,' Wesley suddenly switched tack, 'is it far from here?'

Ted stood up and walked over to the sink. 'It's just . . .' his voice shook a little as he removed the washing up bowl, carefully tipped the contents of the mug down the plughole, and then turned on the tap to rinse it, 'a couple of doors down from the Agency. Opposite the Leisure Centre. It's an American bar. They sell food and . . . and . . . and beer.'

'Of course. Now I remember.'

'You slept *inside* a horse?' Katherine was gazing up at him. 'Was it dead already?' She was obviously unfamiliar with this story.

'I found the animal,' Wesley explained, bored.

Why all these explanations?

(He didn't *want* to backtrack any more, he longed to *consolidate*. Why did nobody ever want to consolidate with him? The repetition was so . . . so dull, so boring . . . so *repetitious*.)

'It was dying,' he continued, 'I sat with it until it stopped breathing and then I ate some of it. I was starving. Later on I climbed inside it to keep warm. It's a basic survival technique. I was alone on the Yorkshire Moors. It was snowing.'

Wesley turned and peered into the depths of the fridge again where – apart from the chocolate – he saw a blue-tinged loaf of Jamaican tea bread (unused), a plastic bag of celery (half-rotted), a carrot, two jars of Dijon mustard, half a cold omelette on a paper plate, a handful of butter (he stuck his finger in, sucked on it – *hmmm*, unsalted) reduced to ghee and left mouldering in a saucer.

'A dead *horse*?'

Katherine was finding this concept difficult to digest.

'Aren't you worried about your daughter?' Ted asked, still running the tap, thinking about her out there – like Wesley had been – in the cold and the dark.

Katherine's head jerked up, but it might've been the chilli in her chocolate bar.

'What?'

The tone of Wesley's voice implied a very strong warning. This was patently not the kind of question he wanted to be asked. He instinctively raised his hand to his cheek, then realised what he was doing and pulled it away again so violently that he slapped the door of the fridge with it.

Ted noticed – out of the corner of his eye – and flinched –

The bad hand

A bad sign

'I just . . . I only wondered . . .'

Pond

Pond

'It wasn't *my* horse,' Wesley addressed Katherine again, 'and I didn't kill it. But when I cut into it, the flesh was still warm. I got arrested two days after. Charged with theft. Two lesser charges of cruelty.'

'If you . . . if you . . .' Ted continued, indomitably, 'if you were putting on an *act*, by any chance – I mean for the Police . . .'

Wesley straightened his damaged hand, then knuckled it. The good hand rushed towards it, as though in some kind of complex damage-limitation manoeuvre.

'If you . . .' Ted finally glanced over properly, his forehead creasing, 'I mean if you were . . . putting it on or something . . . it was very . . .' he paused, his throat tightening, '*convincing*,' he almost gibbered.

'Did I possibly detect . . .' Wesley spoke directly into the scandalously empty salad compartment, trying to push the dead horse from his mind –

The flop of the intestine

The stink

The steam

'Did I inadvertently pick up a tiny smattering of *sexual* tension back there, Ted? Between you and the young officer? Is that why you're asking? Is that what you're really interested in?'

An instinct to be cruel – deep within him – to purge –

Fine to brag about the horse

But it was different in fact

Nearly died in that cold night
Not brave
Not outrageous
Not clever . . .

Oh that beautiful pony
Velvet belly –
New-dead –
Not clever or funny
No
Only –
Only pathetic
Like the judge had said

Nobody ever remembered the bad . . .

Brother Christopher
Bright summer morning
Such blackness inside of it
So much dark inside of it

Remember the warm –
Daughter
The warm –
Horse
The warm –
Christopher
Warm – velvet – closeness

Wesley suddenly pushed the nails on his good hand into the flesh on the palm of his bad. Five nails. Felt them cutting. Celebrated the wound –
The absence
The absences

Blood –
Blood

Over

Ted looked up, bemused, 'But she's not . . .'

'Not the *woman*, stupid,' Wesley interrupted harshly.

Ted's face was a picture –

Shocked

Hurt

Wesley immediately felt better. He reached into the fridge and grabbed the carrot and the celery.

Ted hung his head. His chest caved. He blushed. He pushed his fist into Katherine's blue mug –

Pushed

Wesley shoved the carrot and celery under his elbow, opened a jar of mustard, sniffed, saw a moss-green coating of mould around the top of the glass . . .

Ouch

– a sudden, stinging impact in the region of his ear. A rubber band. Katherine had yanked it deftly from her hair, taken aim and fired. He glared at her.

She was smiling. Dark chocolate on her teeth.

'You're just like the rest of us,' she said.

'Pardon?'

'Just the same. Yes you are.'

He shrugged, listlessly, 'Did I ever say I wasn't?'

'You didn't *say* it,' Katherine mused, 'but you certainly *think* it. You need to believe you're decent – deep inside – but sometimes you worry that you've lost the facility – on your travels. And you may well be right.'

He pondered this for a moment, 'But it's not *about* decency,' he said thickly, 'is it?'

He wasn't asserting so much as asking. Her answer plainly mattered to him.

Katherine shrugged, tipped forward slightly, inspected her skirt –

Drunk

'Nothing is immaculate,' he suddenly quoted, 'until it is consumed or distressed.'

'*Wuh?*'

She looked up again.

'It's from a song.'

Katherine struggled to pull herself out of her niche. Couldn't manage it. Wesley bent down, grabbed the band from the place it'd landed and dropped it, dismissively, into her lap. *'I welcome hurt,'* he whispered.

Katherine positioned the band between her fingers again and aimed it at him.

'Don't you fuck with Ted,' she said – her tone was menacing – 'that's *my* job.' She hiccuped. Wesley turned back to the fridge. He suddenly felt like he'd been staring into that fridge forever.

'To use a device like this,' he grumbled, 'in the middle of fucking winter. Where's the *sense* in it?'

'Oh bugger off,' Katherine mumbled, staring through the lip of the bottle to inspect the floating stub of her cigarette –

Apricot

Liquid

Burned sugar

'We'll have to run down to that bar at eight,' Wesley told Ted, his voice gentler than previously. 'I arranged to meet somebody. He said he'd take a squint at your computer.'

Ted spun around, 'He did?'

'If you're lucky.'

'It's an *Apple Mac*. Does he know about *Apple Macs*?'

'Arthur Young,' Wesley declared, 'is the fucking *Godhead* of *Apple Macs*.'

Katherine began coughing. Ted inspected his watch. His delight promptly dissipated. 'It's already eight-thirty,' he said.

'What of it?'

Wesley slammed the fridge shut (Katherine finished spluttering, wiped her nose on her arm and stretched out her legs again with a groan of relief). He took the carrot and the celery over to the table where he chopped them up, tossed them into the pot, secured the lid and slammed the whole thing into the oven.

'Now I need paper,' he told Ted. He had something to prove to her.

Ted was still standing by the sink, picking tufts of fluff from his jacket and trousers. He was looking dishevelled. His tie was askew. His jacket was off. There were spots of blood on his cuffs. He was hot.

Wesley was hot too. Even the chinchilla was panting. He strolled over and checked its water, saw it was low, took out the bottle, filled it and replaced it.

In that same corner of the kitchen (in the background Katherine was humming a paradoxically sombre version of Kabalevsky's *The Clown*) Wesley came across a stray handout from Holland and Barrett (shoved between a First Edition of Antonio Gramsci's *Prison Notebooks* and Iris Murdoch's *Nuns and Soldiers*) about the benefits of Spirulina (he'd found a jar of it languishing unopened in the empty freezer – had added four capsules to dinner). He turned it over and grabbed a pen from the table-top.

'If you refuse to come into the living room and see for yourself *you lazy, pissed-up freak,*' (the last part he murmured provocatively under his breath and Ted indicated his unease with a tiny flinch), 'then I'll prove it to you here.'

'What?'

She'd already forgotten their earlier disagreement.

(*Now she liked him. Yes she did. The way he'd taken her judgement of him and had swallowed it. She liked that. He'd never know how much – of course – until she got him into bed.*)

Wesley began writing, 'I want your opinion on this, Ted.'

Ted looked up from his watch for the second time. 'It's eight-forty,' he said, 'weren't we . . . ?'

'The way I see it,' Wesley spoke as he wrote (in longhand) the same word several times over, 'the only real threat to the future of our culture – insofar as the concept of "our culture" means a damn thing any more – is the universal inclination towards what Alvin Toffler calls *The Alien Time Sense.*' He glanced up. 'People no longer have any concept of real time, Ted. You must see this every day in your own particular line of work; the breaking of appointments, the financial overstretching, the desire to represent the self through the conduit of property – wall colour – decoration – the *hunger* . . . Toffler says the rot set in with the burger.'

Ted struggled to grasp what Wesley was telling him. The struggle ended with his use of the word *alien*.

'Everything takes,' Wesley continued (writing again), 'just as long as it takes. Never lose the sense of how long something should be in *actual* time, Ted. A death. A dream. A meal. A transaction. To wait well is to truly express your lack of alienation from what is *actual*. When I make people take pause it's really a kind of reaching out. It's like a giant bear-hug from an alternate time-frame.' He shrugged, 'I think about this kind of stuff a lot when I'm out walking.'

Katherine expectorated, noisily, from the corner.

'Alien Time . . .' Ted parroted, endearingly.

'*We* are the aliens, Ted. The alien is progress. We scapegoat the stranger, but the stranger is the alien within us. The alien is what we aspire to. He abducts. He steals the earth and brings modernity. He comes from another planet. He laughs at the mundanity of nature. His world is *nowhere* to him. He seeks only to invade and to pilfer . . .'

'*You* are the alien, then, you pretentious fucker,' Katherine interjected, gurgling on cocoa.

Wesley ignored her. He continued talking, without drawing breath, 'The alien, Ted, has no constraints. He is both what we crave and what we fear. We have wrung the neck of time, Ted. And in the process we have asphyxiated *our own reality*. Urban man lives only in dreaming.'

Wesley completed his task the same moment he finished speaking. He carried the results of his labours to Ted, flashed them at him, then squatted down next to Katherine.

'Take a squint.'

He passed the paper to her. Katherine took it, frowned and peered. She read it, laboriously, '*C-u-n-t,*' she said.

'No. Try the one below. Take your time. Experience the complexity.'

'*C-u-n-t,*' she repeated, jiggling her knees –
Pale knees
Two field mushrooms on a damp Autumn pasture

Wesley inspected the paper again himself, 'No. Make some bloody effort.'

She opened her mouth for the third time.

'*Aunt,*' Wesley interrupted, snatching the paper back again, 'a-u-n-t. That's what I wrote. But I did it longhand. I never join my downstrokes to my . . . It's my style. It means . . .'

'Unreliable,' Katherine said, 'you're an unreliable little turd. Sometimes vicious. You kill birds. You hide inside horses. You reject good chocolate. You abuse the gentle.'

'The point I'm making,' Wesley talked over her, 'is that I have an *aunt* in the area. And I was thinking about her a little earlier when I was playing with your sand. I wrote aunt. Therein lies the confusion. I did not call you a cunt. You called yourself that.'

'Where?' Ted glanced up from his fluff-infested trousers.

'South Benfleet. My father's younger sister, Penelope. Married to an ex-vicar. We don't speak.'

'So you're telling me,' Katherine was suddenly slurring her words, 'that your aunt is a *cunt*?'

(She pronounced it *caaant* for added humour.)

'You're so *funny*,' Wesley chuckled, 'it's no wonder every twelve-year-old boy in this town beats a path to your door.'

Ted's eyes widened. His thoughts turned to Bo.

Katherine scowled.

'This woman I once dated . . .' Wesley turned back to Ted, 'the female with the antique pond . . .'

Ted's head jerked up –

Pond

'she was a Careers Consultant with a major Bank. They analysed your writing – just as a matter of course – before they'd make you a job offer. I write with my left hand now the right one's gone. It makes me a whole lot scruffier.

'But what do they read into that? The truth is that these people will fuck you up just for being *who you are*, they will *reject* you for being yourself – the product of their environment – the product of *capitalism* – and that is fucking *sinful*.'

'I need a fag,' Katherine said, reaching up and grappling around blindly on the counter above her.

'This guy I knew on the markets,' Wesley continued, reaching for the cigarette packet and knocking one out for her – finding a lighter hidden inside the packet too, removing it – 'got pissed up then fell asleep in the shed where we all stored our stalls at night. Had a fag in his hand. Burned everything to shit. Himself included.'

'Did he die?'

(A flutter of interest in Katherine's grey-blue eyes.)

'Nope,' Wesley sounded regretful, 'just burned his palm very badly. So drunk it didn't even wake him at the time. My work associate – Trevor – pulled him from the flames. Said he burned off all his pubic hair. He was having a . . . you know: markets – stalls – sheds . . .'

'No I don't know,' Katherine interjected.

'What did you sell?' Ted asked.

Katherine was battling with her lighter.

'Fruit.'

Wesley grabbed the lighter and lit the cigarette for her.

'What kind of fruit?' Ted asked.

'*Fruit.*'

He looked around him. 'There's no ashtrays,' he said.

'It's actually ten to nine,' Ted interjected.

Wesley ignored him and sat down on the floor next to Katherine, stretching out his legs and placing the piece of paper between his knees. He then deftly folded it, tore it into two perfect squares, took one of these squares and began folding again in earnest.

'What're you doing?' Katherine exhaled smoke at him.

'You stink of violets,' Wesley said.

'Pardon?'

'You smell of violets.'

'Pardon?'

'According to Freud, violets have strong psychological implications.'

'Pardon?'

'Violence.'

'Huh?'

'Violets . . . *Violence.* You have an aggressive scent.'

'*Grrrrrrrrr.*' Katherine snarled at him.

Wesley smiled. '*Katherine Turpin suddenly found herself possessed . . .*' he told her softly, folding all the more deftly, pulling corners, inverting points, twisting, doubling back, '*by the uncontrollable spirit,*' he finished with a flourish and held what he'd made out to her, '*of a bear.*'

Katherine peered at it.

'Just like Jim Morrison,' she said.

'I believe it was a Native American in that instance.'

'You are so clever,' she said, and took the object from him, 'although it's a shitty little *squirrel*, in actual fact.'

'Squirrels can be very aggressive,' Wesley demurred, 'and they have a profound spiritual aspect.'

'Can I have a look?' Ted asked.

Wesley snatched the squirrel from Katherine and passed it over. Ted smiled at it.

'How'd you learn to do that?' Katherine asked.

'Therapy for my hand. I had a specialist who recommended origami to improve coordination. This was during the short phase when I convinced myself that I *wanted* to be better. Now I understand that the concept of "better" is just an evil myth put about by fascist medical practitioners.'

While he was speaking, Wesley was folding. This time the object was easier to assemble.

'Guess,' he said, holding it up to Ted.

Ted frowned.

'Your parents named you after this man.'

'Ted fucking *Heath*,' Katherine spluttered.

'Correct.'

He handed the plain *origami* head to her.

'I must learn how to do that,' she mused, 'do you play mah'jong by any chance?'

'I have a book in my rucksack by Robert Harbin,' he said, ignoring her question. 'He's the best we British have: a serious folder, but with a great sense of humour. The Japs and the Yanks are rather more po-faced about it.'

Wesley unfolded Ted Heath and refolded. Katherine watched on, fascinated.

'Ashtray,' he said, pushing it across the tiles at her and springing to his feet, 'dinner will be in about an hour. Take that wing off. It's cutting into your neck. We're going to the pub.'

'Bar.' Ted picked up his jacket.

'Spot on, Ted,' Wes smiled, grabbing a chunk of Katherine's chocolate, 'you're so reliably . . .' he placed it on his tongue and sucked for a moment, '*chilli*,' he said.

Ted frowned, struggling to assimilate this compliment as he followed him out.

Twenty-five

Oh yes he was *in* alright, but he'd left the lights off as a precaution;
a safeguard –
All the better to . . .
Shut-up
   Preferred the calm of the dark after the strain of work. There was
nothing . . . nothing *untoward* in it. Nothing at all. It was simply a
quirk. A preference.
   Came home – in fact – slightly later than usual –
No hard and fast rules in this line of business
– once the sun had set and the coy suggestion of rain (its soothing,
fog-tinged sussurations) looked like turning into something more
chilling –
No point . . .
   Outdoor job, close to the Dutch Village; pulling down a turn-of-
the-century summerhouse –
Criminal
– beautiful old thing –
Hooligan
   Doing what he could to salvage the best of the fine painted
timber –
That gorgeous, old-fashioned lead-based grey-green colour
Peeling off in voluptuous curls under the heavy pressure of a
clumsy finger
– piled it into the back of his Mazda. Threw a heavy plastic sheet
over, for the journey –

Cat sat under a Euphorbia bush

Just watching
Gold eye
Jumped out of its bones when the roof caved in
Belted towards the conservatory

After all that commotion (and during, even, basking beneath it) . . .
That high-pitched stillness of ocean-floor
Canvey
Quiet
Birds a-bed by three
      No point in . . .
   Shoved the wood into storage on the Charfleets at the workshop.
Might make a –
Time allowing . . .
– Might make a fine, glass-fronted bookcase, like his Great Aunt
Mathilda in Poole'd had, when he was a boy – full of fascinating
books about mineralogy.
      Arrived home at six, work and worry-weary. Anxiety still grinding
away inside of him – not stationary, but moving –
Back and forth, back and forth
– like a sharp-toothed saw, hacking and hewing.
      Parked the car in the lock-up out the rear. Crept into the house
the back way –
Nothing to apologise for
– took a quick shower. Was standing at that window twenty
minutes later; scent of Brylcreem and Imperial Leather . . .
Hmmn
      Slow, to begin with.
      Then the two old boys came; the one whose son had . . . but
who still persisted (he was the first – sat down under the streetlight and messed about with his bootlaces). Next up, the igno-
rant one in the hat and the glasses clambering out of a white
van –
Contravening just about every bloody . . .
      The Police –
Double yellow
There's justice for you
– and the girl – the boy-girl from earlier – walking in the gutter:

hood up – forward – back. Light striking her face; like a small, sharp, well-peeled shallot –

Plain

Clean

Neat as . . .

Small terrier, dancing hyperactively –

Despicable breed

Estate agent at Katherine's front window –

Briefly

The Police making their way over, knocking . . .

Dewi held his breath.

Had a suspicion – more than a suspicion – that he was *in* there (should've got home earlier. Should've ripped that senseless agent limb-from-limb: Edward – *Edward*, damn him – he of *all* people should've known better).

Ted opened the door and ushered . . . ushered . . .

Everybody but the one person who . . .

Dewi rubbed his hands across his face (hands still smelled of wood varnish, underneath). The rain came again, light as icing sugar tipped from a shaker.

He waited –

Waited

The white van suddenly left with a ferocious screeeeech.

He closed his eyes –

Barn Owl

Keening for its mate in the damp-blanket night

He opened his eyes again.

Now only the girl remained –

Little cocktail onion

Clean as a whistle

Pickled in sweet vinegar

And then –

No

– almost as if she suddenly –

No

– almost as if she instinctively –

No

She turned around and looked straight into him –

Blackness
Tiny pickling
– and spoke –
Little lamb
Bleating into steam
Bleating into nothing
   It was then, and then only, that he finally knew Josephine.

These situations were the stuff of comedy, Katherine mused, if it wasn't *you*, and they weren't constantly happening, and you weren't constantly *pissed*, and your bladder wasn't *exploding*, and the doorbell wasn't ringing and ringing and *ringing* –
Stuck
   Managed to drop her fag into her lap. Retrieved it with a yelp, but moved much too quickly, yanking the wire (if possible) even tighter around her throat –
Stuck
The indignity!
   How did she . . . ?
   How had she . . . ?
   And to be discovered by *Dewi*. To be *found* that way –
Spare key under the little pot-bound bay tree
– and then to try and explain, but the words wouldn't come and . . .
And the way he'd *looked* –

'Did he do this to you?'

He kept . . . He kept . . .

'Did he push you in here?'
'Did he tie this wire around your throat?'
'Why do I smell burning?'
'Why are you bleeding?'
'Why all these feathers everywhere?'

When he lifted her – like she was a newborn kitten – so gently –

Those reliable hands
Voice running fast and smooth as a sea-bound river
– and pulled her free and untangled her and re-aligned her and rearranged her . . .

She was . . .

She *felt* . . .

But to see her so . . .

Urgh!

'Just . . . just hold on a second, Katherine . . . Why are . . . ? Where are you . . . ?'

Hand over her mouth, she ran to the toilet, nearly pissing on the tiles before she made it there. Found the door – the bolt – pulled it sharply across – lunged for the bowl – the pan – the sink –

Anywhere

He kept on calling through the door –

And calling

Like in a dream

– and the calling would only –

It must end

It must end

– the calling would only *stop* once she'd told him where they were –

The *bar*. The fucking *BAR*.

It was *torture*.

And then, once she'd told him –

I TOLD YOU, DIDN'T I?

– he'd only go when he was *entirely* certain that she was . . .

That she'd be . . .

Oh the caring! So unbearable!

'I'M FINE. *GET THE FUCK OUT OF HERE!*'

She told the towel and the tiles and the toilet paper. She told her knickers and her elbows and her pubic hair –

So sordid, this thin body

So soiled

– 'GET OUT AND *JUST LEAVE ME!*'

He promised her faithfully – pressing down on the door handle,

whispering, his lips pressed first into the wood, then into the metal
– that he wouldn't, he *wouldn't* . . .

He would not interfere.

Ted made them pause for a moment under the bus shelter so that
he could call his aunt and warn her . . .

'Just leave it in the oven, Auntie. I can't . . . Well, if you're
worried, turn it off. I can always heat it up later . . . No, that's . . .
I . . . It's very . . . Don't miss your . . .'

(Wesley'd kindly loaned him his phone for the call's duration,
then briskly took it off him again once the conversation was
over.)

And they'd hardly . . . they'd barely got in through the door –
Smoke and beer and condensation
Fug
The sudden quiet
The stink of chicken wings in spicy . . .
– before this crazy fucking Welsh *mountain* came tumbling in after
them; howling, *wounded*. Like an injured stag after the rut. Tossing
his head. *Baying*. Rearing up.

Wesley (in the three previous seconds) saw the thin man – Art –
straightening up by the bar – his face – a look of . . .

The Policewoman, deep in conversation . . .

The ceiling fan . . .

A spare chair by the . . .
Huh!

Ted had . . . Ted put out his . . . Ted was grabbing his . . .
Didn't . . .
Tried to . . .
Turned towards . . .

FUUURRGH!!

Nose-spit-teeth-splinter-feet-neck-hand-table-elbow
Floor-Floor-Floor

Had to –
Wuh?
– had to stand up –
If I am to die then let it at least be on my . . .
– stand up –
Woooooooo-oooo-ooooh!
That was . . . that was . . .
Air like a merry-go-colour-splattered-whizzz-sniff-blood
   He glanced around him –
Each and every individual thing as bright as bright as . . .

CRUNCH!

– Was felled like a tree for a second time.

Hang on . . .
   – Wooden boards. Soles and shoes and fag butts and bottle
tops and –
Dé-jà . . .
Did I not just do this before?
Must . . . must get up . . .
I am . . .
I am . . .
Geauuuurgh!
– Up.
   He cocked his head –
If only I could just . . .
   Wesley blinked, bemused –
Ox, bellowing
– he blinked again –
Is this connected to me?
These strange sounds?
This garble?
Should I perhaps . . . ?
Uh . . .
   Ears: atten-*shun!*

'WHY ARE YOU *DOING* THIS TO HER?'

Ox-arm swings to contain the entire . . . the *entire* . . .

Wesley glances around the room, but not really seeing anything.

We are *all* in this, he thinks, with satisfaction – even glasses and ashtrays are implicated. What a grand *sweep* he has there. What a grand . . .

But why am I the only one he's hitting?

Wesley focusses, finally, on the ox-mountain, the fist –

Jeeeees!

– light smearing out of him –

Hooooo

Nearly slipped over . . .

Feel of table under palm – so firm – so solid

He loved that feeling, then.

This table feeling goes straight into my top ten

Oh shit

He's going to hit me again

Prepare for it

(Preparing makes it worse, actually)

Who said that?

Uh . . .

Wah?

He spun around, unsteadily –

There is other stuff

Other

Something high-pitched

From the . . . the . . . the . . .

Back

I hear a little bird singing

She is saying . . .

Hang –

Hang –

Hang on . . .

Whisky-whisky-whisky-eyes?

I think I saw this girl in a dream once and she stabbed me to death with an icicle

And Ted is . . . Ted is . . .
Wesley turned his head –
The thin man . . .
I am . . .

There is a big, black gap, and it . . .
Wooahh!
. . . and it doesn't make any . . .
Wesley took one huge, exploratory step –
I am Mr Neil Armstrong,
And I need to . . . to . . . to . . . to
. . . guh . . .

Twenty-six

Barflies,
This is just a stopover;
105, maximum.
Please do not tarry,
For the sense God gave you will not do you good
Where all is equal – twelve foot under.
Remember The Phoenician
Whose handsome bones were picked in whispers?
Remember Phlebas?
Listen to the waves,
Hear them calling . . .
Kew-we-we-wu
Leading you ever-onward to sweeter nothing

A tall, rather ineffectual looking, ginger-haired man was suddenly introducing himself to Arthur – gently and very formally – halfway up the seven front steps of the old Rio Bingo Hall (or, to give it its proper title – and neither man was anything if not absolutely punctilious in such matters – the *Canvey Leisure Centre*; substantial physical evidence of which buzzed and blinked balefully above them in foot-high, luminous, black and yellow lettering).

He snaked his hand across the front of Wesley's belly.

'I'm Edward, Wesley's estate agent,' he said, stammering a little, 'and I'm not . . . I'm not *involved*, directly.' His eyes unfocussed for a moment and his hand went limp. 'I mean, not . . . not *directly*,' he repeated, with just a fraction less certainty.

Wesley was currently unable to stand unsupported. He had an arm around each of Ted and Arthur's shoulders. His chin was cut and pinkening-up, while the usually unobtrusive cheekbone under his left eye was highlighted by a white-green bump.

Many people watched them from the opposite pavement, restrained by – and lounging against – the pedestrian railings. About a dozen or so; fifteen, maybe.

Arthur heartily wished it would rain and drive them all back inside again. He wasn't accustomed to the attention. Didn't thrill to it, particularly.

He adjusted Wesley's weight and then shook Edward's hand.

'I'm Art,' he said, 'we were supposed to be meeting up in the bar. My involvement is . . .' he paused, thoughtfully, '*tangential.*'

Ted looked impressed (to understand so completely – so *effortlessly* – your relation to a situation was creditable enough, but then to have a wide-ranging *vocabulary* with which to express it? That was . . . that truly *was* compelling).

In those few, brief seconds Arthur fully apprehended Ted's gullible nature –

Oh Arthur Young

You stinking liar

'I suppose it might be . . .' he muttered, glancing around him shiftily –

Stinking

Stinking

'It might be a good idea to take him somewhere a little more . . .'

Not long before the rest of the pack get wind of this in the Lobster Smack

Come storming on over

'To take him somewhere a little more . . .' he repeated, staggering slightly.

Wesley was heavy. Arthur'd seen the punches he'd taken. Wouldn't be surprised if he suffered major concussion, although –

Frankly

– this might be . . . *uh* . . .

Quite useful, really

'I have the keys . . .' Ted whispered, pointing back across the road,

274

'to the agency. But with the picture window and everything . . . it's all fairly public. There's a back room – a bathroom – but it's really much too tiny . . .'

Arthur was momentarily concerned about his rucksack – still in the bar. And the girl. The local girl. He couldn't help wondering whether . . . if she . . .

That was quite some display she'd put on in there. Saved Wesley's bacon –

More's the damn pity

– although he couldn't –

This is ridiculous

– help – *well* – secretly admiring her *chutzpah* (however deranged), her crazed intrepidity.

The big, wild, Welsh *moose*, meanwhile – Arthur surreptitiously noted –

A coward? Moi?

– was being led – unrestrained – to the back of a police car. He offered no resistance. He seemed perfectly sober. Even in the unhealthy, inconsistent yellow-white of several passing headlights he looked to be a . . . a *reasonable* enough chap –

We're on the same side here

Remember that

A black-haired man clambered up the steps behind them and patted Arthur (Arthur flinched) –

Oi! Hands off!

– on the shoulder (a greasy looking creature in a mac. He'd noticed him tormenting the local girl earlier. He'd seen him go through the pockets of her coat. Wouldn't trust him an *inch* if it actually came down to it).

'Excuse me,' Bo panted jovially, proffering Arthur his rucksack, 'I believe this is yours.'

He handed it over, with a puff, 'What've you *got* in there, mate? Solid gold ingots? A 200cc bike engine? Your horse-shoe collection?'

He was speaking to Arthur but had eyes only for Wesley.

'Thanks,' Arthur took the bag – God it *was* heavy – and half-slung it over his shoulder.

Wesley lifted his head, blinked twice at the stranger and spoke an entire sentence, in perfect order, 'I will never sleep again,' he stated emphatically. 'And that is very, very *fucking* sad.'

'Not feeling too good there, then, Wes?' Bo asked.

Wesley shook his head, violently. 'I will *not* feel,' he told him, 'and you will not *bloody* make me.'

Ted glanced over at Arthur, trying to send him a warning look. 'Perhaps we should . . .' he said. (Needed to get Wesley away from . . . as a matter of some . . . but without . . .)

'Oh *shit* man. My nails are growing like *ivy* . . .'

Wesley was staring at his right hand now, full of wonder.

There were no fingers on this hand. No nails. No greenery.

Fortunately they were saved by the doctor.

'I'm the doctor,' he barked, materialising – without any kind of prompting – at Ted's elbow, and holding up his doctor's briefcase. He was a very small man but exceedingly charismatic.

'Where can we take him? We need to sit him down. We need clean water. We need calm. We need . . .'

'I'm wondering if there's any particular *reason* that you should choose to return to Canvey at this point, Wes . . . ?' Bo continued, doggedly.

'Hydrangea . . . *stranger*,' Wesley pondered this distinction.

Bo whipped a high-tech palm from his pocket, flipped it open and removed the metal pen.

'A kind of . . . of plant . . . or . . . or *flower* . . . ?' he questioned, starting to scribble.

'*Quiet*,' the doctor snapped, 'for *God's sake* let's get him out of this circus.'

'Over the road,' Arthur nodded to the bag-bringer a second time. 'Much obliged again,' he said, pushing past him.

'I can carry it for you, if you like,' the greasy-haired man offered, finishing scribbling and then sticking the contraption hurriedly back into his pocket . . . 'or take a turn with Wes, even . . .'

The doctor, however (almost as if sensing the threat Bo posed), was having none of it. 'No stragglers,' he growled, 'just give *me* the bag and let's get moving shall we?'

Arthur passed the bag over and they staggered off down the steps again, around the railings, across the road, back through the small crowd of onlookers. Ted found his keys and opened the agency's front door. He reached over for the light switch, automatically.

'No lights,' the doctor instructed, dumping Arthur's bag with a grunt and pointing to the swivel chair, 'put him down on that. Do you have a bathroom, a secure room? Anything approaching?'

Ted pointed, 'But it isn't very . . .'

The doctor indicated towards the front door, 'I want you to lock it and stand guard. And you . . .' he nodded to Arthur, 'help me push him out into the back space.'

Arthur did as he was instructed. Wesley sat slackly on the chair, meanwhile, emitting a curious whistling sound – as if communicating in whale – while they struggled to shove him. The chair's wheels kept buckling. He almost fell off and tried to stand. The doctor pushed him back down again, a fraction aggressively, Arthur felt – *no finesse* – Arthur hated doctors. They were all fucking Luddites.

Once they'd found their way into it, the small bathroom did indeed seem exceptionally cramped. Smelled of . . . (Arthur sneezed. He was echoed, in kind, by Wesley) . . . of *wax*. The doctor had a torch in his pocket. He took it out and turned it on. He shone it into Wesley's face. Wesley closed his eyes.

'*Owwwwww*,' he groaned, abandoning all pretensions to bravery.

'Open your eyes,' the doctor said.

Wesley just smiled.

'You need to help me, Wesley, to help yourself,' the doctor yapped.

Over by the front door, meanwhile, Art noticed how –
Oh come on
– greasy-locks was trying to persuade Ted (through the window and by a series of intimidating mimes) that he should open up. Ted was at the point of yielding when Art swung rapidly past him to check on his bag. The buckles were all secure, but he still wasn't . . .

'Journalist?' he muttered, keeping his head down.

'Uh, *yes*,' Ted said, nodding, smiling bravely at Bo, trying to look obliging.

'Hand the keys over,' Arthur straightened up. He tried his best to look officious. To look menacing.

277

This small charade had little effect, however, since Bo had already been distracted by a second man at the window who was mouthing the words, 'My *case* . . . he's got my . . .'

'Go keep an eye on Wesley,' Art said.

Bo was now engaging in conversation with this second man. A woman joined the fray. She seemed equally fascinated by what he was saying.

'I don't know if Wesley mentioned,' Ted murmured as he made his way haltingly over to the back room, 'but he did say you might take a look at my . . .'

He pointed, limply –

Computer

The woman was now indicating to Arthur that he should unlock the door. She was very pushy. Arthur recognised her from the bar as the infernally opinionated blabbermouth who'd been bending the local girl's ear –

Bitch

'Not *now*, obviously,' Ted continued, 'but maybe . . .'

He stopped abruptly.

'Oh.'

Art glanced over his shoulder, 'What's up?'

Ted was frowning back at him, through the half-light. The bossy woman was now knocking on the glass, very emphatically.

'I'm afraid the doctor's locked the door,' Ted announced.

'*You* locked the door,' Art answered, 'and I'm glad you did. This woman's a bloody menace.'

'Her name's Anna,' Ted mumbled, 'and she's a plain clothes police officer.'

'*Balls*,' Art turned back to inspect her properly. She'd taken out her wallet and was holding up her badge.

'. . . although for what it's worth I actually meant the *bathroom* door,' Ted tentatively continued.

'*Huh*?'

Arthur wasn't concentrating.

'I said the doctor's locked himself in with Wesley. I just heard the catch slip . . .' Ted tried the handle. It was definitely locked.

'*What*?' Art was befuddled. He turned back around again. Ted had his ear pressed to the crack.

'and whatever's going on in there, it doesn't sound . . . well not . . . not *medical* . . . more . . .' Art jogged over, tried the handle, pushed the door, swore.

'more like a kind of *water* torture,' Ted finished up.

Art put his own ear to the doorframe.

Yes indeed

Something . . .

Something distinctly liquid . . .

The policewoman was now knocking so loudly that he could barely make out the words . . . but what he *could* hear sounded suspiciously . . .

Phlebas? What's *that* all about, *huh*?

(Water splashing)

Huh? . . . The . . . stupid *cat* poems. I know *exactly* what you're playing at . . .

(More water)

Are . . . *hearing* me, you slippery little . . .

(Still more water)

'How could we be so *stupid*?' Arthur yelled, and kicked the door in fury, then looked down at the offending boot, slightly shocked –

Did I just say that?

Out loud?

Did I just . . .

He spun around. 'We need to get inside there, and quick,' he said, 'that guy's obviously some kind of maniac.'

Ted nodded – but nervously – as if Arthur himself might just as easily be the one worth worrying about. He stood awaiting instructions, though, perfectly obligingly.

Arthur was inspecting the handle. He tested it again with his hand. His mind was turning –

If this man . . .

If he . . .

It'll save me the . . .

'We'll have to knock it down,' he announced, 'go and let the cop in.'

He threw the keys to Ted. Ted missed the catch. Arthur took a few steps back and braced himself. Ted picked up the keys and ran. 'You could always try . . .' he called.

Arthur threw himself, bodily – shoulder first – against the door-frame. The door shook.

'. . . *reasoning* with him,' Ted concluded, wincing in tandem with the wood's shuddering. He unlocked the front door and Anna charged in, dragging another straggler behind her but slamming it – unceremoniously – in Bo's face.

'This man has had his case stolen,' she announced. 'Where's the light?'

She found the light switch and turned it on just in time to see Arthur flinging himself against the door for a second time. It shook again, but not very impressively.

'*Police!*' he gasped, trying to put the impostor on his mettle.

'Don't be yelling that,' Anna calmly interrupted, walking over, 'it's not your place.'

Arthur turned and gave her a look of critical incomprehension.

'The doctor's got Wesley locked in the back,' Ted jumped in, 'we think he's . . .'.

'It wasn't one of these two,' the new man clarified (over the babble), 'but a tiny, funny-looking *little* chap . . .'

A loud crash resounded inside the small room. A subsequent *kerfuffle* (rather drawn out) sounding not unlike a fist fight interspersed with successive shards of glass falling.

Ted covered his mouth with his hand. 'Not the *mirror*,' he whispered.

'Stand back,' the officer instructed. Arthur was barely out of the way before she'd karate kicked the door open (it shuddered defiantly in its frame, but remained aligned) and entered.
Shit

Wesley stood, his hair, face and chest dripping wet – eyebrows raised slightly – over by the toilet cubicle, brown tape looped around his wrists and covering his mouth. The doctor was crushed behind the door, bent over the sink, his forehead bleeding (the swivel chair pinning him into an uneasy submission).

'I want to charge this man with assault,' he gurgled in a worryingly high-pitched voice, pointing over towards Wesley.

'I want this man charged with *theft*,' the second stranger

announced, pushing his arm around the door and pulling his briefcase out of the fray.

The officer yanked off Wesley's mouth tape, 'Well we're certainly keeping very *busy* tonight, aren't we, sir?'

Wesley drew a deep breath.

She was standing very close to him.

Arthur could've sworn –

Oh God forbid

– that some kind of subterranean sexual *frisson* passed between them.

Wesley turned to Arthur. '*Never* the shoulder, Art,' he panted informatively, trying to flick some of the water from his eyes, '*always* the foot . . .' he tiredly re-enacted the relevant manoeuvre, 'and as near-as-dammit to the lock.'

The policewoman pulled the tape from his wrists as Arthur watched on. Ted continued staring at the doctor as if still unable to entirely comprehend his shattered credibility. The doctor – apparently in no hurry to make any kind of escape – was gazing into the only remaining piece of mirror still hanging above the sink – a tiny oblong – hungrily exploring the depth and extent of the wound to his forehead.

'I just don't understand . . .' Ted said (suddenly almost angry), 'why you'd tape up his mouth if all you wanted was *answers* . . .'

Wesley smiled at Ted's indignance. 'This is *Furby*, Ted,' he explained gently, pulling some extraneous tape adhesive from around his lips, 'he's my greatest fan. He gave me . . .' he pulled back his sleeve – matter-of-factly – to reveal the vicious scar from what looked like a long stab wound to his left forearm, '*this* little beauty while I was still sleeping, Christmas morning, two years ago, and *this* . . .' he pulled back his shirt collar to reveal a shorter less specific area of scarring across the top of his right shoulder, 'last February when he ran me down on a stolen moped. He isn't really interested in answers. He's much more interested in . . .' he chuckled, almost fondly, 'in celebrating the whole process of *asking*.'

Ted frowned. He didn't understand why it was that Wesley was being so flippant. Shouldn't he at least be angry – or indignant – or . . . or scared?

Wes pointed towards the mirror, weakly, 'Seven long years . . . huh?' He rubbed his hands over his face, slicked back his wet hair, grinned.

'I'm afraid I'm going to have to insist that you accompany . . .' the female officer interrupted him (as further back-up started arriving).

'And screw me . . .' Wesley deadpanned smartly –

He loved the pain

Oh God he loved it

'if it hasn't already bloody started.'

Twenty-seven

Her face was now so well acquainted with the tiles at the base of the toilet that the shallow dip – the path, the furrow, the *indentation* – between the particular two upon which she'd rested her heavy head had etched a matching ridge into the soft flesh of her cheek. Even her lower lip had a special . . . a brief and tender little *pucker* in it.

Katherine gently ran her thumb across this fault-line – this rift – as she gazed – red-eyed – at her reflection in the mirror. Her bath was running –

Hot

Steaming

– and the mirror was gradually condensing over. She coughed, clutched at her head, shivered –

That's no bad thing, either

– and turned away.

In the roar of the water she could just about decipher the softest –

Knocking, was it?

– pounding.

A fault with the plumbing? A kink in the boiler? Her heart racing? Her blood pumping? The early warning signs of a migraine?

She slowly rotated her head on her shoulders – so stiff it made a sound like a pepper grinder – then took off her apricot dress (the burn on her lap made her tut, miserably), her vests, her shift, her bra and dropped them all onto the floor. She stood there in her knickers, pushing a heavy hand through her knotted hair. She rubbed her eyes and suddenly remembered that her essential bath oil –

Six sweet drops
Lavender
– was still sitting on her bedside table, next to her oil-burner.

She staggered to the door, shoved back the bolt and yanked it open; a plume of hot, misty air burst out ahead of her, almost entirely enveloping the person standing there.

Katherine screamed.

Even as she screamed she realised that she wasn't really the screaming kind. Her voice was too low. She sounded like a drag queen who'd just broken a false nail five minutes before a big show. It made her head hurt, her throat, tensed the muscles in her neck; and valuable seconds were all but throttled inside this vile and piercing clamour.

But –

Aw, heck
– it was too late to take it back.

'I'm so *sorry*,' Eileen gasped – pushing herself up hard against the opposite wall, utterly panicked (almost tripping over a broken coffee percolator Katherine had casually stored down there) – 'but the front door was . . . and I wanted . . . I've come about . . . Wesley said . . .' She was staring – round-eyed, aghast – at Katherine's breasts.

Katherine made no effort to cover herself up. She stood tall and puffy-eyed in just her knickers and her scratches.

'Wesley isn't here,' she put her hand to her throat, scowling, 'but it's open fucking *house* in this place today, so you just come right in – stroll through my front door – swan about in my hallway – kick my old percolator – gaze at my *tits* like they're out on display in a tabloid fucking *newspaper*. You do *just* as you like, okay?'

Eileen shifted her stare. Her eyes were almost teary. She was shaking slightly.

'I came about the . . . the *bird*,' she murmured –

Not . . . Not . . . Not . . .

Katherine continued to scowl at her. 'It's in the kitchen,' she pointed – slightly mystified, 'through there.'

Eileen followed the direction of Katherine's finger with her dreamy blue eyes –

'Is it alright if I just . . . ?'

She ducked her head, apologetically.

'Sure.' Katherine grabbed a towel and wrapped it around her as Eileen scurried on ahead. She was wearing a pair of tan, stretch-fabric ski-pants, some little brown boots, a caramel-coloured winter coat with a silk scarf tied around her head. The scarf was pink with tiny, beautifully-painted cowrie-shells and whelk-shells and sting-winkles on it.

'I like your scarf,' Katherine growled, still finding some difficulty in placing one foot in front of the other.

'Thank you.' Eileen smoothed a nervous hand over it as she disappeared into the kitchen.

When Katherine re-entered this room herself, everything seemed very bright to her. She tried to adjust her eyes, blinked a few times. The whole area was still awash in feathers. Wesley's rucksack sat in the corner. It was very hot – smelled of booze and sweat and cigarettes.

'So he invited you to dinner?' Katherine croaked, trying not to see the room the way Eileen was seeing it, but grabbing a broom from behind the door and circling the table, leaning heavily on it. She bent down – almost lost her towel, nearly toppled right over – and picked up the heron's wings; hanging the one still on its wire over the back of the chair, placing the other onto the seat.

Eileen was looking around her, confusedly. She was staring at the wings, frowning at the feathers.

'I don't understand,' she said, 'where is he?'

She gazed over towards the chinchilla's cage, almost as though half-expecting to see the wild bird crammed in there.

'The oven,' Katherine indicated with her head (winced), 'it's been cooking for just over an hour.'

Eileen still didn't seem to understand, so she pointed towards the bird's head, still lying – gold-green-eyed, harpoon-beaked – on the table. Wesley's vicious bone-handled hunting knife lay just beyond it.

Eileen's scarf fell back from her face. Her mouth dropped open. She put up her hand to try and disguise her astonishment.

'Oh my God,' Katherine murmured, 'how did you scratch . . .'

And then – hard upon it – 'Oh *fuck*, my *bath*.'

She careered off, unsteadily, down the corridor.

When she finally got there the water was almost running over. She turned off the tap, reached down for the plug, released it, discovered – with a gurgle of rage and a shudder – that the tap had run cold. The bath was lukewarm.

She let it drain –

Screw the bloody environment

– cursing.

When she returned to the kitchen, pulling on her clothes again – catching her fingers in her clasps – noisily haranguing her ineffectual water-heating system; the librarian, the *chief* librarian: her brown boots, her shell scarf, her ski-pants, her scratches, her look of gently haunted bemusement, had all miraculously evaporated.

Along with – Katherine harrumphed so violently that a single, thin apricot strap fell charmingly from her shoulder – Wesley's best knife, and that poor, that old, that undeniably beautiful but exceedingly dead heron's head.

Twenty-eight

Doc held up his hands to silence the others.

'Furby's back,' he announced (to general consternation), 'and there's been an almighty rumpus. Wesley got punched out in a bar by a local man. The girl – Josephine Bean – stepped in and saved him; breaching pretty much every notable Law of Following in the process, God Bless her. Then immediately after, Michael Furby – posing as a doctor – locked Wesley inside a toilet cubicle, gagged him, bound him, and tried to drown him in the pan.'

Doc's initial words were greeted by a shocked – if appreciative – silence, but by the time he'd finished, derisory snorts and hoots were sounding from all quarters. Ale had been drunk (in prodigious quantities. Even the terrier had partaken – his blood-sugar levels having been soberly calculated, well prior). A game of trumps was still in progress.

'I'm serious,' Doc hotly defended his bulletin, 'the shit's really hit the fan out there. Wesley smashed Furby into a bathroom mirror – my source tells me that they were in the toilets out the back of the estate agency – gave him thirteen stitches in his forehead, apparently, and now he's fully intent on pressing charges.'

Hands of cards were placed down onto the table. Shoes had been winning. He placed his hand down last of all.

'What happened with the girl?' he asked – he had a special interest in the girl; the nurse. 'How exactly did she save him?'

At this point Herbie arrived back from the urinal, his white stick tapping firmly into legs and tiles and tables, his free hand still fiddling with his fly.

'So you finally wound up your little *tête-à-tête* with the journalist?' he muttered, having recognised the timbre of Doc's voice from a distance.

'I did,' Doc nodded, 'it's been absolute bloody chaos out there. Wesley's over at the Cop Shop. He got soundly thrashed by a local lad. And Furby's back with a vengeance. This time . . .' there was almost a chuckle in Doc's voice, 'this time posing as a medical practitioner.'

Herbie's face remained blank. He found nothing to amuse him in Furby's antics. Furby was a pest. At best.

'Did you think to ask your source whether Wesley plans to press charges himself?' Hooch enquired, a canny expression enveloping his features.

'Course I did. He said he didn't think so – and seemed rather surprised at it – which I was very happy with, as answers go.'

'But Wesley *never* presses . . .' Shoes interjected.

'Exactly,' Herbie turned on him, 'that's how he went about testing the calibre of our informant, you cretin.'

'Ah.' Shoes looked down, somewhat regretfully, at his hand again.

'And so you swallowed all that crap he told you about Richard F and the toilet bowl?' the blind man persisted.

Doc looked up. Herbie hadn't been party to the earlier segments of his exposition. This meant . . . He rapidly mapped out the pub's geography in his mind – distance between the men's lavatories and the icy back beer patio where his conversation with The Source had been furtively undertaken (waves splashing against the shingle just a few feet behind them).

Hmmn

It wasn't inconceivable that Herb'd been eavesdropping. He certainly didn't trust him (forget what he'd said to Hooch, previously. He could be as full of bluster as the best of them. And if a certain level of disingenuousness was the price he had to pay to maintain his seniority – that peerless, nay legendary combination of involvement and fairness, distance and intimacy – then so be it.

Oh yes. It was all very finely judged. It was all riding on a thread. It was all so . . . so marginal, so *tenuous*. That was the whole point . . . that was the very *bedrock* of intelligent Following).

Doc couldn't successfully shake the suspicion that Herbie had it in mind – had always had it in mind, frankly – to impose some spuriously . . . well, *crass* sense of . . . of . . . justice on the whole exquisitely convoluted Wesley equation. To curtail him. To make him comply in some way. To watch him, to oversee, to take an active pleasure in some sort of humbling. A submission. But Wesley would never submit. He just *couldn't*. Because that would be the end of him –

The end of everything

(Herb took too much interest – point of fact – in all the money-making crap. The insignificant mechanics of the thing. Way too much interest. Tried to cover it up. Didn't always succeed. Doc'd seen him interrogating the barstaff about backhanders earlier, under the spurious guise of something more piddling.)

To make Wesley *comply*. Like some kind of hard-faced but upstanding sheriff in one of those wild west books Wesley took such delight in reading.

But why, exactly? And was he outside the game or inside it?

That was the vital thing.

'It was the sink, I reckon . . .' Shoes interrupted, 'I bet Furby was holding him over a sink full of water when Wes shot his arse back, unexpectedly, straightened up, and lifted Furby – face-first – into the mirror in front of them.'

Shoes rapidly re-enacted this manoeuvre, nearly knocking over his pint glass in the process. Hooch shot out his hand and rescued it, sucking on his teeth in fury.

'It has to be that way,' Shoes didn't appear to notice, 'nobody in their right mind hangs a mirror above a toilet. Not even an estate agent'd do that.'

'Was there a gag?' Hooch asked (keen to quickly dispel this strangely insidious agent/toilet image from his pristine consciousness).

Doc nodded, 'A Welshman, an Englishman and some fella of dubious nationality, all locked up in this toilet cubicle together . . .'

A short, confused silence . . . then Shoes guffawed. Herbie smiled, thinly. Hooch scowled. Doc put up a hand to his hot cheek –

Cracking jokes now, eh?

Only two pints down . . .

Peter, Paul and Bloody Mary, that infernal booze must be getting to me

'Ha very *ha*,' Hooch enunciated crisply.

'He did say there was tape, actually,' Doc conceded, 'brown tape.'

'That's classic Furby,' Shoes purred, 'that's him alright.'

'So he got hit in a pub . . .' Hooch had his pad out and his pencil at the ready.

'A bar. Saks. On the High Street . . .'

'But he had a deal with The Smack, didn't he? Wasn't this place supposed to be his designated watering hole in Canvey? That's why we're all sitting here, after all, forking out wadfuls of cash to cover the astronomically over-inflated beer prices . . .'

Doc suddenly began talking again, over the top of Hooch's complaining, 'About nine o'clock it was. Two punches. Very nasty. Felled him both times, apparently. Wes'd just that second walked in there with the estate agent. The other guy powered in through the door straight after . . .'

'*Ouch*,' Shoes winced, 'Double *ouch*, in fact.'

'So what did you trade with the hack, to get all this stuff out of him?' Herbie interrupted, feeling the table-top and making his way gradually back to his seat.

'I told him that the local constabulary had visited Katherine Turpin's at around nineteen-hundred hours this evening. I said I thought Wes was renting a room from her. I told him I thought it was about some of the stuff that went on in Rye over Christmas. Or maybe something to do with the Van Hougstraten prank in Brighton at New Year. All guesswork, to be honest, and stuff I'd've given to the website anyway. But he seemed satisfied with it.'

'Used to be a local hero, that bloke,' Herbie said.

'Who did?' Hooch appraised him, briefly.

'The sneak did.'

'Really?' Hooch turned back to look at him a second time.

'Bobby Mackenzie. Tennis champion. Always wears a raincoat. Notorious tit. Usually does the sports coverage for the local press. He's obviously planning to expand his brief with this.'

'Better him than that twat from the *Express*,' Hooch grimaced, 'or the slut from the *Mirror*, for that matter. She was a real handful. The Nationals are a bloody nightmare.'

'*Au contraire*,' Shoes interjected, 'the local ones are hungrier. They're the fuckers to watch out for.'

'Point is,' Doc pulled up a stool and sat down on it –

Piles

– 'we're going to have to be a little bit more flexible when it comes to information garnering while the website's down. This guy's a treat. He's a fool. He has no background in Wesley. He's not bothered by the Loiter. He's out for what he can get but he won't be a problem.'

'In your opinion,' Hooch muttered.

'I think we're always best off keeping *schtum* with the media,' Shoes cautioned. 'It's a slippery old slope, otherwise, and it makes things tricky for Wesley to have the local press snapping at his heels every second he's in a place.'

'*Fuck* Wes,' Hooch murmured, still scribbling.

'Goes with the territory,' Herbie added.

Snug on Shoes' feet beneath the table, Dennis suddenly sat up and burp-yawned, noisily.

'So tell us everything about the bar,' Hooch turned a page and continued writing. 'Where was Wes hit exactly, and what, if anything, was said?'

Doc took a sip of his pint and then brusquely back-handed his lips. '*Uh* . . . Well, like I said, Wes had just got in there, with the agent – the source said the agent's name's Edward, or Ted, and that he's great pals with the Turpin girl – and then this other guy, a local, who goes by the name of . . .' Doc inspected the palm of his hand where he'd scribbled down the details in biro, 'Dewi. Spelled with an "e". Welsh. Was in love with the Turpin girl before all the problems with the graffiti and everything . . .'

'The *moose*,' Hooch interrupted, 'from this morning. Gotta be. The shadow. The dusty one. The nut.'

'The very same,' Doc confirmed. 'Anyhow, Wes'd barely got in there before this Dewi bloke came in after him and punched him twice. Felled him twice, too. Chin, cheek . . .'

'Did he say anything,' Shoes asked, 'before he punched him?'

'No. Not at first. But he did say something in the middle of the

291

fight. He apparently shouted . . .' Doc inspected his palm, 'he said, *Why are you tormenting my Katherine? Why won't you leave her alone?* Or something approximate.'

Hooch clucked under his breath. He hated approximations.

'Turpin girl was always a slapper,' Herbie picked up his pint glass, 'she enjoys the notoriety. Her father left town after the scandal broke. And it was all something and nothing. Just a group of kids, gossiping. He was a great headmaster. Top class bloke. Marriage hit the rocks. The mother stayed on here for a while then went to Kenya. He's up in Scotland, I believe. Runs an exclusive boys' boarding school. They were Dutch, originally,' he took a deep breath, 'she can't help herself, that one. The young lad's wasting his time there.'

'And did Wesley say anything back?' Hooch asked, ignoring Herb's soliloquy.

'Nothing. Although later, outside, the young fella said he'd muttered something vague about not being able to sleep. And he mentioned a flower, very particularly. He mentioned a . . .' Doc looked to his palm, 'a *gardenia*.'

'Fantastic.'

Hooch liked this detail, 'He was punch drunk, presumably. Might've let something slip relating to the Loiter in the heat of the moment.'

'That's what the lad thought, certainly.'

'But what about Furby?' Shoes interrupted. 'How did Furby know we were all here in Canvey if the website's down? Nobody else seems to have clicked yet. We usually have a crowd of at least thirty by Friday.'

'Somebody must've told him,' Hooch shrugged, 'or he checked in on the site a couple of days back. Wesley's location was definitely pinpointed then, although usually – by now – he'd've moved on.'

'Last I knew,' Herbie interjected, 'he was in secure accommodation, somewhere in Hertfordshire.'

'Somebody must've got him out of there,' Hooch shrugged.

Doc frowned at this. 'Good point, Hooch,' he scratched his old ear with a gnarled finger, 'but who? And *why?*'

'We're getting off the point Old Man,' Hooch groaned, licking his pencil tip, 'I need to know how Furby got Wesley tied up.'

'*Sicko*,' Shoes whispered, semi-ironically.

'*You* should talk,' Hooch sniped back.

'And what about this girl,' Herbie asked, 'I don't know anything about the girl. Who is she?'

'Josephine Bean,' Doc clarified, 'fresh as a daisy. Only started Following at dawn today.'

'A Behindling?'

'Claims she is,' Doc nodded.

'I told you about the books,' Shoes interrupted, 'on the walk, before. The L'Amour. That was her idea.'

'Oh yes,' Herbie slowly recollected.

'I think she is, anyway,' Shoes drained his glass.

'Pardon?' (Hooch, with a belch.)

'A Behindling. I think she's to be trusted. I like her. She's ballsy.'

'And you're so bloody discriminating, Shoes, eh?'

'She's from Southend. She works as a nurse,' Doc enlightened The Blind Man, holding back his counsel on the other stuff.

'She has some kind of profile as an environmental campaigner,' Hooch added, 'which I found a little bit . . . *challenging*.'

Doc gave him a warning look. Hooch didn't catch it. Shoes caught it, though, and nudged Hooch for him.

'What was that?' Herbie asked, sensing the movement.

'She works with sanitary products,' Hooch smiled, glancing up and shrugging at the Old Man. Herbie wrinkled his nose. Doc tapped his own with his middle finger. Hooch grimaced.

'But what did she *do*,' Shoes interrupted, 'to stop the fight?'

'Well that's the crazy bit,' Doc explained. 'She threatened to harm herself.'

'Come again?' Herbie frowned.

'This Dewi guy – a big guy, I mean you've seen how big he is – he was preparing to smash into Wes for the third time. The source . . .' Doc inspected his palm, 'Bo . . . He said he thought he was going to kill him. He was probably exaggerating. And coincidentally, there was an off-duty cop in there . . . The one Hooch and I saw earlier outside the Turpin house. The woman. Knew Josephine Bean from their schooldays, it seems. They were in there having a drink together.'

'Jesus H,' Hooch shook his head, inspecting his notebook, 'this is a bloody jigsaw.'

'And she was getting ready to try and do something,' Doc continued, 'I mean the cop; to step in – when the Behindling . . .'

'Or not, as the case may be,' Hooch said.

'This girl Josephine comes rushing forward, into the fray, soaking wet from the rain – he called her . . .' Doc looked to his palm again, 'the source called her . . . a little *fury*.

'Anyway, she had a beer bottle in her hand. She smashed it open on a table-top, put the sharp end to her wrist and shouted . . .'

'*What?*' Shoes was plainly astonished by this.

'shouted . . . uh . . . *Stop or I'll cut myself, I'll cut myself* . . . three or four times over. And then she starts to slash at her arm with the bottle. He said it looked bad for her. Drew a deal of blood, at any rate.'

'Fucking *madness*,' Shoes gasped.

'You said it.'

'And how did Dewi react?' Herbie asked.

'Like he'd been punched himself. Everybody was stunned. Even Wesley was stunned. But that might well've been concussion.'

'*I'm* stunned,' Shoes said, picking up his poker hand (his pint was finished).

'Let's get on to Furby,' Hooch interrupted.

'Well, Wes was punch drunk. The agent took him outside with the help of another chap. Thin man in a baseball cap. A stranger. Carrying a rucksack full of electronic stuff.'

'A thin man, you say?' Herbie butted in.

'Apparently so.'

'That'll be the bloke on the boat,' Shoes nudged Herbie, 'he was thin and wearing a beige cap, wasn't he?'

'*Uh* . . . yes,' Herbie responded, irritably.

'And he had some kind of portable computer thing. Battery-fed, we imagined, since there was no power to speak of on the craft. Herb here heard it beeping,' Shoes continued.

Herbie's top row of teeth were methodically gnashing against his lower lip.

'And the hack says he *wasn't* local?' Shoes enquired.

'I think he did, yes,' Doc nodded.

Herbie nodded to himself, irritably, yet smugly.

'Who's this, then?' Hooch asked.

'On the craft, by Wesley's camp,' Herbie explained, keeping it casual, 'we had a little chat with him on the perimeter walk. It was nothing important. I thought he might be Wesley's go-between, for the . . . for the *negotiations* . . .' Herbie pulled a significant expression. He was obviously fishing.

Doc didn't like the direction this conversation was heading, 'I don't recollect seeing him myself,' he said, struggling to remember a thin man on the walk, 'I saw some foreign-looking bloke, though, down by the river. But I was bloody whacked at that stage. It was foggy . . . you mean on that boat on stilts with the messed-up walkway, presumably?'

'Yep.'

'So who was he?' Hooch looked up.

'We don't know,' Shoes answered, glancing over to Herb who was distractedly tapping his stick on the floor. Doc observed his unease and resolved to follow it up, later.

'Did they arrest the Welsh chap?' Hooch asked.

'Didn't ask. I imagine they must've.'

'Was he pissed?'

'As a bloody newt, I imagine, but don't quote me.'

'And so Wes got carried outside and then Furby approached?'

'It's all a little confused,' Doc said. 'Some guy had his case stolen – by Furby – and he reported it to the policewoman. Furby used the bag to help him pose as a medical man.'

They all sniggered at this, except Shoes.

'I hate that little prick,' the Hippie murmured, with unusual vehemence.

'God yes,' Herbie turned to face him, 'he broke your knee, didn't he? During that whole moped catastrophe?'

'*Scooter.*'

Shoes nodded, his hand now protectively stroking the fabric covering the affected area, 'Ruined my Following habits for almost a year. Totally out of order.'

'Nobody's going to dispute the fact,' Doc intervened, counselling reason, 'that he's the kind of person who gives Following a bad reputation. He even had a small run-in with . . .' Doc paused –

My boy
Set fire to his tent when he refused to give him money for a taxi fare . . .
– then he shook his head, irritably, 'anyway . . .'

He attempted to continue, inspecting his palm, clearing his throat.

The rest of the group caught up, became sober, exchanged looks.

'So Furby stole a case and then posed as a doctor . . .' Doc finally got back on track, 'God only knows how he got Wes alone after that . . .'

'The really odd thing is,' Shoes interrupted, 'that Wes doesn't seem to have a problem with him. He tolerates Furby in a way that he doesn't tolerate some of the others. Even after the knife attack.'

'True.'

'Recognises a fellow maniac,' Hooch growled.

'Landlord's going to be pissed off,' Shoes sighed, gazing over poignantly towards the bar (as if he'd only just that second become sensitive to his glass's dryness), 'if the website's down and nobody knows to come in here. I guess Wes got some cash off him, up front, as usual.'

'You could be right,' Hooch conceded, disinterestedly.

Herbie tapped his stick again, excitedly. Hooch frowned. It wasn't a relaxing sound.

Doc slid his hand into his pocket and drew out a fiver.

'Get me another stout, Shoes, will you? And whatever you're after having.'

Shoes took the note and stood up, still staring at the bar, a mite distractedly. 'Need a quick slash first,' he said, 'if you don't mind waiting, Old Man.'

'Remember to wash your hands, love,' Hooch trilled after him.

Ladies . . . Ladies . . . *Ladies'* toilets. Or had she . . . *uh* . . .
Nope
(The Sanitary Towel Dispenser on the wall to the left of her was a sure-fire give-away.)

Jo craned her neck around to confirm in fact the distinctively *male* reflection which'd quietly materialised in the mirror before her (she was standing at the basins, the tap running, washing and washing).

Not simply . . . not . . .

Not hiding

Shoes.

She shuddered, careful to keep her body angled strictly away from him, her wrist hidden.

'I think you're in . . . This is meant to be . . .'

She felt a million miles away from everybody (and what did rules matter, anyway, in this alien, fucked-up, Wesley-informed environ?).

Why am I still here?

'We were just talking about you,' Shoes said, smiling at her (his reflected image transformed – in person – by her frazzled neurons into something ever skewed – buckling – distorted).

His toenails made a subtle kind of clattering on the lino as he walked over and casually rested his bulk against the hand dryer.

Jo wiggled her wet hands in the air ineffectually, the left hand more gently. She didn't . . .

'Is it bad?' Shoes asked, matter of factly.

'What?'

Hunted rabbit

'The cut. Didn't you wrap it up?'

'No I . . . But how did . . . ? I was just rinsing it . . . under the warm tap . . .'

'I'm a wholehearted fan of pain myself,' Shoes informed her. 'It's the root of my connection to both the Following and to Wesley. Are you the same way inclined yourself, Josephine?'

Jo stared over at him, confused.

He straightened up and pressed the wide silver button on the hand dryer, activating it.

'Hold the wound under here,' he advised, 'to dry it out. I'm just going for a slash . . .' He disappeared into a cubicle, but didn't close the door.

Jo walked over to the dryer. She held her hands under it. Her wrist. The wrist was bleeding, the blood still mixing and diluting with what remained of the tap water.

It was stinging now. A good two hours since she'd cut it. Had tried to start her car. Had tried to flee. Had failed, abysmally –

Damp in the pistons

Dried them

Dripping blood

Snivelling

Sat inside there for an hour

The pain singing

Motherfucking Mini

'Remember how I told you . . .' Shoes' voice emerged affably from the cubicle, over the splash of urine hitting the pan, the purr of the machine, her own breathing, 'that I had your name tattooed on my . . .'

'Pardon?'

Shoes popped his head around the door, halting his flow of urine to order.

'My arse. Remember I told you earlier how I had your name tattooed on it? Do you remember that?'

Jo held her slashed arm under the dryer. The cubicle was at an exact halfway point between the handbasins and the door. She felt the wounds instinctively tightening as the blood released its moisture. They weren't as bad as all . . . as all . . . saw much worse every half-hour on her training stints in Casualty.

She nodded. She did remember about the name, her name, tattooed on . . .

'I do remember,' she said –

Too left-field for any kind of reason

'So what d'you make of it?' he continued smiling.

Had he been drinking, maybe?

Silly question

'I didn't . . .' Jo frowned, 'I wasn't . . .'

'Well I'm currently in a good position to prove it,' Shoes said, 'would you like that, Josephine Bean? Would you like to see the proof of the pudding?'

'*Uh* . . .' Jo blinked.

'Would you?'

This is just silly

Need a nurse's curt voice

Need to call on all those old . . .
Defences
All that . . .

'Go ahead,' she said. Utterly obeisant.

'Well you'll have to excuse . . .'

Shoes indicated delightedly to his lower regions (not so much an excuse as an outright celebration), finished urinating, shook himself clean, hitched up his trousers – but not fully, just to the base of his sumptuous shudder of buttocks – emerged from the cubicle and walked casually towards her.

He was in an awkward state of semi-arousal (yet seemed to find no embarrassment in it), but that wasn't the worst part. He had . . . he . . .

Every kind of genital piercing known to man
And then some

Balls like two pin-cushions. Punched and peppered. Sleepered and studded. The shaft a complex silver lattice-work, base to tip.

On his belly –

That belly
That magnificent tub of manly blubber –
Hanging, swaying
Regal as an obese bantam after a henhouse seduction –

she saw (among the many tattoos, one in *particular*, a badly-drawn hangman; still pink with new-infection: the gallows completed, the rope, the body – the head, the torso, the legs and the feet – everything, in fact, but the right hand, which was missing.

Underneath, two words, seven letters and five –

G – – D – I – / S – – DS

Jo stared at these letters, her mind struggling to make sense of it –

Why am I . . .
How thoroughly . . .

'That's not it.' Shoes looked down at himself, relishing his work-of-art status, completely at ease with it. He turned around and pointed.

His arse was bare at the back – not just naked, but without any notable embellishments except for a further two words, written in a faded blue ink at the precise point where his momentous buttocks joined into the base of his spine: YOUR NAME

Jo stared at these two words for a few seconds –

Your name

Shoes peeked over his shoulder, 'Get it? I have *your* . . . ?'

Jo nodded. She wasn't quite smiling.

Shoes yanked up his trousers (they were elastic-waisted – his penis caught on the waistband and flipped high before being tightly enveloped).

'See you back in the bar, *gorgeous*,' he whispered, clicking his fingers, swishing his hips, and sashaying pertly away from her.

Twenty-nine

Ted was struggling valiantly to convince a twenty-four hour glazier that it would be worth his while driving over from Benfleet (on the night of his Twelfth Wedding Anniversary, as luck would have it) to undertake the pointless-seeming task of installing a mirror, while Arthur (a prodigiously ironic expression tightening one corner of his lips and feeding through, automatically, to the outer edge of his adjacent eye) tapped away diligently at the virus-ridden computer.

The agency lights had been cautiously turned off again (a detail which hardly aided Arthur's quiet endeavours) but he was a competent touch-typist and seemed a skilful technician – if not exactly the genius that Wesley had proclaimed him.

The room was coolly bathed by a spooky-seeming, almost-undulating, semi-aquatic blue-grey glow (generated, in its entirety, by the defective hardware), yet both men seemed quite at their ease floating around inside this dreamy liquidity.

'Lucky you kept the back-up disks to hand,' Art murmured, once Ted's abortive-sounding conversation had finally concluded (Ted saw his words emerging in a series of shimmering air pockets, which trickled from his mouth and then hung, vibrating gently, just above his head), 'there's nothing too bad gone on here, really. It's only a question of . . .' he tapped. He tapped again. '. . . feeding it all in. Setting it all up again. You should let me show you how, then you could easily do it yourself next time.'

Ted paddled over and stood at his shoulder.

'There won't be a next time,' he gurgled.

He was certain of it.

'I don't know how much general information you were keeping on the desktop . . .' Arthur mused, still tapping.

'A whole stack of it,' Ted affirmed, not appreciating – at first – the negative implications of Arthur's musings –

Gone

All gone

Drifted clean away . . .

'You didn't copy any of it onto a spare *floppy* by any . . . ?'

He glanced up. He clocked Ted's expression –

Drowning

He looked down again.

Tap tap

'I'm dead in the water,' Ted pronounced miserably.

Arthur rapidly switched tack, 'So will the glazier be coming over later?'

'Much later. He's taking his wife out to dinner. It's their wedding anniversary.'

Arthur grimaced, sympathetically, 'And the carpenter? For the door?'

'That'd be Dewi. I left him a message . . .'

'*Great*,' Arthur suddenly exclaimed, 'your mouse is finally up and running, now we're *really* getting somewhere . . .'

'But I have the distinct feeling,' Ted continued, 'that he might be otherwise engaged this evening.'

Tap tap . . .

Tap tap tap . . .

'Why's that, then?' Arthur glanced up distractedly.

'He's the big fellow who clouted Wesley.'

'*Ah.*'

'In love with Katherine. Works mainly in flooring. Did these floors . . .' Ted tapped his foot (the sound held back, trapped in liquid, then echoing eerily, seconds later), 'did them rather beautifully, in actual fact.'

Ted leaned across Arthur's shoulder and inspected the screen more closely. 'The worst part,' he said, still sounding suitably traumatised by the whole experience, 'was the way the information just kept on . . . kept on *spurting*. There was this real sense of . . . of viciousness . . . a *redness*. Then everything just went *click*. Dead.'

'I think you might've . . .' Arthur suddenly reached down to his feet and felt around blindly, 'I think you might've unplugged it, inadvertently. The socket's extremely overloaded down there. You should definitely consider getting a second adaptor . . .' he straightened up again, '. . . but we're working through it. Don't worry. And it all seems pretty much . . . pretty much . . . *uh . . .*'

He was frowning at the screen. An arbitrary snatch of debris was floating past them;

HOUSE FOR SALE: Semi-detached, quiet cul-de-sac, all local amenities, three bedrooms, no chain

Then another –

UNUSED GASOMETER for Auction: 5th February; Set in 2 1/2 acres. Road access available. No planning permission as yet for full residency. Suit artist as studio or other

Then –

Splat!

Ted blanched as a man – a square-headed soldier – beamed out of the screen at them with seven giant marbles packed under his foreskin (an eighth – held jauntily – between his thumb and forefinger).

'*Gracious,*' Arthur murmured, 'I guess that's one way of keeping active during those long winter nights in Kosovo.'

'It's not . . . it belongs . . .'

Ted couldn't muster up the moral fibre.

Tap tap tap . . .

Tap

'If the virus arrived in an email attachment . . .' Arthur paused, speculatively, 'you should definitely put in some work to try and stop it getting any further.'

'It wasn't an email,' Ted said.

Arthur turned sharply, mid-procedure (a series of ripples spreading out dramatically behind him), 'You downloaded this thing from the web?'

Ted rubbed an uneasy shoe – still spotlessly clean – onto the back of its opposite calf.

'From a Wesley site, actually,' he admitted, feeling himself, his surroundings, the *atmosphere*, mysteriously dry up.

Arthur almost smiled.

'How very . . .'

He shrugged –

Appropriate

He didn't seem shocked (Ted was relieved to note – I mean there were *rules* in this business, weren't there? And not just Following rules, either, but fundamental codes of common . . . of common . . .)

'So which site was it, exactly?'

Arthur was back at work already. Ted frowned, 'I thought there was only . . .'

Tap tap . . .

Hiatus

'Nope. There are several.'

. . . Tap

'The main one, then. The big one. The one all the Followings use, and the newspaper people . . .'

'Behindlings.'

'Pardon?'

'Behindlings.'

'Yes . . . *Yes*, precisely.'

Arthur grabbed a pen and scribbled an address down. He showed it to him.

'This lot are notoriously shonky.'

Ted stared at it, frowning. He shook his head.

Arthur adjusted the pen and began writing out another.

'Nope,' Ted said, grabbing the pen himself, the paper, pressing down on the desk and writing out the address he'd used in bold, clear lettering.

'Here.'

He pushed it over.

Arthur took the pad, glanced at the address, shook his head. 'No,' he said, pushing it away, 'you must've got that wrong.'

Ted half-smiled, 'Which is *exactly* what Wesley said when the police questioned him about it earlier.'

Arthur twisted around on his stool – all pretence of indifference suddenly gone, 'I don't understand. Did Wesley put you up to this? Because please don't think for a *minute* that you can fuck with me and get away with it.'

He was prodigiously emphatic.

Ted stepped back, nervously. It hadn't dawned on him . . . It hadn't occurred to him that this person might be . . . I mean after the interlude with the would-be doctor and everything . . .

'Don't be frightened,' Arthur said (even his tone – its demand for calm – seeming intimidating).

'I'm not . . .' Ted stuttered –

Think of the pond

The lilies

The hiss of bullrushes

'And I'm not *wrong*, either. The local constabulary accessed the site this afternoon – probably round about the same time I did – and they were burned by it too. That's what they said.'

'*This* site?'

Arthur held up the pad again. He pointed.

'Yes. I think they had a suspicion that Wesley himself might be behind it. But he obviously wasn't by the way he . . .'

'Don't be ridiculous,' Arthur snapped, 'this site has absolutely *nothing* to do with Wesley.'

Ted paused, took stock, then shook his head, slowly. 'I'm not being ridiculous,' he discurred, 'and it has *everything* to do with him.'

Arthur took this gentle rebuff on the chin. 'So what did Wesley have to say about the site being down?' he asked, reviving his sympathetic side, softening his tone slightly.

'He said there had to be a mistake. Same as you did. And he seemed . . .' Ted paused, 'I'm not very . . .' he scratched his head, 'I'm not terribly *familiar* with all this Wesley . . . all the rules and the etiquette and everything . . .'

'That's why he chose you, presumably,' Arthur mumbled.

Chose?

Ted considered this concept, momentarily.

To be chosen

'Do you at least know *why* the police were visiting him?' Arthur was feeling around inside his pocket for his phone. 'Was it about the site or about the Loiter? Did he mention?'

Ted seemed to experience some difficulty in answering.

Arthur found his phone, tried to turn it on – realised that it was turned on already – swore – then attempted to call up his text messages.

'It's *important*, Ted . . .'

Had to use the name

'Was it about the competition, perhaps?'

'No. No it was . . . it was nothing . . .'

Ted watched on as Arthur jabbed away at his phone, unsuccessfully.

'It was something more . . .'

He fell silent. Arthur didn't seem to be listening, anyway.

'Was it to do with New Year, by any chance? The stuff in Brighton?'

Ted shook his head.

Arthur snapped the phone shut with a growl and slipped it into his pocket. He turned back to the computer again. He seemed deeply preoccupied, if not necessarily by it –

Profound absence of tap

He turned back around again. 'I have some equipment in my bag,' he said, 'and I need to charge it. Is it okay to use the plug here?' He pointed.

'What kind of stuff?' Ted felt uneasy. He was in enough bloody trouble with Leo already. Didn't feel the need to *add* to it particularly.

'Portable computer. Nothing risky. I'd charge it at home but I'm staying on a boat. I have no mains power there.'

'I suppose it'd be churlish to refuse . . .' Ted murmured – wishing he could be churlish for once in his damn life. But this man was fixing his . . . Doing him a . . . And Wesley seemed to . . . to *trust* . . . He'd invited him back for dinner, after all. Katherine's. In an hour (had seemed pretty confident that he'd be finished with the police by then).

Ted glanced at his watch. The hour was almost done.

'It's nearly time to meet Wesley at the bungalow. I could walk you over, then dash back here and sit it out for the glazier. I'm certain Katherine would let you re-charge there if you asked her.'

Arthur shrugged.

Tap tap tap

'I still can't . . .' he promptly changed the subject, 'I still can't get over that girl in the bar. The skinny girl with the short . . .'

306

'Yes,' Ted said. 'It was . . .' He couldn't think of a word. 'Odd,' he said, finally.

'Is she local? She seemed to know her way around the place. She was having a drink with the police officer.'

'Right.'

Ted seemed indifferent.

'She drew blood,' Arthur continued, 'I don't know how bad the wounds were. Wesley always seems to inspire that kind of . . .'

Crazy

'that kind of . . .'

Lunatic . . .

'that kind of mind-boggling loyalty.'

'I do know her . . .' Ted interrupted – as if only just patching it all together, 'she's a Bean. She's the Bean girl.'

Arthur didn't seem to be listening. He just shrugged, 'I figured she must be . . .'

Tap tap tap

'. . . *connected* in some way. Because of the Welsh lad. Because of the extremity of his reaction.'

'Yes it was . . .' Ted nodded, '. . . it was extreme, certainly.'

Arthur peered up, 'A Behindling, then, d'you reckon?'

'I . . . uh . . .' Ted scratched his head, 'I'm afraid I don't really know what that *means*.'

Arthur opened his mouth as if to tell him, but Ted interrupted, 'And I think I'm happier *not* knowing,' he gently resisted, 'I mean if you don't know the rules you can't be . . . it's less . . .'

Arthur shrugged. He seemed to be evaluating something –

This level of naivety

Suspicious

And he was very well placed . . .

'We went to school together,' Ted continued, misconstruing Arthur's silence as hostility, wanting to mollify him, 'and she has brothers in Canvey. Three brothers. One runs a minicab business. One manages the sports centre. The other owns a salvage company on the Charfleet Estate, along with her father.'

'I see.'

'But she had very long hair before.'

'Really?'

'Yes. That's why I didn't . . . She had very long hair. Blonde. Wesley actually spoke to her, earlier this afternoon. She said she was over from Southend for the day. But I'm certain it was her, and that she was from Canvey, originally.'

Ted noticed – with some irritation – how Arthur sprang to attention at the mention of Wesley's name. As if everything gained its significance through its connection to him.

'Well placed, too, then, eh?' Arthur murmured.

'Pardon?'

'I said she's *well placed*. Like you are.'

Arthur gave Ted a significant look. But Ted seemed mystified by it, if not a little disturbed. Perhaps the strange light wasn't helping.

Ted shifted his weight.

'Don't worry about it,' Arthur turned back to the computer, smiling –

That kind of innocence

You couldn't fuck with it

He dwelled briefly on the broken bottle and the blood. There was something . . . there was something not quite . . . that *level* of . . .

Outrageous

Bean. *Bean*. Needed to remember . . .

Then he gradually began tapping again; curtailing, re-configuring, tidying things up.

Ted padded slowly to the front door (couldn't risk the picture window – too open – too bare). He peeked through it and over towards the Leisure Centre where the last few stragglers for the night's second Bingo session were doggedly accumulating. Still raining. That deep, that steady, that *ineffable* Winter-deep Canvey *drear*.

Then he blinked. He drew a sharp breath. He pulled back. He double-checked. He pulled back even further.

'*Duck*,' he whispered urgently.

Arthur ducked, immediately – under the table – bones creaking.

Ted's mouth had fallen open, his eyes were improbably wide.

Could've *sworn* he just saw . . . Could've *sworn* he just . . .

Eileen.

But she wasn't . . . she seemed . . . she wasn't looking over. She was staring down, fixedly. Scuttling along. Scarf pulled around her head, over her cheek, as if . . . yanked across . . . like in . . . a kind of . . . a mad . . . a desperate . . .

Purdah

She always played Bingo with her mother on a Friday, but tonight she was walking in the opposite direction. Head down. Straight past. Scurrying . . . *uh* . . .

Home – would that be?

'Can I . . . ?' Arthur's face was ruddy with the exertion of his position.

Ted's head jerked around.

'Sorry,' he whispered. 'Boss's wife. She usually plays Bingo on a Friday.'

Didn't need to mention . . .

How distressed . . .

Shouldn't . . .

Or Wesley . . .

Arthur straightened up again, grimacing.

'Quick response, though,' Ted added –

Must be military

Or very . . .

Arthur shrugged. He whizzed the mouse around, clicked it a few times, waited, then flipped off the power.

'That's about it,' he said, stretching and yawning.

As the screen went black, so too did his corner.

'We're back to all the basics,' he continued, matter-of-factly, through the darkness (Ted was still visible by the door), 'I've not been able to save everything, but you've been pretty fortunate, all in all.'

Ted chuckled to himself, weakly, touching his head, his hair, not a little derangedly. 'Must be my lucky day,' he said.

Outside, meanwhile, a small van was pulling up, flanked – on both sides – by the distinctive metal struts denoting the largescale transportation of breakable material.

Arthur's ironic eyes trailed the van, its driver (improbably well-attired – for Service – in a smart shirt and tie and blazer).

'I think it *must* be,' he replied.

Thirty

'You've checked the points, presumably . . .'

A voice spoke – a male voice – from directly behind her, 'they're always the first thing to go with a Mini. In damp weather, especially.'

Josephine carefully withdrew her head from under the small bonnet of her car. 'Several times already,' she said, turning and instinctively bringing the screwdriver she was holding (her hands so cold she could barely cling onto it) to the front of her belly.

But it was Wesley.

She stared up at him, astonished.

He peered past her, into the engine, his face (even in the steady murk of semi-darkness) enlivened by a clutch of painful-looking reddish blotches. 'I'm mechanically-minded,' he said, squinting myopically, 'but I eschew the car ideologically.'

She shifted left, to allow him full access, while surreptitiously stealing her injured arm behind her back (something she instantly regretted – it created a furtive impression, as if she was now intent upon hiding the screwdriver from him, for some inexplicable reason).

Wesley didn't miss a thing. He leaned sideways to try and spot what she was concealing. She shifted her feet (heavy as a shire horse's hooves after a full day's ploughing) and sheepishly brought the tool back around again, her cheeks reddening. She seemed painfully aware of his sudden proximity.

He pulled out the points and blew on them, drying them on the lining of his jacket.

'I t-t-tried the points,' she repeated, shivering (so cold her lips were almost frozen; her words might shatter if he breathed any warmth on them).

Wesley pushed the points firmly back into place again. 'Anti-freeze?'

She nodded, 'Last thing yesterday. F-first thing this morning.'

'Checked the oil?'

She nodded.

'Petrol? Water? Battery?'

She nodded again.

He stepped back, wiping the grease from his fingers onto his trousers.

That injured hand

A baby bird

Opening and closing like a hungry fledgling

'Then you should probably get a cab back to Southend. You'll kill yourself if you stay out here much longer.'

'I'd get a c-cab if I was anywhere else,' she said, her teeth clashing pitiably, 'but I can't here. N-not in C-Canvey.'

Canvey

Pronounced the name like it was something heinous – polluted – despicable.

Wesley mused this over – staring at her intently – clearly impressed by her particular brand of evasive straightforwardness. Then he smiled. He shrugged. He turned away –

So let her die

'It was m-me who sent you that letter,' she chattered after him, wrapping her arms around her shoulders to try and cushion her juddering chin, 'about my . . . about . . .'

'I have no address,' Wesley cut her off, contemptuously, 'I receive no . . .'

'When you were staying down in Devon. With the p-p-potter. The cr-crazy potter. Last year. Early. After the book first came out. It was about Katherine, about the gr-graffiti . . .'

Wesley walked on a few paces.

He never talked to the Followers. There were perfectly good reasons for it. He had to keep things separate. It was a kind of self-preservation.

'But I wasn't F-Following then,' she said (as if reading his thoughts). 'And it isn't . . .' She dropped the screwdriver and bent down to pick it up again, 'it isn't *f-fair* . . .'

'What isn't?' Wesley paused for a second, half-smiling, but keeping his back turned deliberately towards her, 'What isn't *f-fair?*' He bleated out the word in a cruel impersonation.

(The concept of fairness seemed so laughable to him, so thin, so weedy, so conceptually pointless. *Fair?* What kind of rankly amateur, blithering shallow-wit was this woman, anyway?)

Josephine felt her nose running. Was unable to stop it. Tasted the salt of snot on her upper lip. 'It's impossible to approach you without . . . without F-Following. I st-started unintentionally. I was . . . I got . . . It's not what I . . .'

'I didn't *get* any letter,' he repeated, ominously, 'and the potter, for your information, isn't remotely crazy.'

He was facing into the wind. He'd been released from custody less than ten minutes earlier. He'd had no intention of happening across her. Of getting . . . getting . . .

Button-holed

He hated that kind of . . . of . . .

Responsibility

It was well past eleven (although time meant nothing to him; time was merely the interval between sleeping and waking, eating and shitting). He briefly half-remembered his promises for dinner. He half-remembered Katherine – the stink of drink – the milky neck – the lazy temptation.

They were standing on a quiet, flat, unremarkable street only five minutes walk from the town centre and the Furtherwick (the Police Station two roads off to their left).

It was foggy, threatening to snow. He felt his own face slowly freezing. His cheek – his chin – his bruises were aching.

'I only n-need . . .' she said – trying to walk forward a step but her legs kept on seizing, 'just to *explain*, b-before . . .'

'You'll freeze to death out here,' he warned her, not sounding particularly concerned by this prospect (more bored by it), but even so . . .

He weakened for a moment and peered over his shoulder. She was a pathetic sight. Slight as a feather. Shaking like a puppy in a sudden bout of thunder. She was licked and whipped. She was stopped. She was *fucked*.

'You were wet,' he said, suddenly remembering (in a blurry haze, a fug), 'earlier, in the bar . . .' He squinted at her, 'and you're *still* wet. You'll catch hypothermia. Stop being a fool. You can't possibly stay out here.'

'I ha-have to stay,' she said, 'I *n-need* to . . . I'm in a . . .'

He growled under his breath and strode impatiently towards her. 'Show me the arm.'

Her arm was hidden again. She didn't want to show it. She was humiliated now, by everything. And if he was kind – admittedly, it seemed a remote possibility – but if he was, she would surely start crying. And he would really hate her, then. And deservedly.

He reached out his bad hand – the sheer, shiny pincer of palm and thumb – grabbed a hold of her elbow, yanked it forward and roughly shoved back the sleeve of her jumper. She winced.

'I thought you were working for the company,' he said, staring at the cuts as if he couldn't quite believe in them – four in all, each two inches long, bottle shaped – curving into smiles – a couple thick with dried blood and new scab, the third and fourth still oozing, 'and even if you aren't,' he released her arm dispassionately, 'you're only complicating matters unnecessarily.'

'I'm not wo-working for anybody,' she chattered.

'Except yourself,' he sneered.

He was just as cruel as she'd anticipated. *Hateful.* It was what she'd wanted. She needed punishing. Pain was her motivator.

'Get back in the car and start up the engine,' he ordered.

Jo shuffled around the Mini, pulling her sleeve down, miserably. She opened the door, climbed stiffly inside, pressed down the pedals, turned the key in the ignition.

The car squealed, unresponsively.

She tried again.

A third time.

Wesley slammed down the bonnet. He circled the car, twice (like a predator negotiating a rival's territory), then he yanked the door open on the passenger side and clambered in.

'Any talking about specifics,' he warned her, sticking his seat into recline (but sitting bolt upright in it) 'about the Loiter, the letter, the Turpin girl, and I'm straight out of here.'

314

He slammed his door shut, pulled off his waterproof, his jacket and his sweater.

'Fuck the battery,' he said, pushing back her hood, yanking off her wet scarf and tossing it onto the back seat, 'put on the bloody heater.'

'Just keep ringing,' Ted said, backing off slowly down the neat, brick pathway and colliding with a conifer (clipping it with his shoulder and starting – not a little comically, Arthur felt – like he'd been cornered, unexpectedly, by an irritable green ogre) then continuing to ease himself – still backwards, still slowly – across the parquet-style driveway (like he was a big saloon car, or an improbably large Pleasure Cruiser on an impossibly small river) carefully maintaining eye-contact – for the best part – so Arthur wouldn't get all jittery (perhaps) or lose his nerve and follow him – like a lost kitten – all the way back to the agency again, 'she might've fallen asleep or something, but she's bound to answer eventually . . .'

He paused, on the roadway, 'I'm sorry I can't stay any longer, it's just . . .' He pointed, dumbly –

Glazier

'Simply tell her who you are and that you've arranged to meet up with Wesley here. She'll be fine about it, honestly. Contrary to what people like to say about her, Katherine can often be very . . .' he bit his lip, 'very *accommodating*,' he murmured faintly (as if suddenly – or not so suddenly – having serious doubts about the overall situation, his unenviable part in it, the actual implications of what he was saying), then smiling (a little weakly), turning, waving, and promptly scarpering.

Arthur frowned. Accommodating? *Contrary* to her reputation? He pulled the rucksack off his shoulder, tipped back his hat, pushed his finger towards the bell, made contact and sat on it.

Ted had him all wrong. He felt no anxiety about meeting Miss Turpin. He had a very distinct idea of how she would be: sallow-skinned, auburn haired, thick-set, defeated. Like a young Pat Phoenix but without the fight. Like a rough-cut Liz Taylor circa *Virginia Woolf*, fluffy-slippered, sullen, puffy, ruined, fag-ended.

He had no particular concerns about the thought of encountering her. He believed himself an expert in the laws of human behaviour.

He was tough as hide. He could handle anything.

Katherine finally answered during Arthur's third resounding climax of Sinatra's *My Way* (no frills or flourishes in his particular rendition – marginally slower, perhaps, than the more famous original; on the good side of monotonous, the cusp of funereal).

Arthur's jaw went slack as she opened the door –

Good God

Who would've . . . ?

That husky-mouthed, milky-faced, heavy-smoking, fold-up-biking . . .

That vicious . . .

She barely glanced at him, though, as she ushered him – rather crabbily – within.

'*Hate* that damn song,' she muttered, clutching her ear –

What was it with the ear?

But it wasn't so much the *ear* – it soon transpired – as her whole strange, pale head in all its fabulous entirety. She was savagely hung over.

The hallway – Arthur put his hand to his nose, instinctively, his eyes prickling – was full of smoke.

'I fell asleep,' she croaked. 'It feels like the bell's been sounding off for hours.'

'Is something burning?' he asked, closing the door, putting down his rucksack (there were bags and bottles everywhere) glancing around him – slightly aghast at the mess – and then following her, carefully, down the corridor.

'Your guess is as good as mine.'

She suddenly stopped and turned and stared up at him, 'What brought you here, exactly?' She scratched her head, vaguely, 'I can't for the life of me . . .'

'Wesley,' he promptly answered, 'we're meant to be meeting for dinner. He went off with the police about an hour ago . . .' Arthur glanced at his watch, 'in fact closer on two.'

'Was it about the librarian?' Katherine asked, frowning doubtfully, turning back around, still not focussing properly. 'Or was it about his daughter?'

'His . . .' Arthur stopped in his tracks, '. . . *pardon*?'

Katherine rubbed her right eye, yawned, started walking again.

'The daughter,' she repeated, over her shoulder, 'like earlier . . . when the police . . .'

She paused a second time, and shook her head (as if something had come loose inside her skull and the consequent rattle was truly provoking her) '. . . and talking of earlier, didn't we meet before? I'm experiencing a disturbing *déjà* . . .'

She walked on, coughing, without waiting for an answer.

He followed her into the kitchen where the smoke was billowing (much to Katherine's disinterest, and Arthur's horror) in graceful plumes through the occasional crack in the oven's perished rubber lining. The floor was covered in feathers and paper. No – stranger still – in feathers and *origami*.

A heron's wing was hung over the back of a chair by a piece of wire.

Katherine pointed to this wing, rather querulously, 'Dinner,' she announced, placing her hand onto her belly, 'in case you weren't yet acquainted with the menu.'

She went over to the sink, turned on the cold tap, ran it for a while, bent over and drank from it. When she eventually straightened up, the excess fluid dribbled onto her chin, her jaw, then down her neck. She made no effort to wipe it away.

Arthur struggled not to focus on the droplets – their fascinating –

Uh . . .

– descent. Instead he went over and switched off the oven. He opened the back door. He waved his arms around a little.

'We met on the road, this morning,' he said, trying to keep things casual, 'when your tyre got a puncture.'

Katherine had grabbed her cigarettes from the counter-top. Her hands were shaking.

'Oh God yes,' she murmured emphatically, not even looking at him, 'you're a lovely walker.'

'You have a fold-up bike,' he said, slightly embarrassed, inspecting the marks across the back of her shoulders –

Friction burns

Blood prints

317

'I do', she readily agreed, her low voice quavering. She turned to face him as she lit up. 'Smoke?'

'Why not?' he found himself saying –

You've given up

She was still wearing peach, in many layers –

Or was that apricot?

'Please shut the fucking door,' she whispered, hugging herself and shivering, 'before I freeze my bony arse off.'

The house was improbably hot. The kitchen was still smoky. But he closed the door anyway.

She'd lit up a fag for him and made as if to pass it over. He reached out a hand for it. She dropped it onto the floor. Purposefully.

'I am *very* . . .' she said, smiling at him alluringly (as if she'd finished this sentence and not just left it hanging), 'and not only that,' she continued, 'but *painfully* . . .'

He bent over to retrieve the cigarette, uncertain how to respond to her. When he straightened up, though, holding it firmly, she casually dropped the other.

'. . . disappointed,' she concluded, with a sigh.

It rolled towards the cabinets. He bent down again, automatically.

When he'd plucked it from the tiles (they were warm under his fingers – he rested his palms there, for a second) and stood up again, holding a cigarette in both hands now (what better way to give up giving up?), he noticed – with a kind of alarm, but also a kind of . . . a kind of thudding . . . *delight*, was it? – that she'd removed a prodigious cross-section of her copious silky layers. They'd slid to the floor, as if of their own volition.

She was now all but naked, except for an old-fashioned bra (which looked like it was made from a combination of cream-coloured tent fabric and some coordinated boot-laces) and a pair of loosely-fitting, almost contemporaneous (1920s? '30s? – what did *he* know of historical trends in female undergarments?) cami-knickers. The knickers hung off her hips revealing . . .

What was the word for the nape, the dimple of no-flesh, the cleft that lay so desirably underneath the knuckle of a girl's hip?

What was the name for that?

Her body was hairless. She was white as a maggot. Her breasts –
inside those hockey-shoe-lace-cricket-white contraptions –
Oh shit
– deliriously full and slack.

Arthur closed his mouth. It had fallen open. He took a puff on a
cigarette.
its fire crackled into him –
Why am I here again?
Back in this effortless, hungry, instinctive place I so confidently
believed I'd left behind me?

'I have some terrible knots,' Katherine said, perching her marbled
hip onto the corner of the table –
The whiteness, like a joint of flesh, all pearled in death; all
plucked, un-hung . . .
The grain of old pine underneath
Its ancient creak
The shower of grey-black feathers
A Still Life-
Corbieres-
They were calling it . . .

Arthur stole another puff –
They were calling it . . .

She was pointing to her brassiere. The laces were all . . .
This has to happen
– he moved closer, like a man passionately engaged by a fascinating
dilemma – a puzzle . . . They were all . . . all *co . . . co . . . co . . .*
coagulated.

A kind of miniature bodice, knotted to the fore – a tangle of
closed-openings – an impossibility.

He put out his hands to untie them; clumsily, at first – a blind
man reaching for the kettle cord; a schoolboy wiping down the
classroom blackboard . . .
These huge brown hands
How could they achieve anything useful here?

He drew his face in close, was now down on his knees, miraculously . . .

The smell of . . . of *violence* from the tiny pleats in her belly.
The clefts between . . .

319

Made the hairs on his . . .

No –

No

– the smell of *Violets* –

Spring flowering so sweetly-mauve in the moist shelter of shady corners –

Uh . . .

– and cigarettes.

Where had he put them?

But the tangle was too . . . too important. He stared even harder at it. His nose was very nearly . . . and his fingers . . . the pale skin – when he brushed it, inadvertently – hot as seared chicken, straight from the spit of frying –

The tangle . . .

His fingers pulled and teased and twisted and wound and interwound. Then his teeth were pulling too, but only very gently, and the laces were dampened and the ancient moth-smelling, cricket-pad, english-lawn-green-wax-rubbing cotton and the flesh just to the left of it – and to the right of it – and the damper flesh, pinkened by the pressure of fabric just under –

The tightness . . .

They were suddenly on the . . .

Tiles hot below the scrape of pale and the knickers loose as butter-fabric slipping with the ineluctable pleat of . . .

Five fingers each with . . . She had five fingers and they had that pressure-warm-push-and-determined force of . . . of . . .

Snout

Busy as any kind of sharp-nosed wild white woodland creature you might care to mention in the ice-snow-cold of winter with the searing-hot-scarlet of . . . of . . .

Snow Fox!

Teeth!

Fur!

Claw!

Arthur Young – Man of History – lay there, pulsating, whipped and panting, eyes without irises purple-flowering, calm as a log split and crashed into the moss-sodden forest of infinite languor, while she bit and tunnelled and dug him over.

'We worked on the markets together,' Wesley said. 'Have you ever been to Bow? It's in the East of London. An infernal shit-hole, point of fact, but I almost considered making my permanent home there . . . until things . . . *uh* . . .'

Caught up

They always catch up

Josephine shook her head (perhaps a little too quickly). 'I don't know it,' she lied, then changed tack slightly, 'I've never *been* there,' she modified.

Of course she'd heard of it. She'd read the name, frequently; the famous old Roman Road Market, Bow . . . *The Story of the Freeing of the Eels*. The first Wesley story. It was the start of everything. It was all but legendary.

She blinked. She felt her heart banging. She saw her breath condensing, right there, just in front of her.

Here he was, in *person*, and it wasn't so much a story, to him, as a bundle of memories, none really connecting. And he was telling it to her now. Haltingly.

She held her breath, staring at him –

Please don't let me spoil anything

'I've never been there,' she carefully repeated, 'I don't know London well.'

She was down to her grey, thermal vest – thankfully still dry in patches – and some matching grey, calf-length leggings. Her feet were bare.

'Your feet . . .' Wesley told her, inspecting them dispassionately –

Like tiny, dried-out bat's claws

Long-toed

Tender

'seem to have fared worse than the rest of you. Ears aside . . .'

Pink as a piglet's with the sun shining behind them

'and your neat hands, obviously.'

Neat hands

The windows were already steamed to capacity. Wesley had

discovered an old blanket in the back. She didn't remember ever having seen it there before –

Can this really be my car?

The blanket was covered in dog hair. It smelled of stale sick. Wesley didn't care. He was towelling her dry with it. She might as well have been an itinerant pony or a muck-drenched lurcher for all the pains he took to preserve her dignity. And when he got down to her toes, he threw aside the blanket and smacked her feet – *hard* – until she could feel it.

Only when she gasped (three times, four) did he stop, with a smile, and without apology.

He made her put on his jumper and his jacket –

The smell of them . . .

Like juniper and off-milk and pipe-smoke-tangerine-old-pelt-grandfather

– then he wrapped up her legs – like a tortilla – in the blanket.

There was no room inside that tiny car for anything. He flipped her seat back, lay back himself, pulled her feet onto his lap, rubbed them.

'So why didn't you?' she asked, still shivering.

'Why didn't I what?'

He leaned forward, scrabbled around inside his coat pocket and removed a sweet, some matches and a cigarette stub.

He unfurled the sweet and popped it into her mouth.

He lit the cigarette for himself.

She pushed the sweet –

Barley sugar

– into her cheek, 'Why didn't you make a home there?'

Wesley obviously disliked this question.

'I was involved in a dispute,' he muttered, 'with a foreman on a job . . . And you know what?'

She shook her head.

'I should probably go out and find you some dock leaves, later . . .' he opened his door and tossed the spent match into the gutter. 'For the cuts,' he added.

'In Bow?' she persisted.

He slammed the door shut.

'Nope,' he gave up evading her, 'Holloway. He fell off a ladder.

Broke four ribs. So I ended up working on the markets in the East with this character called Trevor . . .'

Wesley inspected his cigarette, his bad hand still resting casually on her foot.

She felt his hand there. In that moment she *was* her foot.

'Trevor was the potter you mentioned earlier . . .' he lifted his bad hand and pulled open the ashtray on the dash –
Hand gone

'He wasn't the world's most conscientious co-worker – not back then – but we were solid together for almost a year. It was alright for a while. Got a little . . .' Wesley paused, 'claustrophobic,' he tapped the ash off his stub then rested his hand – without thinking – on her foot again –
Hand back

Jo shivered. Wesley misconstrued it as the cold, and began rubbing, distractedly, 'Anyhow I got involved in some other stuff – at a pie and mash shop, releasing a few eels – and I fucked the situation up . . .'

He sniffed. He was starting to feel the cold himself. He grimly hunched his shoulders against its steady encroachments, continued talking to try and keep his mind off the breeze whistling through the crack in his side-window.

'A long old while after, Trev pulled himself together and became a potter. At first just casual labour in one of the big Staffordshire factories – in the warehouse or something – then he gradually worked his way up. Got involved in some of the actual . . . the hands-on . . . the creative stuff . . .'

Wesley was distractedly rubbing his own arm with his smoking hand. Jo quickly pulled some of the blanket free and placed it, demurely, across his knees.

'What happened then?' she tentatively asked.

Wesley accepted the blanket without comment. He adjusted its placement slightly. He dragged on his cigarette.

'We met again – years later – while I was Loitering near there. He looked me up. He was fairly desperate – and angry about some of the things that'd gone wrong – pissed off about . . . had a gambling problem. Marriage was . . .'

Wesley shrugged, choosing not to specify the exact locus of

Trevor's irritability, 'So we walked down to Devon together. Started talking about trying to do something special with all the stuff he'd learned in Staffordshire. Setting up our own pottery, maybe. Something old-fashioned, because Trev's traditional to the core, but in the loveliest . . . in a very primitive . . . he has this overwhelming . . . an innocence. A real innocence. And that makes him hot-headed sometimes, which is a pity. A few weeks in each other's company and we end up almost killing each other.'

Wesley shot her a look. He hadn't made eye contact with her since he'd climbed into the car.

'Was he violent?' Jo whispered, frightened that if she spoke too loudly she might kill the story.

Wesley cleared his throat. Drew on his cigarette.

'We built this traditional Anagama kiln,' he continued, 'or a round-about version of it; approximately four-hundred-and-fifty cubic feet in diameter . . .' he exhaled, using both hands to outline its shape, 'takes a couple of months to fill, ten days to pack, five days to fire, a week – at least – to cool . . .'

'And this was Trevor's idea?'

Wesley shifted in his seat, 'You can flog it as art – that's the clever thing – and folk'll swallow it whole, because the entire set-up's so *fantastically* arse about face . . .'

Wesley smiled at the thought. It was the first time she'd seen him smile properly – ever. She gazed at the smile, proprietorially.

'For most potters,' Wesley explained, 'the clay is the crucial factor, the moulding, the glaze, the artistry. And that's how it was for Trev, initially. He'd developed this really *precise* streak – never had it when we worked on the markets – don't know where it came from, really. But it wasn't right for him. It was part of the problem. He needed . . .' Wesley pondered, for a moment, '. . . to exorcise it. Which is why the new techniques have been so liberating. Because now it's not all about creating the perfect *object* so much as creating the most legitimate *process* . . .'

Wesley's hand returned – under the blanket now – to Jo's foot, and stroked it, unthinkingly, 'Out of every fifty mugs or plates he sticks into that kiln, he gets – at best – fifteen back. And they are *fucked*, let me tell you. Crazy-looking things. All the glaze cracked. All the purity gone. Takes literally days to clean them. And Trevor rages against it. He *rages*. But that's . . . What he doesn't quite understand yet is how that's just as it *should* be, because it's all about . . . the whole process is all about . . . not finish or perfection, but *turbulence* . . .'

'Does he make a living at it?'

Wesley frowned at this question, then shrugged, as if he couldn't be bothered trying to understand it, 'The pieces that survive – and this is the whole point, really, the way I see it – the things that somehow *survive* this chaos are absolutely . . . they're dazzling . . .'

That smile again

'They're without compare. They're magical. Like old soldiers marching on VE day, proudly carrying their medals and their scars of battle.'

Josephine nodded.

'To have a thing,' Wesley explained, his cigarette stub burning down to nothing, 'that isn't so much an entity in the present sense – I mean entirely functional or anything – so much as an object with its whole history, its whole journey, physically *embedded* . . .'

'And is Trevor happy?'

Jo immediately regretted this question. It seemed so . . . so . . .

Prissy

Wesley shrugged (not appearing, on the surface, to object). 'He's perfectly viable.'

Viable?

Josephine pondered this concept for a while. This word.

'For Trevor,' Wesley didn't notice her marginal retreat, 'for him it's just a different kind of gambling. It's another channel. It's very physical.'

Wesley stubbed out his cigarette and squinted through the windscreen. 'Looks like . . . *bollocks*,' he shrank down in his seat, 'it's the Old Man. I recognise the glow of his torch. Cover me over with the blanket. He shouldn't see me here.'

Wesley pushed himself down onto the floor, using the segment of the blanket he already had to cover himself as best he could. Jo stared at him confusedly, then at herself – his distinctive jacket wrapped so tightly around her – then out through the windscreen.

In the distance she saw a flashlight wavering. She pulled the blanket off her legs and covered him more thoroughly, then took off the jacket, the jumper, wound down her window and peeked out, cautiously.

The cold teared her eyes up. She blinked. She focussed again.

It was Doc. He was walking unsteadily (either his feet were still a mess or he was slightly tipsy). As he drew even closer, she wound the window down further – but not too far – so that her whole face was now visible, and the top of her shoulder. She hoped the dark (and the condensation) would protect the car's interior.

'I had a gut feeling this was yours when we drove past it earlier,' Doc shouted at her, kicking the tyre tread, 'can't you get the bugger started?'

Jo shook her head.

'Did you try the points? They're always the first thing to play up with a Mini.'

Jo nodded, 'I did try them. But I think it might be the carburettor. It's squealing. It went once before.'

'Not with the AA, eh?'

She shook her head. Doc clucked to himself, 'Hooch couldn't possibly survive without it. Calls them at the drop of a hat. Got banned by the RAC for taking the piss. He's useless with technical stuff.'

He peered over her shoulder and into the car. She straightened up a little to impede his view.

'Shoes said he saw you a few hours back in the Lobster Smack,' Doc continued benignly. 'You should've come through to the bar. We were all in there, getting royally pissed up.'

Jo nodded again. 'I should've,' she said, 'but I was very . . .' she paused, embarrassed.

'I brought you a bit of stuff over, anyway,' Doc tactfully interrupted her, 'a spare sleeping bag, a flask, a few sandwiches we had left. It's a filthy night to be sleeping out if you're not . . .'

'That's very kind . . .' Jo smiled at him (he shrugged, as if momentarily resenting his own amiability) then she wound the window down further and pushed out her hands, 'I'm actually in my . . .'

She glanced modestly towards her chest, 'so it's a little . . .'

Doc stepped back, circumspectly –

326

Pissed, he was

For certain

– then leaned forward, trepidatiously, from his new position (careful not to encroach even a half-inch further) and handed her each item, individually. The bag was a stretch, but she managed to pull it through, with a tug.

'That's Hooch's. He'll definitely be wanting it back first thing,' Doc warned her, 'it's a good one.'

'Of course,' Jo nodded, 'I'm very grateful to you, Doc.'

Used the name

Doc shrugged, 'I only hope Shoes didn't scare you off earlier. He said he saw you in the bathroom. He likes to use the Ladies when he's had a few. Means no harm by it.'

Jo smiled, said nothing.

'He went out and collected you some dock leaves. For the cuts. Wes always uses dock. He swears by it. And he wanted me to give you this; to pass the hours, he said.'

Doc offered her some large, glossy green leaves, and under these, a book –

Utah Blaine

Jo took them both, her heart almost missing a beat, immediately slipping the book – surreptitiously – down the side of her seat, 'Well thank him from me, Doc.'

Doc nodded, 'Better close that window before you lose all your heat.'

'Thanks.'

Jo started winding. Doc turned away, paused –

Just please don't ask . . .

– then spun back around to face her again.

'So your police friend didn't say anything important? Didn't shed any interesting light on what was happening earlier?'

Jo froze. '*Uh* . . .' She stopped winding and peeked evasively through the remaining gap. 'No. Sorry. *No.* It was all slightly . . .' she grimaced. He put his head to one side, as if he couldn't quite hear her.

She removed her eyes from the gap and replaced them with her lips, 'It was all just a little bit *complicated.*' She ducked down, reconnecting her eyes with the gap to gauge his reaction.

Doc was shrugging, off-handedly.

'Let's catch up in the morning,' he said, still not moving, but standing and watching her, calmly, as she placed her lips to the gap again, whispered, 'Thanks, Doc, goodnight then . . .' and gladly recommenced her last few inches of winding.

But he stayed.

He remained in place until that keen, water-drenched pane of glass firmly hit its snug rubber lining; still as an old egret in a fertile rice paddy; rigid as a doubting nun at her thrice-nightly prayers; quiet as a dishonest clerk creeping around after hours; firm as Gibraltar – and just as imperturbable – he held and he held and he kept on holding.

Thirty-one

They sat in a kind of *anti*-communion around the table; Katherine and Dewi at either end (making no physical or visual contact whatsoever), Ted and Arthur on opposite sides (their feet and shins occasionally knocking together). Nobody spoke a word. The atmosphere (although by no means every individual contributing to it) was sober.

Four places were set – Dewi had taken Wesley's; knew damn well he had; didn't care – but there was no sign, as yet, of the guest of honour. Dinner was burned. It sat congealing in the oven.

Ted politely stifled a yawn and shifted his foot (knocked Arthur's boot, quickly shifted it back). He nodded a shy apology.

Where on earth *was* Wesley, anyway? He'd taken the precaution of ringing his own phone (which Wes was still in firm possession of – no answer, turned off) and then the Police Station (on first arriving at the bungalow). They claimed they'd released him an hour before.

(Was he in trouble? Was he taking the Mick? Would it be sensible, or appropriate even, to go out and search for him; this being a man who evaded pursuit semi-professionally – made a kind of . . . of *living* from it?).

How the heck did we all end up here, Ted wondered, turning his glass over, superstitiously (they'd been placed upside down, as if in preparation for a game of Ouija) and glancing around the table at the other three. This whole situation just seemed so . . . so . . .
So infernally Wesley
– but what did that mean?

Ted still hadn't entirely come to terms with the whole . . . the whole 'Following' wheeze. Couldn't really grasp the ins and the outs of it; the numerous subtle permutations of what you were meant to do – or not to do – as the case may be.

One thing was for certain, though . . .
He suddenly sneezed –
Katherine's perfume
Old-fashioned breath cashews
Industrial-strength fly killer
– snatched his hanky – with dispatch – from his top pocket (frowning fastidiously), patted his nose and the back of his wrist with it.

They were definitely –
Phew
That was better
(he shook his head, shuddering)
– they were definitely all waiting for some *thing* to happen. And it wasn't just Wesley (the bugger) or the meal (Goddammit). It was . . . and this really *did* sound like a bit of a . . . *uh* . . .
A cockamamie . . .
– they were waiting –
I mean just look at them all . . .
   (Ted lifted his head and gazed around the table)
– they were all waiting for life –
For life
Yes
– they were all waiting for life to take over; in all its sheer, crushing . . . the *sap* . . . the brutality . . . the horror . . . the actual, candid . . . the cruel . . . the unexpurgated . . .
Yes
– because that was what he stood for –
Wasn't it?
– that was what he represented –
Didn't he?
– the independent stroke – the cocking a snook – the kick in the pants – the gently raised middle . . . index . . . *uh* . . .
What am I thinking?
   Ted abruptly abandoned his attempt to make sense of things –
Futile

He felt ridiculously ill-equipped for the struggle. He felt over-powered by circumstance; like a tiny fieldmouse (he told himself) foetal-ing up as it feels the plough's first horrible tremor. I'm a purely defensive kind of rodent, he gently mused. I'm not a fighter. I'm a huddler. A curler. I cannot –

I will not

– flee.

I stay in place, no matter what. I do my best to hold my head up. And they can mock me, if they like –

And they do mock, too

– they can mock me, but it's a kind of . . .

I won't run

– a kind of . . . of . . .

Sincerity?

Was that it?

Ted glanced down at his watch. Wesley was two hours –

Free – he was – indisputably

  two *whole* hours late.

No gentle little field-rodent, he –

Not Wesley

– Ted visualised him as some kind of unashamedly big-boned, scruffy-whiskered, fast-perambulating, ginger-coated puss.

A predator to the core –

Never comes home on time

Won't do as you say

Takes what he wants and then buggers off

Tail held high

Arse neat and tight as a spinster's kiss

With big old teeth (Ted smiled to himself, secretly), three-pawed, one-eared, vagabond-suited, hob-nail booted. Carrying a twig –

A stick

– with a spotted 'kerchief held over one shoulder –

Whistling

– ridiculously jaunty. Sun shining down on him. Obligatory blue jay singing somewhere in the . . . in the . . .

Rear of the picture

Ted couldn't help remembering – with a kind of perplexed awe – the way Wes'd reacted to the news about his daughter. The way he took those punches in the bar. The way he'd faced up to Katherine –

Just stormed on in there

The way he'd slaughtered that bird and forgave the . . . the . . . the . . .

Impostor

And the Pond –

The pond

Ah

He also remembered (equally irresistibly) the way Dewi had behaved (just an hour before) when he'd turned up at the agency ready to mend the lock and reset that door. The hostility. The intensity. The . . . the . . .

Life!

. . . the magnificent *involvement* –

Yes!

'Are you on his side, Edward? Has he talked you around? Has he worked his magic? Is it admiration, Edward, or confusion? Are you overwhelmed? Is it fear?'

And Ted had said –

'Does it have to be a question of taking sides?'

Taking sides?

Pshaw!

That was such . . . such . . .

Playground behaviour

And Dewi had shaken his head, and he had looked at him, sadly –

Like he's never looked at me before –

Hang on

Hang . . .

Isn't that because he's never actually looked –

Never actually seen me before now?

Is this what it took?

To be visible?

And Dewi said –

It's like bloodsports, Edward, or prostitution or public executions. It's something that you instinctively take a side on. Look into your heart, Edward. Read what's written there.'

And Ted had looked (in all sincerity). And he saw –
A pond
In the summer
Heat sizzling on the algae
Releasing the sour scent of kelp
Angry spinach
Sticking to his fingers as he swished a limp hand . . .
As he . . .
Hmmn
– he saw nothing in particular.

Ted slid his tongue across his upper plate –
Bubbles from the fish rising to the top
The occasional water . . .
– and that was it, really –
The occasional water snail . . .
– that was –
Fin

Ted flipped himself back into the present. He found himself fingering his tie (mentally re-processing the neat lines of hand-stitching). He licked his lips, relinquished his grip, weaved his ten fingers together on his lap (feeling that reassuring callus on his index finger), jiggled his shoulders, stretched his neck, gazed over briefly at his table setting. He was missing –
A dessert spoon

He peered around. Everybody else had . . . had . . .
No pudding for Ted

He sank back down into his chair. Lowered his head (as if saying grace) and rested his chin (like a golf ball upon its tee) onto the hard, neat knot of his tie –
My poor back
In agony

He and Arthur were less 'sat' at that table, more 'sunk' (like two well-hammered tent pegs) into a couple of old-fashioned deck chairs which Katherine had dragged inside from the back conservatory upon Ted's arrival (no comment offered on the fact of Dewi. Not a smile, a frown, a wisecrack. Just a quiet –
A howling
– indifference).

333

She'd looked on keenly as Ted'd battled to set the chairs up (refusing to let the others help him), clucking her tongue sarcastically with each more clumsy attempt, finally chastising him roundly –

Ah

So this is to be my punishment

– then shoving him aside and taking over herself (if she'd had sleeves she'd have rolled them up), instructing Arthur –

Since when did these two get so tight?

– to time her, and setting both chairs up at just under . . .

'Five seconds, *per*,' he said, deftly tapping the glass on his watch-face with his finger.

The chairs – built for lounging – were so low that only their occupants' heads and necks were visible above the table-top. Katherine and Dewi perched primly on stools which – as the fates decreed – were just fractionally too high (Dewi, at the cutlery drawer end, couldn't fit his knees under comfortably, so sat sideways, tipped – as was his preference – towards Ted; conspicuously ignoring the now diminutive Arthur).

It was 12.15 a.m. Ted silently thanked the Lord that he'd rung on ahead (crossed himself, inconspicuously).

Katherine snorted, for no apparent reason –

Did she just see?

Dewi'd had him over a barrel. Either they promptly returned to Katherine's aid – as he touchingly described it – with the help of Ted's handy house key (Dewi'd known she wouldn't let him in if he tried to gain access the traditional way. She could recognise his ring. It was actually quite uncanny), or the agency's bathroom door would remain unhinged, as, doubtless, would Pathfinder, on uncovering the extent of Ted's wrongdoing the following morning.

Even so – warning or no warning – Katherine was still clad in only her underwear, with a tea towel (decorated in gypsy caravans – one approaching, one in retreat, a barge, a shire horse, a watering can and a calendar: 1994) tucked into her bra. The towel was newly stained at its centre.

Ted was no expert in these matters, but there were definitely the voracious marks of sex all over her (bite marks, scuff marks, suck-marks, finger-prints, general but unspecific wear and tear) and she exuded (even up against the stink of burnt poultry, chinchilla pee, cigarettes, apricot brandy) an exquisitely piquant post-coital aroma.

In the corner, on the sideboard (Ted could only see over there at a stretch from his painfully reduced position) he noted that Arthur was successfully re-energising his computer –
Fast worker, eh?

Dewi re-adjusted his knife and fork into their more traditional positions, straightened his spoon (Katherine – apparently not look-ing, but patently still seeing – groaned under her breath. He flinched) and then silently followed Ted's eye-line. He stared at the computer for a long, long while. Then he pointed towards it.

'What's that?' he asked (with all the quizzical moral zeal of a four-year-old child at the public zoo on espying a fully aroused male gorilla approaching an unsuspecting female from the rear). It was the first time he'd actually spoken (they had been in *situ* now for almost half-an-hour).

'It *talks*,' Katherine exclaimed, kicking Arthur under the table (as if she was now the child, but visiting a science lab, where Dewi was being held hostage as a creature of experimental interest).

Arthur – ignoring the kick as best he could – glanced over to the sideboard. 'It's my computer . . .' he said, sounding suitably non-plussed –
What is this?
The Stone Age?

'It's just recharging.'

'What's it *for*?' Dewi asked (still talking to Ted, ignoring Arthur).

'*Computering*, you imbecile,' Katherine snarled, 'what else?'
Good Heavens
– Arthur cleared his throat, anxiously –
A whole shit-load of hostility at work here, apparently

A further silence.

'Who *is* he?' Dewi asked (Ted again – and his timing so exquis-itely snail-like that even the agent felt his hackles rising). Dewi tipped his head fractionally in Arthur's direction (just to make sure), 'and what's he think he's doing here?'

Nobody answered (not least because no one could actually

remember Arthur's name). Arthur himself was struggling . . . the
sex had been . . . had been . . .

Bewildering

No

No . . .

Luminous

No

No . . .

Nu-minous

(Uh . . . Was that it?)

'Who *is* he?' Dewi repeated, this time using his thumb (hitching
it rudely in Arthur's direction) and addressing the question directly
to Katherine.

He'd crossed a line – Ted could tell, Art could tell – but nobody
knew what that line was, precisely, or what crossing it meant.

Katherine stared back blankly (her eyes as bold and empty as
a cuckoo's conscience) then turned to Ted, 'This is stupid. I'm
ravenous. Should we get started on dinner?'

'I *love* you, Katy,' Dewi murmured.

Oh God

Arthur raised his brows, stared at his crotch, chewed on his lip.
Ted sank down even lower into his chair. Katherine stood up,
grabbed her glass, turned it over, picked up the jug of water close
by, stepped back, and poured an exact glassful onto the floor.

Then she placed the jug back down again, walked to the cooker
(stepping daintily through the mess), grabbed an oven glove and
opened the door.

They all watched, in unison, as she bent over – the stool's curved
wooden edge pinkly printed onto the lower segment of her bottom
– removed Wesley's casserole and carried it over.

Arthur cleared his throat. He remembered Dewi – with a spectacular clarity; in technicolor, in 3D – from the fight in the bar.
Dewi's left fist, in fact (currently resting like a flesh-rock on the
table-top) was very slightly grazed across the knuckle –

And I just screwed her on the tiles?

Was I off my . . . ?

'I'm Arthur,' he said, 'Arthur *Young*. I'm . . .'

How to explain it?

336

Which side to take?
How to avoid . . .
To . . .
'. . . I'm a . . . I'm actually a . . . a *charity* worker.'
Wow

They all turned to look at him.

'To be fucked out of *charity* in my own kitchen,' Katherine eventually mused, placing down the casserole pot and lifting the lid, 'that's *got* to be a first.'

Dewi stood up, leaned over the table (Arthur flinched), picked up the water jug and poured himself a glass. He drank it. Still towering above them. Seven huge glugs, his prodigious Adam's apple bobbing like a locomotive piston.

'Tell a lie,' Katherine continued, grabbing a ladle for dishing up, 'Ted actually fucked me three times out of charity in October last year. I forced you to,' Katherine cuffed his cheek fondly with the ladle, 'didn't I, darling?'

Arthur suddenly began talking. Off the top of his head. Whatever he could . . . whatever came to . . .
Had no . . .
No long-term . . .
No . . .
. . . whatever he could dish-up-serve-*present* at such short notice . . .
Like a kind of –
Socially-ambivalent free-association
– totally arbitrary mental ratatouille –
Tomato, onion, egg-plant, courgette . . .

'I don't know if you're familiar with a man called Jonathan . . . uh . . . *Routh*,' Arthur cracked his finger-joints – with relief – on remembering the name – from the book – on the bedside table – in the boat – a few hours before, 'he was one of the . . . uh . . . the first . . . uh . . .'

Dewi sat down again, abruptly.

'He was actually – or he claimed to be – one of the foremost practical jokers of the second half of the last . . . uh . . . the last . . . uh . . . century. He was behind some awful television programme called . . . called . . . called something like . . . uh . . .'

'*Candid Camera*,' Katherine said.

'Yes. *Yes,*' he bounced back, 'I think that's right.'

'It is right. I loved that programme.'

'Yes,' Arthur paused for a moment, confusedly –

Need to change tack, quick

'Yes, well . . . I suppose he *was* an interesting figure. I was just looking through his . . . his autobiography. And apparently after he left university he took out an ad in the personal columns of *The Times*, advertising himself as a practical joker. He didn't . . .'

As he spoke Arthur was focussing principally on Ted.

'He didn't feel like he was fit for much else . . . which, *uh*, I suppose says a lot about what people consider a top flight . . . *uh* . . . education . . .'

Ted glanced up and caught his eye at this point, then rapidly looked down again, wincing, 'But he had a novel way of looking at things and he . . . *uh* . . .'

Arthur peeked over at Dewi. Averted his eyes –

Quick-smart

'And people . . . people would . . .' Arthur reached out his arm and pushed his plate towards the casserole pot, 'people would actually pay him to play these . . . these practical *jokes* on . . . *uh* . . .'

Why does this feel so familiar?

He gazed up at Katherine, almost beseechingly. Katherine shrugged and delved into the pot.

'But he always said that the . . . *uh* . . . the only reason to play a joke on someone – or a hoax or anything – was to create an atmosphere of bewilderment and *men-men-mental* confusion. It's never a moral . . . *uh* . . . morality doesn't . . . for the *real* practical joker morality doesn't ever enter into the . . . *uh* . . .'

Arthur glanced towards Dewi again, 'But Wesley would say – and *wrongly*, in my opinion – because of his reading of pop-sociological works like those of, say, Alvin Toffler . . .' he half-inclined his head, 'I don't know if you're . . . you're *familiar* with . . . *uh* . . . with . . . ?'

Katherine snorted.

Dewi remained perfectly still, staring quietly at Katherine, saying nothing. Katherine pulled some burned skin off the top of the casserole (placed it onto Ted's plate) then proceeded to delve inside again.

'Well . . .' Arthur was slightly discombobulated by this (his eyes flying from one person to the next). 'Well, anyway, Toffler – did I say *Toffler* before?'

Ted nodded, still refusing eye contact.

'Yes. Well, Toffler talks about how change is achieved by the combination of confusion or chaos and . . . *uh* . . . natural . . . natural disaster . . .'

Dewi suddenly turned his head and stared at Arthur, frowning (as if he'd only just noticed him again). 'What *kind* of charity?' he asked.

Arthur stared back at him blankly, then held out his hand, 'I don't think we were formally introduced before. I'm Arthur Young.'

Dewi ignored his hand.

'What *kind* of charity?' he repeated.

Arthur paused, withdrew his hand. Katherine filled the pause by pushing Arthur's plate back towards him. 'I served you first,' she whispered, 'because we had such a first class *fuck.*'

'A . . . a . . . a *children's* charity,' Arthur swallowed, hard –

Was she insane?

– and took the plate. 'Thanks. You were saying earlier that Dewi here was a talented carpenter, weren't you, Katherine?'

She looked over at him, smiling, '*Huh?*'

'You . . . you were saying that Dewi here was a brilliant carpenter, weren't you?'

'He *is* a carpenter,' Katherine confirmed, pushing aside the burned stuff on Ted's plate then ladling out some of the unburned, 'but I don't know when we'd've had time to discuss it . . .' she frowned, 'although I suppose we did squeeze in a couple of minutes' small-talk directly before the second blow job.'

'Not too much,' Ted murmured, hoarsely.

'And that's *just* what I said when you showed me your sweet, little dick last October, eh, Ted?'

Silence

'Because in the same book . . .' Arthur began speaking again, 'the same book I mentioned before . . . *uh* . . . Toffler says . . . I did cite Toffler, previously, didn't I?'

Ted nodded.

'Yes. Yes. Well Toffler said that it's the people who live slower and more practical . . . *uh* . . . lives who will ultimately reap the benefits of . . . *uh* . . . of our accelerated . . . *uh* . . .'

What am I doing?

What am I saying?

Arthur scooped up a spoonful of food and pushed it into his mouth, chewed, swallowed.

'That's very good,' he said, 'in actual fact.'

'*Children's* charity?'

Dewi had finally re-connected.

Arthur scooped up a second spoonful.

Dewi was staring at him again, pointedly, 'You said a *children's* charity?'

Ted pushed his spoon into his mouth and nodded, 'Yes.'

He spoke through the casserole.

Katherine dished herself up a tiny portion and sat down. She removed a feather from the edge of her plate.

'What *kind* of children's charity?' she asked, nonchalantly.

'*Eh* . . . ?' Arthur glanced up, 'for . . . *uh* . . . for . . .'

'Children,' Katherine filled in. 'I do believe we've all fully grasped that difficult concept.'

Arthur pulled himself straight. He pushed his hand into his trouser pocket and pulled out his wallet. He opened it. He closed it again. He un-poppered the back section, turned the wallet over and drew out a clutch of business cards and credit cards. Mixed up between them was a tiny photograph. He removed it; a little girl, about seven years old, thin, anxious-seeming, brown eyed, wearing a plain jumper and a matching pale blue alice-band to pull the loose wisps of brown hair away from her face.

Arthur pushed the picture over the table towards Dewi.

'My . . . my . . .' he said, stammering, swallowing. 'She has a condition called Cystic Fibrosis. It means her body produces excessive amounts of . . . of . . .' he cleared his throat, 'of phlegm which tends to settle on her chest. She finds it difficult to . . .' he filled his lungs, 'to breathe.'

Dewi put out his hand and picked up the picture. He cradled it inside his huge hand, gently.

'Some other . . . complications,' Arthur continued, 'I . . . I raise

340

money to increase awareness of the condition in Britain. We . . . we're saving for a h-h-h-heart and lung transplant. In America . . .'

'What's her name?' Dewi asked.

Arthur started at this question. 'Harmony,' he stuttered. 'She's not a . . . a transplant priority over here because she has other . . . other problems. Which is . . .'

He scrabbled for the word.

'Sad,' Dewi said.

'Wrong,' Ted said.

'Crap,' Katherine said.

All at the same time.

Arthur nodded.

'Yes.'

He smiled shakily.

Dewi suddenly stood up. 'I have a bundle of cash from a job I did today. I want you to have it,' he said. 'Come over and get it. I live directly opposite.'

Arthur was shocked. He put down his spoon.

'Right *now*?' he asked, glancing anxiously towards his computer, towards Katherine, his dinner plate, 'this very minute?'

'Why not?'

Dewi was already pulling at the door and walking through it.

'*Uh* . . .' Arthur stood up. 'Fine,' he said, looking towards Katherine again, hoping for reassurance – finding none – then Ted. Ted was biting his lip and pushing aside a piece of the burned stuff on his plate.

Arthur took a deep breath, pushed back his deckchair, turned and followed the Welshman – slowly at first, then gradually picking up speed – like a boy who'd just casually released his grip on the string of a balloon, and yet suddenly longed – once more – to feel the reassuring tug of it.

Thirty-two

Doc was hardly five yards from the car before Wesley had yanked himself straight and tossed off the blanket. His hair was ruffled, his T-shirt pulled skew – one sleeve pushed right up (over his shoulder, under his armpit) and the remaining bulk concertinaed rather fetchingly across his midriff (Jo caught a quick glimpse of his skinny stomach – an object lesson in unswerving muscularity – and felt her ears –

Ears?

– tingling in a bizarre response). His face was no longer swollen, but definitely pinkened in places, his chin –

That determined chin

– grazed very slightly. Not too bad, though, really, all things considered.

'Sleeping bag,' Josephine murmured, turning her eyes away from his belly and towards the ceiling. It was rolled up, fatly, on her lap. She put her arms around it. Squeezed it, furtively. Rested her head on top –

My cover's blown

It's over

He knows for sure now that I'm a real Follower

Wesley gave her a curious look, almost as if he could read what her thoughts were –

Mustn't think

– then he turned his head away and stared (although there was no view, only moisture) at his side window. A few seconds later he turned and gazed at her again, his expression not so much hostile as profoundly heedful; like a too skinny dog sitting hard and fast against a well-laden trestle table.

'There's a flask,' Josephine added, somewhat fatuously (as if he hadn't heard her conversation with Doc perfectly well himself), 'something hot.'

'Seems like we're all *very* well set up, then,' Wesley responded, stretching (confinedly) –

Being sarcastic . . . (Was he?)

– pulling down his T-shirt, then brushing his good hand through his hair –

We . . . (Did he just say?)

Josephine nodded, modestly. They were well set up. She felt a brief glow of optimism. Perhaps misguidedly.

'Good old *Doc*,' Wesley added, his tone prodigiously jocular.

Jo nodded again, but slower this time, as she watched his –

False . . .

Had to be . . .

– grin turn into a scowl.

'He admires you a great deal,' she said, 'if that helps.'

Oh God, just listen to me

'I mean they all do – for the most part.'

'It doesn't help,' Wesley snapped, 'and it isn't true. You plainly have absolutely no *conception* of what Following represents, what it consists of, in real terms.'

Not so much aggressive as . . . as . . . well, yes *aggressive*.

He snatched the flask, which was almost rolling from her lap, unscrewed the cup and then the lid.

'It might seem novel to you,' he said, 'all this . . . this unexpected *solidarity*. But I've had four solid godforsaken fucking *years* of it.'

Josephine stared straight ahead, her shoulders rolled forward defensively –

I screwed up

'Note,' Wesley continued, jiggling the flask at her, 'this is the kind of flask *I* have.'

He suddenly chuckled to himself, as if she wasn't actually there and he was quietly partaking in a perfectly cheery yet despicably below average interior monologue.

'*My flask*,' he murmured.

'What's in it?' she asked brightly.

Is mundanity the answer?

Avoidance?

'I predict . . .' Wesley sniffed, '*yup*. Oxtail. That devious old prick virtually lives on the stuff.'

Josephine grimaced.

'What's with the face?' he snapped.

She stopped grimacing.

'You loathe oxtail, is that it?' he asked. 'You were force-fed it as a kid. Thought it'd put hairs on your chest, but they never actually sprouted . . . at least,' he shrugged, gazing at her flat breasts, provokingly, 'I don't *think* they did, anyway.'

She slowly untied the sleeping bag.

'I thought,' she eventually muttered (utterly composed), 'we weren't meant to be talking about all that.'

'That's *right*,' Wesley congratulated her, perhaps a little too robustly.

He tipped some soup into the cup, still talking as he poured, 'So what did Shoes do to you exactly in that cosy pub toilet? Did he show you his piercings? His etchings? Did he . . .' he stopped pouring, glanced over, mischievously, 'did he fuck you senseless? Did he shit you up?'

'You were right. I'm not a great fan of oxtail,' she said primly.

'Not a great fan,' Wesley repeated.

He blew on the soup then knocked it back. He poured her a cup.

'Did you see his tattoos, Josephine Bean?' he asked, offering it to her, cordially. 'Weren't you terribly impressed?'

Josephine took the soup. She sniffed it. She nodded. Her affirmation was suitably non-specific. Wesley grabbed the sandwich container. He pulled off its tupperware lid.

'For your information, Josephine,' he said, 'I have a tupperware container *exactly* like this one in my rucksack.'

Josephine took a sip of the soup. Almost burned her tongue on it (it was extremely salty, but wonderfully hot). Then she took another sip, cradled her hands around the cup and allowed its steam to warm her nose, her chin, her cheek.

Wesley snaked out his hand and plucked a stray dock leaf from her lap.

'Dock,' he said, '*I* was about to go out and gather some of that.'

He screwed the soft leaf up, menacingly, and tossed it at the windscreen. Her side.

He was –

Bully

– intimidating her.

And quite successfully –

I don't care, I don't care, just so long as he stays here

She cleared her throat. 'He had . . . he . . . Shoes had a strange one on his stomach,' she said, struggling to maintain a rather puny sense of decorum, 'a very . . . very strange tattoo.'

'Really.'

Wesley wasn't interested. He was inspecting the sandwiches.

'Salmon paste,' he muttered, peeling one open. He pushed it into his mouth, whole, and peeled open a second. 'Chocolate spread,' he said, through his mouthful.

She turned to look at him, her eyebrows raised.

'Not together,' he clarified, sensing her sudden interest, 'obviously.'

'Obviously,' she echoed, still watching him, pointedly.

'*What?*'

He scowled at her, his jaw working resentfully.

She shrugged, 'I just . . . I only thought they might be *exactly* like the kind that *you* eat, usually, or . . . or something like that.'

Wesley jumped back, sharply, as if she'd burned him with her wit. Her sarcasm. 'You're a fucking *razor*,' he said.

They were both quiet for a while. Wesley devoured the second sandwich.

'Hangman,' Jo eventually continued (once she'd mustered the requisite stamina).

'Pardon?' He glanced at her, still chewing.

'Two words. Seven and five. Like in the game you play on paper. And the little figure hanging there on the gallows with everything intact but a . . .' she paused, swallowed.

Wesley picked up a third sandwich and took a bite. Spoke with his mouth full, 'But a *what?* My God it's like squeezing blood from a stone with you, Bean.'

'But a *hand*,' she said, 'a right hand.'

She glanced towards his – held hers up – took a final sip of the soup then passed it back. He delivered a scorching glance as he grabbed the cup, 'You really love all this stuff, huh? All this fatuous, this . . . this pointless riddle-puzzle *cack*.'

Jo didn't answer.

He shook his head, 'I never thought anyone would fall for it – least of all anyone remotely intelligent. A *girl* for fuck's sake . . .'

He burped.

'Pardon me.'

'Fall for what?'

'*Look* at you,' Wesley suddenly guffawed, pointing at her, 'you really *are* one of them. You're slotting in, Bean . . . *Bean from Southend.* I mean Doc bringing you some soup and a fucking . . .' he pointed, 'for Christ's sake, a fucking *sleeping* bag.'

He rolled back in his seat, then rocked energetically forward again, as though fuelled by his piss-taking. '*Waah!*' he yelled, waving his hands at her and smiling gummily like a black and white minstrel caught mid-ditty.

Josephine looked stiff. Hurt. She embraced the bag tightly again.

'*Man*, it's like a *disease* with you people . . .'

He peeked at her, hugging himself – grinning, plainly delighted by his own psychological acuity. She looked crushed. She was shivering again.

Cold

'Oh for *fuck's* sake,' Wesley's cheer evaporated, 'I gave you my jacket didn't I? We're having a *conversation*, aren't we? I could be . . .'

Having sex with the white skinned girl in that disgracefully hot kitchen, the bird well cooked, full of brandy

'I know I must seem rather ridiculous to you,' Josephine murmured softly, 'and that I made a real fool of myself, earlier, in the bar. It was a . . . an unnecessary *complication* – like you said – a distraction – a misjudgement. I can see that now. But I felt so . . .' she shrugged, poignantly, 'so *terrible* for Dewi. All that hurt – all that *upset* – it's all been so unnecessary.'

Wesley's eyes widened a fraction, 'You felt sorry for the *moose?*'

He was taken aback.

Josephine nodded, 'He's the most decent man.'

Wesley put a tentative hand to his jaw, his cheek, 'For some *inexplicable* reason,' he growled, 'I hadn't really considered it from his side before.'

'Sometimes it's actually harder hitting than just being . . . just being a . . . a *target*,' Josephine continued, her confidence growing.

'And did anybody ever punch *you* in the face before?' he asked, forming his bad hand into a fingerless fist, as if seriously considering trying it out for himself.

(Down on his lap, however, his good hand was quietly sneaking its way over towards his bad, pulling it back, loosening it up and then gently touching the scars there – as if they represented a novel kind of braille which he never tired of reading; the primitive topography for a beloved journey.)

'No,' Josephine shook her head, 'and anyway, we're not meant to be talking about all of that,' she smiled, 'are we?'

She stared ahead of her, at the windscreen, staunchly.

Wesley didn't say anything for a while. Then he pulled his hands apart, reached forward and drew a series of short lines into the moisture on the windscreen. Seven, a small gap, then five

'So how many letters did Shoes have in place?' he asked. 'Can you remember?'

Josephine straightened slightly, peeked at him, side-long.

Is this a test?

Should I dare answer?

She quietly tried to visualise it all in her head; Shoes' prodigious dough-rise stomach; that inescapably sensuous blue-pale hillock of unassailable flesh.

Wesley drained her cup, meanwhile, then screwed it – and the cap – back into place.

'He had one D, I think, and two Ns. G at the start. Maybe an E somewhere . . .'

She leaned forward in her seat, reached out her finger and wrote the letters into the requisite gaps.

G – – D – – N – EN – –

Wesley stuck out his lip and mulled this over. 'I think you'll find it's two Ds,' he said, pointing to the penultimate letter in the second word, 'not one. And no E either,' he added, scratching it out with his thumb.

G – – D – – N – – ND –

Josephine frowned, then reconsidered, 'You could be right . . .'

'Oh I *am* right,' he butted in.

'Really?' she smiled. 'Have you seen it yourself, then? Did he show it to you? Wasn't it amazing?'

Wesley shook his head (he smirked at *amazing*, though).

'So how do you know?' she asked, plainly bewildered, 'and what's the answer? Is it something clever? Or . . .' she wrinkled up her nose, suspiciously, 'or something dirty?'

Dirty

Wesley smiled again at her choice of vocabulary. She was so *clean*, this Bean. 'It's just a little joke,' he said. 'It's like *your name* written on his arse. About the same league as that.'

'And it has something to do with *you*, presumably?'

Wesley shrugged. He paused. 'Do you remember the sound of his toenails tippy-tapping on the tiles from behind you?'

She nodded. She did remember. She almost shuddered.

Wesley nodded, 'Yeah. Well I hear that sound constantly. I hear that sound in my dreams. I've been Followed by fuck-ups quite a bit. It goes with the territory. But he really shits me up sometimes with his gentleness and his fatness and his infernal fucking *tippy-tippy-tap*.'

He leaned forward (Jo sunk back, instinctively) and wiped the screen clean with his palm. 'Pass me the leaves,' he said, observing her retreat with a half-smile, 'and give me your arm.'

Josephine did as he asked, then stared at the smudged windscreen again, deep in thought. 'Here's a sandwich,' he said. 'Eat.'

She took the sandwich with her spare hand while he rolled up her sleeve. Underneath, the flesh was still icy. He found a wad of toilet paper half-covering the cut which must've been shifted back when he'd stared at it previously. He carefully unwound it. Then he pulled her arm nearer to his face and inspected it closely.

Josephine's glazed-over eyes flickered left. She could feel his warm breath. Her skin goose-bumped. She stared down at the sandwich –

Salmon paste

– and took a bite –

No. Tuna

Wesley turned on his side-light. 'Think you need stitches?' he asked.

She shook her head.

'Well I suppose you're the expert.'

The sandwich was halfway to her mouth. She halted its simple trajectory.

'Pardon?'

'You're the nurse.'

'Who told you that?'

'Your nails told me. And your hands. And the way you made the cut. And the way you've cleaned it up.'

She blinked.

He'd barely finished speaking when he pushed his lips up close to the first wound and . . . and . . .

Licked

Not impetuously. Not sensuously. But gently and determinedly, like a well-trained cat.

Jo's arm stiffened.

'I'm an expert,' she said, her voice slightly huskier than normal, 'in the subject of female gynaecology. I campaign for . . .' she took a deep breath, 'for a more environmentally responsible . . . *uh* . . . use of sanitary . . .'

Her arm relaxed –

Like a neat-mouthed, clean-tongued . . .

'Your professional life is of fuck-all interest to me,' Wesley murmured, 'and you have a real *pig* of an iron deficiency.'

He reached out his good hand, rested it lightly on her cheek and pulled down her left eye's lower lid. She did not resist, merely gazed at him, passively.

'*Bingo*,' he said, returning to her arm again.

The cuts were now all sting and prickle, but she wished he'd lick her forever, just the same.

Everywhere.

He released her arm for a moment and rubbed each dock leaf roughly between his palms (to release the sap, she presumed) and then applied them, individually, to the cuts.

She closed her eyes. She drew a deep breath. The sandwich fell from her hand.

'So which of the books was it Shoes gave you before?'

Her eyes flew open again, 'Sorry?'

(She hadn't realised that she'd closed them. That was half the shock.)

'The librarian told me what he took out. But he's not a great reader, Shoes.' Wesley grabbed the discarded tissue paper and gently wound it around her arm again. When he'd finished, he carefully pulled her sleeve down over the top.

'So which book was it?'

Josephine pushed her hand down the side of her chair. She retrieved the book. He took it from her. She stared at his face –

Looking for clues

Can't . . .

Can't help myself

– but he gave nothing away.

'There's this ridiculously prevalent myth about Louis L'Amour . . .' he said, flicking idly through it, 'that his whole existence as a writer-hero of the American West has been fabricated. That he isn't American at all. That he's English. That he lives in Stansted or Woking or somewhere. All complete bullshit, by the way. Because he was the real thing; hobo, writer, marine, cattle rancher, explorer. Entirely self-educated. Bare-knuckle boxer. I love all that stuff . . .'

He slapped it shut and passed it back to her.

'Good choice,' he said.

She took the book and pushed it back down the side of her seat. 'I don't know much about Westerns,' she said, 'but apparently the Estuary is meant to bear a strong resemblance to the American . . .'

'It's the English psyche,' Wesley interrupted, 'we love to de-vitalise – suck out the sap – it's our most fundamental instinct. We mistrust passion. We think it's a sign of weakness or deviance. And we loathe sincerity. It makes us uneasy . . .'

He shrugged, 'It's an automatic gut reaction, a knee-jerk thing. And it's only because we don't actually know who we are, because we're all spent as a nation. Even a cow understands its own essence better than we can – understands its *cowness* – but we don't have a clue. We don't know what it is to be *human*. And we sorely resent all those creatures, those nationalities, those non-conformists who do.'

'D'you reckon L'Amour would be less of a hero if he *did* write all his stuff in a bedsit in Woking?' she asked, idly touching her arm where he'd touched it before.

'That's a bullshit question,' he yawned, 'you obviously haven't been paying attention.' He scratched his head then collapsed back on his seat. 'I'm going to sleep,' he said, 'turn off the heater, put my jumper and coat back on, unzip the sleeping bag, we'll need to share it.'

Then he switched the light off, shifted onto his right hip and turned slightly to the left. 'I'll take on the doorhandle,' he told her, grudgingly, 'if you don't mind the gearstick.'

Thirty-three

'It's so damn *Catholic*,' Katherine told him, 'the way you always clean your plate off like that.'

Ted put down his fork, looked up. 'I don't always,' he said, a hint of childish rebellion entering his voice, 'and it has nothing to do with being . . .'

'Yes you do,' she interrupted.

'Not if it's cabbage or broad beans,' he said.

'You really need to cast off those shackles, Ted. The permanent stain of the armed *bloody* forces, the infernal, strangulating *noose* of the papacy. Cast them off! Stop being so ridiculously *compliant*. It's so boring for everybody.'

'Navy,' he murmured obdurately, glancing over towards the door.

'Same thing,' she said.

'No,' he said.

She gazed down at him, opened her mouth and covered it with her hand in a demonstration of *faux*-shock.

He shrugged

'Let's face it, Teddy, once the church *and* the army have had their portion,' she continued, like a puppy worrying a discarded sock, 'there's only a very tiny little piece of the original Ted left. And this significant part is defined *entirely* by its absolute rejection of the broad bean.'

Ted shook his head. She was always like this. Would never leave things where they were. He glanced over towards the door for a second time.

'Why's the door suddenly so fascinating?'

353

'If you must know,' he said (as if seeing the door had somehow given him confidence – the certain confirmation of a quick exit, maybe), 'I didn't entirely like the way that you . . .'

Entirely

Such a compromise word

Wesley wouldn't use it

Wesley wouldn't compromise with his words like that

'I didn't *at all* like . . .'

Nope

That's just not me

He tried to push himself away from the table (eating at such an acute angle had given him indigestion. His neck was aching. He was slightly worried about Arthur – and Wesley, too, for that matter, however gratuitously).

Katherine put out a restraining hand, grabbed a firm hold of his arm, stopped him. '*Hates* broad beans, *loves* the door,' she announced. 'That's almost a manifesto, Ted. You could run for political office on it. It's a fucking *platform*.'

'True,' he said.

'And *that's* a good one;' Katherine smiled, '*agrees with anything to avoid conflict*. It's just *got* to be a central plank in your electoral strategy.'

Ted shrugged.

'So what . . .' she tightened her grip on his arm, '*what* was it that you didn't like before?'

Ted cleared his throat. Now he was in for it.

'And *where* did Wesley get to, anyway,' she continued, picking up her plate, stacking it on top of his and then leaving it there. 'Nobody's filled me in yet.'

Ted half-smiled to himself –

Off the hook

He straightened his head.

'Your cryptic smile,' Katherine informed him, 'is pissing me off.'

'I'm worried about Arthur,' he said, wiping his smile away, jiggling his stiff shoulder, 'I'm worried Dewi might be . . .' he paused.

'Might be what?'

'Dewi thinks he's one of the Behindlings. He thinks it's a question of taking sides. Or that's what he told me.'

'I can see why,' Katherine concurred (somewhat unexpectedly, Ted thought, considering), 'and *I* thought he was, too, to begin with, but not any more,' she put her finger to her nose, 'he doesn't *smell* like someone who'd Follow. He smells of boot polish and resin. Like *repression*. He smells like a leader of men, but all kind of . . . kind of *stunted* . . . *misdirected* . . .'

Ted was frowning –

Resin?

'All the charity stuff,' Katherine continued, 'was absolutely inspired. And he fucks like a wolf. He's *fantastically* sinewy.'

Ted winced at this.

'God. You and your damn *wincing*,' Katherine muttered, pulling her hair away from her face, 'let's see . . .' she counted each thing off, on her fingers, individually, 'so we've got wincing, broad beans, love of the door . . .'

'Talking of . . . *uh* . . . I saw . . .' Ted put his own hand to his neck, his tie.

'Pardon?' Katherine didn't like being interrupted, especially by him.

'I saw the *Bean* girl, earlier. She was in the bar. And I've seen her outside here, twice, with the Followers . . .'

No reaction from Katherine.

'You still haven't clarified what you meant,' she said, screwing up her eyes, 'when you said *I didn't like the way that you* . . .'

Ted pulled himself up from his deck chair, grabbed their two plates and walked over to the sink.

'It tasted like pheasant,' he said, tipping them in and turning on the tap (no hot water, *dammit*), 'don't you think?'

'It tasted like *heron*,' Katherine said, scowling, debating her options. Either she could sulk it out of him or launch a full-frontal attack.

Ted peeked over his shoulder (almost as if sensing that she was preparing an assault).

'If you must know,' he said, but very hands-off, very conversational, without – he hoped – a trace of criticism . . .

Remember how he took that punch?

Remember?

'I didn't like the way that you behaved with Dewi, earlier.'

'How did I behave?' Katherine was unrepentant.

Ted almost lost his nerve (his nerve was like a go-cart on a sharp corner. It needed handling). •

'Slightly cruel. And a little bit . . .' he tried to find the most appropriate adverb. 'A little bit *provocative* . . . Provocative-*ly*,' he added, as if suddenly uncertain of the grammar.

'But it's my long-term project, Ted,' Katherine patiently explained without a hint of humour, 'to injure him as much as he injured me. It's my life's work. I thought you already knew that.' She was serious. But mocking. Like she always was.

'That's a very . . .' he scratched his neck –

Collar chafing

'I just think you should maybe consider . . .'

Moving on

'If you dare say "moving on", I'm going to rip off your insignificant little prick,' she said, standing up and walking over to Bron's cage, 'and feed it to the damn *chinchilla*.'

Bron was asleep in his box. Blissfully vegetarian. His water bottle was empty again.

'Don't forget that *you* were the person who got us into this shitty situation in the first place. If you hadn't peeked into my Dad's office that day and mistaken me for . . . for . . .'

'But I didn't spread *anything*,' Ted mumbled, 'that was Bo. Bo thought it'd be funny . . .'

'An innocent *hug*,' Katherine bellowed, 'with his own *daughter*.'

Ted nodded, submissively.

'And if Dewi feels the need to take some kind of crazy stance on Following,' Katherine continued, ignoring him, 'or on Wesley, for that matter, then he should look to his laurels. The man's an out-and-out *stalker* – he's a pest – a *betrayer*. And he causes me more mental anguish per *inch* than two thousand stunted, bifocal-wearing weirdoes ever could.'

'That's harsh,' Ted said.

'I think Bron may be too hot,' she grunted. 'Open the back door, will you? I'm going to carry him through to the conservatory.'

Ted did as he was asked. Katherine removed the rodent's water bottle, meanwhile, and walked over to the sink to fill it up. On her way across, she paused in front of Arthur's computer. She put down the bottle and expertly opened the lid.

Ted walked over himself. 'What are you doing?'

'I'm just looking.'

'Why?'

Katherine was bending over to inspect the side of the laptop for its on-off switch.

'Because I *can*, Ted.'

'I really don't think . . .' Ted tried to sound dynamic, 'I *really* don't think that's a good idea.'

'Why not?'

'Because it's private.'

'If it's so fucking *private*, Teddy, then he shouldn't just have left it in my kitchen, should he, using up all my bloody electricity?' She located the button and turned it on. The machine zipped into life. She inspected the keyboard intently as it downloaded.

'A nipple,' she said, 'instead of a mouse. *Ah.* Must've been breast-fed.'

She touched her finger to it. 'And so *responsive.*'

Ted grimaced, stepped back.

'So do you trust him, Ted?' she asked, apparently preoccupied by what she was doing.

'Arthur? Yes,' he answered, almost without thinking.

'Really?'

Ted thought for a moment. 'I don't know. *Yes.* I mean I can't really . . . I don't really understand all this trusting/not-trusting . . .'

'Well *that's* good then.'

She balanced herself neatly on the good side of withering.

'Why?' Ted was daunted. 'Don't you trust him?'

She chuckled, 'Absolutely *not.*'

Ted stared at her for a while, frowning.

'I mean . . .' he conceded, '. . . well, he did seem slightly . . .'

'What?'

She was inspecting his desktop. She seemed very interested in it.

'He was saying some stuff to me – back at the office when he was helping out with the computer – he was saying some stuff about how I was in a perfect position to . . . I mean he said that I was *well placed*. And he said that the Bean girl was *well placed* too. I didn't know what he meant by it. But he gave me a very distinct *look*, like he was trying to make a . . . as if he thought we might be in some kind of . . .'

'Collusion.'

'Yes.'

No

That wasn't the word

Ted frowned, 'He seemed to want to find things out that I wasn't entirely at ease with. Stuff about Wesley . . .'

'*Fuck* Wesley already,' Katherine murmured, turning from the computer to look at him. 'So where does he think the Bean girl fits in? I mean what does the *Bean* girl have to do with anything?'

'The Bean girl . . .' Ted rubbed his hand over his face, tiredly, 'the Bean girl was in Saks when Wesley and I went in there to meet up with Arthur. But before we'd even made it to the bar, Dewi'd charged in and knocked him for six.'

'He hit Wesley?'

The computer beeped. Katherine turned back around to inspect it. 'That was probably my fault,' she mused, 'come to think of it.'

She didn't seem bothered.

'Right. Well . . . anyhow, after he'd hit him a couple of times – knocked him flat, in actual fact, the Bean girl came running through the bar telling him to stop with a smashed beer bottle in her hand, which she held to her arm, and then *sliced* into her wrist with it.'

Katherine turned back around again. 'Why the *fuck* would she do something as stupid as that?'

'That's what *I* thought. I mean that's what I . . . what I wondered.'

Ted shrugged.

Katherine gave him a straight look.

'It just seemed . . .' Ted expanded (couldn't help himself), 'I mean the time-scale and everything, in relation to the Bean girl . . . her hair's all gone now. Cut off . . . her blonde . . .'

Katherine raised her finger in warning.

'Don't you *dare*,' she said.

Ted closed his mouth.

She turned back to the computer and began messing around on it.

'In case you were wondering,' she said (and very casually), 'they have one of these at work. Only bigger.'

Ted seemed surprised by this information.

'What are you doing?' he asked, peering over her shoulder.

On the desktop a series of files had appeared. Katherine went to the first – entitled Gumble Inc – and double clicked on it.

The file consisted of a letter, dated from twelve weeks before . . .

Dear Sir,

they read together,

We are a specialist Austrian plastics manufacturer (specialising mainly in high-impact vegetarian footwear), and are great fans of your website. We would be very interested in taking out a series of high-profile adverts . . .

Katherine exited the document. She entered another one, entitled *Gumble Exclusivity* . . .

Dear Mr Young,

they read

Gumble Inc are extremely satisfied with our participation in the Behindlings enterprise, to the extent that we now feel a major investment in the site would be in our interest. We are currently willing to offer you a lump sum to ensure Gumble Inc exclusivity on the site . . .

Katherine exited the document. She entered another one entitled *No Sale* . . .

Dear Sir,

they read

Thank you for your offer, but after a considerable period of heart-searching I have decided that I am unable to sell the

Behindling site. I do hope that this will not impact on the successful relationship we currently have between Gumble Inc and the site . . .

Katherine exited the document. She was about to enter a third one, entitled *Murdoch*, but then changed her mind. Instead she moved the cursor to *Edit*, ran it down the menu to *Rename* and clicked onto that. The document entitled *Murdoch* turned blue and began to flash.

'Should you be doing that?' Ted asked.

'I'm leaving a little . . .' she chuckled to herself, 'a little *message* for our sinewy friend. Something to give him pause, later on, once I've fucked him again and sent him off home with a flea in his ear . . .'

She thought for a moment, 'Think I'll call it . . .'

She fell silent, typed . . .

BETTER WATCH YOUR STEP, ARTHUR

'I don't get it,' Ted said.

'Of course you don't,' Katherine flapped her hand, dismissively.

She moved the nipple to *Start*, rolled up the menu to *Shut down*, clicked on it, waited . . .

'And you *are* well placed,' she said, tapping her foot, filling in time, 'even if you haven't quite realised it yet.'

Ted frowned confusedly, as she cocked her head, slid her hand rapidly down the side of the laptop and turned it off. It bleeped in protest. She abruptly shut the lid and moved over towards the washing up.

Ted moved with her, glancing anxiously towards the door.

'Mr Arthur Young is back,' she whispered, twisting around, grabbing Ted's face between her hands, pulling it down towards her lips and giving the tip of his snout a gentle kiss, 'I think it's about time baby bear went home to bed.'

Thirty-four

By the time Arthur had negotiated the tiny – but inexplicably cumbersome – front gate, had clambered through the garden and marched onto the verandah (the house was painted a funny colour – the mint of the mint-choc-chip he remembered devouring on idyllic caravanning holidays in Minehead as a kid), the Welshman appeared to have completely evaporated.

The bungalow – as he entered – had an unoccupied feel about it (the smell of dust, the creak of the door), and there was only a single – ineffectual – source of light; a standard lamp with a shabby frill, standing lopsidedly in the far corner.

Arthur peered around, wiping his feet on the mat, stepping inside and pushing the door nearly – but not –
Not
– quite shut.

He still couldn't determine the Welshman's exact whereabouts.

The room was full (*packed* full) of furniture. Good stuff. Wooden pieces (he couldn't, for the most part, tell if they were modern or antique). It had the air of a showroom. A store-room. The boards echoed hollowly, under his feet.

He flashed back to the agency –
The gentle agent stamping his foot in that dreamily aquatic grey-blue light
'Close the door.'

Arthur jerked around sharply at the sound of his voice. It seemed closer than was really feasible. His arms stiffened, defensively, his heart – he noticed – was pumping violently.

The huge Welshman was crouched down low, directly to the left
of him –
Hackles

He seemed to be –
Hunting
– fiddling around with something –
Knife?
Gun?
Arrow?
Spear?

Arthur blinked and stared harder –
Eyes oiled up with fear

He blinked a second time, more in surprise than anything.

Dewi had struck a match and was busy –
Good Lord
– lighting a fire. A log fire. He was down on his knees, holding out
a long, thin strip of –
Tallow?
Was it?
– something keen and flammable (burning brightly at its tip) and
poking it into the heart of a bundle of kindling.

Arthur closed the door – as he'd been instructed – but remained
in place (like a nervous sentry to his own imminent departure).

'I find I freeze up when I leave her,' Dewi said, with a shake –
Was that a shake?
– in his voice.

'She certainly has an extremely efficient underfloor heating system,'
Arthur conceded, then despised himself for being so . . . so . . .
Heartless

So dispassionate. So poker-faced.

He struggled to make up for it. But they were two men – strangers
– united only – in the main – by their hatred of another –
There are more outlandish things to have in common, I guess
A common fuck, for one

Arthur tensed his knees, guiltily, 'She's an extraordinary woman,'
he murmured, 'and . . . and strong . . .'
The grip of her thighs, like a pair of pliers
The tickle of her tongue

The slap of her soft-white stomach

He shook his head, swallowed.

Who am I?

D.H. bloody . . . uh . . . ?

It was as if another – far more emotionally reactive – creature was temporarily conducting his thoughts for him (the real Arthur Young was now way off camera – taking it easy – in the canteen – drinking filter coffee – eating a sandwich – feet up – reading the classifieds in the local paper).

'She's had to be tough,' Dewi murmured, holding the flaming stick in place until the twigs began smoking, then crackling; until the flame finally took.

He remained – hunkered down – on his haunches. 'I've loved her since the very beginning,' he whispered, 'and she can fuck the whole town if needs be, because it won't make any difference to me. I was here before all of the slander and the bullshit and the betrayals, and I will be here long after.'

Arthur took a few unsteady steps into the room. He leaned his hand onto a free-standing chest of drawers and struck what he hoped to be a –

Please don't hit me

I'm on a pension

I have a disa . . . disa . . . disa . . .

– sympathetic posture.

'How long?' he asked. His voice was even croakier than usual. He cleared his throat, exaggeratedly. Dewi reached behind him and pulled a small, padded footrest in closer to the fireplace. He perched himself upon it (like a full-grown elephant sat on a drum during a badly-choreographed circus performance). He kept his back to Arthur.

'She was seventeen,' he said.

'That's a *hell* of a long time ago,' Arthur murmured (impressed by the sheer breadth of this human tragedy), then suddenly appreciated how ungallant he must've sounded.

Dewi nodded (he hadn't noticed). 'Thirteen years,' he said.

'But how . . .'

Arthur was suddenly intrigued by the basic practicalities – began quietly calculating –

'So if Wesley wrote the book three years ago . . . how on earth did the graffiti stay in place all that while? An entire decade? Didn't it fade? Wasn't it ever painted over?'

Dewi shrugged. His back was curved. His elbows pressed deep dimples into his muscular knees. His huge hands cupped his face.

'In the clock of the heart,' he murmured, his accent thickening with emotion, 'thirteen years is a single *tick*.'

Arthur glanced behind him, towards the door –

How long am I staying here?

'Sit,' Dewi said, and pointed towards a straight-backed armchair at the other side of the fire.

The wood was smoking heavily. Arthur could smell beech-pine-*fir*. He flashed back to Epping Forest –

The crackle of needles, underfoot

The yaffle of the woodpecker

The bark of the deer

– then came to again, seated –

How long have I been here?

He felt the faded velvet of the chair's upholstery, the polished wood at the tip of its arm. He stared at Dewi's magnificent profile –

A bison

A bear

– gilt-dipped in the fitful yellow of the fire's flickering.

'Was it true?' he found himself asking. 'What they . . . what they . . .'

KATHERINE (whore) TURPIN ABORTED HER OWN FATHER'S BASTARD

Couldn't say it

'What they wrote about her – the graffiti?'

Dewi shook his head, 'Katherine had a reputation, and she was no angel, but she was hardly . . .' he shrugged, 'and her father was a decent man – much loved . . .' Dewi nearly smiled, remembering, 'a great educationalist. Energetic. Motivated. Enthusiastic. A real innovator. A real *improver* . . .'

A long silence.

'But then there's never smoke without . . .' he indicated towards the hearth, then rubbed his knees, resignedly, 'and I suppose that's

364

what people thought. And they weren't entirely . . . they weren't absolutely wrong to think it, either.'

Arthur struggled to comprehend this answer. He tried to recall whatever it was that Wesley had written on the subject –

Hard to bring it to . . .

Hard to conjure . . .

– all the stuff about perimeters; those 'savagely drawn margins of small-town orthodoxy . . .' 'Who will we side with, ultimately? Those coddled straight-jackets, walled in by their own convention-ality? Or the giant, impassive gush of wave and foam and spray – fearless, remorseless, *free* . . . ?'

Sheer hyperbole

KATHERINE (whore) TURPIN ABORTED HER OWN FATHER'S BASTARD

Fact

Scrawled onto the grey concrete of that tall sea wall. One foot by seven. Contravening just about every . . .

Did salt actually work as a preservative for graffiti?

And in mentioning it –

Back to the point, Arthur

– in mentioning it Wesley had *celebrated* that contravention (hadn't he?). Under the guise of celebrating her. Had made her humiliation a kerbstone, a signpost, a *landmark* attraction on his map of the estuary –

A *Rubicon* for the people Following.

'She slept with her *father*?'

He couldn't help himself.

Dewi smiled, tiredly, 'No. That's the whole . . . it was never as simple . . . never as *literal*. I thought you people were meant to be fond of riddles.'

You people

Arthur grimaced, sourly, then tried to think.

'Her father was the local headmaster . . .'

Dewi nodded.

'. . . and her mother was active in the church in some capacity?'

Dewi rubbed his two huge hands together. 'Low church. They were descended from Dutch stock.'

'So where are they now? Do you know? Do you keep in touch?'

'The father's in Scotland. He runs a boys' boarding school there. The mother was a missionary – New Guinea. Died last year. Pancreatic cancer.'

'But Katherine stayed here? Why?'

'Because she wouldn't walk away from it . . . and . . . and because if she stayed, nobody got away with anything.'

'Least of all you, eh?'

Dewi shook his head, 'Least of all her. I was the weak link. I made things worse by caring about all the wrong things. I deserved to suffer.'

'But the graffiti's still there, you say? After – what is it – thirteen years? And it still *matters*? Isn't that . . . ?'

Dewi smiled, leaned forward, poked the fire. 'It's a landmark.'

Arthur leaned forward himself, in his chair, struck by a sudden thought. 'Somebody must've hated her. Who was it? Do you know? Did you ever find out?'

Dewi shrugged, 'It's a small town. People feel things deeply here.'

'And you didn't ever feel tempted to defend her in any way?'

Dewi twisted around on his stool, gazed at Arthur, blankly. 'I did,' he said, 'I painted over it. Twice. She begged me not to. We'd been dating for over a year when it all first blew up. She told me there was no truth in it and I believed her. She said if you destroy a thing it gives it more power. She thought no one would dream of taking it seriously. But she was naive. And she was wrong. And I did paint over it. And she hated me for it – she hated that conformist side of me. She took it as a lack of faith. Which it was. And then when it came back – which it did – it was like . . .' he turned towards the fire again, 'like a splinter. Under the skin. Fighting, *pushing*, to get out again.'

Arthur closed his eyes for a second. 'It must've . . .' he visualised the splinter. The image touched him. 'It must've *hurt*.'

Dewi nodded, slowly, 'At first, perhaps, but it grew . . . it grew familiar,' he murmured, 'and after a while I resigned myself to it. It was my own mess, my own fault. I learned that to love someone is to accept everything. Even the bullshit. The self-deceit. Even the lying. The graffiti meant nothing. It was a public act, yet a strangely *private* thing. It was faded . . . it was *history* – part of

366

the grain,' Dewi slid his flat hand through the air, unthinkingly, 'part of the weft, the *weave* of my life with Katherine . . .'

'Then Wesley happened along,' Arthur interrupted, 'and made it all feel fresh again.'

Dewi's profile hardened. 'I think he imagined that he was championing her in some way,' he shook his head, as if unable to comprehend, 'but it was an act of such staggering . . . such revolting *vandalism*. He used her . . .'

Dewi glanced over at Arthur, fleetingly, 'Katherine was always *used* you see.'

Arthur knotted his fingers together, rested them on his lap, covered his crotch, unconsciously.

'The point was,' Dewi turned back to the fire, 'the words he read on that wall – the ones he repeated in his stupid book – took no account of *anything*. He pretended he was defending her, but all he really did was make her into some kind of *tourist* attraction. He made her the same as . . . he pulled her into *his* story. He made her into *him*.'

'God I know how that feels,' Arthur whispered, covering his face with his hands, falling back into his chair again, '*I know that pain*.'

Dewi remained motionless. Arthur almost considered repeating what he'd whispered. Louder –
Louder
For the drama
– but he held off.

'Katherine's been through the fire,' Dewi murmured, 'and she's grown very accustomed to the burn of it. I've watched her acclimatise. I've seen her skin harden. But after Wesley, I finally saw her do something I never thought she'd do. I saw her *becoming* the lie. I saw her *living* it. And he did that to her. *He* made that happen.'

Arthur nodded –
Yes he did
He did

'And all of the others,' Dewi continued, 'they're just as bad: the people who Follow, the sad Old Man with his dead son, the business corporation behind that stupid competition, the people running those computer sites who repeat those lies about her, the publishers . . . *they're* all implicated. They spread the lie too. They revitalise it. They re-energise it. Make it real. Give it its power.'

Arthur suddenly stopped nodding.

'No,' he said. 'It's more . . .' he frowned, 'if you don't mind my saying so, it's much more *subtle* than that – and this is what you have to try and take some kind of *solace* in – because the people Following, the site on the Net tracking Wesley, the articles in the paper; these apparent trappings of his success are actually its very *opposite*. These people aren't his allies – you'd have to be a fool to think that. These people are his punishment.

'And those . . . those institutions which on the one hand seem to celebrate his so-called individuality, are the very same institutions which unwittingly curtail it. They dog him. They smother him. They torment and they *control* him.'

As he spoke, Dewi observed Arthur's hands moving between his knees; as though they were playing some kind of invisible instrument – a harmonium, a small organ, maybe . . . slowly at first, and then faster . . .

He frowned at them. For some reason those hands made him feel uneasy.

Arthur was still speaking. Dewi tuned in again.

'Wesley likes to project this enviable sense of . . . of *freedom* – from care, responsibility, from any kind of con . . . con . . .' Arthur squinted, 'con*ven*tional moral life, even – but he's like a wild hare trapped in a jeep's headlights. He's *frozen* inside that glare. He's *blinded* by it. He's incapacitated. There's no release, no reprieve, no . . . no *escape* from it.'

On *escape*, Arthur's frantic hands quietened, and in the calm following the tumult – the peace after the climax – Arthur's thin face broke into a gentle half-smile. 'Perhaps,' he spoke kindly, 'perhaps you should try and take some kind of comfort from that fact, Dewi.'

Ah . . .

Used the name

Finally

Dewi leaned forward and threw another log onto the fire, choosing not to comment on Arthur's assessment of things, not to give any inkling as to whether he'd accepted or digested the stuff he was telling him.

'When you have sex with Katherine again,' he murmured (settling back down onto his stool, not changing his tone of voice, not meeting Arthur's benign gaze, but speaking directly into the fire, almost tenderly), 'could I ask you to use protection? And to bear in mind the things I've said? And to be gentle with her. And to be kind. She has a . . .' he suddenly chuckled, fondly, 'she has a sensitive spot just behind the lobe of her left ear. There's a small birthmark . . . I don't know if you . . . I don't know if you . . . but she always laughs when you touch her there.'

As he spoke he pushed his hand into his shirt pocket and took hold of something. For a second, for a brief –
Awful
– moment, Arthur thought it might be a neat packet of prophy-lactics –
With spermicide
Ribbed
Unflavoured
'Here's that money I promised . . . for Harmony,' Dewi stretched his arm towards Arthur. There was a roll of notes in it. He did not look at him as he handed it over, but kept his eyes fixed – all the while – on the licking flames ahead of him.

Arthur stood up to take the money, feeling slightly like a boy who's been asked to vacate the cub-house after using bad language –
Akela's arse is grass
Baden-Powell's a knob-head
– feeling low and vulgar and somewhat flustered.

'That's very . . . very generous,' he muttered, gauging the density of the roll; instinctively weighing up its financial content –
Significant
He remained standing for a minute or so, longing to say something –
To exonerate
– but this was no time – no place – for justifications. He knew it –
I am dismissed
He stood still for a second longer, then moved off, almost sloping

369

(hyena-like) towards the door, shoving the bundle into his pocket, pulling up the collar on his jacket – as if protecting himself, but not from the cold outside so much as something . . . something *interior* –

He instinctively knew I could be bought off

Is it really that obvious?

Exactly the same way Wesley knew, earlier

He pulled the door open, stepped through, then softly closed it behind him. Once outside –

Deep breath

Deep breath

– instead of fleeing, Arthur paused for a second on the Welshman's wide verandah.

The evening was still foggy. He looked up. He smelled the fruity smoke from the woodfire; saw it hanging in the air. He saw a slip of moon, peeking, just momentarily – undelineated, a *fuzz* of potentiality – through the moist and whited cloud around him. He observed the green paint on the timber, too, reflected in that nearly-shine –

Cool mint

– and he was suddenly caught up and transported on that mild patina – that *green* – through winter, through spring, to the middle of an unimagined – an *unimaginable* – summer –

Yet here I am

Here I am . . .

Imagining

– found himself reborn, standing tall on that roomy porch, early evening; a loose-limbed boy, full of anticipation –

Ah yes . . .

Possibility

– his head flung back, his mouth hung open, his innocent eyes roundly gazing as the clouds of fireflies commenced their nightly swarming – rising from the swamps, the high-tide-line, the marshes – and then rapidly descending, *en masse* (who gave the instruction? Who was it? Who *told* them?), to candy-coat that smooth, creamy-clean-leaf-ice-green facade into a billion strong, crazy-black-speck-*fidget* of double-*double*-chocolate chipping.

Thirty-five

She was still –
Like a corpse
– for the first hour, at least. He was still, too. Seemed almost
unconscious –
Motionless
– his breathing shallow but regular.
   They were touching –
Shoulder
Hip
Bottom
Inside thigh
Inside knee
Foot
   His arm was looped around –
Breath – on – my – neck
– her scrawny waist, holding them close together –
For the warmth
   There was –
Yes
– a certain pressure –
A firmness
– to the back of her –
No suggestion of impropriety
– which after forty minutes she realised –
God
– was actually the pocket on his jacket, fallen open –
Fallen back

– full of stuff, acting as a tiny yet very distinct –

Push

– barrier between them. Against her buttocks.

The front pocket – when she started thinking about it – was directly beneath her left arm – which was slung –

light/heavy/mad with tension

– over the top of his.

Josephine Angela Bean steadied her breathing and considered that pocket for a very long time. She opened her eyes; the sleeping bag was pulled up and tucked firmly under her chin. Down lower she was covered by it entirely, like a small insect encased in its silky pupa – could see nothing. It was more a question of –

Of feeling

– of moving slightly, perhaps adjusting her position. But very –

Very

– casually.

She sighed – a dozy sigh, almost a snore – and shifted sleepily – just those parts that were necessary –

Shoulder

Thigh

Fingers especially . . .

– so that her hand was now gently positioned on top of the pocket, her thumb already pretty much pushed inside it. She felt a mixture of –

Can't – help – myself

– intriguing sensations; tantalising objects –

Paper, foil, loose tobacco . . .

– but needed to . . . to investigate still more thoroughly –

To pilfer

– so gradually moved her index finger deep inside to join the other.

This is my job, she told herself; I am trained for it. I am *good* at it –

Talented . . .

A vocation to enter

To pry

To gain gentle access to those secret recesses

To check out

To investigate
To gauge
To be firm and calm and unobtrusive
　Between her finger and thumb she slowly gripped a folded wad of . . . of . . .
Like those machines in the Amusement Arcade
Full of prizes
The chocolate bunnies
The cheap watches in bubbled plastic
The teddies
The silver pincer; swinging, dipping, tightening . . .
　She remained still –
Holding
– for what seemed like forever. Listened. Wesley's breath on her neck was exactly – if not more –
Was that possible?
– regular than before. She –
Oh Lord, can't help it
– suddenly shuddered –
　The thrill
– then quickly pulled herself together. Was cautious –
Excitable
– as an adder – early evening – public park – hiding under a discarded sheet of corrugated metal –
Old roof – wall – shed –
Sharp-edged
Orange with rust
– waiting, only, to slither free – unblinking – frozen – heightened.
　Slowly –
Slowly
– she began to withdraw –
Thumb
Finger
Elbow
In the slightest coordination
Many minutes –
So many
– passed. Millimetre by millimetre. Until finally –

YES

– that papery object was free. She had it.

I have it!

'No you don't,' Wesley leaned a fraction closer (whispering softly into the hairs on the back of her neck), placed his hand firmly over her hand and took the object from her.

Josephine froze – gave it up readily –

'I was . . .' she said, 'it must've just *slipped* into . . .'

'Your arse is *grass*, Bean,' Wesley murmured (his voice wicked with grin – *or vindictive, was it?*) into the brushed-cut softness of the hair behind her ear. 'Give me my jacket back you sneaky little viper.'

She felt his fingers on her, around her neck. Froze harder –

Will he kill me? Like he killed his brother?

– but the hands did not tighten there, merely gripped the lapels of the jacket and slid it firmly from her shoulders. She pushed herself up a little, onto her elbow, to facilitate the coat's removal. He yanked the sleeves down to just above her wrists then left it there, pulled her down again, roughly –

Arms all constricted . . .

Behind my . . .

Cannot . . .

– then leaned up onto his forearm, curving around her – like an insinuating sepal, cupping a wildflower – slightly higher now than before, breathing onto her left cheek, his lips close to the line of her jaw.

Electric tickle from ear to nipple

Then – even – uh –

Lower

He opened his right hand –

Firm – index-finger

– and traced the curve from the back of her ear to the tip of her chin –

As if rehearsing some kind of incision

– then brushed his thumb over her cheek, to the corner of her lips.

Her mouth fell open. She breathed through it. A tiny expulsion. 'Tell me who you are,' he said –

No longer a smile there

'I'm just a . . . just a Follower, like all of the others.'

Her voice was shaking; more, even, than she'd imagined. Her mouth was dry.

He chuckled at this, 'No . . .'

Bent in closer, whispered into her ear, '. . . if you were just a Follower I wouldn't be here. The sugar people sent you. The fat man with his gold-buttoned blazer. They're panicking.'

She tried to shake her head, '*No* . . . I don't . . .'

Her arms were already aching –

Twisted neck

– the cuts were stinging.

'My *arms* . . .'

Woolcy slid his finger from her mouth, over the contour of her jaw, down her throat, across her chest, around her waist, to her elbow. 'Boo-*hoo*,' he whispered, gripping it, hurting. He pushed his face into the nape of her neck. She could feel his lips –

Tongue

– tracing an inexplicable pattern there. She felt like a mystical deer –

Shot

Bleeding

– fatally injured by its huntsman-lover.

'Then *who*?' his chin –

Stubble

– was tucked –

Rubbing

– into the curve of her shoulder, making her throat tighten and her chin jerk forward, unintentionally.

'Or is it local industry? Is it the Gas Terminal people? Have they sent you down here to try and bribe me?'

'No.'

She felt the badger-cold of his nose behind her ear again –

His breath

'Your friend told me that you're involved in environmental causes.'

He gripped her ear-lobe between his teeth, tugged at it, enough to –

Hurt

– make her expostulate. He seemed to enjoy the small noise she uttered.

'Is that the sound you made,' he murmured, 'when you were fucking the headmaster?'

No

She tried to twist her head away, disgusted.

'*Poor* baby Bean,' he said, clucking.

'Which friend?' she asked, angrily –

Hurt

– but shaken. Her neck curving away from him.

He pushed his cheek into it again. Grazed its soft skin. She turned her head back around – a few inches –

Strained

– suddenly found her mouth right –

Right

– next to his. He kissed her then, but from a strange angle, so that their lips met like two silver sprats tangling together quickly in a fishing net –

No –

But –

Uh –

– his hand was flat on her belly –

Thumb circling belly button, in a crazy constellation of twinkling

– then firm on the sharp bone of her thigh –

Pushed it open

– brushed over her hip, then moved lower –

Have to –

Need to –

Must turn around, to feel his . . .

She pushed herself flat onto her back, her arms still bound and pushing up her chest. His hand was now resting on her opposite hip. She reached her chin up to find his lips.

'The policewoman,' he said, then kissed her. She could feel his mouth pulling into a smile, and then softening, opening, his teeth snagging the soft, top corner of her lip, pulling it up, his tongue following, like a tiny asp, slithering along her gumline, withdrawing.

She blinked. His hand –

Left hand

– moved from her waist, under the tight material of her vest, over her ribs –

Wide hand

– his thumb tracing a firm line through the centre of her diaphragm, the remaining fingers strumming each curving bone like individual harp strings –

The soft flesh under her arm tingling

Wind-chiming

Jangling

– until those two disparate hand-parts came together again, curling, gently – like a gardener caressing the cool head of his prize chrysanthemum – to cup the tender bulb of her breast –

Tightening

– until she winced.

He kissed her. This time like a grazing animal plucking a mouthful of grass from the pasture – a nuzzle – a brush – soft-faced – almost lipless. Then back again. But on the return movement he pressed into her – shifted his body over – between hers –

Pushed

– lifted her. She lifted.

'I'll be needing to punish you,' his wet lips warned her burning ear, his flat hand instructed the dip in her spine, his bruising hip scolded her tender thigh, 'and very *harshly*, for this.'

Thirty-six

What time was it?

  What *time* was it?

I am . . .

I . . .

Jesus bollocks

A bloody mess!

A bloody . . .

  It'd been –

God. Had to admit it

– quite the most *horrible*, the most *distressing* walk he could ever remember. And there had been thousands of walks –

Countless

– and hundreds of night walks, in particular; Arthur Young *liked* night walking; could often be seen striding along purposefully until late into the evening –

Often

– and quite happily (in the summer, mainly, admittedly). But this? This was –

Absolutely Godawful

– *very* different, somehow from other walks: the mud – the sea – the fog – the *struggle*. The pitch dark, dark, *dark*.

  The pervasive sense of being . . . of being . . .

Don't think it

Of being watched –

I said . . .

– of being . . .

Please . . .

– of being . . .
Don't . . .
– of being . . .
Followed-Ambushed-Trapped-Killed-Ripped-Cut-Skinned-Devoured
– Oh God . . .
Deep breath – deep breath – deep breath
 And then the bloody torch –
Ah yes . . .
The torch
Totally –
Fucking
– unreliable. Batteries went dead after approximately fifteen . . .
 (Katherine's face. That look she'd pulled when he'd bolted. Got out of there so quick –
In/out
Just like that
– he even overtook the agent on the driveway – still dragging on his jacket, still holding his rucksack open in one hand – laptop inside, all higgledy-piggledy – still struggling to get the lead rolled up, still muttering a pack of inconsequential rubbish about having to get . . . to get . . . to get . . .
Back
 But for what?
 And Dewi. Standing at his window –
Indomitably
– tiger-striped from the front by the thick slats of his wooden shutters, from behind by the flickering, orange-tinged glow of the fire.)
 Arthur shuddered. He felt the torch in his pocket. Blinked. Rewound –
Dark
 Can you do a special test for n-n-n-night-blindness?
 Is it an actual condition?
 Is it a . . .
 Could it be a . . .
 A symptom?
 He was barely past the first oil storage complex before the torch began to weaken, then flicker – barely past the Lobster Smack, in fact (shut) and the caravan sites (dead).

The want of light had been almost . . .
Should fucking sue that battery company
     . . . almost *lethal*, in places –
Fucking rain came down
Fucking relentless fucking rain
The later, less well-delineated segments on the muddy bank had been especially treacherous. He'd fallen countless times –
Countless
So undignified for a . . .
Arthur snatched the offending torch from his pocket and threw it into the soup of darkness, just about as far as he could possibly muster. Tried to hear the sound of it landing. The *plop*. Couldn't. Only the gentle splat of the rain. *Swore.*
But there were so many subsidiary noises; all competing furiously for their place in the darkness – scrabbling to scratch their print into the deep night ink: squeals and whispers, cracklings and rustlings, hoots and splashes –
Fifty thousand rats, launching themselves into the water like a huge, utterly coherent, sharp-toothed Armada . . .
Badgers running riot, under the bastard bramble bushes . . .
Snipe. Screaming. Flapping from their low roosts up into the air . . .
The infernal
The fucking, bloody, infernal rip and squeak and scurry of the limitless Big Black
He reached a tentative hand towards the wooden rail – (had clambered down the bank backwards – skulking like a crab – on his hands and knees. Abandoning all remaining vestiges of locomotive dignity. Clawing into the mud with his bare hands and fingers –
Clinging on
Desperate).
The boat was dark. The water was vile and black and treacherous – he peered sideways, over the rail, squinting into the sleeting rain (which duly blinded him for a moment), looking for confirmation –
Where was the water?
In? Out?
Couldn't actually see anything, only hear the smack and the suck and the gurgle of it –

Same as ever

The walkway wobbled under him –

Or is it actually my legs, wobbling under me?

I am wobbling . . .

Totally

He staggered across it, wiping his eyes with his fingers, grumbling (more for effect than anything; to *bolster*). Wrestled with the knob on the door. Finally mastered –

Thank God

– the dodgy mechanism, and yanked it open. Paused on the brink. Felt –

Scared, dammit

– a brief moment of unease. Swallowed it back. Entered. The door slammed shut behind him.

Tried to remember the exact whereabouts of the two gas-fired lamps. Felt for the lighter in his pocket. Staggered around blindly with his outstretched –

Uh . . .

– hands –

What the . . . ?!

– then suddenly began –

Sweet Jesus!

The stink!

– sniffing obsessively. Turning his head around, reaching out his hands, just . . . just sniffing –

Badly rotting egg?

Pure sulphur?

Horse shit?

Total decomposition?

He stopped moving. Drew his arms in. Stood very still. Could hear . . .

Oh Jesus –

Worst-case-scenario

. . . could hear *breathing*.

And it was . . . it was . . .

Big

Is that possible?

Can breathing have a size?

A stature!

. . . like the breathing of a boxer, or a . . . a wrestler. An American WWF monster with biceps like pineapples and a head like twenty-two pounds of pink boiled ham.

Arthur backed off a-way, towards the door. His rucksack hit a picture or a bookshelf or a cabinet. Made it clatter. He jumped rorward –

Like a silly tart

– jibbering, then turned and rushed – headfirst – towards the exit. The door, when he grabbed it –

Oh yes,

Of course

– was stuck.

'I wouldn't . . .'

Aaaaaargh!

A horrible –

Tiny

– little voice was squeaking. It was –

Directly

– behind him.

Uh . . .

Vindictive-woman-dwarf

Uh . . .

Red cape

Uh . . .

Intent on murder

'Just *listen* to me,' the small voice said.

Art had somehow contrived to push his hand –

How did . . . ?

Fuck!

– through the glass in the window. He pulled it quickly back –

Mistake

Seconds after – long seconds – he could hear the fragments tinkling down onto the gangplank, into the water.

'I'm only a small *girl*,' the voice said (not a little irritably), 'I don't mean you any harm.'

'Just do what you have to do,' Arthur found himself whimpering, withering up inside with fear, 'just do what you have to do. And do it *quickly*.' He was holding his bloody hand out in front of him, like a bit-part actress in a horror movie.

A small patch of light suddenly appeared, to the far end of the cabin. Arthur blinked towards it

A torch

It was low, held by – it swung around – a small hand – an arm (fur-encased) – Arthur shuddered – a shoulder (more fur, grey in colour) – then a little head. Not a crazy-ugly-killer dwarf face. A nice enough face. Gappy-toothed. Boyish.

'I'm Sasha,' the mouth in the head announced, 'and this is Brion.'

The torch dipped left, its beam illuminating a monkey-puzzle of horn, a wide brown eye. A long – a very long – nose. A suggestion of whisker.

'Don't panic. Brion is from Norwegian breeding stock and *very* meek . . .'

Arthur stared at the deer, blankly.

'Unless he's provoked.'

Bri-on . . . ?

'I mean he kicked a boy once who poked him in his privates . . .' she sniggered, 'but who wouldn't?'

Bri-on . . . ?

The beast grumbled at the unwelcome torch-light; a sound not unlike an old Douglas motorbike struggling up a steep incline.

'What are you doing here?' Arthur asked, bringing his hand even closer to his face, confusedly, trying to focus in on it –

Warm

Wet

'Before I give anything else away,' she said, 'if you don't mind . . .'

She shone the torch directly at him. Arthur covered his face with his arm, pained by the light, grimacing.

'You definitely aren't the person I was expecting,' the girl mused, after a brief period of quiet scrutiny, 'and you're not my stupid Uncle Toby, either. Are you renting this craft, or are you just an impostor?'

'No. I'm . . . *Yes*, of course I'm renting. I'm Arthur *Young*,' Arthur said, 'and I've actually . . .' he indicated towards his hand, speaking very slowly and clearly, as if presenting an item of general interest during a primary school Show and Tell, 'I've cut my hand. I'm bleeding.'

'That's the least of your problems,' she informed him, twirling the torch around flamboyantly. He blinked over at her, suspiciously, through the moving light –

Is she a poltergeist?

He felt confused. Not a little nauseous.

'Take a look . . .'

She walked towards him (as if in slow motion) –

Is it her?

Is it me?

– then paused, turned briefly, pointed firmly at the reindeer, '*Stay,* Brion.'

She was about nine years old, warmly ensconced in a thick fur jacket –

Rabbit, mostly, by the look of it

– and waterproof trousers which rustled as she moved. Heavy boots. A red knitted deerstalker-style hat, tied under her chin, with a white pom-pom on top. Red gloves; matching pom-poms dangling at either wrist.

Arthur couldn't tell if it was the girl or the animal, but as she drew closer there was definitely the sense of an encroaching scent; a powerful musk-based aroma of some kind or other.

She stood next to him, pushed open the door and shone the torch out onto the bridge.

'Oh my . . . *God.*' Arthur's jaw dropped.

There *was* no bridge. Half of it was gone. The other half. He briefly remembered part of the rail rotting away under his fingers – the left-hand-side – earlier – but this was . . .

Wow

Now all that remained was the right-hand rail (his knees went weak – *Didn't I just . . . ?*) and some arbitrary slats of wood breaking off almost into thin –

Pretty much into thin

– air.

'Don't know how you made it over,' the girl ruminated, 'I

thought about trying to cross back myself, but it seemed too shaky. And I wouldn't leave Brion,' she continued passionately, 'he's my rock.'

'I did think it was a little . . .' Arthur murmured, still staring at the walkway, confounded, 'a little *wobbly*.'

'Understatement of the *year*,' she snorted, 'the whole bloody *structure's* collapsing. I noticed soon after I climbed on board. I told Brion to stay outside – at the bottom of the bank – but he came on over anyhow – to investigate – while I was busy snooping. The bridge must've fallen in under the weight of him. Luckily he's sure-footed. And he has a very level head . . .' she paused. 'For a *deer*,' she conceded.

'We should definitely get out of . . .' Arthur let go of his wrist, pulled his hat down, decisively, 'if I go first you . . . *whoops*'.

The entire structure tipped as the reindeer shifted its weight.

'*Stay*, Brion,' the girl barked. The reindeer moved back to its original position. The structure righted itself again.

'Just hold the torch out ahead of me.'

Arthur adjusted the girl's hand with the torch so that he could see exactly what he was up against. 'You didn't think,' he asked, gazing at the full horror of the ruined bridge anew, 'to try and warn me in some way before I stepped out onto that thing?'

'I was hiding,' she shrugged, gazing up at him.
There was something . . . a certain . . .
A quality . . .
Arthur blinked.

'Anyway, I thought you might be one of the bad people . . .' she put out her hand to adjust the pom-pom on her hat, 'but I changed my mind when you started screaming. We have a fish eagle back home who screams exactly like that . . .' She paused, delicately, 'a *lady* fish eagle,' she elucidated, releasing the pom-pom and smiling.

Arthur half-smiled himself, more from –
Pain
Embarrassment
– exhaustion than anything.

'Which bad people did you have in mind?' he asked, trying –
Failing

– to conjure up an air of gentle superiority.

'The ones who sabotaged this craft, *silly*,' the girl performed a rapid guide with the torch, 'see? I was hiding out in that blackthorn copse,' she pointed (the torch's beam didn't reach that far), 'for a good hour at least before I came over. There was someone on board. Making a real racket. Once they'd gone I decided to have a quick poke around. Saw straight off that there were deep cuts into all of the major supporting struts. So if the wind rises – and with your added weight on board, obviously – we are well and truly . . .' she smiled sweetly, '*shafted*.'

As she spoke, the girl shifted her torch to one of the several side beams. It had been hacked up with an axe. Clumsily.

'And look . . .' she continued, pointing the torch to one of the oil lamps.

Smashed

'Oil everywhere. I'm only glad you didn't try and strike a . . .'

Before she'd completed her sentence, a crashing outside made her calmly adjust the torch's focus. The section of the gangplank closest to them had just fallen clean away. Seven, maybe eight planks in total.

Arthur stepped back. The boat shifted, infinitesimally.

'*match*,' the girl concluded – but somewhat distractedly – placing her hand onto the doorframe for added support, then leaning boldly forward and shining the torch down and down and down, into the distant swirl of icy black water.

Thirty-seven

Katherine sat – like a pony-club princess – bolt upright astride her burnished-brass bed, supported from the rear by two large cream-coloured, quilted-nylon pillows (heavily frilled and fully co-ordinated with her cream-coloured wheat-and-cornflower-design counterpane). She had Wesley's rucksack held firmly between her thighs, and the lamb's tail he'd given her shoved – like a pen – behind her ear.

She was steaming slightly – from a recent bath – and her white hair was parted and divided into two wonky plaits (the ends bound up tightly by thin pieces of lilac ribbon) which hung – still damp – across either shoulder.

In the gentle light of her two matching wicker-work bedside lamps, her chin and nose appeared slightly pink and raw from her energetic sexual exploits of earlier.

Protruding from beneath her right thigh – and crushed into the counterpane – lay a letter, already opened, the envelope post-marked from two days before. On her left-hand side lay an old, blue, pocket-Oxford dictionary, its spine broken and its cover partially torn.

Katherine gazed around her bedroom (her eyes alighting on her white and gold Barbie-style dressing table covered in an incongru-ous collection of stylish 1930s bowls and boxes in a combination of glass, porcelain and *decoupage*, her matching white and gold bookshelf – a well-maintained group of period-costume orien-tal dolls sitting pertly on top – her built-in wardrobe – neatly shut, with an incongruous *No Smoking* sign hung casually on the protruding key – and on its own small, free-standing table; her magnificent two-floored front-hinged Georgian-style doll's house, shining in a luminous top-of-the-milk white, with eight windows – all hung in matching velvet – and a bright blue front door with gold-plated letterbox, number, knob and knocker).

Everything – as she appraised it – seemed in tolerably good order. Having finally convinced herself of this fact, Katherine reached down for the letter – tipped herself up slightly to facilitate its removal – and closely re-scrutinised the post mark on the envelope's top left-hand corner.

She was wearing only a dressing gown in antique satin, smothered in wild orange and black blotches, edged with a contrasting – and luminous – shocking-pink trim and tied loosely at its waist by a belt carefully handcrafted in lime green wool from the simple method of crochet she'd been taught – as a child – involving a hooked needle and a cotton reel with four nails banged into the top of it. She twiddled at the end of this belt with her spare hand, distractedly.

The letter was signed; *A well-wisher*. It had been typed – she immediately deduced – on a word processor, and printed onto an A4 sheet of unrecycled – she winced – general office paper (she flipped it fully open, her top lip curling). The post mark – as she inspected it again – informed her that it had been sent from a mailbox in Southend.

Dear Miss Turpin,

She read, supporting it on top of Wesley's fat rucksack;

First, please let me apologise in advance for my contacting you in such an impromptu manner. Second, let me assure you that there are very good reasons for my needing to do so under the protective – if somewhat disreputable – guise of anonymity. Thirdly, while there is little point in my struggling to explain what these (very personal) reasons are here, let me at least hope that you will try and believe me when I say that my motivations in this matter are entirely reputable, above board, even sisterly.

To the point: –

*If, by chance, a man called **Arthur Young** tries to make contact with you over the next few days, please be sure to treat him – and the things he says – with due caution. Arthur is an incredibly kind, gentle and honourable man, but suffers from a condition called Korsikov Syndrome which affects him in a variety of ways; both physical and mental.*

Arthur is not – I repeat NOT – a dangerous or a vindictive person, but may sometimes suffer from periods of paranoia and confusion.

I've taken it upon myself to contact you in this direct manner because of your (I don't doubt) unwitting connection with the Wesley situation. Arthur also feels himself to be 'involved' (however spuriously) in that situation. On this basis he may well feel tempted to contact you while he – and Wesley – are in the Canvey vicinity.

Please, please, please do not feel any undue concern about Arthur's temporary presence in your home town, and let me stress again that in the normal run of things Arthur is a good, kind and highly altruistic individual. You are in no physical danger and have nothing whatsoever to fear from him so long as you bear my friendly counsel in mind.

Yours, in all good faith,

A well-wisher.

Katherine read the letter twice over, harrumphed, tossed one of her two plaits behind her shoulder and then grabbed her dictionary. She turned to the letter K and tried to find the word

Korsikov –

Nothing

She quickly flipped back to A and searched out the dictionary definition of the word *Altruistic*. Under *Altruism* she read: *regard for others as a principle of action.*

She frowned, trying to make sense of this for a second –

Regard for others as a principle of action

She snorted, flung down the dictionary, folded up the letter murmuring, 'Sisterly my *fanny*,' pushed it back into its envelope and tossed it onto the floor.

She stared at Wesley's rucksack for a moment, drew a deep breath, then reached out both hands to touch it (using only the centre of her palms; lifting the tips of her fingers, sensuously).
Ah . . .

After a minute or so she shuddered – her knees tightening – and shifted herself further forward, away from her cushions and down the bed, pulling up her skinny, white legs and weaving them tightly around the rucksack – as if to try and preclude its sudden escape from her.

The rucksack was a large, black, packed-full, decidedly weighty, heavily-pocketed canvas object. The buckles were a scuffed silver, the tags, a cracked and browning leather. The maker's mark had been torn away – almost damaging the integrity of the bag's canvas – and in its place – or partially – were glued a series of cub-scout patches. One was for road safety. Another for fire-starting. A third was for bird identification. The fourth Katherine couldn't entirely decipher – it was too heavily damaged – but might've possibly been sailing –
Or sumo
Or scuba-diving

She bent down and sniffed, just above where the badges were – her head nudging unmelodiously into the short neck of Wesley's banjo which protruded – rather vulnerably – from the left-hand side.
Wood smoke
Beef jerky
Cat-sick
Lavender

She snorted under her breath, then reached out for the bag's buckles, starting in on the main central ones, rolling them through, pulling them up, yanking them free, flipping the whole central flap back in a single smooth motion –
Good

She peeked inside. Pushed carefully to the left – and totally supported by a well-formed, self-contained plywood partition – was Wesley's banjo. She'd been longing to see it properly. She carefully manoeuvred it up and out, held it aloft with both hands and inspected it closely.

It was tiny – much smaller than she'd expected it to be – plainly very old, had hardly any back to it (wasn't *contained*, wasn't *boxed-up* like a guitar. Could that be right? Would it still work that way?), bore virtually no ornamentation or design – the pegs and supports were all clumsily fashioned from a worn, dark wood (walnut? Oak?) and there were a series of strong steel clips to the side holding the pigskin frontal-piece (which had the look of a sheet of well-used, oil-stained baking parchment) into place.

This pigskin was firm to the touch. She tapped at it with her knuckle – the way you'd tap a tambourine – then she plucked at a string with her index finger. She sniggered, guiltily. It produced that deliciously tinny, utterly distinctive banjo sound – that dizzy twang – that stifled yowl of an angry tabby with its tail caught in a malfunctioning cat-flap. She liked it.

Katherine gently placed the banjo down by the bed and peered inside the bag again. Next she removed a rolled up, tightly bound sleeping bag, an old plastic ground sheet, a pillow case stuffed with – she peeked inside, grimaced – two worn pairs of brown socks, some old, white y-fronts, three vests, a black T shirt, five handkerchiefs, all mixed up with some sprigs of lavender (*Hmmn*), several pieces of rosemary, a tuft of sage, at least ten bay leaves and twenty or more cardamom pods.

She took out two further T-shirts, both short-sleeved. One had a picture of a cockroach on its front and the address of an exterminating firm in Hoboken, New Jersey. The other was blue and bore a cartoon of a camel's face with the word *Palace* inscribed underneath it in fancy white lettering. This T-shirt was well-worn and had a small tear under the armpit.

A pair of jeans. Extremely scruffy. Some baggy shorts – brown corduroy. Some combat trousers (German, apparently). Another pair of combats cut down to knee-length. Another jumper. Brown. Heavy wool. Slightly ragged.

A plastic bag containing several animal pelts. Some still fairly aromatic. Katherine carefully removed two rabbit skins, a badger skin, three rat pelts. Even the skin of a tiny field mouse.

She stared at the field-mouse skin for a long time, flattened it out between her fingers, uncrossed her legs from around the rucksack and bounced off her bed, still holding it. She walked over to her doll's house, gently unclipped the latch on the right-hand-side, opened the front, peeked into the living room (on the ground floor), shoved a couple of pieces of furniture aside – leaving a space before the hearth – then pushed the little mouse-skin inside, placed it next to the fire, adjusted it, drew a rocking chair in close again, pulled back, smiling.

She returned to her bed, and to Wesley's rucksack. Next she found a scarf. Hand knitted. Grey. White skull and crossbones at either end. Matching gloves. Fingerless.

At the bottom of the central section she discovered a home-made (yet rather lovely) wooden box. Inside this (she opened it cautiously; it was hinged and squeaked a little) were two improvised wooden banjo picks and one in imitation tortoiseshell, several fragments of ancient-seeming pottery – all unpatterned – burned. An envelope with what seemed to be – but *couldn't* be, surely? – gunpowder inside of it.

About ten old buttons. A cotton reel and needle. A ball of string. Several rubber bands. A comb with most of its teeth missing. A strip of velcro. Three hypo-allergenic plasters. Five thick black marker pens. Two small HB pencils. A rubber. A packet of condoms (*Durex*, half used). A pack of playing cards (hailing from Jamaica). A small tin of Germolene. An even smaller tin of Tiger Balm. Some *Rizla* papers –
Ah-ha

Two tiny fossils. An owl dropping made out of hair (this made her shiver a little). A photo of two young boys sitting on two swings, both smiling wildly. The one slightly older, the other . . . it had to be Wesley: green eyes, a mop of brown hair, a striped jumper, flares. Gappy teeth.

Katherine stared at this picture for a long while. She turned it over. On the back was written – but very faded – Wes and Chris, Portmeirion, 1973.

She drew a deep breath, and – for the first time in a good while – looked over towards the door, uneasily, then replaced the picture back inside the box, very carefully.

Three postcards; two from the British Museum. One depicting a simple-seeming Egyptian-style tapestry, the other an old jug shaped like an owl. She turned them over. The first was addressed simply to King's Lynn, Norfolk, and said *Wes you fucking cunt! Marty*. The other had just an address in Barnstaple (Three Chimneys, Pembury Road) but no message. The third was a picture of 'The New Penguin Enclosure at London Zoo', was very dog-eared, had a foreign stamp on the back – postmark . . . *uh* . . . somewhere in Japan?

To Wes, it said, *Wish you were here, son. Dad*

Katherine frowned at this, confused. The address it'd been sent to was somewhere in Gloucester.

A small locket – a woman's locket, by the look of things; gold, tiny – with . . . (Katherine struggled to open it. Her clumsy nail seemed so huge by comparison to the clasp of the thing) . . . a tiny lock of hair inside and a photo of a man and woman – the man in some kind of military uniform – sitting on the deck of a ship, their arms wrapped around each other, smiling, perhaps slightly uncomfortably.

Katherine closed this locket, carefully.

Last of all, and perhaps most eerily: two plaster casts – joined together by wire – of the teeth of a mouth; a child's mouth. The kind of cast dentists made when they were moulding the jaw for braces (maybe) or a cap, or some kind of serious dental surgery.

A curiously tiny but neat set of teeth. Not particularly gappy. The top front two slightly overlapping.

Katherine shuddered. She put the mould away. She sat still for a while, deep in thought, frowning.

Finally she closed the box and placed it back into the rucksack, followed by every other item, refolded and put back in meticulous order. Last of all – and most regretfully – the banjo.

Next she started in on the side pockets. On the left-hand side she found a tartan Thermos, three spoons, a fork and a knife inside a plastic tupperware sandwich box. A small pale blue enamel plate with dark blue trim. A matching bowl. Some strange metal prongs which seemed darkened at their tips by – she sniffed – meat juices. Old blood. A very small saucepan. Very battered. Stained black.

A wooden spoon. A strange – this was hard to pull out, there was obviously a special technique – metal rack thing like you'd have in a grill pan, which unfolded, from its centre, so was pretty handy (for cooking fish or fillets over a fire, she presumed).

Matches, matches, *matches*. Tiny boxes, from all over the place.

Pubs and bars mainly. A tiny tin of – she opened it – gravy browning? Cocoa? Coffee?

Hard to tell.

Dozens of sugar sachets.

The other side. Mainly cosmetics. There was an old tube of smoker's toothpaste. A toothbrush – so ancient its bristles were flat and yellow. A half-used bottle of Rescue Remedy (she raised her brows at this). A damp brown towel. A small bottle of cardamom oil (an amateur pressing; on the front was written; CARDAMOM, FOR INDIGESTION. DO NOT APPLY DIRECT TO SKIN OR SWALLOW (two exclamation marks).

Katherine unscrewed the lid and inhaled. She smiled. It was a good smell. It reminded her of Wesley (that moment when he'd leaned forward to kiss her. She closed her eyes. Remembered that moment, her lips moving, unconsciously. She opened her eyes again. Cleared her throat. Twitched her shoulder).

An old fashioned razor – bone handled – wrapped up in a small off-white face towel (Katherine almost cut herself upon it. She squeaked. Gazed. Tested its sharpness on her thumb. Was impressed. Wrapped it carefully back up again). A whole pile of –

Urgh

– goo (how else to describe it?). In an old shaving tin. Bits of stringy green stuff and some kind of cactusy foamy . . .

She closed the tin, rapidly.

A pill bottle containing a series of odd-looking tablets. Several kinds. Homeopathic. An ancient – very battered – hip flask –

Yip yip!

– containing (Katherine unscrewed it) bourbon or sour mash whiskey. She put it to her lips, swigged, coughed, grinned.

A cream fabric bag with a draw-string top containing (she thought it'd be dope or something) grass, but of the seed variety, poppy seeds, too, and countless other kinds –

Sweet

She had a vision of Wesley strolling along in high summer, haphazardly scattering seed into the hedgerows, out of pure . . . pure . . .

Altruism

Or was that just naive of her?

Three books. One called (deep breath) *Famous Utopias; an omnibus containing the complete texts of More's Utopia, Campanella's City of the Sun, Rousseau's Social Contract, Bacon's New Atlantis.*

Katherine scowled tiredly as she paged through it. It seemed ancient – so old, in fact, that the pages were raw and uncut. But the cover was beautiful – black and white, with freaky lettering – of several different styles and all just sort of shoved up together, willy-nilly.

Inside was an inscription;

For Wes, (it said, in a beautiful hand; real green ink) *For laughing and feeling,*

Stevie

Two kisses.

Katherine raised her brows at this, almost jealously, and as she flipped through it again something fell out – a picture. A photo. She picked it up from her lap and gazed at it. She blinked and stared harder.

A little girl. Oddly familiar. Katherine gazed up at the ceiling for a moment, then back down at it, as though testing herself: small girl, dark haired, wearing an alice band, not smiling, serious-seeming, thin, sickly-looking.

It was the same –

Wasn't it?

– almost the same photograph Arthur had shown them during dinner (perhaps taken at the same sitting, on the same occasion? Christmas? Birthday?). The same little girl, she was certain.

Katherine scrutinised the photo closely again. Nodded to herself, frowning. Idly turned it over. On the back was written – in pen, but very neatly – *This is the daughter. 9 yrs. Birthday Jan 7th. Lives with the mother.*

Now that was definitely –

Hmmn

– more than a little strange. She gazed over briefly to the letter she'd tossed down onto the floor –

A well-wisher

– then slipped the picture into the front pocket of her dressing gown. Almost surreptitiously. She closed the book gently and put

397

it down. Took a deep breath. Exhaled it, slowly. Snapped back to the task in hand.

The second volume – this one a paperback – was called *Ravens in Winter* by Bernd Heinrich. She paged through it (one field biologist's struggle to uncover the mysteries of raven behaviour in Canada or North America or *somewhere*). The book was marked by a series of feathers. She drew every feather out, one by one. They were all perfect. All iridescent. A deep blue-black-green (hard to see it properly in the muted light), with the occasional sidelong smear of white –

Magpie

Whatever else?

Next to each feather – in the book's margins – she discovered that Wesley had scribbled a series of comments – seemingly unconnected to the text – in pencil.

NB. Contact: (one such comment read) *Michael Hitchens; re. Goodwin;* then a phone number. There were other numbers too. Other names. Another scribble said *In Madagascar an acceptable unit of time is 'rice-cooking time', or shorter; 'the frying of a locust'. Toffler (TTW).*

There were plenty of these cryptic comments (all saying Toffler *TTW* afterwards – Katherine presumed Toffler was a person – a writer – a seer of some kind).

Somewhere else Wesley had written: *Edward Albee: 'the permanent transient'.*

Elsewhere; *Support the GPO!* In big letters.

'Social decay is the compost-bed of our civilisation', then after, in capitals, *BUT THAT'S SO FUCKING PRAGMATIC!*

Katherine grabbed her dictionary again. Under *Pragmatic(al)* she read; *meddlesome, positive, dictatorial* (she snorted, irritably). Then later; *doctrine that the conception of an object is no more than the conception of its possible practical effects.*

She slammed the dictionary shut and threw it at her cupboard. She continued to inspect Wesley's Raven book, crossly.

Next to another feather marker was written: *Joseph Williamson; King of Edge Hill. Tunnels. Must see.* Then further on: *Time: circular or linear?*

As she read, Katherine carefully returned each feather to its original position. Towards the back, her eyes suddenly tightened as she struggled to decipher an especially interesting but rather badly written scribble. She stared at it for a long while. Eventually she made out . . .

Korsikov;

Alcohol abuse.

Short term memory-Liver-Testicular

She straightened her neck, flipped her second plait over her shoulder, growled, slotted away the last feather and sat still for a long while, rocking – almost imperceptibly – and quietly musing.

Finally, she grabbed hold of the third book – gazed at the cover –

Ah

Now *this* was more like it – *Bottersnikes and Gumbles* by S.A. Wakefield. A slim children's story about some squidgy but very *pliant* creatures called . . .

She frowned . . . called . . .

Gumbles

(Now why did that mean something to her? Why was that ringing an alarm bell, somewhere?)

She inspected the picture. A small, white and rather adorable koala-type animal . . . Her forehead cleared. She grinned.

And they were relentlessly bullied and manipulated, these . . . these Gumbles (and kept in old tin cans) by an angry but regal pointy-red-eared creature called Chank who lived in a dump with his furiously lazy Bottersnike compadres. Fully illustrated.

Katherine collapsed back onto her pillows with Wesley's flask in her spare hand, emitted a gentle burp, licked the remaining slick of spirit from her lips and commenced reading.

Thirty-eight

Of course this was Wesley's child. He'd known it – he told himself (if a touch unconvincingly) –
An instinct, call it . . .
– from the very first moment, the first *instant* he'd laid eyes on her

Wesley's own little Sasha. The freak-girl who lived among the deer at her grandparents' Norfolk-based Menagerie-cum-Garden Centre.

She looked like him, too. Arthur shot her a sly glance. But not exactly. He'd seen pictures of the mother (blonde, angry, angular) and she appeared to resemble that side of the family in no way whatsoever.

The mother was a hard-nut. Had gone to the papers – several times – during all the maintenance complications the previous year. Seemed to actively enjoy unburdening on the subject of her ex-lover. Told everything and yet – Arthur's brow rose, minutely – nobody could ever tell quite *enough*, could they?

He visualised the page on the website;
Uh . . .

Food: 'When we lived by the sea in the little bed and breakfast in Hunstanton, we'd cook macaroni cheese from the tin on our tiny cooker – share a bowl of it – curled up in bed together.'
Hygiene: 'He was never all that big on changing his clothes or dressing up or having a bath. He'd swim in the sea, though, all

401

the time. Even in winter. He was like a seal. Or a *machine*. He never seemed to feel the cold.'

Sex: 'He was straight down the line, but sometimes he liked me to *bite* and pinch. Once he'd lost his hand we didn't really sleep together any more – he lost interest, but I was heavily pregnant by then, with Sasha.'

And of course:

Wildlife: 'At first – when he raised his hand – I thought he was going to hit me. But then he turned and pushed his fingers into the cage instead. It was dark . . . very dark. There was a scream. But it wasn't him. It was the bird, the owl. This horrible . . . this unforgettable squealing noise. Like an animal in terrible pain.'

At this point Iris turns towards her fiancé for support. He takes her hand and squeezes it, comfortingly. The small, dark girl – Wesley's daughter – sits by the window, apparently lost in her own childish world, smiling at a sparrow on the lawn, playing with her hair . . .

'He said it was . . .' *Iris's voice falters,* 'he tried to pretend it was me – when we talked about it, after – but it wasn't. It *wasn't*. It was the bird. And later on, Derek – the keeper – said that Wes'd asked to feed that particular owl himself over the previous couple of weeks – said he'd been paying it a lot of personal attention.

'He actually thought Wes'd been disposing of its food, that he'd been starving it, in secret. On purpose. He thought he'd been planning the whole thing for quite a while . . .'

Iris clears her throat, her eyes fill with tears, 'I mean he's charming when he feels like it, but he's a real manipulator. He plays with people's feelings. I think he's a . . .' *Iris lowers her voice, for the sake of the child, but she seems terrified,* 'a *schizophrenic*. He has two personalities. You can't trust him. Especially after – well, his *history* – what he did to the younger brother*. That's why I never want him to have anything to do with my Sasha.'

© *Printed with kind permission of William Harvey*

* _correction_: William Harvey would like it to be stated here that Wesley's brother was not – as Iris specifies in the

interview – younger than him, but older, by approximately sixteen months.

Arthur blinked –

Was I asleep?

He blinked again –

Why do I always remember the Wesley things?

And with such painful – such inexcusable – clarity?

He shivered, struggling to switch himself back into the present.

They were sitting together, close to the doorway. It was freezing. Arthur didn't want to move any further inside – couldn't risk it – and they'd kept the door open, in case of –

If the girl – the daughter – fell into the water

If she was lost in the water

That would be just . . .

Stop

That would be just . . .

STOP!

'Snowing,' the girl suddenly murmured. They'd been quiet for a long while. The only sounds were the gurgle of the low tide hitting the boat's stilts, the boat creaking, the slight wind, the distant and intermittent throb of the flyover.

Arthur looked down at his wrist –

Time

– it was three forty a.m. –

Late

– then he gazed up into the sky. She was right. Snow. Improbably large flakes. His heart sank.

He took out his phone and gazed at it – the third time in as many minutes – pressed some buttons, but it still wasn't working. Almost – kind of – *blocked* – in some way –

Is that possible?

Seriously?

Wesley's call had been the last he'd received. But did that . . . could that make him culpable?

Am I going crazy?

'The man who wrecked the boat,' Arthur said –

It had to be . . .

– 'did you get a good look at him by any chance?'

Sasha shook her head, 'Too dark, and it was raining.'

Arthur pushed his phone back into his pocket and gently pulled his rucksack from his shoulders, careful not to do anything too abruptly. He was cold. She must be too. He pulled out his sleeping bag and unfolded it, propped it around them and loosely tucked it in.

His cut arm was aching. And warm. And numb. It was still bleeding. Felt heavy. He'd tied a handkerchief around it, but wasn't entirely sure what good that was doing. His stomach rumbled –
Hungry

He was sure he had a small packet of honey and sesame crackers hidden away inside his rucksack, somewhere.

'Do you swim?' he asked, scrabbling around – eventually removing his computer, a flask, some spare socks. 'I mean if the worst comes to the worst?'

The girl nodded, 'But there's rocks down below. That's why my grandad settled the boat here. The tide'd need to be pretty high before we could risk jumping without getting hurt on them.'

'Pardon?'

Arthur had the sesame crackers in his hand. But his hand had frozen, mid-air.

'Rocks,' she reiterated slowly, 'down below.'

'Oh,' Arthur nodded his head, then forced himself to start moving again. He offered her the packet.

'What are they?' she frowned.

'Honey and sesame crackers. Good for energy. Take one. It'll keep you lively.'

'Giraffes,' she told him morosely, reaching out for the bag and carefully removing one, 'only ever sleep for three minutes a night.'

Arthur was piling the other stuff back into his rucksack again – everything so far but the computer, which remained on his lap. 'Not so,' he said.

He couldn't let her have it. He was Arthur Anthony Young, after all.

'Is so too,' she answered.

Arthur shook his head, 'I think you'll find that they only ever doze for three minute *durations*. In total – throughout the day – they sleep for about half an hour . . .'

Silence

'Which isn't very *long*,' he conceded, 'admittedly.'

She handed him back his cracker packet, grumpily.

'How about deer?' he asked, taking them and removing one for himself, then glancing over his shoulder towards Brion. Brion was still standing firmly and implacably between the kitchen cabinets. He'd barely moved an inch in the past twenty minutes.

'Brion likes the cold,' she said, 'reindeer live on the ice-caps out of preference. This is nothing to him. This is a walk in the park for Brion.'

'Well that's a weight off my mind, then,' Arthur said, shocked to discover his lip curling. He took a bite from his cracker and chewed on it, thoughtfully.

Sasha – as if looking to him for a lead – took a nibble of hers then pulled a face.

'Although in actual fact creatures rarely adapt to something out of preference,' Arthur continued. 'It's more often a case of biological necessity. For all we know Brion could dislike the cold as much as you do, but his body just happens to *cope* with it better than yours does.'

'*Yeah*,' the little girl sighed, shoving her finger into her mouth to try and prise the glutinous layer of honey and sesame away from her back molars.

'So why are you here?' Arthur asked.

Sasha removed her finger from her mouth and inspected it. Then she took another bite of her cracker and chewed on it, deliberately.

'I was just wondering,' she said, her mouth still full, 'how long it would be before you asked me that.'

She nodded towards his lap, 'Is that a computer?'

'Yes. Laptop.'

'Can I take a look?'

'No.'

'What kind is it?'

Arthur frowned, '*Uh . . . Toshiba*.'

'Piece of shit, huh?'

'Not at all.'

She sniffed.

'So this was your grandfather's boat?'

'Did *I* say that?' Her eyes widened.

'Yes.'

'Then I suppose it must be true, dammit.'

She pushed out her hand into the darkness to try and catch a snowflake on it. Brion shifted. The boat shifted. Arthur grabbed hold of the doorframe, as if in preparation for hurling himself through it. But the boat slowly settled back into place again.

'That *pesky* reindeer,' the girl tutted, rolling her eyes, unfazed. Arthur released his grip, humiliated. He looked down at his hand, his arm. The handkerchief had been white. Now it was dark.

'Aren't you afraid?' he asked the girl, quietly.

'Aren't you?' she backhanded.

'Slightly.'

'Are there games on your computer?'

'No.'

She snorted, 'I bet there are, too.'

'No,' he shook his head. 'No games. I've never seen games on it.'

'I bet there are.'

'And the battery's almost flat.'

'I bet there are, though.'

Arthur was silent.

'Games,' she persisted.

Arthur remained silent.

'I *bet*.'

He drew a deep breath. 'We're going to have to wait until dawn. I don't really see what other choices we have. The big question is whether when the water eventually rises the boat becomes more insecure.'

'Are you familiar with the tides?' Sasha asked. 'I imagine you must be if you live here permanently.'

Her eyes were still on the computer.

'I've not lived here long,' he acknowledged, 'not really.'

'Oh.'

She nodded. She shrugged.

They listened to the boat creaking. Brion sighed, noisily.

'It should be light enough by seven, seven-thirty. And you never know, someone might ... A *rambler* or a *hiker* or a *farmer* or *someone* ...'

'Or *someone*,' the girl repeated, echoing his curious emphasis. He glanced up –

Is she taking the piss?

'I bet you *do* have games,' she continued, fiddling with the pom-poms on her wrists.

Arthur pulled open his laptop, turned it on. He blinked at the sudden light it generated.

'Go to *Start* and call up the menu. Then roll up to *Programs*,' she instructed, leaning over. He ignored her, heading instead for the battery sign in the bottom right-hand corner, pressing it for more information. 1hr20 flashed up –

Okay

Arthur whizzed over to *Start*.

'*Programs*,' she reminded him impatiently, pressing her finger onto the screen.

'Keep your hands off,' he warned. 'It's ... it's ...'

Couldn't think of the word. She ignored him, anyway.

'Now over to *Accessories*,' she wheedled.

Arthur went to *Accessories*.

'*Games*,' she chuckled. 'See? *See?*'

She was pointing, rocking excitedly.

But Arthur wasn't looking at *Games* (a choice of four: *Free Cell, Hearts, Minesweeper, Solitaire*). He wasn't itching to play, or cursing his ignorance or celebrating his laptop's extraordinary multiplicity. He was looking at the desktop, at his files (peeking out reliably from under the sudden city-scape of menu-boxes) and he was seeing,

Better watch your step, Arthur

'Let's play Minesweeper,' the girl said, moving in closer, inching a proprietorial finger towards the keyboard.

WATCH YOUR STEP, ARTHUR

'What?'

What?

This time Arthur didn't try and stop her.

Thirty-nine

It was still dark – still night – when he slowly unwound his arms
from around her and –
Oh the smell of him
Like sweet ginger and leaf-mould and Polyfilla
– quietly left the car murmuring
That voice
Like the wind through an ash tree
– something about –
Don't wake up
Don't worry
I just need a . . .
– not being gone a minute. Not a *minute* – he'd said, breathing
into her ear. She remembered that breath –
Warm
– then a blast of cold air as he'd opened the door, pulled on his
jacket, his waterproof, slammed it.

  She remembered yanking the sleeping bag over her shoulder, her
arm throbbing. She remembered her knee being punctured by the
gear-stick –
Don't care
– and her feet feeling like solid blocks of –
Stuff that falls from the septic tanks of aeroplanes
A bright blue colour
Crashes through the air and lands –
Oh God!
On the heads of an innocent couple going cycling
In a newly established country park near . . .

She woke up –

Wah?

Her feet *were* frozen. Crampy. She tried to shake them –

Where am I?

She was suddenly jolted. Sat upright, gasping –

Where's Wesley?

The sun was rising. But it was cloudy. The windows were icy. There was snow – just a thin layer – and the simple reflection was making everything whiter –

Lighter

– than it otherwise might be.

The clock on her dash said 2.23. But that clock wasn't working –

Actually

– so there was no point in looking. She was guessing 7.00 . . . 7.30?

Jo threw off the sleeping bag, grabbed her clothes (still damp, for the most part) threw them back on (without even a murmur) found *Utah Blaine*, rolled the bag up, grabbed the flask –

Uh . . .

– Doc's tupperware container –

Okay – Okay – Okay

She was almost panting –

Panicking

Then something occurred to her –

Footprints

– there was *snow* out there. There would be . . .

She threw open the passenger door, gazed down. *There* they were . . . relatively clear. Although a certain – and quite inevitable – amount of back-and-forthing –

Uh . . .

She slammed the car door behind her, stamped her feet to try and bring the life back into them, yanked down her hat (over her ears), secured the bag under her arm – shoved the flask into one coat pocket (pulling the seams too tight – not caring), the tupperware into the other, the book . . . *the book* . . . down the front of her jeans –

Only place for it

– and strode out, her brown eyes glued to the floor . . .

But it was never as –
Whoops
Arms rotating like a wind up wooden toy
Almost fell over
– but it was never as simple as it should be –
No
– because there were other footprints too –
And bird and dog and . . .
Bloody hell
– a total mish-mash.

It was still blessedly early, though. She turned a corner. A blast of cold sea air hit her –
Full in the face
A huge, perishing . . .
Fist
A mighty, spiralling
Whooah . . . !

She teetered on the edge of the pavement, blinking. The prints were even less decipherable here – and leading off in *both* directions. She tossed a coin in her head, rubbed her nose –
God, the tickling
– turned left, kept walking until
Ahh
Ahhhh
Ahhh-tish-u!
Urgh

'Bless you.'

Jo looked up, dazed, her eyes streaming. She'd been concentrating so hard it'd been almost like dreaming. Doc reached out his arm and took the sleeping bag from her. They were standing near the gates of the caravan site, the sea wall rearing above them like the precipitous brow of Frankenstein's monster –
Did he come this way?
The other?

Gulls were circling, their keening cries at once muffled and amplified by the fleecy sky. 'He's long gone,' Doc said, 'and the phone and the internet sites are both still down.'

'I was just bringing you back . . . *uh* . . .'

411

Jo grabbed the flask from her pocket, the tupperware.

She glanced down at the footprints. Up again. Doc was offering her a tissue.

'Those prints you're following are mine,' he said, 'I came to check up on you about an hour ago – just before first light – and he was already well-gone by that time.'

'Oh . . .'

Jo took the tissue, pained, 'So you knew?'

'Of *course* I knew,' Doc looked suitably irritated. 'It's my *job* to know. I'm *Doc*.'

As he spoke he glanced around him with an air of slight anxiety (as if uttering his own name so brazenly might prove inexplicably risky). Jo gazed around her too. Her eyes settled on a man – still in the middle distance, but heading towards them, at speed – wearing a smart coat, holding a white stick. He was being led by another man, much younger, and sighted. Shoes was just behind, following in their slipstream.

'This Internet stuff's causing chaos, huh?' Jo said. 'Are you in direct contact with the site? I thought you were their man on the ground. Are they likely to sort it all out?'

Doc didn't answer. He tipped his head stiffly towards the approaching threesome. 'The Blind Man,' he murmured, 'have you had the pleasure yet?'

'No.'

'I strongly recommend you keep it that way.'

'Why?'

'Ex-cop.'

She glanced up. Doc gave her a straight look. Shrugged. Turned back to appraise the advancing party. 'I'm a little worried,' he mused, 'that Shoes might've gone over to the other side.'

'Pardon?'

'Why not just walk on,' Doc advised her, his voice suddenly lower, more urgent, as if he'd made a decision, a snap one, 'and be casual. Say nothing about Wesley. Give nothing away. Meet me in the Wimpy. We need to talk privately.'

'When?'

'Ten minutes. If anyone starts bothering you, pretend you're still crazy. They all really fell for that clever little tactic yesterday.'

'But I . . .'

I wasn't pretending

'The whole *shebang*,' he expanded, raising his white brows at her. Jo scowled, gazed up at the sea wall. 'What about Wesley?'

'I've got it covered,' Doc casually rested his hand on his coat pocket, tapped it 'tracking device,' he muttered, 'Dennis is working undercover.'

'The *dog*?'

'Scarper,' Doc growled, 'I'll fill you in later. And for *God's sake . . .*'

He pointed towards her chest, grimacing.

Jo looked down –

Bollocks

The jumper

– she pulled her coat tighter, blushing, then cleared her throat and raised her voice, 'Tell Hooch thanks for the bag. I suppose I'd better be getting back to my car . . .'

She thrust the thermos and the tupperware into his huge, old hands. Doc nodded, 'You do that.'

She started walking, zigzagging across the road, to the opposite pavement, peering keenly to the right of her as if looking for something (a key or a sign or some money). As she drew adjacent to the others she could hear the sighted guide talking, 'A young woman,' he described, 'skinny, wearing a knitted hat . . .'

'The nurse,' Shoes butted in, 'the one from the bar.'

'*Hey*,' the Blind Man pointed his stick towards her. Jo pretended she hadn't noticed. Walked even faster.

'*Hey*,' the Blind Man repeated. His tone was stentorian

She continued to ignore it.

'Jo,' Shoes called, '*Jo*. Hold up a minute. This is Herbie. He's *blind*. He wants a . . .'

Jo turned around, still very much on the move. 'I've got . . . uh . . .' she shouted back, then almost tripped up, 'the *AA*,' she continued, jerkily, readjusting her posture, 'coming over to check out my car. I have to get . . .'

She threw up her arms in a gesture of apology.

'Did you get the book?' Shoes asked (normal volume, making quite a mockery out of all the yelling).

'Yes,' she answered (still loud, still moving. But he didn't seem to catch her).

'*Yes*,' she shouted louder. 'Thanks. I'll give it you back *later* . . .'

'HOW'S YOUR ARM?' he bellowed –

Taking the piss

Has to be

She lifted it into the air, like a wing. 'Good. *Better*.'

The Blind Man turned and began saying something. Jo turned herself and started jogging. Her feet were heavy, though, and the ground was slippy.

Thirty seconds later, the young guide was bobbing along at her shoulder. He'd plainly been dispatched. She glanced over at him. He was black haired, wide-eyed, with a sprinkling of acne on his jaw.

'So Doc got to you first, huh?' he panted. He had a good accent. Well modulated.

'What do you want?' she asked.

'Could you just . . .' The guide was breathing heavily, 'just *stop* for a second?'

He skidded.

Jo stopped automatically, grabbed his arm and steadied him.

'Thanks,' he blew out his cheeks, relieved.

She glanced behind them. The others had met up and were now all in a huddle. The Blind Man was tapping Doc's leg with his stick. Doc was smiling, raising his voice . . . he seemed . . . he seemed *jovial* . . .

Was that . . . ?

Was that the right . . . ?

Jo realised that she was still clutching the tissue he'd given her. Her nose was dripping. She patted her face with it.

'What do you want?' she asked brusquely, finishing with it, screwing it up and pushing it deep inside her coat pocket.

'*Uh* . . .'

The guide lifted his arm and inspected his right wrist (although there was patently no watch on it). '*Damn*,' he cursed, 'is it that time already?'

He wasn't much of an actor.

'You're not wearing a watch,' Jo said.

'Okay . . .' he swallowed and then looked up into the sky as if struggling to call something to mind, 'just quickly, then. Herbie wants me to tell you,' he counted each statement off onto his fingers (in case he should forget), 'that Doc's playing a double game. That he's started keeping stuff back. That he's got too involved. That he's gone a little crazy. That he wants to spoil it for the rest of us . . . sorry . . .' he chuckled, raising his brows, 'the rest of *them.*'

As he chuckled he made eye contact. He had cold eyes. And they weren't chuckling. Jo's expression remained impassive. The guide shrugged, 'Don't even ask me what this all *means* . . .' There was something engagingly feminine about him.

He lifted his right hand and checked his non-watch again (Jo presumed it was just some kind of crazy *tick*), 'You're not heading into the centre of town by any chance?'

'Nope.' Jo shook her head.

'Oh. *Okay.* It's just . . .' he scratched his chin – the patch of acne there, 'I was meant to be heading home *hours* ago but Herbie will insist on *careering* off at every given opportunity . . .'

'I'm sorry,' Jo was frowning, 'I don't . . .'

'God it's *nothing*,' the man interrupted, 'I'm Herbie's temporary careworker. Someone just happened to mention that you were in the nursing profession . . .'

Jo slowly began walking again. He paused for a second and then slowly walked with her.

'Yes,' she said, 'but I'm not . . . I'm on sick leave. I'm . . . I'm . . .' she swallowed down her pride, 'currently suspended.'

Hard to say it

'A touch of depression.'

That was easier

The guide didn't quite seem to hear her. 'I had someone due to take over from me over twenty minutes ago,' he persisted, 'they'll be waiting outside the library in a silver car . . .'

'And?'

Jo stopped walking, faced him.

'And I thought if you were in the area – and had a moment to spare – that you might nip on over there and tell him where I am. He'd be very . . .' he tipped his head, 'very *appreciative*, I'm sure.'

415

Jo smiled, sympathetically, 'I already explained that I'm going back to my car. I'm waiting for the *AA*. My car's *way* over . . .'

She pointed towards her car, then radically altered the direction she was pointing (almost hitting the guide, the swing of her arm was so spectacular) –

Oh Lord

'Over there.'

'Of course.'

The guide shrugged. He looked depressed.

'Can't you just phone him?' Jo asked.

'Forgotten the number,' he shrugged again.

'Can't *Shoes* go and find him, then?'

The guide *pooh-poohed* this, 'It's nothing. It's fine. Don't worry. I must've . . .' he smiled, '*misconstrued* . . .'

He put his hand up to his hair, pushed his fringe back from his forehead. Used his left hand. As he raised his arm and the sleeve of his coat fell away, Jo saw that he was wearing a watch on that left wrist. A good watch. Swiss Army.

'Guess I'll see you later.'

He turned and jogged back to join the others. Jo remained where she was for a moment. She shook her head, slowly – stopped – gazed blankly ahead of her, frowned – then shook it a second time, for a little longer.

The little kid – the boy – Patty –

Was that his name?

– had taken up residence on the pavement directly opposite Katherine's. He looked, Ted thought – if possible – even grimier than he had done the day before. He was devouring a cheese and salad sandwich, its plastic wrapper casually discarded in the gutter, along with most of the tomato and most of the cheese.

'Where's Wesley?' the kid asked – his gums white with bread – as Ted crossed the road in front of him.

'I have no idea.'

Ted tried to sound civil (he knew what a potential powder-keg the kid could be).

'*Prick*,' the kid murmured darkly – although barely audibly. Then, '*Stupid damn wanker.*' Then (Ted stiffened his back, prepared himself) . . .

'*Ginger winger.*'

He made it to the opposite pavement, smartly eclipsed Katherine's conifers, turned into the driveway and drew to an abrupt halt.

Bo was leaning in Katherine's porchway, smoking a fag, casually perusing her paper.

'Another loyal member of your ever-expanding fanclub, eh, Ted?' he grinned.

'Bo,' Ted muttered, 'it's you.'

'Ever the one for stating the fucking obvious,' Bo responded, deftly re-folding the paper and shoving it through Katherine's letterbox, 'and it can't be any coincidence, can it, *sir*, that your appearing here this morning happens to coincide with a series of rumours about a certain celebrity-troublemaker having taken up temporary residence at this address?'

'*Uh* . . .' Ted tried to think on his feet but they were already fully engaged in the act of supporting him. So he went with his gut, instead.

'No,' he said.

This wasn't quite the answer Bo'd been expecting (a pathetic attempt to lie would've been marginally more satisfying). His mono-brow rose, fractionally. His black eyes glimmered.

Unfortunately this wasn't quite the answer *Ted'd* anticipated delivering, either –

That damn gut

'Because . . .' Ted continued (perhaps ill-advisedly), 'because *Pathfinder* set it up, late yesterday evening. Very late. After all that trouble in the bar . . .'

'And was this before,' Bo rubbed his wide jaw, speculatively, 'or *after* that same charming lodger physically assaulted his wife?'

Ted stared at him blankly. 'Wesley's married?'

'Oh *God*,' Bo bit on his knuckles, *faux*-dramatically, 'and you actually hold down a *responsible position* in this town, Ted?'

Ted frowned (was this question purely rhetorical?), then he nodded – slowly – almost imperceptibly (on the off-chance that it wasn't).

417

Bo threw down his cigarette, crushed it underfoot and turned to the door.

'I thought we had an agreement,' Ted said (his gut working overtime; transcending his head), 'I thought we'd agreed that you wouldn't be bothering Katherine with any of this mess.'

'The *Bean* girl,' Bo smiled, caustically, 'needs to *vamoose*. And who better to persuade her?'

'How does the Bean girl enter into any of this?' Ted asked, frowning confusedly.

'If I can't get what I want from the monkey . . .' Bo shrugged, letting the second half of his sentence unfold silently, mid-air.

Ted stared at him.

I'm waiting for life to start – he thought – just the same as the rest of them. I'm not the original picture anymore. I have become a *duplication* of the real me. I am a *copy*.

'Just go to the office, Ted.'

Bo made a dismissive finger-walking gesture, then turned to the door and lifted the knocker. Ted did as he was instructed, obligingly, then suddenly – and without warning – rotated back sharply to his former position.

'You were *never* any good at tennis, Bo,' he said.

Forty

He hadn't thought it possible he could feel this tired. The Solitaire had played its part. Thirty or more games. Her idiotic *banter*. She'd developed a series of theories about the peculiar mind-set of his computer –

Tosh-eeee-baaa

– she kept muttering

Tosh-eeee-baaa

She thought this particular game's designers were incorrigible bastards.

'These people are just *scoundrels*,' she'd say, 'I *salute* them.'

Then she'd salute (quite traditionally) but integrating a v-sign into the second half of the gesture. She plainly found herself terribly amusing.

'It's Solitaire,' Arthur kept interrupting her. 'They don't have to *do* anything to make it interesting. It was interesting *before* someone put it onto the machine. It's only chance that keeps you playing. Nobody can design chance. It just happens. It's random.'

She wasn't convinced. 'Of *course* they can design it. That's the whole *point*. They have to keep you interested. It's their job.'

'It's just random,' he repeated.

Just random

'When I grow up I'm going to . . .' she paused for a second, considered – gazed over her shoulder towards the deer. Brion yawned. Then farted.

'. . . Work with animals,' she concluded, flatly (all emotional declarations of Game Designing instantaneously evaporating). 'That's my destiny.'

'Do you have a computer at home?' Arthur asked, trying – unsuccessfully – to tie a sock around his wrist using just his other hand and his teeth.

'Give it here.' Sasha put the computer aside, grabbed the sock and tied it around, firmly. 'You've made a mess,' she observed, pointing to his trousers. A dark stain covered the knee-area, but the sight of blood didn't seem to bother her.

Arthur's mind turned – for a moment – to the short-haired girl in the bar. The broken bottle. The slashes on her arm. He supposed – tiredly, idly – that through this wound he'd forged a kind of inadvertent kinship with her –

Hate that thought

It's stupid

Sasha picked up the computer and recommenced her playing. 'I keep in touch with my dad through the Internet,' she suddenly announced, 'and nobody knows a *thing* about it.'

Arthur's head swung around – he'd been peering out through the door, listening to the groans of the boat above the *tap tap* of her fingers, '*Do* you?'

She nodded.

'So how does that work exactly?'

'Easy. There's a special site I can connect to which gives me up-to-date reports on everything he's doing. Sometimes hour by hour.'

She cleared her throat. 'He works for a kind of Secret Service,' she confided. 'It's all very *hush-hush-hush*.'

Arthur mulled this over for a second (that endearing one *hush* too many), 'Do you ever get to see him?'

She nodded, cheerfully, 'All the time. In pictures. And he has charisma,' she peered up at him, proudly, 'most people have to pay a *bundle* to get that.'

She continued to gaze at him. '*You* have it,' she said (a smiling vision of shameless insincerity).

Arthur wasn't taken in, obviously.

'You've never seen him in person, though?' he asked, already knowing the answer (wanting to knock some of the perkiness out of her – but failing, quite markedly, and feeling secretly relieved that he had).

She shrugged her shoulders, 'When it's a question of National Security, people's feelings don't really . . .' she paused, '*damn* . . .' peered even closer at the screen, 'I thought that'd be the Ace of Clubs. I don't *need* another red four . . .'

Arthur gazed at the screen himself. 'Six on your seven,' he nudged.

'Do you have any children, Arthur?' she asked.

Arthur felt both surprised and infantilised by her using his name so confidently. He shook his head.

'Yes,' he said.

She gave him a perplexed look.

'A boy?' she eventually continued.

'No. A daughter. A couple of years younger than you are.'

'Does she live here? On this boat?'

'No,' he smiled, wryly, 'she lives with her mother.'

Sasha completed one game, then promptly began another. 'Are you divorced?'

'I was never married.'

'Why not?'

'She was . . .' he paused –

Preoccupied

Lost

Ruined

Undone

'She just didn't want to. Not in the end.'

'What's her name?'

'Bethan. She was in love with somebody else. Someone she knew from before we met each other . . .' he paused, 'not in *love*, exactly . . . she just couldn't . . . couldn't get over the effect he had on her. She went a little bit mad. He made her *feel* differently. He invaded her.'

'Sex?' she asked, scowling.

He almost smiled at this. 'No.'

Yes

'One of the strangest facts of life,' he murmured, 'is that some people have more of an impact on you when they aren't even there. As absences. Like your dad.'

Sasha continued scowling. 'I'm still not getting it,' she said.

'Well, when our daughter was born,' Arthur tried to explain further, 'Bethan became very . . . very *preoccupied* by her. That was all part of it – of the effect this man had. Our daughter was extremely ill. She thought it was all connected – that it was her . . . her *punishment*. Or a kind of justice.'

'And was it?'

Arthur scowled, 'Yes . . . *No* . . .' he fought with himself, '*Yes.*'

Sasha's eyes widened, 'What kind of ill?'

'Serious . . .' Arthur said. 'She gets . . .' he struggled to find the word. She waited for it, patiently.

'. . . im-im-imperfections,' he said, then frowned.

'Pardon?'

'She gets . . . *infections*. Chest infections. She's in hospital much of the time. She needs a big operation. I do a lot of fund-raising.'

'How?'

He paused, considered his answer carefully. 'Walking,' he said, 'long distances . . .'

Running

He quickly cleared his throat. 'Getting sponsorship.'

'And is that enough?' she asked brutally.

Art's eyes widened. He was cut. 'No,' he said, tightly, 'it isn't. I do some other things too, which help.'

Sasha didn't notice the tightness.

'What's her name?' she asked, turning over a red King in the game and moving it into a gap.

'Harmony.'

'No kidding?' She glanced up.

He shook his head. 'I don't . . .' he paused, couldn't finish –

Kid

'Brion had an aunt called Harmony. Like the hairspray. But she broke her leg so my Grandad shot her. This was years ago, when I was still tiny. Of course I was *devastated*,' she said, with a roll of her eyes, 'I loved her . . .' she paused – just like Arthur had – and groped for the word she needed, 'to . . . to destruction.'

Arthur frowned suspiciously at her malapropism.

'To *distraction*,' she corrected herself, smiling.

'That's . . .' he said, his eyes focussing on the computer.

'Do you see your daughter much?' she persisted.

Arthur didn't appear to like this question.

'When I can,' he said. 'It's sometimes difficult.'

'Why?'

'I've been unwell myself. I have certain . . . *obligations*. Certain . . . *interests* that keep us apart.'

'Same as my dad,' she nodded, as if comforted by this thought.

Arthur looked upset. He plainly didn't like this comparison.

'And do you have the same thing your daughter has?'

Arthur glanced up, 'Pardon?'

'The illness?'

'*God* no. No. I was a heavy drinker for a long while . . . for a long while after . . . I have a . . .' he struggled, 'a *condition*. It affects my memory. My short term . . . my kidneys.'

'Yours is a *tragic* tale,' Sasha announced portentously.

Her eyes followed his, down onto the desktop. She gazed at the files which protruded from under the game she was playing.

'I *love* Gumbles,' she announced passionately, 'I *knew* you were a friend when I saw that Gumble on your hat.'

'What?'

He frowned, putting his hand to his head, removing his hat, staring at it, blankly.

'Oh,' he said, 'but this isn't really . . .'

My hat

'Can I try it?' she asked.

She took it from him, inspected it closely, squinting at it in the darkness. 'Yup,' she said, 'exactly like in the story.'

'I'm not . . .' Arthur murmured, '. . . not *acquainted* with it.'

'*Bottersnikes and Gumbles*. S. A. Wakefield. He's an Australian. My gran gave me a copy my dad once had when he was still a little boy. I keep it hidden under my bed.'

Arthur was shaking his head, slowly, trying to comprehend what she was telling him.

'There are two groups,' she explained, needing no further prompting, 'the Bottersnikes who have ears which turn red when they're angry and who are very lazy but rule the rubbish dump just the same, and the Gumbles who are very squidgy and white and get shoved into jam-jars and tins and stored there as slaves until the Bottersnikes want to use them to do their bidding . . .' she paused, 'and the Bottersnikes say *Foo!* when they're cross. They're very funny.'

He didn't react to this. His mind was suddenly elsewhere . . .

A rubbish dump

The early 1970s

One little boy was pushing another towards a disused refrigerator

Shoving him inside there

Closing him in

Preserving him for ever

He shuddered.

'It sounds . . . *in* . . . interesting,' he said, finally. His voice was hoarse.

Sasha adjusted his hat on her head and then recommenced her play.

The reindeer shifted.

The boat shifted.

'Do you keep other animals,' Arthur asked, gazing tiredly over his shoulder, 'apart from reindeer?'

She nodded, distractedly.

'What kind?'

'Hawks. Birds of prey. Owls.'

The computer commenced a high-pitched beeping.

'Battery,' Arthur said, taking the machine from her, using his bad hand to turn it off, clumsily.

Sasha yawned – wide – making no attempt to cover it; her jaw snapping smartly shut like a tightly-hinged letterbox. 'I don't know if you've noticed,' she said, 'but we seem to be tipping back slightly.'

'I hadn't noticed,' Arthur lied.

She shuffled up closer to him, rested her head on his shoulder and closed her eyes.

'Probably for the best,' she murmured.

Forty-one

The penny finally dropped on the short walk over. It wasn't *Wesley's* wife (Wesley didn't have a wife), it was *Pathfinder's*. It was Eileen.

Ted burst into the office just in time to witness an effervescent Leo (his moustache as wayward as an ill-constructed corn dolly) going online – the familiar whistle, the clang, the *boink* . . .

'When I finally track him down,' he said, pointing at Ted with one accusing hand, hurriedly typing in an address with the other, 'I am going to swing for him first, then *you*, straight after.'

'Is Eileen alright?' Ted asked – his eyes travelling, ineluctably, towards the cloakroom door (the paintwork around the hinges still detectably shabby), the new mirror beyond it – however – in pristine good order (if fractionally larger). He swallowed hard but maintained a veneer of calm, removing his coat, his scarf, and neatly hanging them on the pegs provided.

He was certain Eileen must be okay. Fundamentally. Wesley was – he frowned, thoughtfully – like a funfair ride; if you agreed to climb on board (if you paid for your ticket and passed all the restrictions regarding age and size), then you were pretty much *dutybound* to feel a little weak and wobbly by the time you clambered off again at the other side. That was the whole . . .
But what if . . . ?
No.

I *need* to believe . . . (Ted's thoughts tripped over each other like the pages of an open book blowing in the breeze; like a daydreaming schoolgirl stumbling on a chink in a city pavement.)
I need to believe in someone –

So let it be him

'Extremely distressed,' Leo snarled, 'her face – her neck – all scratched up. Her nails broken. Tearful. And refuses to breathe a word about it to anybody, has offered *no* convincing . . .'

The phone began to ring. Ted walked over to answer it, keeping his eyes fixed – all the while – on Leo and the computer.

'Hello?'

'I need you,' Wesley said. 'Bring me some rope. Heavy rope. At least twenty foot of it, and a box of eggs, and the librarian. Meet me by the flyover.'

He hung up.

Ted slowly replaced the receiver, feeling the strangely unruly burden of this new responsibility – and yet the corresponding *light-ness* of suddenly not giving a shit about anything else or anybody.

I am his *sop*, he thought.

There

Leo was still frowning at the computer, twitching the mouse around, grumbling. He was patently accessing the Wesley site.

I should say something, Ted thought, but he didn't. He merely watched on, instead, as the screen went dark, lit up, and the now familiar graphics for the Behindlings Home Page slowly down-loaded.

'Where is she?'

'At home. Getting ready for work.'

'Is there anything I can do for her?'

Leo was frowning at the screen and twiddling his moustache.

'What possible good could *you* do anybody?'

'I thought I might . . .'

'Think again. It's currently a police matter.'

Ted's eyes widened, 'She called in the police?'

'Nope. I did. I bumped into Bo earlier, on my way over here. He said he'd seen her conferring with that Wesley character – yesterday – in the library. He said Wesley had a *reputation* for dalliances with library staff.'

'That's just a silly rumour,' Ted asserted, 'and Bo of all people should know better.'

Leo glanced up, combatively, and that exact-same moment – as if in retaliation – the computer commenced a quite abominable squealing. He winced. Turned. The screen went black. It went red. It went absolutely haywire.

'What the *fuck's* going on here?'

He fought with it for a minute, then swore, yanked the mouse from its socket and threw it into the air. He swiped it – like a shuttlecock – with the palm of his hand. Made a hit (brought down the details of a Shop To Let display in the forefront of the window with it).

'That'll be the virus,' Ted calmly observed.

'What?' Leo turned. 'You *knew* there was a virus and you didn't think to warn me about it?'

Ted did not flinch. He stood his ground.

'Everybody knew about the virus, Leo,' he said –

Used the name

Must use the name

– then he tipped his head to one side, his face a mask of determined impunity. 'I'm *needed* somewhere,' he announced, looking on coolly – was there even a glimmer of *mockery* in that stare? – as Leo bent down to grapple with the plug, then banged his head on the drawer, then swore.

Ted walked to the door, took his jacket and scarf down from the peg, pulled them back on again. 'What a terrible . . .' he paused, turned, caught sight of the short-haired girl – Josephine Bean – rapidly disappearing down a skinny alleyway, the stately arrival of a police car, flashed back to that hollow moment the night before when he'd stood in the same spot and had witnessed Eileen scurrying past in her curious purdah (Arthur crouched down low in Leo's chair) . . . and yet . . . and yet best of all – and most vividly – he saw that pond –

Pond

– in his mind's eye; that *floating* pond; that exquisite unlikelihood of weed and water and fish and air . . .

'What an unbelievable *fuck up*, eh?' he sighed distractedly, feeling an impious flutter in his belly –

No –

– a capricious *tingle* (more-like), rapidly succeeded by a voluptuous *spasm* –

Oh God –

Oh Jesus Christ!
I finally belong somewhere
– as he nipped smartly, neatly, through the door.

'I need you to come with me,' Hooch informed her; appearing almost from nowhere, grabbing her arm as she stood by the counter, and then steering her – at full speed – out of the Wimpy and onto the High Street.

'I *can't*,' Jo almost yelped, dashing down her money (he was pinching her, she was struggling to hold two steaming cartons of coffee), 'I'm waiting . . .'

'Doc,' Hooch said, 'I know *exactly* who you're waiting for.'

They arrived on the pavement in perfect tandem with a police car which was pulling up, with sinuous efficiency, outside the agency (Jo thought she could see the agent inside, newly arrived; he hadn't been there five minutes before – she'd checked – and another man, a short man with a mad, ginger moustache, sitting at his desk with a face as bright as a matador's flag).

'Double *shit*.' Hooch swore, espying the police and yanking her a hard, sharp left into a thin nook between two shops. This unsalubrious alley smelled of piss and sulphur. It contained several rubbish bins and quantities of litter.

'The fucking police are everywhere in this town.'

He let go of her arm and ripped off his hat (in such a way – with such gusto, such aplomb – that she wouldn't have been surprised if a trained white dove had been left sitting there, its pink feet poignantly skedaddling on his waxy pate). He struggled to catch his breath.

'I've had enough of you,' he finally said.

Jo smiled. She thought he must be kidding.

'And before you . . .' he held up his hand, 'before you do all of this *blah blah blah* . . .' (he waved the hand around, dismissively), 'I know exactly who you are and why you're here.'

Josephine's fingers tightened around her paper coffee cartons, but she didn't utter a word, she just waited, benignly, for some kind of explanation.

'The Turpin girl . . .' Hooch continued (fully intent upon providing her with one), 'rumour has it that you slept with her father. You were still a schoolgirl. He was the local headmaster . . .' Hooch sounded unbelievably bored by the facts he was disclosing, 'but you weren't terribly discreet, were you? Or careful, for that matter. You got yourself pregnant. Katherine helped you to get rid of it – presumably to try and salvage what remained of her dad's career. Your family became involved. Your three hulking brothers . . . and whatever they did . . .' he ruminated on this fact for a moment, 'well, it must've been pretty, bloody persuasive, because everything suddenly got all *twisted*; what with the graffiti; your comparable hair colours – Katherine's bad reputation . . .'

He shrugged, phlegmatically, 'Somewhere along the line she got well and truly shafted, while you, on the other hand, toddled off to Southend and became . . .' he grinned, devilishly (well aware of the irony), 'an *Angel* of friggin' *Mercy*.'

'Who told you?'

She seemed astonished.

'The local hack. We did a part-exchange with him. He was very forthcoming.'

'No.'

She was definite. 'No,' she repeated, 'Bo wouldn't have had anything to *gain* from telling . . .' She paused for a second, her mind obviously racing, 'Was it the estate agent?' she asked. 'He's the only real weak link here . . .'

Hooch shook his head (although patently now registering the agent's involvement in the affair). 'Let's just say that I put two and two together. Stuff I've been observing since I first arrived in this town . . . the contents of a letter which I'd all but forgotten about . . .'

Jo's eyes tightened. 'Which letter?'

Hooch smirked at her disquiet. 'Something I picked up over a year ago, sent care of a certain lunatic West-Country potter . . .'

'I don't understand.'

'He had one of those free-standing postboxes at the end of his driveway . . .' Hooch grinned as he described it, gleefully outlining the shape of it with his hands, 'irresistibly easy to pilfer.'

Jo was aghast. 'You *stole* my letter to Wesley?'

'No big deal,' he shrugged, 'I always put everything back once I've . . .' He put his hand into his pocket and withdrew a couple of neatly-folded sheets of paper, 'once I've *photocopied.*'

Josephine stared down – aghast – as he unfolded them. She saw her letter, her handwriting. Hooch snorted at her expression. 'Look,' he sneered, shoving them away again, 'before you feel the need to go and get all righteous on me, I don't happen to give a *shit* about the various permutations of your vulgar little story. I only care about Wesley and his involvement with it.'

'Well that's touching.' She sounded suitably caustic.

Hooch smiled, 'He's not a *swan*, darling. He doesn't fuck a girl once and then bond for *life* with her.'

Josephine glanced off, sideways.

'And even on the understanding that Wes knows or remembers – or gives a *damn* – about your sordid teenage activities,' he continued, 'that wouldn't be enough. Because you Followed. You fucked up. And your case – no matter what it is, how worthy – will be permanently contaminated by that.'

Hooch placed his hat back onto his head again. Jo stared at it, at the distinctive logo, somewhat blankly, frowning slightly.

'What does that mean?' she asked, pointing.

'He's a creature of habit, our Wes,' Hooch talked on, as if he hadn't heard her. 'He protects himself with these rituals. They give him a sense of security. They allow him to keep people at a distance, to push people away. I've seen it all a thousand times before, believe me.'

As Hooch spoke, Jo rolled her eyes skywards, staring intently into the thin, grey ruler of cloud neatly measuring the two buildings above them.

Hooch wasn't buying her nonchalance. 'You probably think it's your charming *personality* that's attracted him,' he scoffed, 'or your excruciatingly embarrassing display in the bar yesterday. But it isn't. It can't be. There has to be something extra. Or at least he *thinks* there is, and that's what's keeping him interested . . .'

'Well there *isn't* anything extra,' she interrupted, defiantly, 'and even if there were, I'd hardly go out of my way to tell you all about it, would I? Or him, for that matter.'

'Not good enough,' Hooch shook his head (delighted to have snapped her out of her complacent posture), 'because Wesley *never* interacts with the people Following – and it's not even because he doesn't want to, but because he knows that it wouldn't work; the whole Following system – the institution – would collapse, would lose all its meaning if he did. He *knows* that. And the Loiters – the Following – the Behindlings, are vital to him. He wouldn't be viable, he wouldn't be anything without them.'

Viable

– Jo frowned –

That word again

'No,' she eventually spoke out, 'I'm not swallowing it. Wesley hates the Following. You're totally deluded if you think otherwise.'

Hooch stared at her, in silence, for a short duration, then he continued on talking, as if what she'd just said had barely registered with him. 'I'd've guessed,' he mused thoughtfully, 'on first glance – obviously – that you were working on behalf of local industry. But it doesn't make sense. You've got environmental interests, so they wouldn't touch you with a . . .'

Josephine snorted, under her breath, looked up into the air again. This did niggle him.

'What's so amusing?'

'For all you know,' she told him, 'that might make me *exactly* the kind of person they'd want on side.'

'Bollocks.'

He wasn't swallowing it. But she expanded this idea, nevertheless, in a blatant attempt to provoke him, 'For all you know, they might've offered me some kind of humanitarian *incentive* to trail Wesley around. Or maybe . . . maybe they thought my reputation as a local Mata Hari might work as a cunning smoke-screen to veil over some fantastically audacious *plot* they're hatching . . . or . . . or perhaps they agreed to make some fundamental environmental *concessions* if I agreed to help them out with a little bit of harmless surveillance activity, or to fund a worthwhile . . . a . . . a *pamphlet* on The Pill or Cystitis or some other criminally under-publicised feminine health issue . . .'

Hooch was unimpressed. 'Who do you think you are?' he asked dourly. 'The Joan of Arc of the fucking Uterus?'

She laughed out loud at this. An anxious laugh. He was too close for comfort. He was too close by half.

'You must be *very* proud,' he said, 'to have made that difficult transition from local ride to local saviour.'

Jo gazed over his shoulder, her face hardening. 'I'm meant to be meeting Doc,' she muttered.

'There's something *clever* about you,' Hooch whispered back, 'and that's precisely why I want you out of here.'

Her eyeline shifted.

'I want you gone,' he said (in case she remained in any doubt about what he'd meant the first time).

She shook her head, confusedly. 'I really must be missing something,' she murmured, 'are you actually threatening me, Hooch? Or are you threatened *by* me? D'you think I've got too close to Wesley or to the big *prize* money? D'you think I might try and steal them both away?'

Hooch adjusted his glasses on his long, wide nose. They slid down again, immediately. 'The Loiter isn't an issue,' he announced calmly, 'the Loiter's old news. It's a done deal already.'

'How?'

He shrugged.

She stared at him; his long face, his dolorous expression, his unbelievable aura of insufferable complacency. 'I don't believe you.'

'You can believe what you like,' he grimaced, 'I don't *care* what you believe.'

'Then why haven't you claimed it, yet?' she persisted. 'Why hasn't there been any fuss?'

'There are some things,' he placed his hat back onto his head then calmly reached out his hand and took one of the coffees from her, gently prising the lid open with his thumb, 'far more *important* than prizes, Bean. That's something you don't yet seem to have grasped about this whole situation. We were Following long before this competition ever began, and we'll be Following for a long time after. It's a long-term *investment*. We're in this for the long haul.'

Jo wasn't entirely satisfied with his answer, but before she could puzzle it out, he'd suddenly turned the tables on her.

'Tell me,' he asked (taking a careful sip of his coffee, his glasses partially steaming up), 'what kind of person d'you think you are?'

Jo was unimpressed by this question. It was plainly pure verbiage. Bored she fired it straight back at him.

'What kind of person do *you* think I am, Hooch?'

'I think,' Hooch leaned back against the opposite wall, unmoved by her hostility, 'I think you're a fundamentally decent girl. And responsible. You obviously commit to things. You're cunning. You don't give up easily . . .'

He paused, took another sip of his coffee, pointedly ignoring her look of astonishment. 'I definitely think you're the kind of person,' he continued, 'who doesn't like the idea of somebody else taking the rap for her.'

'Why would you think that?' Jo's lips suddenly twisted, 'since – according to you – I famously *did* once let somebody else take the rap for me?'

'I think that,' he replied calmly, 'because of what happened in the bar yesterday.'

'Pardon?' Jo was having none of it. 'My *excruciatingly embarrassing* display, if I recall your words correctly.'

She automatically placed her free hand onto the arm of her coat – underneath which the four stinging cuts lay – as if somehow hoping to defend her wounds from his cruel accusations of insincerity.

Hooch watched this movement. It was thoroughly instinctive. It reminded him of the way Wesley moved. The way he touched his cheek sometimes, or brought his good hand across his belly to caress his fingerless stump.

'I'm pretty certain that the Turpin girl won't thank you for sticking your oar in around here again,' he said, moving on swiftly, 'whatever your motivations are. Because the more fuss you cause – the more attention you draw to yourself – the more likely you are to stir up all those old . . .' he paused, ruminatively, 'those old *complications*.

'And let's face it,' he continued, 'that kind of scandal never really dies away in this kind of place, does it? The graffiti's still there, still fresh, after all this time, which means that *somebody* in this town is still heartily committed to the whole affair.'

'I have a right to try and make things better,' Jo muttered –

almost sulkily. 'Wesley had no *business* interfering in matters he didn't understand.'

'But that's *Wesley*,' Hooch sneered, 'that's his *knack*.'

Jo looked down at her coffee cup for a while, dug her neat thumb-nail into the paper. She looked up again. 'So Doc already knows the answer to the Loiter, then? And Shoes? And the rest of them?'

Hooch wouldn't be drawn on this. 'The Blind Man,' he said, tipping the dregs of his coffee onto the floor, pushing the toe of his boot into this brown pool he'd created, 'now there's a *real* live wire for you. Almost a local. Ex-copper. Then there's the *journalist* boy. Your letter'd certainly provide a juicy little exclusive for a man like him, eh?'

Jo shook her head firmly, 'My father happens to run the biggest local Salvage Centre on the *Charfleets*. He offers regular financial support to all local good causes, including the local paper. He funded that nasty, talentless little geek's entire *tennis* career. Bo has nothing to gain from making fools of my family.'

Hooch shrugged, 'But there's always someone, somewhere, who'll gain something from making a monkey out of you, Bean. And now Wesley's involved the stakes are that much higher . . .'

'I don't care about myself,' Jo said, 'but I do care about Katherine . . .'

'And Katherine still cares for her father,' Hooch interrupted, 'or she wouldn't be happy to continue taking the brunt of all this stuff on his behalf, would she?'

Jo was forced to concede his point. She did it ungracefully, though, with a scowl and a half-shrug. But this was good enough for Hooch. He crumpled up the coffee carton and tossed it towards one of the bins at the far end of the passageway.

'What you need to understand, Bean,' he said gently, 'is that I'm not personally threatened by you in any way. I don't care about what you've done or what you intend to do. I don't even care about whoever – or whichever interest – you happen to represent . . .'

'Then what's the problem?'

'Doc.'

Jo blinked.

'Sorry?'

'It's my concerns over Doc – *for* Doc – that oblige me to warn

434

you off. The way I see it, so long as you're hanging around here you're posing a threat to him. To his general wellbeing. To the structure of the group. To the Behindlings. The Behindlings are his *life* . . .'

Jo was already shaking her head. But Hooch kept on talking. 'I don't feel the need to offer any explanation to you, Bean. I won't justify what I'm saying or simplify it. I merely want Doc left in peace. He's in a vulnerable position. People tend to predate on him. They take advantage – sometimes without even realising . . .'

Jo looked uncomfortable, briefly. Hooch noticed. 'He lost his *boy*,' he continued, 'he lost some of his anonymity. And he's a little bit excitable – susceptible, even. He's confused. People have been saying that he's all washed-up. That he's losing it. The truth is that he's *exhausted*. He just needs to Follow, to be quiet, to muddle, along at his own pace . . .'

'I'm sorry,' Jo suddenly wasn't having any of it, 'that's just rubbish. I've *seen* you around Doc, Hooch. I've seen the way you constantly undermine him, the way you criticise him behind his back, the way you clearly resent his status among the others . . .'

'You're interfering with things – with situations – that you don't understand,' Hooch spoke slowly and calmly, 'and these are bad situations. Painful situations. Doc and I have a complicated relationship – I'll make no bones about it – but it's a relationship which someone from outside of the group couldn't *possibly* be expected to understand. And I don't *want* you to understand it. What I do want you to register – and it's very simple – is that you need to get out of here. To go. Today. Immediately. Because if you don't, you're going to end up hurting him – unintentionally, maybe, but hurting him nonetheless – the same way you hurt Katherine, Katherine's family, all the rest of them.'

Jo stared at him, blankly.

'I'll leave first,' Hooch murmured, touching the brim of his hat in a show of unexpected civility, then turning and moving off – rapidly – back down the alleyway, 'just give it a few minutes before you come on out after me . . .' he paused, peeked over his shoulder, winked at her, 'for the sake of propriety, eh?'

Forty-two

His instincts led him anti-clockwise, and the wind – on this occasion – conveniently caught the back of him, prodded him forward, actively encouraged him. So he took a sharp right and just kept on going –
No reason
No need to justify anything
– until he hit the sea wall and scaled it without thinking.

Still dark. All too soon it was snowing.

He glanced behind him.

He'd been walking for almost forty minutes and this was the first time he'd looked back –
Not a soul

He shuddered, closed his eyes, put his hand to his cheek, rubbed at it gently for a while and then progressed (an almost imperceptible crossover) into slapping at it, ruminatively – the way you'd slap the arse of a newly delivered baby – as if the cheek had grown numb and he was fighting to bring back some feeling into it.

He wobbled. His eyes flew open. He threw out his arms (like a professional unicyclist), regained his balance, then dropped them, briskly, to his sides again.

He peered down to his right, where the sea wall fell deeply – ten feet, fifteen, maybe – onto a concrete pathway (just above what was now marshland – he was headed inland – and a tidal tributary). His eyes suddenly glimmered with a vague sense of recognition.

He continued walking, but now much more purposefully, scanning ahead of him as though hoping for some kind of quick access onto the lower causeway.

He soon found it; a glorified ladder; metal, virtually free-standing; two fireman's poles with skinny rungs slung between them – bolted into the wall, the bolts all rusting.

He swung himself down, nimbly (the flesh of his palms almost sticking to the metal, it was so icy) reached the bottom, kept on walking – still in the same direction – but slower now, and as he walked he closely scrutinised the dark wall above him. Three minutes – possibly four – passed in this way. Then he stopped, squinted, stepped back, read something:

Katherine Turpin (in a luminous spray – 'whore' scribbled over the top of her name in a different colour) *aborted her own father's bastard*

He stepped forward and touched his hand to it, smiled, then kept his hand on the wall – its rough concrete – as he continued walking, trailing it behind him like a child running a stick against metal railings.

He stopped for a second time when he felt the quality of the concrete changing. He drew close to the wall and found himself analysing another, shorter line of graffiti (much smaller, this time), hacked into the concrete with a knife or a flint or a broken bottle. He stuck out his lower lip – such was the light and the level of concentration required – and struggled to read it (painstakingly tracing his fingers through each letter for further confirmation)
I
am
the
fucking . . .

He tried to find a noun at the end of the sentence (he imagined; I am the fucking *king*; I am the fucking *end*; I am the fucking *champion*; I am the fucking *best fuck in the whole fucking WORLD so FUCK YOU*) but there was nothing.

He frowned.

'I am the fucking . . .' he murmured. Leaving space for expansion

– an opening, a question mark, even . . .

Then, 'I am the . . .'

He began chuckling (the path between his nose and his lips so frozen he thought it might be in imminent danger of splitting).

'I am the *fucking*,' he proclaimed proudly, finally making sense of it, turning back into the wind, throwing his chin into the air (his eyes instantly pummelled by snowflakes, his lashes gently clogged and weighed down by them).

I AM THE FUCKING

Without thinking he shoved his fingertips into his mouth, sucked on them and realised that they were bleeding.

He began walking again. He kept walking –

I am the **fucking**

– past the putting green –

I **am** *the* . . .

– left onto the roadway –

I *am* . . .

– just beyond the bridge . . . the –

Calvin

– No –

Culvin

– No –

Colvin

Hah!

He punched the air, victoriously, then clutched at his stomach –

Sharp pain

The snow was falling faster. He paused for a moment and saw – as if the whole tragic spectacle had been specifically timed for him, or *caused* by him (his spectral presence standing there on the edge of that tarmac) – a slow-moving jeep hitting a fast-moving fox.

The jeep honked, braked, made a sudden, thudding contact, but did not stop. Wesley walked forward. The fox lay on its side in the heart of the road; panting, eyes blueing up with shock; a vixen.

One of her back legs was hanging loose, broken, and there was an inconceivably huge gash on her stomach. He saw that her teats were red and still swollen from feeding. He put his hand into his pocket for his knife –

Nothing

– he cursed, walked to the side of the road, saw a dilapidated road sign –

Leisure Centre

– appraised it, kicked it over, grabbed the loosest supporting metal pole, yanked it free (it took some while to give entirely – the base was weighed down with concrete) carried it over to the fox –

God bless you

Hit

And hit

– killed her.

Another car drove over the bridge, caught him in its headlights, braked, then sounded its horn. He tossed the pole aside, shuddering, picked her up and slung her warm carcass across his shoulders – her blood sweet on his neck, his back, his fingers – and headed for the long grass on the opposite siding. He crouched low there, laying down the body gently, waiting for a while and then emitting a sharp and ghostly bark into the icy early morning.

It must've been half an hour before the first cub appeared. It was shy of the stranger; hesitant. Wesley made a crying sound; a kind of whining. He had inadvertently smeared some of the vixen's blood onto his cheeks. He had cut off her tail with a piece of broken glass and tied it to his wrist with a bundle of tightly-wound grass.

The small fox drew closer.

'Your mother's dead, little man,' Wesley whispered, 'come on over here and have a smell of her.'

The cub was thin. His coat was coarse and uneven. His ribs protruded like the individual struts on an old-fashioned, oil-fired hospital radiator. He came close and sniffed tentatively at the corpse of his mother. He licked some of the blood from her. He emitted a tiny squeak. He pushed his nose to her teat – selfishly, almost angrily – and tried to suckle there.

Wesley made a series of gentle cooing sounds until the cub had finished and pulled away, then he picked up the vixen again, lifted her over his shoulders, turned – but very slowly – holding the vixen's four feet together in his one good hand and trailing her tail onto the ground behind him, still affixed to the other.

He walked on; over the makeshift wooden bridge (slippy with ice – treacherous) and onto the mud embankment which snaked alongside the river. He did not look back to check if the cub was following. He looked forward, and from side to side, struggling – in the darkness – to locate the vixen's spore.

He paid special attention to any large rocks or tree-stumps (although there were precious few in these snow-peppered, mud-splattered flatlands) where he imagined the vixen might've left territorial markings. He found several. But the first was goose – he bent down, sifted through the snow and pressed the frozen faeces loosely between his fingers, sniffed. Clucked. The second was badger. The third –

Ah

He glanced back. Two cubs now, both following anxiously, ten, maybe twenty paces behind him. Ahead lay the dawn – he drew a deep breath – but only the faintest suggestion of it, and the concrete flyover; arching its long back and yawning resignedly into the possibility of morning.

Beyond that?

What a question

Beyond that?

The future:

Pissed-up

Blood-smattered

Blister-raw

The flyover – when he reached it – was still all but deserted and pitch dark underneath. But he remembered from walking here before (and could tell by the smell; deadened by the snow, but still perceptibly there) that the den was very near. He waited for his eyes to adjust, looked around for the give away pile of dirt. Found it.

A truck rumbled over.

He staggered out the other side, straightened up (his back protesting – his fingers numb now, his nose, his lips), peered behind him –

the cubs were close together, shoulder rubbing shoulder, entering the den, joggling for first access, for precedence. He shifted the weight of the mother, put one foot onto the stile and stared ahead.

White had made everything brighter. And he'd turned a corner. The snow was now hitting the left side of him. He half-squinted into it. He frowned. He stepped onto the stile for added height. He stared. He swore. He glanced up onto the roadway –

Quiet

– he felt around inside his pockets, located the agent's mobile, turned it on, pressed the first digit, experimentally.

Ted's aunt answered –

Hello?

He cut her off.

The second –

Work

Ted's voice.

'I need you,' Wesley said, 'bring me some rope. Heavy rope. At least twenty foot of it . . .' he paused, 'and a box of eggs, and the librarian. Meet me by the flyover.'

He completed his instructions and dialled another number. He tapped his foot, impatiently. The set of his expression indicated some kind of call-answering service. He did not seem surprised by this. He waited for the beep, then spoke.

'I've got your message, Gumble *Inc*,' he said, bending forward slightly as he spoke, clutching his stomach, his lips white with fury, 'that was my *father's* boat. I know exactly what you're doing. We had a *deal*. Doesn't matter how things turned out. *Fuck* the bloody context . . .'

He paused and gazed at the boat awhile, and then something strange suddenly struck him. 'Arthur's not *playing*,' he said, his voice quite astonished, '*is* he?'

He chuckled, shook his head, then focussed again. 'Back off, or I'll do as I threatened. I don't *care* about the Old Man. I'll *sacrifice* the Old Man . . .' he paused, squinted towards the boat, saw it move – saw it shuddering – as a choppy incoming wave hit a supporting strut.

He swore under his breath, cut the line and tossed Ted's phone into the river, adjusted the vixen and jumped over the stile, butting his head like an angry ram into the flurry of snow as it fell on him.

Forty-three

She had thought it might be the postman, or Wesley, even –
Had Ted actually given him a key?
– but it wasn't either of them. It was Bo.

He was standing on her doorstep, cheerfully exuding his own
special kind of vitality (the kind male models cultivate on the
back of wholegrain cereal packets) and he was smiling widely at
her – gloating, more precisely – larger than life, smugger than hell,
thicker than shit – and that was the worst part of it –
The ignorance

So she smiled right back at him, wished him a hearty good
morning, kicked him hard in the gonads (was pleased by the accuracy
of her attack, considering she was wearing her slippers and they were
liable to fly off without warning) watched calmly as he bent over,
clutching himself, squeaking (you'd think a man of his stature
might produce a better sound than *that*), then (never one to let
an opportunity pass) she lifted her knee, brought down her hands
(meshed forcibly together), united these two disparate body-parts
in a sterling manoeuvre, heard a *gnuff*, then his nose crack (or at
least she hoped she had – hoped it wasn't a tile on her front step),
shoved him off her porch, told him to watch out for her *fucking*
hydrangea (he didn't) clucked her tongue furiously, glanced up,
saw Dewi walking out onto his verandah, snorted, showed him the
finger, went back inside and slammed her door shut behind her.
Have I gone too far?

Two minutes passed.
Silence

Then the shouting commenced.

Bo's voice – in the road – but directed away from her; towards another . . .
She did it HERSELF!
– he yelled –
You fucking love-lorn IDIOT
She wrote it HERSELF
And she MAINTAINED it
All these fucking YEARS
She MAINTAINED IT HERSELF
D'you HEAR me?
She maintained it HERSELF
I HAD NO BLOODY PART IN IT

Katherine burst out laughing – a loud laugh, violent, almost hysterical – then turned, smacked her head into the wall – her clenched fists flying out behind her – and commenced crying so fiercely that her snot ran in a waterfall down onto the floor.

The rope had been the easy bit – he was on good terms with the local chandler (sold him his premises, August 1997), and the eggs were a cinch, but the librarian – the fragrant *Eileen* – proved a trickier proposition altogether.

He was lucky to catch her. She was half way up her street, picking an unsteady route along the icy pavement in some exceedingly inappropriate footwear – little lime green boots with spiky heels (at the sight of their inappropriateness, his mouth twisted up at its corners). Not dressed for the cold particularly (a lemon-yellow raincoat, a pale yellow cashmere frock, a silk scarf with seashells on it). Ted pulled up and hailed her from his old, white company Fiesta.

'I'm a little late for work, Ted,' she lied, turning her face away and flapping her hand at him like he was a persistent middle-eastern child beggar who'd – quite meanly yet miraculously – detected some unfathomable sign of weakness in her.

Ted knew for a fact that the library didn't open for a further two hours. But she looked exhausted –

His heart went out to her.

He noticed the scratch on her cheek. Just one scratch. Yet deep. It trickled down stickily onto her neck, like the viscid tail of a sweet, raspberry jam pip. Her nails were clean, though, and neat and newly painted. She was holding a yellow mesh shopping bag dotted with perky plastic daisies.

'I have a message from Wesley,' Ted murmured, almost swallowing the name whole he was so anxious about offending her with it.

Eileen glanced sharply into the back of his car (perhaps Wesley might be hiding there, ready to spring out at her, unprovoked?) and saw the rope, coiled up, like a boa constrictor. She put her hand to her throat, automatically. 'Why?' she asked distrustfully, 'what does he want with me?'

'I don't know. I've arranged to meet him just out of town. He asked me to bring you along. And some rope. And some eggs.'

Her eyes immediately filled with tears. 'Does he plan to humiliate me again?' she asked tremulously (as if humiliation was all she deserved, all she could ever really hope for).

It suddenly dawned on Ted what kind of a picture his shopping list had painted for her. He winced. And yet . . .

'Did he humiliate you before?' he asked, battling to evict the image of Eileen in awful bondage, her yellow cashmere sweater dress irrevocably yanked asunder . . .

The gradual drip of the yolk down the front of her cleavage
The slither of the albumen down her pale, porcelain shoulder

She nodded. Sniffed. Lifted her glasses. Patted at her eyes with the knuckle of her index finger.

'Did he *hurt* you?'

Ted's hand clenched his leg. He wasn't sure why, exactly. But he enjoyed the tantalising pinch of his thumb and his index finger.

She nodded again, lifted her bag, looked inside it for a tissue to try and salvage her mascara.

'Did he . . .' Ted indicated towards her cheek.

She glanced up and shook her head.

'No. A beak,' she muttered.

'Oh.'

'He hurt my pride,' she said, then shrugged, modestly, 'that's all. And I probably deserved it. I've let things . . . I've let things *slide . . .'*

Ted couldn't work out whether her modest shrug made things better or worse. He did note however, a corresponding – an *unexpected* twitch in his genitalia.

Eileen removed her purse from her handbag along with a powder compact, a bone-handled hunting knife, some throat pastilles and a heron's head preserved for posterity inside a transparent plastic bag.

Ted's gentle erection immediately subsided.

She finally located her tissues, took one out of the packet, and dabbed softly at her injured cheek with it.

'Isn't that Wesley's knife?' Ted asked, eyeing the decapitated bird's head, worriedly.

She looked down, almost aghast, automatically opened her hand and dropped it.

'I don't know why I took it,' she said, panicked (as if she'd only just that second committed the theft – had been caught red-handed), 'I just wanted to stop him from . . . from *hurting . . .'*

Ted climbed out of his car and retrieved the knife for her. He handed it back, blunt-end first. She thanked him and thrust it into her bag.

'Leo said he'd called the police,' Ted said, glancing over his shoulder.

Her eyes widened behind her glasses.

'I don't think you'd want them to find you with that . . .' he indicated towards the bird, 'I believe they're protected. Wesley was very . . .'

She looked down, shaking a little.

'He was very *specific* on that point,' Ted concluded.

'I was intending to bury it somewhere,' she explained.

'We could do it together,' Ted heard himself saying gently, 'I could drive you to the beach or to . . . to the flyover, underneath it, where the soil is soft. We could bury it there.'

'Are you laughing at me Ted,' she suddenly asked, 'just like he did? And just like the *Turpin* girl did? Is there something . . . something *funny* about me? Am I *very* silly?'

Ted's gut told him to put out his hand and touch her hair. He put out his hand. He touched her hair.

It was *unbelievably* stiff.

'I think you're magnificent,' he said, leaning forward, as if to sniff where he'd touched (what was the logic in that?) but he kissed her, instead. On the ear. This wasn't exactly the place he'd been gunning for. But it was a start –

Wasn't it?

Eileen hiccuped – quite unromantically – turned her nose sharply into his cheek and then dropped her bag, heavily, onto his feet.

Forty-four

Beyond the quick and the dead
Lies Sirius, First God of Dogs,
Who stood up
51 times
Who fell
Only 8,
But who spawned
Sweet Beauty and his Angel
So the gone might gander

She scampered past the Wimpy (head down, hood up) but she was a fool – she told herself –
A fool
– if she honestly believed she was going to get away with it. To pursue was his life-blood; the hunting, the hounding, the heeling, the trailing . . .
   She suddenly didn't –
I don't
– she suddenly didn't –
I don't . . .
I don't . . .
– she suddenly didn't *like* it –
This feeling
– she suddenly began to appreciate . . .
Damn
   He was out of there like a shot – she heard the door slamming, a

muffled curse, his oilskin flapping like an ill-adjusted mainsail as he jogged heavily – unevenly –

Was that a limp?

– behind her.

'Where've you been?' he finally gasped, placing his hand onto her shoulder, exerting a certain amount of pressure. He *was* limping. Just slightly. And the ground was slippy. The snow was still coming down in unpredictable flurries. It was fiercely cold.

'I got distracted,' she said flatly and struggled to keep on walking (like a girl who'd stormed out on her faithless lover – a girl who *wanted* to stop but whose pride wouldn't let her).

'Distracted by what?'

He struggled to keep up.

'By the past.'

He didn't seem to want to register this answer. It was too bald. Too pretentious.

'What did the guide want? Did he give anything away? Is he working with the fraud squad? Did he say?'

She shook her head. Her eyes were burning –

Strained

– by all that persistent gazing; that staring outward, that squinting forward. They were approaching the intersection opposite the Bingo hall, alongside the pub. It was relatively busy for the time of day it was. She picked up her pace.

Doc – and quite unexpectedly – did the complete opposite. He stalled. He stopped in his tracks. Jo tried to walk on – almost oblivious – tried to cross, but the lights changed and she was obliged to turn back again. She puffed out her cheeks, frustratedly.

'They got to you,' he said. His voice sounded the same. His facial expression did not alter. But there was a palpable difference in him – a transformation. She glanced over, slightly alarmed, unsure what her own face was doing –

Can't trust it

– only wanting not to engage him or to encourage him, or to offend.

'Nobody got to me,' she retorted blankly.

'I can tell they did,' he answered, staring at her intently, 'I can *see*.'

She shrugged. She felt like a heel. But she was out of her depth here. Hooch'd been right –

The miserable little shit

'Well that's . . . that's just too bad,' he murmured, gently shaking his head. His voice was soft now. He seemed – she frowned – almost disappointed. No –

No . . .

– Fascinated?

No . . .

– Fearful?

Yes

She suddenly remembered how Shoes had looked, the previous day, after their stint in the library. That same look of . . . that same . . .

Loss?

And she felt it too. She was feeling –

An absence?

A short-fall?

A deficiency?

'Please don't be . . .' she grappled for the appropriate adjective, brushing some snow from her eyelid.

He began to back off, very slowly, as if he'd inadvertently kicked a dozing cobra. She felt alarm, as though – by some miraculous process – the real Josephine Bean was suddenly standing behind her, perhaps laughing maniacally, brandishing a firearm, resting it insolently across her shoulder.

'Something bad's happening here,' Doc said ominously, his shoulders hunching up, glancing around him. 'He keeps walking the island, and walking, and *walking* . . . like he's . . . like he's *locked*. Like he's *stuck*. I've never seen it before. Never. Something's missing. Something's gone *wrong*,' he gazed straight at her, 'and now *you've* become party to it . . .'

'No,' Jo shook her head, 'I just got . . . I'm just . . . *caught* up . . . I'm not . . . not . . .'

Involved

The light had changed. The traffic was now stationary.

'He doesn't . . .' Doc said, then stopped abruptly, looking around him, patting at his pockets as if he'd momentarily forgotten something.

'Are you alright, Doc?'

She was worried for him.

'He doesn't *talk* . . .' he started up again, then he stopped, like an old-fashioned record player with a faulty wind-up-mechanism.

'Doc?'

She took a step closer. She held out her hand.

'He doesn't . . .' he was briefly re-energised, 'Wesley doesn't *talk* to the people Following . . . that's the whole . . . the whole *point*.'

He concluded his mantra, then gazed at her, balefully, as if she'd contravened something inviolable.

'He thinks I'm . . .' Jo pushed back her hood, as though this small gesture might underline her irreproachability, 'he thinks I'm a fraud,' she said, 'but I'm . . .'

Aren't I?

'Hooch warned me about you,' Doc said, 'but I didn't . . .' he shook his head, confusedly. A woman walked past them with a tartan shopping cart; one of the wheels was squeaking fiercely. He grimaced, 'Because they've been keeping stuff back . . .' he continued, doggedly, 'and it's not just the . . .'

His eyes were moving, from place to place, unfocussed, 'It's not just the *confectionery* thing. It's bigger. And they won't . . . it's like they're *devouring* him. Like the whole of the Following is gradually . . .'

Doc was visibly unravelling. Like an old reel of cotton. There. On the street. Right in front of her.

'Oh God knows I was a bad father,' he suddenly whimpered, wiping his mouth with the back of his arm, 'never had time for my boy. First it was the model replicas – the traction engines – but he was never remotely mechanical. *Never*. And then after Hilly passed . . .' He was smiling, hopelessly. 'The Following just . . . it just . . .'

He made a mushroom-cloud gesture with his hands, gazed at her imploringly.

'Ballooned,' Jo struggled to fill in.

'No,' he was definite.

'*Exploded?*' Jo tried again.

He shrugged. He let her have it. He moved on.

'Wes was working with the crop circle people. Then it broadened out into that whole anti-pesticide thing.' He turned – for no apparent reason – and began directing his words towards the pub noticeboard, which was hung on the wall directly to the right of him. 'He wrote THIS IS POISON in the barley close to where I was living – a place called Bletchley – in *huge* lettering. And it was . . .' he chuckled, 'it was *glorious*. I went along to see it, just to take a quick . . . and that was the start. I was . . .'

He was quiet for a while, still gazing dreamily at *Sky TV – Snooker – Home-Cooked Pub Grub Served Daily* in chalk-effect paint.

'It's no coincidence,' he murmured, 'that the website's gone down. They're isolating him. They're planning something.'

'Who?' Jo asked. She couldn't help herself.

Doc didn't appear to have heard her.

'Doc?' she said, gently.

His looked over, almost shocked by her being there, his eyes focussing in on the lapels of her coat. 'I never had time for Colin . . .' he mumbled, 'Colin just wanted to *join in*. I should've made time for him, away from all of this . . . this . . .' his eyes moved idly over her shoulder, then widened.

'They've got my dog,' he gurgled. Josephine gazed at him, stolidly.

'They've got my *dog*,' he repeated, with rather more urgency. Jo turned around, slowly. A silver car was pulling across the lights, turning a lazy left. Inside it the guide – the *young* guide – on the passenger side, and another man – older – driving. On the young man's lap sat the dog. He seemed perfectly at his ease there.

'*Dennis!*' Doc yelled, grabbing Jo's coffee cup and throwing it at the car as it glided magisterially past them. Both men were smiling. The man driving lifted his hand off the steering wheel and waved as the coffee carton connected. The lid bounced off but there was precious little liquid left inside of it.

Doc tried to hurl himself at them, but he was blocked by railings, so he charged a sharp right, onto the crossing. The traffic was still moving. One car honked its horn. Another – a white car – braked sharply and veered into the neighbouring lane. A bike swerved, the rider struggling to stay upright by running his trainered shoe at high speed along the tarmac.

'*Doc!*'

Jo sprinted out after him.

She could smell rubber, burning.

A second car sounded its horn. She grabbed his arm but he resisted.

He was much stronger than she might've anticipated. He broke free and just ran –
He ran
– straight into the path of an oncoming mail van.

Two-three-five seconds later and –
Is this my fault?
Did I . . . ?
Fuck
– everything had just . . . just . . .
Stopped
– and the grey stuff – the . . . the . . .
Tarmac
  Its . . . Its . . . Its . . .
Hardness
  The way he . . . he . . .
Jolted
  The way it – the way . . .
The bounce
  All his clothes . . . the way they'd . . . the way –
Shuddered
  And it was only –
What was it?
  Bumper –
  Light –
  Bonnet –

'I am a . . .' she gasped, 'I am a *qualified* medical . . .'
A nurse

They all drew around him, like petals around a flower. She glanced up –
Where did they . . . ?
– then she looked down again and loosened his collar.
They all drew back slightly.

A murmur
Blood
Corner of his lip
The pulse of it
The un-ex-purgated tick-tick-tick . . .

'He's bitten his tongue,' she murmured.
    Doc was still conscious, but not . . .
    'Take . . .' he said, his eyes bulging wider. He put his hand to his pocket but everything inside it had flown out in the collision –
On impact . . .
Saliva . . .
A small pool of it on the . . .
Darkening
    Someone had gathered all the discarded things together.

How long had it been already?
No time?
Forever?

A shoe –
Hat –
Dog leash –
Bus pass –
Wallet –
Pager –

Some
One
Good
Person
Had
Kindly
Done
That

'It's *okay*,' she said, 'it was just a . . . it doesn't look . . .'
    He was staring past her, trying to shake his head.

There was a tiny –
A tiny . . .
– a tiny little nick on his ear.

The guide was suddenly there – 'Oh *shit*. Oh my *God* . . .' – bending over and gasping, 'We only just *found* the dog, wandering around in the Charfleets. We were bringing it straight . . .'

'Will everybody just move *back* . . .' she shouted.

She could see –
Just keep on breathing

She could see the beginnings of a cataract on his left eye. She was mesmerised by it as she squeezed his hand.

The dog arrived, pulling along the driver of the silver car who'd tied his belt around his neck in an attempt to secure him and was holding his trousers up – comically –
Funny
This isn't funny
– with his other hand.

'Dennis is back,' she said, 'Doc?'

'*Doc?*'

The dog shunted its way forward and licked the Old Man's neck.

The Old Man had closed his eyes.

She looked up. She saw the tennis player, holding a handkerchief over his face, staring down, amazed. He was talking to the man who ran the Bingo hall. He had his notebook out. Pen. Didn't have enough hands.

The boy . . .

Patty . . .

Mugging dumbly in confusion, hugging himself with anxiety . . .

I am alone

'Where's Wesley?' Doc had opened his eyes. He was panting.

'It's alright,' Jo whispered.

'No . . .' Doc tried to turn his head, 'you don't . . . he *needs* . . .'

'Don't worry,' she said. She could hear sirens. 'I'll take care of him. *Trust* me.'

The traffic was still flowing past them –
Slowly
Quietly
With the minimum of disruption
– as she gently made her pledge to annihilate everything.

Forty-five

Quiescence
   The only real option available to them.
   He'd thought his way around it –
Solidly
– and even *thinking* about doing anything –
Even thinking it
– seemed incalculably perilous.
   He'd been awake for so long now – was so tired –
Tired
– that his thoughts were shaping themselves into a repetitive pattern; a sing-song; a nursery rhyme; an exhaustive –
Exhausting
– rhythm; until all other noise, all other stimulus –
Outside
Within
– lost its independent significance; became just so much –
Wholly unnecessary
– additional percussion.
   Sasha was sleeping.
   She shifted when the boat creaked –
   Then the reindeer shifted –
   The boat shifted –
   It creaked –
   Sasha shifted –
   Arthur flinched, held his breath –
Expecting the . . .
Expecting . . .

– then everything, very gradually, righted itself again.
Or did it?
Huh?

He was sure that she must be frozen –
Wesley's child
He was –
C . . . c . . . c . . . c . . .
– so *icy*. He couldn't feel –
Cheeks
Nose
Fingers
Feet
– hardly anything, in fact, and he no longer understood the angle he was at. How acute was it? How far back?

He could tell – could sense, somehow – that the door was now rather more like a kind of a *lip* (a pike's mouth, on the diagonal, snarling out of the water).

The mud of the bank seemed further off, and the tide was obviously higher –
Higher
– but not quite high enough. He could feel it lapping at the back of the craft, could hear its eager wavelets keenly whispering their perpetual brown commentary.

It was definitely getting brighter. By rights he should've felt a sense of relief, but instead he felt the illogical fury of the industrious miner, on leaving –
Blink
– the close dark –
Blink
– of the cruel shaft
Blink
– and cringing into the light.

'If *I* go,' Sasha lifted her head, abruptly, as though talking in her sleep, 'then Brion will come after me. And that's exactly how we got into this stupid mess in the first place.'

'Perhaps the boat will float,' Arthur said, sounding hopeless, even to himself.

'Are you a good swimmer?' she asked.

'Are you?'

He gazed down at her. She rubbed her nose on her knuckles. Neither party felt inclined to answer.

Brion began micturating. Out of the blue –

The black

– and it seemed to go on for hours – this piss. Arthur suddenly found himself on the verge of a titter –

What's wrong with me?

– he disguised it with a hiccup, and turned to stare at the deer, accusingly. It was too dark to see much, but he thought he saw the urine flowing, at an alarming rate, down onto the floor and then streaming away –

Gone

'Just thank your lucky stars that we aren't sitting *behind* him,' Sasha murmured.

'You're right, Sasha,' Arthur affirmed blankly, 'we have so much to be grateful for.'

She peered up at him, her brows raised slightly – he could *sense* it – under his *Gumble* hat. He stared at that hat –

I'm a fool

A stooge

A cat's paw

– and then his wrist began stinging; brought him sharply back.

'Sorry,' he said, 'I'm feeling . . .' he cleared his throat, '*giddy.*'

Sasha wasn't paying attention. She quietly shushed him, raised her hand, whispered, 'Do you hear anything?' gradually inching her way forward, then peering – blinking like a new-born kitten – out into the wide and unrelenting winter maw.

'Motorway,' Arthur tried to focus again. But he was struggling. 'No . . .'

Sasha moved still further, until the snow landed softly onto the brim of her hat.

'It's a man,' she said, trying to suppress her excitement, 'carrying some kind of . . . of red-coloured *sack* . . .'

On *sack*, Arthur moved forward himself. There was the sharp sound of something shearing. A plank fell from the roof above them. The reindeer jerked back – hit a cabinet (a drawer had tipped open behind him; its cutlery rattled, several pieces spilled out onto the

461

floor) – the rear-end of the boat plummeted.

'*For fuck sake HELP us!*' Arthur bellowed. He scrabbled onto his knees and lunged for the door. Sasha had tipped sideways – then back. She lay flat on her belly, holding – for dear life – onto his right foot. She looked up at him from this new position, wearing an expression of genial bemusement.

'*Yikes,*' she said.

He squinted out into the snow, still panicked.

Wesley. Standing on the bank. Ruddy-faced. A dead fox slung around his neck. That same dead red fox's tail tied – mystifyingly – onto his wrist.

'I admire your *ardour*, Art,' he yelled over, carefully lowering the fox onto the ground, 'but I couldn't really guarantee that vessel *floating* anywhere . . .'

'There's an eight-year-old girl in here,' Arthur yelled back, and a . . .' he paused (he hated this moment), 'and a *reindeer.*'

Wesley slowly straightened up. 'How very . . .' he peered past Arthur's shoulder, 'how extremely *festive* for you,' he shouted.

'I'm *nine*,' a small voice interrupted them.

'Not for long, the way things are going,' Wesley smiled at Arthur, winningly, then turned around, as if something rather more significant was taking place behind him.

Perhaps a rare breed of stork was landing on a tree-top . . .

Perhaps he'd dropped a glove on the path . . .

Perhaps . . .

'We need to get *out*,' Arthur bawled, barely biting back his hysteria.

Wesley turned around again. 'Of course you do,' he said – at normal volume – barely audibly. He proceeded to make his way – carefully – down the mud bank. He stood at the river's edge and peered down into the water. 'The tide's got a way to go yet,' he said, 'that's still quite a drop.'

'Mud,' the voice yelled from within, 'and some very sharp rocks.'

'An unappealing conjunction,' he said, nodding.

Arthur glared at him, in silence, his knuckles tightening on the doorframe.

Wes didn't move.

A crashing sound emerged from the back of the vessel as a pot or a cup fell off a counter. *'Ouch,'* the young voice intoned.

Wesley raised his eyebrows. He glanced right. Close to where he stood was a thick wooden pike, driven into the bank. A good length of rope had been tied around it. Wesley carefully unwound it while Arthur watched him. His fingers were definitely beginning to go numb. He tried to concentrate on them. He tried to bully them into clinging on.

Once he'd untied it from the pike, Wesley got as close to the craft as he possibly could. 'Tie yourselves together with that,' he said, 'to be going on with.'

Arthur frowned, 'Is that a good idea? If the boat collapses and one of us gets trapped . . .'

'Three of us,' a voice hollered from within, 'I'm going *nowhere* without my deer.'

Wesley pondered this for a moment. 'Well here's wishing you and your antlered companion a wonderful new life together at the bottom of the river,' he shouted.

He threw the rope.

Arthur wasn't ready. He missed the catch. His arms barely moved. It fell down into the water. Wesley watched the rope sink. He gazed back up at Arthur. 'You're off the team, buddy,' he said, then clambered back up the bank again and wandered off.

'What's happening?'

The girl's voice again, but this time slightly tremulous, 'Is he still going to help us?'

'Of *course* he is,' Arthur snapped, in his most adult manner.

'Where's the rope?'

'It fell in the water.'

Silence

'What's he doing now?'

'He's . . . he's just . . . *uh* . . .'

Arthur watched Wesley retreating into the distance. Not at a run. Not at a trot. But at a pace best described as a casual meander.

He turned his head, 'How's the deer?'

Sasha peered under her arm. 'He seems quite cheerful,' she said.

Arthur grimaced. 'That's *good,*' he said, 'but what's holding him up?'

'Oh.' Sasha glanced back again, 'He's resting his rump against an open drawer. I suppose if that goes then we're all . . . *uh* . . .'

Scuppered

'*Hurry*,' Arthur yelled.

When he opened his mouth wide his teeth hurt.

Wesley waved his hand. He disappeared from view.

The back of the boat was bobbing. Arthur could feel this new motion. He didn't know how long it had been there. He felt an acute sense of disorientation.

'Maybe he won't come back,' the girl pondered, slightly breathlessly.

'Don't be *ridiculous*,' Arthur blurted.

'All things considered,' she adjusted her grip on his foot, grunted, 'I do think Brion's been quite a star.'

'Let's all give Brion a great *big* hand, shall we?' Arthur murmured.

'Good idea.'

He felt her hold loosen and twisted around, panicked. The boat groaned, like Moby Dick, harpooned.

She sniggered. Her grip tightened again.

'Stop fucking around,' he said, secretly admiring her capacity not to take the prospect of imminent death seriously.

'I'll clap with my feet, shall I?'

He heard her feet flapping. He tensed himself for any unexpected repercussions.

Nothing

'I applaud you, Brion,' she said.

Brion wuffled appreciatively.

Arthur relaxed slightly and bit his lip.

Would Wesley come back again?

Does he know who I am?

Am I here because of him?

'Survival in a crisis is eighty percent attitude,' Sasha cordially informed Brion, from under her armpit.

'Where did you read that?' Arthur asked, tetchily.

'My grandad was in the SAS. He knows everything about everything.'

Arthur rolled his eyes.

'He taught me how to fight a crocodile,' Sasha maintained, smugly.

Arthur said nothing.

'You hit them on the nose,' she said, 'then jab their eyes out with your fingers . . . *Foo!*' (She thoughtfully provided her own batch of sound effects.)

'I'm sure you'll have the entire reptilian population of Canvey quaking in its scales at that,' Arthur growled.

'If a big dog comes at you,' she continued, 'then grab both of its front legs, pull them out sideways – *eeeee-yo!* – and snap its back.'

Arthur snorted, unimpressed.

'I know how to deal with a Mountain Lion,' she wheedled.

'How?' Arthur asked.

'Flash.'

Arthur struggled to register this.

'Open your coat,' she expanded, 'to make yourself look bigger.'

'What if you're not wearing a coat?' Arthur tried his best to deflate her. 'What if it's the height of summer?'

'Then talk in a *VERY LOW VOICE*,' she boomed.

Arthur didn't comment.

'I know how to jump from a high cliff down into a river,' she continued, 'and I also know how to identify a terrorist bomb in the post.'

'How?' he asked.

'If a package has a handwritten address label, but comes from a credible commercial source, then that's suspicious. And if it's unevenly balanced – when you handle it – or tied up in string, those are sure-fire give-aways,' she said.

'Why string?' he asked.

'Because nobody wraps packages in string any more. Only bombers.'

'I do.'

'Terrorists use string because they're very old-fashioned, at heart,' she continued, ignoring his objections.

'*I* wrap packages up in string,' Arthur repeated.

'That's sweet,' she said, adjusting her grip, 'but next time use Sellotape.'

'No string,' Arthur grumbled, 'that's ridiculous.'

'Another sure-fire give-away,' she continued, 'is too much post-age.'

The boat jolted, sideways. Arthur clung onto the door.

A high wave?

A collapsing stanchion?

There was a tearing sound.

'Because that means,' Sasha piped up again, 'that the terrorist didn't want to risk taking it to the . . .'

'How about the river?' Arthur interrupted her, swallowing. His mouth felt dry –

Thirsty

All the damn liquid's gone into my bladder

'Well if you're in a sinking *car*,' she said (plainly being extra-specific about the kind of vehicle to try and safeguard his feelings), 'then you need to open the windows so that when the water eventually flows inside, it'll maintain its balance.'

'Why not open the door?' Arthur tested her. His voice was shaking. His knees were hurting –

Fearfully

'Water pressure would be too great,' she explained.

He nodded.

'Anyway, you might tip the whole thing over. If your engine's in the front you'll sink at a steep angle. Ten foot of water or over and you'll end up on the roof, more than likely.'

'What if you're not in a car?' Arthur enquired, swallowing hard, trying to locate Wesley again, on the horizon.

'Well if you aren't in a car and you're jumping off a bridge – say – then you need to jump in legs first, keeping them very straight, very tight, and covering up your privates with your hands so the leeches don't bite . . .' she paused. 'That's a little joke.'

Arthur didn't react.

'Then squeeze your feet together and clench your buttocks. When you hit the water – if it's deep enough – spread out your arms and legs to try and create . . .'

'He's *back*,' Arthur exclaimed, barely troubling to disguise his relief.

Wesley had reappeared on the edge of his sightline. He wasn't alone, this time.

'He's got a horse,' Arthur murmured.

'Is it piebald?'

'Yes.'

'I saw that stallion yesterday. Do you think he might've rung the fire brigade?'

'If he has,' Arthur quipped, 'then he's a very intelligent animal.'

Sasha was silent for a second, then, 'Good call.'

She was smiling.

'Maybe he did,' Arthur said, five seconds too late to sound convincing –

He hasn't

He wants me dead

If Bethan finds out I'm here she'll never . . .

She'll never . . .

She'll turn the kid against me

She'll make the kid hate me

As Wesley drew closer it became clear that he was also dragging several planks along with him. And more rope – in several sections – but some of it rather shabby-looking.

He led the horse carefully down the bank.

'This horse is a *shit*,' he said, 'it bit my arse when I turned my back.'

There was a furtive snigger from inside the boat.

Arthur frowned –

Silence

Wesley mulled this chuckle over. '*Hell*,' he finally exclaimed, 'let's rescue the deer and ditch the kid.'

'*Bah*,' the girl exclaimed.

Arthur couldn't tell if Wesley was joking or not. He smiled thinly. He'd begun shivering, almost uncontrollably.

Wesley had tied a length of rope around the horse's neck and midriff.

'We've been lucky,' he said, 'there's all kinds of crap hanging around under the bridge. Planks left over from the construction work . . .'

He began knotting the remaining segments of rope together. When he'd finished he tied the end section firmly around his waist.

'What are you doing?' Arthur asked.

'Your hands are too weak,' Wesley explained impassively, 'I'm going to have to come over.'

467

Arthur looked astonished. 'The boat couldn't possibly sustain the extra . . .'

'Bollocks. It's the back section that's fucked. The front's fine.'

Wesley put his good hand onto the remaining guide rail. The rail slowly, but inexorably, collapsed beneath it. He watched the wood hit the water, then shrugged. 'I never *liked* that rail,' he said.

He led the horse to the pike, tethered it, then arranged the planks he'd collected in order of length. The longest he manoeuvred out towards the stricken vessel, sliding it along what remained of the gangplank. It was only just long enough, and the bank's dense muddiness didn't improve its grip. Wesley tested it with his foot. He shrugged. He slid the other planks between the two.

'I certainly hope that deer's sure-footed,' he murmured. Then he stepped out.

Forty-six

She suddenly felt the urge to *clean* –
Everywhere
Everybody
Everything
Started off in the hallway: found an unused roll of black plastic refuse sacks, unwound them, tore them off – one by one – and began piling stuff, *en masse*, inside of them: bottles, *bags* of bottles, junk-mail, the broken coffee filter machine, an old draining board, a shrunken jumper, a cracked flower-pot, a stained sundress, a batch of carpet samples . . .

She pulled her plaits out, yanked her hair back. Tied it up with an old rubber band. Smoothed her hands roughly – matter-of-factly – across her still-wet cheeks. Left a series of long, dirty, finger-strokes there.

Sniffed.
Coughed.
Glanced down at herself. Pulled off her slippers (black and purple Chinese-pattern antique satin, criminally worn-down at the heel) and threw them in. Took off her dressing gown (a small tear under the arm). Did the same again.

Drew a deep breath, panted it out.

She walked through to the living room, dug around under the table, found an old denim overall. Unfolded it. Stepped into it. Pushed the poppers together on the front. The arms were too long. And the legs. It didn't bother her. Found a half-used bottle of pine-scented disinfectant, an old cloth. Poured one onto the other.

Then she started over.

Soon she ran out of bags and surfaces (the disinfectant was making her fingers tingle, her nose run), so she pulled her throw off the armchair and began piling things onto that instead: dried flowers, an old tape recorder, a framed photo of herself, at school, straight-backed, smiling – middle-toothless – into the camera.

She gazed around, her chest heaving.

The nets.

She went to the window, grabbed them from the bottom and yanked. They fell – with a twanging-snap – like a fire-curtain during an intermission.

Dewi stood there –

Huge

– staring through the glass at her.

'Tell me it isn't true,' he said.

His voice sounded like he was speaking underwater. He looked like an indignant hero on an American soap opera, helplessly trapped inside the unmanly bubble of TV forever –

His destiny

She shook her head.

'Tell me it isn't true,' he repeated.

'I can't hear you,' she murmured, applying her disinfected cloth to the window and rubbing at it; not intending to provoke, but provoking, nonetheless.

'Lie to me, at *least*,' he said, 'to spare my feelings.'

'No.'

She shook her head again, speaking calmly through the frenzied squeak of her wrist action.

'Step back,' he said.

She frowned.

He lifted both his arms, his fists – as if about to play a major solo on the bass drum with a touring orchestra – and then held them there, mid-air. She visualised a series of notices slung neatly between them (Bob Dylan's *Subterranean Homesick Blues* style) –

You

Are

Killing

Me

Katherine

He bent his elbows in slightly – as if pulling the handbrake on an old-fashioned freight lorry – and then smashed them forward, forcefully, into the centre of the largest glass pane.

She stepped back –

Quick

The glass collapsed in about five large segments. Some of the smaller pieces made contact with her legs, her feet. But she wasn't hurt. The thick denim protected her.

A moment later – and almost more of a shock – her warm and smeary face was blasted by an unwelcome gust of ice-cold winter air.

'You bitch,' he said, once all the commotion was over.

His voice was very clear. Then he bent down, and with both strong hands – like Samson, blind with rage and righteousness – he ripped up her hydrangea.

The dog didn't want to walk, but she yanked him on, sternly. He responded by stiffening, rocking back onto his hindquarters, glancing yearningly –

The minx kidnapped me –

Do something!

– over his shoulder.

She was struggling up the Furtherwick. The young guide and his associate were trailing five paces behind her. She couldn't shake them. She didn't really know if she was afraid or not –

Should I be?

They seemed . . .

She glanced back –

They seemed . . .

Shell-shocked

'Looks like that fool journalist finally got his story,' the young guide said, trying valiantly to engage her.

She ignored him, lifting her haughty chin, cussing the dog.

'D'you really think the Old Man will be alright?' he persisted, his tone penitent, almost wheedling.

She drew a deep breath. She stopped. She turned around. 'Stop

471

Following me,' she blasted, 'I'm not *him*. I'm not *Wesley*. And I'm not *Doc*, either – you hospitalised him already, *remember!*'

His face was swathed in a look of pure astonishment. She blinked.

'Of course he'll be *fine* . . .' she backtracked, sullenly –

Mollified

'We thought we were doing him a favour,' the older man interjected – he had a strong Northern accent, 'he must've just *misconstrued* it . . .'

'Sure,' she yanked the dog on again. But the dog –

Typical

– was uncooperative. He appeared to hold the older man in inexplicably high esteem. She glanced over at him, irritably, observing his hand in his pocket, detecting –

Huh!

– the subterranean crackle of a crisp packet.

'We're meant to be keeping an *eye* on him,' the older man continued, taking her attention as a sign of encouragement, 'this really is the last thing we wanted.'

She stopped in her tracks.

'Pardon?'

The young guide shot the older man a warning look.

'Let me get this straight,' Josephine turned to face him properly, 'you're saying you've been hired to *protect* Doc?'

The older man looked to the younger for direction. The young guide merely shrugged.

'Who by?' she persisted.

He looked a little shifty.

'More to the point,' she continued, 'who *against!*'

'Hippie. Seven o'clock,' the older man murmured.

The young guide glanced around. 'Head him off, quickly.'

The older man did as he was instructed, striding rapidly towards the Hippie, raising his hands dramatically and embroiling him in a noisy discussion about what'd just befallen the Old Man (his own questionable involvement duly eradicated from the narrative).

Doc turned and then he just ran, he just ran into the roadway . . .

The young guide grabbed Jo's arm and walked on with her. 'The sugar people are determined,' he said, 'that the Loiter should progress without any further complications. Especially where Doc's concerned. We've simply been hired to keep an eye . . .' he faltered, 'to keep a *lid* on things . . .'

'Call me *slow*,' Jo interrupted, 'but from where I'm standing, all you seem to've done so far is undermine him. The poor devil thinks everyone's turned against him – he thinks he's going insane – and *now*, to top it all off . . .'

'Okay,' the young guide stopped walking, was suddenly business-like, 'you've worked out the L'Amour connection already, and I'm presuming the kid unwittingly helped you with some of the other stuff in the Wimpy yesterday . . .'

Jo stared at him, frowning.

Were they Following me, yesterday?

Couldn't I tell?

Didn't I see?

'You're a local girl,' he smiled at her, encouragingly, 'an *environmentalist*, no less. You're genned up on the geography of the whole south-eastern coastal region. You have an *advantage* . . .'

'Why?' she stared at him, bemusedly.

'*Think* about it.'

He pointed behind her and then placed his hand onto his belly. She glanced over her shoulder, back towards Shoes, not really focussing. She was quiet for a second, then her eyes widened. Her heart nearly missed a beat. 'The *Sands* . . .'

She rapidly counted the letters off onto her fingers. '*Shit*. That's *it*. Goodwin *Sands*. Past Deal, near Sandwich . . .'

He watched her, smiling benevolently.

'The prize is on the *Sands*?' she reiterated breathlessly, trying frantically to work things back . . .

'Oh *God* . . .' she suddenly made the connection. 'Clue 2. *That's* the giveaway . . .'

He nodded.

'*Barflies* –' she recited from memory, '*This is just a stop-over, 105, maximum* . . .'

'The rest is all just *filler*, basically . . .'

She frowned. She was quiet for a minute.

'But *hang* on . . .'

'It's clever, though, isn't it?' he said, trying to stall her train of thought. '*Bar*flies. Because it's a sand *bar*, and people can only visit it . . .'

'In June,' she interrupted, taking his bait, 'during the *equinox* – the low spring tides – when it's finally revealed, but for only a few hours . . . so there *were* astronomical directions . . .'

He nodded. 'Clue 4 . . .'

She ran ahead of him. '*There's lamb and lynx and lion, Yet no fish and no fowl either* . . . they're all astrological signs?'

'Yup. The first three are all visible in the Northern Hemisphere during early June.'

She paused for a second, visibly astonished. 'That's actually very . . .' she was awed, '. . . *clever.*'

'Kew-wee-we-wu,' he continued, 'the distinctive song of the God-wit. A *wading* bird. It's rumoured that the Godwit sometimes visits the area at that particular time of year . . .'

She was nodding again, thoughtfully.

'Good-*win*,' she said. 'That's perfect. What a . . .' she unconsciously rolled Dennis's lead tight around her fingers, until his front feet were almost pulled from the ground, 'what an amazing *wind*-up.'

'But nobody can go onto the sands and find the prize, obviously,' the guide continued smartly, 'until the right time of year.'

Jo smiled at this. 'Oh no,' she said, noticing Dennis's predicament, and unwinding him fractionally.

His eyes tightened.

'Oh no,' she repeated, 'it's not quite that simple, though, is it?'

The guide began walking again. Very quickly. Josephine turned and followed, dragging the dog behind her.

'It doesn't add up. L'Amour has to fit into this puzzle somewhere. And Doc.'

'What you need to bear in mind,' the guide explained, curtly, 'is that Doc's son . . .'

'Colin,' Jo reminded him, pointedly.

'It wasn't *our* responsibility that he saw fit to wander around in that Welsh estuary. There were plenty of warnings about the tides there . . .'

'It did look rather bad for your people, though,' she smiled, tightly, 'didn't it?'

He ignored her. 'The Loiter was only intended as a bit of fun . . .'

'Get to the point.'

'The prize isn't *on* Goodwin, as such.'

He was squirming. She noticed, stopped walking. She shook her head, 'I'm not . . .'

He scowled, turned, 'The prize *is* Goodwin.'

'What?' She stared at him, open-mouthed, 'You *bought* The Sands?'

He nodded, 'That was the . . . the twist . . . the *irony*. To give a prize which cost so much – financially – which meant so much, historically, geographically, culturally – as a navigational landmark and all the rest of it – but which was – and *is*, actually – to all intents and purposes – worth absolutely nothing.'

She was loving this. Couldn't resist it.

'And L'Amour?'

'There are references to L'Amour throughout the clues. Wesley's father was a sailor. L'Amour was a sailor and an adventurer and a writer. He had two children, Angelo and Beauty . . .'

'*Sweet Beauty and her Angel* . . .' Jo interrupted.

'Precisely. L'Amour's family published new novels by him, even after his death. Books that were written just before he died, for that very purpose. He was a man who became – in effect, and perfectly voluntarily – almost an *industry*. Those kinds of ideas – those ramifications – have a particular significance to Wesley. The numbers 42 and 8 refer to the number of fights L'Amour won and lost in his career as a professional boxer . . .'

'*So the gone might gander*,' Jo suddenly filled in, slowly catching up.

He nodded, '*Utah Blaine* – Wesley makes a reference to *Hondo*, L'Amour's most famous book, with *Sirius, God of Dogs* – but *Utah Blaine* is the important one. He signposts Utah geographically in Clue One with references to a series of rivers – the Beaver . . . Antelope . . . Bear. In *Utah Blaine* the hero risks his life for something that is not actually his. An abstract principle. For honour. A ranch that belongs to a dead man so is effectively worthless . . . I presume you're starting to see the parallels . . . ?'

Jo nodded, 'Of course. But I still don't understand Doc's connection to all of this.'

The young guide drew a deep breath, 'It was felt – in light of his son's drowning, and the universal *upset* this tragedy generated in the media – that it might seem . . .' he paused, searching for the right word, 'inappropriate if the prize were to be an island whose entire history is a torrid patchwork of drownings and shipwrecks and misery. These sands are held to be one of the most treacherous offshore strands in the world. When Colin' the guide used his name with especial emphasis, 'died, it was then felt that some adjustments should be made to the whole Goodwin arrangement. As it currently stands, the Loiter is a PR disaster. And a very personal one, too, for Murdoch, for Murdoch's family . . .'

'So Wesley happily went along with the idea of a cover-up?' Jo was suspicious.

The guide paused, then nodded, 'Of course. Whatever impression he likes to give, he's as concerned for Doc's feelings as the rest of us. Doc is a key figure in the whole Following diaspora. He's central. It'd be a tragedy if the . . .'

'So when Colin died,' Jo interrupted him, 'and Wesley said he'd won, that he was a winner, he wasn't being quite as perverse as it might've appeared. Because the prize is actually a celebration of a certain kind of . . . of treachery . . .'

The young guide shrugged. He plainly didn't really relish this way of thinking.

'And the subsidiary prize will have to be planted presumably,' she continued, 'as soon as the tide's finally low enough.'

'That's pretty much the sum of it . . .' he turned and gazed back toward his older accomplice, 'and you're obviously now in a prime position,' he turned and grinned, hollowly, 'to join in the search.'

Jo was quiet for a while. She tried to straighten out Hooch's involvement in her mind.

'Gumble,' she suddenly said.

He gazed at her, blankly, 'Sorry?'

She gauged the minutiae of his reactions –

Fists tightening

Nostrils flaring slightly

– then let it pass.

'You've told Hooch all of this, then, presumably,' she continued.

He nodded, 'Hooch was central to our strategy. He's close to Doc, and yet there's that interesting competitive edge between the two of them. Hooch – in turn – told Shoes. He needed Shoes on board to shore things up. But they're the only two who currently know anything . . . so far as we're aware, obviously.'

'Does the Blind Man know?'

The young guide shook his head, 'No. And nor shall he, if I have anything to do with it.'

'Because the fewer people who find out . . .'

He smiled, 'Of course. The more chances the few who *do* know have of winning.'

'And the more chances the company have of keeping the whole original hoax under wraps.'

He passed over this, 'If Shoes or Hooch win, the Behindlings as a whole will benefit. The Following *culture* will benefit. Most importantly, Doc will benefit, if only indirectly . . .'

He paused. 'Today has obviously been . . .' he grimaced.

'A monumental cock-up,' she finished off for him.

He inclined his head, graciously.

In the distance a car horn sounded. Jo's eyes instinctively moved towards it.

'So how many of you are there?' she asked.

'Not many. A few.'

'Does Wesley know who you are?'

'Probably.'

Her eyes focussed in on something, further up the road; Dewi, in the middle distance, piling clothing and furniture – willy-nilly – into the back of his pick-up. And Katherine, also on the road, stopping the traffic, holding up some kind of . . . of . . . *tree* and berating him violently.

'I must go,' she said, and started walking.

'Can we depend upon your cooperation?' the guide called after her, perhaps a mite apprehensively.

She turned and bent down to pick up the dog (grunting at the unexpected weight of him). 'Of *course* you can,' she adjusted him in her arms, 'I mean . . .' she paused, speculatively, her brown eyes glinting, 'insofar as you can depend upon anybody's.'

Forty-seven

He parked the car on the dainty hard shoulder, riding up – with a jolt
(Eileen made a sudden lunge for her seat-belt) – onto the muddy grass
siding, braking gently and stopping. They'd barely spoken during
the journey. Eileen had fiddled nervously with her bag; accidentally
twisting a plastic daisy-head from its mesh and then compulsively
struggling – without success – to work it back into place again.

Ted had turned the radio on, was listening – with an unbelievable
intensity – to an angry man complaining about the lack of adequate
public toilet facilities in the Tilbury/Thameshaven vicinity.

Once the engine was off – and the whining was halted – Ted bent
forward to pick up Eileen's bag, which had fallen from her lap in
the brief commotion. She pulled her legs up, instinctively, at his
unexpected proximity. He grabbed both the bag and its loose daisy,
then in a series of deft hand movements, re-established the whole to
its former glory.

'*There.*'

He passed it back to her.

Eileen snatched the bag from him, staring querulously at the
reinstated plastic flower (as if it was some kind of errant *tick*,
sucking the life out of the surrounding fabric), then she carefully
removed the knife (Ted frowned), the heron's head, and shoved the
bag – as if now repelled by it – down under the dashboard, kicking
it from sight with her neatly-shod feet.

'I hope he'll be alright,' she said, with a shudder.

'Pardon?'

'The Old Man.'

Ted frowned, 'I'm sure he'll be . . .'

'I mean the way he just . . .' she interrupted, flapping her hand, helplessly.

'I know,' he nodded sagely, '*tragic*.'

'Perhaps we should've . . .'

'No,' Ted focussed on the condensation at the corners of the windscreen, 'stopping would've been dangerous – the lights were changing. And there were plenty of witnesses. The Bean girl, for one. She's a qualified nurse. She'll've known what to do for the best.'

'Good,' Eileen said, and climbed out of the car.

He loved that.

He loved the way she dealt with things: careful yet carefree, caring but care*less*.

He loved that.

Outside, the weather was like a truculent two-year-old with a brand new birthday football; sulking and blubbering one minute, whooping and blustering the next. Eileen hunched up her shoulders and put her hand to her hair. It blew sideways – *en masse* – like a compacted serving of organic alfalfa.

Ted clambered out himself, winced (at the weather), and then awkwardly offered Eileen his jacket. She told him not to be so *ridiculous*, then blushed, as if embarrassed by the unnecessary violence of her response.

He quietly chastised himself as he grabbed the eggs and removed the rope (felt the coarse-fibred bump of it on the palm of his hands, the insides of his fingers, and finally – once he'd slung it over his arm – felt it rub heavily against his shoulder through his light woollen suit fabric).

He knew that it was principally just an issue of *approach*. His gut – operating (as it now was), in a consultative capacity – told him that it wasn't *what* you did in life that really mattered, so much as *how* you went about it. Not the actual content (*balls* to achievement, to accomplishment, to the solid things; the big house, the wad of cash, the two kids, the exam result), but the *manner of dispatch* that was truly significant.

I am an Agent of the Future

– his gut told him –

I am an idea

I am a plan

A spark
A thrust
An inkling

'I'd love to make you a dress, Eileen,' he boldly announced, slamming his car door shut and rapidly catching up with her, 'pinched at the waist, tight on the leg, knee length, in a beautiful honey-coloured brushed velvet. A choker to match.' He put his hand to his own neck as he imagined it.

She walked stalwartly into the flurry. 'Do you come here often, Ted?' she asked.

He paused – *cut* – before softly answering, 'Never.'

They staggered forward together – Ted keeping on the outside to protect her from the slush – and when they finally reached the flyover, instead of climbing down from it (there seemed to be no ready means of exit – a clamber, a straddle, a leap being the only technique that sprang readily to mind), Ted strolled up to its centre-point, placed his hands firmly onto its thigh-high concrete ledge and gazed questingly over –

Wesley
Where is he?

'I'd have to be able to *walk* in the damn thing,' Eileen suddenly declared, a hint of irritation hijacking her voice as she tried to wipe wet snow from the lenses of her glasses.

'Pardon?'

She'd caught him off-guard.

'The dress, *Ted*. The honey-coloured dress.'

'Of *course*,' he quickly reassured her, 'a tiny split at the back. And lined – so it doesn't cling – in the thickest, richest, *bloodiest* blood-orange.'

He paused.

Have I gone too far?

Eileen gazed up at him, her eyes illuminating.

'*Blood* orange,' she smiled, 'in shot-silk? I *love* the sound of that.'

'Good,' he nodded – a kind of courteous dismissal, a tender fullstop – then he turned his attention back to the river.

It was impossible to see far in the soft sleet, the half-light. Perhaps God was masquerading – Ted thought, scowling – for *fun* or out of sheer *viciousness*, as some kind of cack-handed amateur artist;

roped in to paint the scenery for a bad school drama; working for nothing and – by the shoddy calibre of his output – without enthusiasm; wholly intent upon making the whole *damn* world into a heavy-handed caricature; a sketch; a border, a wing, a back-drop.

Ted marked it a clumsy effort. Failed him for it.

In the distance –

Ah, that endless thirst for refinement . . .

– the ghostly flare of the oil terminal; its eternally mischievous, up-all-hours industrious twinkle.

His eyes moved in closer again as the mist briefly shifted and he could suddenly just about decipher . . .

Tiny details

A precious little water-colour

Finding its definition inside the wider picture . . .

Eileen grabbed his arm and pointed: towards an ornately-stricken craft, a piebald horse, a dead . . . a dead *fox* –

Was it?

– and a familiar figure clambering unsteadily across a nauseatingly temporary-looking make-piece walkway.

For a moment Ted's starved aesthetic sense was gratified –

Pleasured

– and then –

Shit

– he thrust the eggs into Eileen's hands, 'That's *Wes*. He's . . . Oh *Damnation . . .*'

And he ran –

But why?

– to lend a hand – to prompt – to prop – to light – to ham . . . to . . . to . . . to . . .

What?

– as ticket collector – as previewer – reviewer – enthusiastic applauder . . .

Witness

Audience

Fan

He didn't care. So long as it was *him*, and so long as he was there.

*   *   *

Arthur couldn't quite believe Wesley'd made it over. He'd been preparing for a catastrophe –

Hoping . . .

– and yet here he was, looming solidly above him – all old rope and hard puff and new sweat and *vigour* – and here Arthur still was –

Still

– down on his knees; frozen, inept, the girl clinging to his foot and . . . the . . . the . . . the *deer* skulking around aromatically in the background somewhere . . .

Laughable

   It was almost as if –

Almost

– he'd actually started believing –

And how ridiculous

– in a moment's weakness, or foolishness – that this was actually *his* story, *his* drama . . . but suddenly –

Cruelly

In a flash

– he knew much better. This was Wesley's story (this was *always* Wesley's story). It bore all the familiar hallmarks. It was too complicated, too unlikely, too intense, too lovely . . .

The blood
The pain
The fear
The beauty

Wesley's story

Arthur cursed his own gullibility. Because at some point during that long night – that awful night – their curiously potent little threesome (their *troika*, their *trinity*) had actually started to *mean* something to him . . .

To signify . . .

483

He'd honestly started to think of them –
Oh God
– as . . . as *immutable* in some . . . in some . . .
   As unified, as united, as *destined* to . . . to . . .
   He had actually begun to believe – to focus, to fixate – on some
kind of vital, rooted, essential *equilibrium* –
A balance
– something loosely –
Very loosely
– uh . . . *spiritual*. A twisted sort of divinity (the nativity on stilts.
The nativity on ice, on *water* . . .)
That sense of encroaching peril rendering everything so . . . so . . .
Clear

Hello?
Hello?
   Is this Arthur Young?
   Mr Arthur *Anthony* Young?
Is it?
   Could it . . . ?
Nah

Am I . . . ?
Am I . . . ?
Am I cr . . . cr . . . ?
Is this some kind of falsely retroac-ac-active . . .
Hy . . . hypothermic . . .
Blood-loss-related . . .
Pharmaceu . . . ceutically engendered . . .
Eh?

And yet –
Sure as eggs is fucking eggs
– to get back to the point, to get back to the reality; here was *bloody*
Wesley –
Tah-dah!
– to mess it all up again, to move things on, to make things *happen*,

to tinker with the balance, to save, to relish, to implode, to conquer, to appropriate to . . . to . . . to . . .
Christ I hate him

'*Shit*, man,' Wesley said, clinging to the doorframe, waiting a second for the craft to stop swaying, 'it's no wonder your catching skills were so fucking *abject*, Art, – you've lost a *ton* of blood, there.'

He sounded concerned –
Fibber

'I smashed my hand through the stupid window,' Art sullenly explained, 'in the dark.' Wesley began to try and tie a rope around him, but Arthur pushed him firmly back. 'I want the girl off before me,' he chattered, peering up into his face to try and find evidence of the sound beating he'd received the previous evening. But there was nothing. A slight rash on his left cheek, like a strawberry birthmark –
Is he . . .
Is he real?

Wesley glanced into the boat and saw the girl gazing benignly up at him from the floor. His face stiffened at the sight of her, as if he'd received a sudden sharp jab to his lower intestine –
Christopher

'*Fine*,' he grated (almost short of breath), his former ebullience totally evaporating, 'if that's how you want to play it.'

'But when I go,' the girl immediately began wheedling, 'the deer will come after me, so we should really try and get Brion off before . . .'

'Shut up,' Wesley snapped, forming some of his spare rope into a lassoo.

'You don't *understand*,' the girl persisted, 'if *I* go the deer will . . .'

'Bollocks,' he snarled, 'that deer has much more sense than you do.'

He tossed the looped rope down at her. It landed on her head, slipped onto the brim of Arthur's cap, stuck there. She released one hand from Art's foot – gasping with the exertion – pulled the rope loose and then over her shoulder. She was breathing heavily.

'My *fingers* . . .' she panted, pausing for a moment.

It was the first time Arthur had heard a word of complaint

from her in all the time they'd been together. He twisted around, concerned.

'Cut the *whining*,' Wesley interrupted.

Arthur glared up at him, furiously.

The girl yanked the rope fairly laboriously, first under one armpit, then under the other. The boat protested.

Before she'd even had a chance to prepare herself, Wesley tightened the lassoo, and began pulling her forward.

He was strong. The deer grunted then shuffled as the girl's body shifted.

'You stay the *hell* where you are,' Wesley shouted, pointing at it.

'He doesn't respond to . . .'

'*Blah*,' Wesley said, pushing his shoulder past Arthur and easing her further.

'The boat's *really* swaying,' Arthur warned him.

'Thanks for that, Art,' Wesley muttered as Sasha finally drew close enough for him to offer her his free hand.

The bad hand.

Sasha saw the hand and froze for a millisecond, then frowned, grabbed at it and rose unsteadily to her feet.

Wes indicated briskly towards the walkway, barely looking at her, tying the other end of the lassoo to his waist, then transferring the rope connecting him to the horse from around his hips to hers.

'Run over it quickly,' he said, 'spread your weight evenly between both planks, but lightly. We're linked up in two different ways. Try not to trip. If you do fall, though, you're tied both to me *and* to the pony. We'll get you out . . .' he paused, somewhat meanly, '*eventually*. If you *do* fall,' he repeated (almost as if savouring the thought), 'then try and keep upright, push your legs and knees and feet together. Fall straight. It's safer.'

'I *know* how to fall,' she interrupted, 'but there's rocks under the mud down there . . .'

Wesley grunted and gave her a sharp little push to set her on her way.

The bad hand.

Arthur saw the shove and was appalled, but Sasha responded well to it, setting off at a light, snaking trot and reaching the other side without undue mishap.

Not so the craft, which jolted – side to side – with a horrible creaking and then dropped – even further – at the back. An inch? Three inches?

Sasha turned around, pulled the two ropes off and tied them together, her eyes wide with a sudden anxiety – as if the feel of solid land, the fact of her now almost certain safety, had somehow made everything seem paradoxically scarier. 'Please don't forget *Brion*,' she shouted dramatically, 'he's my only friend in all the *world*.'

'Holy *bosh*,' Wesley muttered, rapidly reeling the rope back in. 'You're next, Art. Try and stand so you can loosen up your legs a little first . . .'

'No,' Arthur was staring at the small girl with an unusually bright – yet exceptionally morbid – expression on his face.

'No,' he repeated, and shook his head, 'the deer.'

Sasha was listening, had heard him. She whooped and bounced, punching her arm into the air.

'*Pardon*?'

Wesley couldn't understand.

'The *deer*,' Arthur repeated, 'rope it up.'

Wesley was silent. 'When the deer goes,' he finally spoke, 'this *whole structure* goes with it. You do know that?'

'I don't care.' Arthur stuck his chin out. 'She's a good girl. She loves that damn animal.'

'*Go* Brion!'

The girl yelled. The deer began moving in response to her call. The boat tipped.

'*Shut* the *fuck* up,' Wesley bellowed.

The deer froze. Sasha froze.

The boat shifted back. Creaked.

'I am climbing off this thing *alone*, Art,' Wes said, barely regaining his composure, 'and *leaving* you here, before I take that moronic bovine off first.'

'Fine,' Arthur shrugged, 'I'll lead the deer off myself.'

'*Thank you* Art,' the girl yelled.

Arthur raised his arm in an uncertain royal salute, like a visiting first-world sovereign attending a mysterious cultural event in the colonies –

I am a visitor here
In this beautiful land

'Don't be *ridiculous*,' Wesley spat. He was clenching his teeth, 'Deer swim perfectly well. I'll lassoo him. He'll be fine. But if this thing goes down with you still on board, you're *fucked*.'

'I thought you liked animals,' Arthur said.

'Pardon?'

'I said I thought you were a *friend* to the animals . . .' he paused, satirically, 'like . . . like *Dr Dolittle* was.'

He suddenly realised that he was having a good time.

'I do,' Wesley muttered (plainly appreciating Arthur's little victory over him, but still confused by it), 'I *am*.'

'Well then.'

Arthur tried to neaten up his appearance. He pushed his hair back, rubbed his hand across his chin.

Wesley watched him, scowling.

'*Urgh*,' the girl said, locating first the fox's tail, then the rest of its cadaver. She picked up the tail and inspected it closely.

'Perhaps,' Wesley said gently, 'your judgement's been clouded a little by lack of *sleep*, Art.' His tone – Arthur noted with some surprise – was almost respectful, if querulous.

'I want the girl,' Arthur's teeth were chattering slightly again, but he was full – almost exploding – with a kind of crazy zeal, 'to have her deer. She *loves* her deer. Didn't you hear what she said before? Weren't you *listening*? The deer is all she has in the *world*.'

The girl looked up from the vixen's carcass, having momentarily abandoned all thoughts of Brion's safety.

'*Yes*,' she cheerleadered, suddenly catching up again, waving the tail in the air. '*Go*, Art.'

Wesley gave Arthur a straight look, 'You can't be serious.'

Art nodded devoutly. Yes. Yes he was.

'She's an eight-year-old *girl*, Art.'

'Nine.'

'What?'

'She's nine.'

Wesley rubbed his hands over his face, 'I don't have enough rope to lassoo both you *and* the animal.'

'And yourself.'

Arthur sniffed, then smiled, thinly. Provocatively.

'Pardon?'

'You don't have enough rope for me, the deer, *and* yourself.'

Wesley was quiet for a second, processing. He detected a challenge. He *liked* challenges.

'Of course you're right,' he mused ruminatively. 'I don't *need* the rope. I was only wearing it in the first place for the girl's safety . . .' He began to take the rope off.

The girl, meanwhile, had clambered part-way up the muddy bank and was peering off keenly to her right, her back as straight – her posture as rapt and attentive – as a wary prairie dog with the scent of a coyote on his territory.

Wesley leaned casually forward as he unwound the rope. He saw Ted, running towards them at full pelt (in his lovely handmade suit; like *Carter*, like *James Bond*), followed – close behind – by Eileen. They looked a delightfully incongruous pair. They were soaking wet. Their legs were splattered with mud. They were both bright-cheeked and out of breath.

'*I have more* . . .' Ted yelled, gesticulating clumsily, '*I've brought* . . .' He pulled the rope from his arm and then slid – hard on his arse – down the steep bank. The rope bounced out of his clutches and rolled straight into the river.

Plop

'*Ouch,*' the girl chuckled, lifting her shoulders, sniggering through her fingers, 'you messed up.' Ted winced and closed his eyes. Agonised.

'Don't worry, Ted,' Wesley shouted over, 'there's more than enough rope here already for Art and the deer.'

'I won't be needing any rope,' Arthur murmured, haughtily.

Wesley stopped smiling.

'Don't be ridiculous.'

'If *you* don't need any rope,' Arthur attempted to struggle to his feet (failed abysmally), 'then nor do I.'

Ted – also struggling to stand up again, and succeeding, but with a slight groan – turned to the girl, 'Did he just say there was a *deer* stuck on that thing?'

She nodded.

Ted gazed at her, dazed. The coin dropped.

'Then you must be . . . ?'

She nodded again, her eyes widening. Ted frowned at her reaction, then suddenly understood it on feeling a violent pressure to the back of his legs as the piebald pony interposed its large nose between his two thighs and flipped him savagely forward. He shrieked and almost toppled. Sasha grabbed him.

'You're so *comical*,' she murmured, staring up at him intently, 'I'm *very* glad you're here.' She nudged him flirtatiously with her fox's tail. Ted stepped back, his face a mixture of fascination and horror.

That was *Wesley's* look (that deliciously, unconsciously *cruel* look).

That was *Wesley's* face, in miniature.

Eileen, who had picked her way – rather more genteelly – down the slope, finally arrived safely at the bottom of it.

'So what's happening?' she asked, still out of breath. 'Has anybody thought to call the Fire Brigade yet?'

'*No*,' Arthur and Wes both shouted from the craft in unison.

Wes was forming a lassoo again, tossing it – the first time; unsuccessfully – the second time . . . Arthur was shaking out his legs.

'My deer's stuck on the boat,' Sasha explained gamely, 'and Art has promised to save him for me,' she paused, 'what are those for?'

She pointed to the box of eggs Eileen was clutching.

'*Fuck the Brigade!*' Wesley yelled, tightening the rope around the deer's neck. 'We reserve the right as *free men* . . .' he grimaced as the rope pulled on his scarred hand, 'to make our *own* bloody mistakes and to suffer the consequences of them . . .'

'*Hear Hear*,' Arthur concurred, passionately. For once – and once only – they were in absolute agreement.

Eileen frowned down at the eggs (as if she hadn't really heard them), then over at Sasha, 'I must admit,' she whispered softly, 'that I was only just wondering about these *myself* . . .'

Then she opened the box, carefully removed a single, perfect, creamy-coloured oval, held it firmly between her finger and thumb, rotated it gently, showing it off to its very best advantage, 'but now I . . .'

She suddenly turned and *hurled* it – with a quite astonishing ferocity, an *intoxicating* accuracy – towards the craft.

When the egg made contact with the back of Wesley's shoulder, the whole thing, the whole *structure* – as if a secret button had been pressed, a cord severed, a hidden brake, released – simply plummeted.

Forty-eight

She dropped the dog and cautiously circled the hydrangea, as if uncertain whether this twiggy beast was stone dead or simply shamming (this was Katherine's brute, after all – might it not jump up and bite her? Or turn and flee? At the last minute? Just when she . . . ?).

Katherine had thrown the plant into the road and left it there. Cars were slowing down and then gingerly overtaking; no one – as yet – feeling sufficiently public-spirited to stop their vehicle, climb out and remove it.

It was a large plant, and beautiful; even in its skeletal winter phase; with numerous dried flower-heads in a subtle medley of pinky-blues and bleached brown-mauves. Jo grabbed it from underneath, just above its roots. Pulled. *Groaned*. It was heavy.

'That's so bloody *Canvey*,' she grunted, dragging it to the side of the road, beaching it on the pavement, 'don't you reckon?'

She glanced over towards Dewi.

Dewi was still arranging his stuff into the back of his pick up; three 18th century walnut captain's chairs, several pieces of bedding, a box of randomly assorted bits of cutlery and crockery, some work tools, a crate crushed full of books and shoes . . .

He wouldn't look at her initially. But after a moment he stopped what he was doing and glanced up.

'Why?'

He seemed bloodless; distressed, as faded as one of the dried hydrangea flower-heads.

'They'd rather sit for an hour in a line of traffic,' she exaggerated, 'than commit to the horrible physical *responsibility* of removing the damn thing that's impeding their way.' Dewi shrugged. Jo smiled, self-consciously, 'Perhaps I've grown a little cynical about this place in my old age.'

'Just get out of here,' Dewi mumbled – but not aggressively – turning away again.

Josephine stood her ground. She cleared her throat, as if preparing to make some kind of public announcement, then patted the dog's rump to make it sit down. The dog, at least, did as it was told; it sat and stared up at her, shivering a little.

'I really loved him,' she said, her voice sounding exceptionally clear – even child-like – under pressure, 'I really *loved* Mr Turpin. I know it can't . . . I know it won't make anyone feel any better about the whole thing . . . but he was unbelievably *kind*, and a great teacher, and it wasn't as wrong or as calculated or as *sordid* as it might've seemed to . . . to *you* or to my family. It wasn't planned. It wasn't . . . it was just . . . just an *accident* . . .'

Dewi was trying to unwind his tarpaulin, but his fingers were clumsy. His arms had been scratched by the plant. His hands and his nails were still muddy. He cursed under his breath.

'We could always dig it back in,' Jo murmured hollowly –
What was I expecting?
A sudden reprieve?
Total exoneration?
A hug?
– turning her attention back to the plant again, adjusting it slightly so its branches wouldn't snap or tear any more than they had done already – 'the roots are still . . .'

He turned on her, furiously, 'If you're trying to use that stupid plant as some kind of ridiculous *symbol* for what's been going on between myself and Katherine, then forget about it. It's just a *hydrangea*, Josephine, a *ridiculous* hydrangea.'

Josephine took a step back –
He used my name
– but only one step.

She gazed down at the plant again.

'I suppose it must symbolise *something*,' she eventually muttered, 'if you felt overwhelmed by the sudden urge to yank it up . . .' she glanced over the road, 'and then smash her window,' she added.

This seemed to irritate him, 'For one thing,' he said letting go of his tarpaulin, 'it's none of your *bloody* business what I do or don't do regarding Katherine, and for another, I smashed the window *before* I pulled up the hydrangea. Smashing the window wasn't *enough*, you see.' He glared at her, vindictively, 'I felt like I wanted to hurt her *more*. To punish her *more*, in the same way she's delighted for so long in punishing me.'

'You punished yourself,' Jo said, 'because she refused to shy away from the lies people spread about her, and you weren't big enough, or *brave* enough just to accept them and move on.'

'I should've given up,' he muttered, returning to his tarpaulin, '*years* ago. I should've done like you did,' he glanced over at her, coldly, 'and crawled away from here. There's been no dignity in remaining.'

'But you had to stay,' Josephine smiled, bitterly, 'didn't you? If only to remind her of what could've been if she'd loved herself a little more.'

'You're as twisted as she is,' he whispered.

'We've all hurt Katherine quite enough to be going on with,' Jo intoned primly, carefully straightening the dog's leash.

Dewi began to laugh. Hollowly. She glanced over at him.

'See how *neat* her house is on the outside?' he asked, his face contorting with a curious energy. Jo turned her focus towards the house. It wasn't looking especially neat any more, but still, she nodded. 'Well when you get *inside*,' he continued, 'it gets really *dirty*. Full of all kinds of crap. Full of *shit . . .*'

Jo's mouth tightened at its corners.

'But then when you go into her *own* room, her *bed*room, it's absolutely *spotless*, and full of *flowers* and *doll's houses* and a ton of other stupid, girlish . . .'

'And what does that mean?' Jo interrupted, harshly.

He paused, then shrugged, his victorious expression suddenly disintegrating. 'I don't know,' he said, his eyes filling, 'and I don't . . . I can't *care* any more. I've given up. I've quit. She's won. *You've* won. Why not just be happy about it?'

Josephine cocked her head, frowning, 'Is this all my fault, then?'

Dewi almost laughed, 'He was *right* about her, you know. Everything he said. Everything he thought . . .'

Jo struggled to follow his reasoning.

'Because *she* wrote it . . .' Dewi almost choked as he spoke, 'she wrote it *herself*. The graffiti. *She* wrote it. And she . . .'

'No,' Jo said; almost a knee-jerk reaction, 'she didn't.'

'. . . and when I painted it out, *she* maintained it. It was *her*.'

'No.' Jo was shaking her head. 'No.'

He turned, his eyes burning.

'She just *admitted* it to me.'

'No,' Jo remained emphatic, even in the face of his considerable anguish, 'she didn't. And I know she didn't, for a fact.'

'*How* do you know?' His tone was insolent.

'Because . . .' the words exploded out of her, in a jumble, 'because of . . . it . . . it was me.' He stared at her, barely grasping what she was saying.

'It was *me*,' she pointed to her own chest, tapped on her own breast-plate, repeatedly. 'It was me. I wrote it, Dewi. *I* wrote it. It was me.'

No answer at the door so she tied the dog to the gatepost, put her gloves back on, removed the worst shards of glass from the window-frame and then climbed inside through the gaping hole. The entire house was in chaos. Everything smelled acrid; a mixture of Marlboro's, old booze and cheap, pine-flavoured household detergent.

Josephine slowly plotted herself a route down the passageway, clambering unsteadily over piles of black refuse sacks, peeking timorously into an old study, a bathroom, and then finally locating Katherine in her bedroom – as neat and clean as Dewi had described it – where she was sitting – crosslegged – on her bed, sipping what looked like crème de menthe from an old-fashioned brandy balloon.

'I really should kill you,' Katherine glanced up from the book she was reading, patently unfazed at seeing Josephine standing there, 'for spreading that evil lie about me.'

She stared at her – po-faced – for three straight seconds, then burst out laughing.

Josephine drew a deep breath. She looked down at her feet. She was shaking. 'Go to hell,' she muttered.

'Well that was certainly . . . *uh* . . .' Katherine leaned over and scrabbled around on the floor by her bed for a piece of paper, picked it up, straightened it out, inspected it, 'that was certainly very . . . *uh* . . . *altruistic* of you, Josephine,' she said, 'and very . . .' she inspected the letter again, 'very *sisterly*. To take the blame like that,' she smiled with a kind of vicious joy, 'after all this time.'

Jo shook her head, refusing to be intimidated. 'That's the last time I'm going to lie,' she said, 'for you, your dad, for me, for *anybody*. I came here to tell you that I don't want to lie any more. I won't. I don't care what the consequences are. I can't and I *shan't*.'

Katherine looked mildly surprised by this outburst. 'Whyever not?'

'Because it's cruel. It's gone too far. It was bad enough already before Wesley took it to another level with the book . . .'

'*Good*,' Katherine snorted, 'you know how I *thrive* on the notoriety . . .'

'Do you?' Josephine gave her a searching look.

Katherine maintained her gaze for a few seconds, but couldn't hold it, turned her eyes away, furtively.

'You saved your dad's career. You protected me. You tested yourself, *and* Dewi. I don't care why you did what you did back then, and I don't give a damn about what you've since become. I'll always . . . I'll *always* admire you for it.'

Katherine shrugged, 'Too little. Too late.' She sipped on her drink, pulled a face at the harsh taste, 'And Dewi won't swallow it,' she gasped, 'the truth always has a particular kind of . . .' she ruminated, frowning, 'of immediacy, don't you think? A *glow*. He'll recognise it, eventually. You're just prolonging his agony this way.'

Jo shook her head, 'The truth is just another fact – you of *all* people should know that.' Katherine merely smiled and turned down the corner on the page of her book.

'I honestly thought my brothers wrote that graffiti,' Josephine continued, watching her dispassionately, 'I haven't exchanged a word with my family in over fourteen years because of it. I never dared show my face in Canvey again, I was so *fucking* ashamed and disgusted by what had happened.'

'God knows,' Katherine rolled her eyes, dramatically, 'I'm almost dying with remorse here.' She burst out laughing again. She seemed slightly hysterical. Drunk, maybe.

'Dewi's leaving,' Jo said coldly, 'he's packing up his pick-up and he's going.'

'Good,' Katherine smacked her lips.

'You don't mean that.'

'Yes I do. Screw the fool. I don't *care*. I hope I never see him again. He was always such a fucking *drag*. Unlike . . .' she continued smartly, flapping the letter at her again, 'our *dear* friend Mr Arthur Young, who turned out to be quite the most *charming* creature. And a remarkable *fuck*. And a *fantastic* liar.'

Jo frowned, 'I don't understand. Why should that matter?'

Katherine's pale eyebrows rose slightly. 'Because you sent me this letter. Southend postmark. Warning me off. You're mixed up to your silly *neck* in all this unsavoury Wesley mess. Probably felt a *tweak* of conscience over the graffiti stuff in the book, and it developed from there. You were always such a *train*spotter, Bean. I think that's why my dad took pity on you. He had an MA in Industrial Engineering, after all.'

Josephine scowled and put out her hand for the letter. Katherine sipped on her drink and then passed it over. Jo rapidly read through it. When she'd finished, she looked up, 'Why on earth would I have sent you this?'

Katherine shrugged, 'Therein lies the mystery, Bean. The rest I can *just* about get my head around . . .'

'The rest of what?'

'*Gumble.*' Katherine held up her book, smiling like a cat.

Josephine blinked, focussed, drew closer. 'What is it?'

'Kid's book. I dug it out of Wesley's rucksack. *Gumbles* are these silly, squidgy little creatures who get shoved into tin cans and bullied and manipulated . . .'

'This is *Wesley's* book?' Josephine looked astonished, reached out her hand. But Katherine refused to let her have it.

'I also found . . .' Katherine opened the book and removed a marker from inside it – a photo. This she did pass over. Josephine stared at the picture of the brown-haired girl, turned it, read the back.

'Who is she?'

'Arthur Young's daughter, so far as I can gather.'

'And why does she matter?'

'She has Cystic Fibrosis. Needs a big operation, in America.'

Josephine handed the picture back, shrugged.

'A charming little company called Gumble Inc, manufacturers of high quality vegetarian *footwear* . . .' Katherine chuckled, then burped (put her hand over her mouth), '*Sorry.*'

Josephine was still struggling to catch up.

'He runs the website, you *prick*. Arthur Young. Gumble Inc are trying to buy him out. They engineered an exclusive advertising deal with him a few months back, then quickly started throwing their weight around . . .'

Josephine continued to stare at her, blankly, 'You're saying . . .' she frowned, a slow realisation gradually dawning, 'you're saying you think *Wesley* . . . ?'

'Seems likely. I mean if you're going to be Followed everywhere, then *hell*, why not take control of the mechanisms organising it?' She paused. 'Obviously it's bound to be slightly more *complicated* than that . . .'

Josephine was shaking her head, 'It doesn't . . .' she paused, speculatively, 'and do you think Arthur Young knows?'

Katherine shrugged, hiccuped, 'The ten million dollar question. But I doubt it. There's no love lost there, that's for certain. I get the impression that the whole Wesley thing is a labour of *love* with our Arthur.'

Josephine frowned.

'Because the punchline is . . .' Katherine continued, 'and the punchline is the *best* thing; Arthur has no *intention* of selling, even though the money could buy his little girl new lungs, new kidneys and – *fuck it* – whatever else her messed-up nine-year-old heart wanted.'

Josephine picked up the letter again and rapidly re-read it, her eye pausing, just for a split second, on the word *sisterly*, the word *altruism*.

'I don't think this letter was sent to warn you off . . .' she suddenly murmured, 'I think it's some kind of alibi.'

Katherine wasn't buying it. 'Who for?'

'If something bad happens.'

'Who to?'

'If something *bad* happens, to Arthur.'

Josephine's head was spinning. She stepped back, rubbed her hands over her face.

'Don't get *too* excited, Bean, dear,' Katherine muttered. She lay back on her pillows and rested her hand on her stomach.

'Have you heard from your dad lately?' Jo suddenly asked – dropping her hands, turning and seeing a picture of him on Katherine's dressing table, walking over to look at it.

'Nope,' she burped, unapologetically, 'he remarried five years ago, has a three-year-old baby boy and is *blissfully* fucking *happy*.'

Jo shot her a sharp look, 'You'll never forgive him, will you, for being almost as much of a slut as you are. That's really what this is all about. It has nothing to do with self-sacrifice. You're just twisting the knife, keeping us all dangling. It makes you feel powerful.'

Katherine merely sniggered at this, gazed up at the ceiling, but she wasn't happy.

Jo walked over to the doll's house. '*Christ*, the white-collar Protestant *hypocrisy* . . .' and touched its neat roof, lightly. Katherine stiffened, visibly, as Josephine's fingers made contact.

She turned, 'How's your mum?'

'Died last year,' Katherine's voice was tight, 'New Guinea. Pancreatic cancer.'

A long silence.

She suddenly gulped. At first Jo thought it was *grief*, but when Katherine gulped a second time, she immediately knew better. Her eye moved calmly to the glass she was holding.

'What are you drinking?' she asked almost tenderly.

'Brandy.'

'But it's the wrong colour.'

Katherine gulped again.

Josephine strode over and took the glass from her. She sniffed it.

'Disinfectant. How much have you had?'

Katherine shrugged, gulped again.

'Sick it up,' Jo ordered.

Katherine shook her head. She swallowed.

'Okay,' Josephine walked over to her dressing-table and picked up a china pot. It was tiny, delicate, decorated in little hand-painted daisies. She threw it against the cupboard doors. It smashed.

Katherine gaped at her. She picked up an oriental doll, snapped its neck, turned. '*SICK IT UP!*' she yelled, tossing the head at her.

Katherine ducked left to avoid it. Her book fell to the floor.

Josephine walked over to the doll's house. She flexed her fingers.

'*No,*' Katherine said. She gulped, then put her hand over her mouth.

'I won't ask you again,' Josephine said, and bent over to pick it up.

Katherine vomited, vociferously, down onto the carpet.

'*MORE!*' Josephine shouted, holding the house suspended in the air, her elbows buckling under the weight of it, the furniture shifting within, the front facade creaking, threatening to fall open.

Katherine vomited again. A third time.

'Put it . . .' she tried to clear her mouth, was sick again, '*down.*'

'Of course.' Josephine nodded. She dropped the doll's house. It landed on its corner, with a crack.

'What a tragedy,' she murmured, 'now you have absolutely *nothing* left worth staying here for.

'I need to borrow your bike . . .' she continued, swooping down to pick up the *Gumble* book, shaking the sick off it, seeing the disinfectant bottle stuffed under Katherine's counterpane. She grabbed that too, inspected the back, '*Jesus,* 3% non-ionic surfactants. A glass of *tap water* has more chemicals in it than that . . .'

She sniggered, 'It's 97% *preservative.* This stuff'd probably *increase* your life expectancy, before it ended it. . . .'

She threw the bottle down, dismissively.

Katherine's eyes were still slowly moving from Josephine to the doll's house (the tiny chair on the floor, the vicious crack on the front of the facade) then back.

'Next time your self-hatred gets too overpowering,' Josephine advised her, 'try pure bleach. It has a little more *kick* . . .'

Jo sprang – in a timely leap – towards the door, as Katherine exploded out of bed and scrambled, gnashing like a chained bull-terrier, across the floor.

Forty-nine

He was suddenly calculating –
Really calculating
– although he'd never –
Very strange
– ever been even *remotely* mathematically-inclined at school (or since) –
Never
– but he found himself tabulating, nonetheless –
All these numbers, just spinning and squeezing and compacting and rotating . . .
Oh Lord
– stuff about the acuteness of the angle at which he'd fallen, and the precise geometrical . . .
Uh
I think I hit my . . .
    Arthur opened his eyes –
If only it wasn't so cold – and if only I could breathe – I might con-con-consider a permanent in-in-investment in the under-water scene
    He couldn't see much –
No views
Just mud
Wood
Stuff
– but he was sharp enough to witness a violent and thoroughly unwarranted –
The bastards!

– desertion by some of his most important, his most *critical* formulas –

Shit

How to survive without 124/6792 +/– 453/009 .8735465489?

Huh?

– saw them writhing away from him, like eels . . .

Come back!

And all those lovely fractions of fractions . . .

All those x's to the power of . . .

   Tried to grab their tails –

Not quick enough

– so he wished them well, with a heavy heart. Tried to make the best of it –

Bye-bye . . .

Bon-voyage . . .

   He even slapped a couple on their backs (for good measure); booted their tiny, arithmetical rumps . . .

Wuh?

Wake-up!

   His head snapped around as he suddenly felt –

Thwhap!

Otter-water-fur

Big

Wood-scrabble

Clip

Limb

Hoof

Bubble

Nuugh!

   Deer

Remember the deer?

And that other life you had?

That old life?

   Rope. Stiff rope . . .

Uuuuhhh . . .

   He felt the irresistible urge to feel his way along it.

So much commotion above . . .

The kick

The white
The panic
He gradually worked his way down; a blind man walking the prom
– it wasn't far – and there he found . . .
No!
Stop!

Everything flooded back:

Wesley

4578/78 + 9/452222

She was a recruitment officer
She lived in Palmer's Green
And I –
He –
I –
He –
Arthur Young . . .
Arthur Anthony Young . . .

And she was called Bethany –
No –
Bethan –
 And he –
I –
He felt very strong things for her
He lo-lo-lo

Wesley
And that hand
And the sheer poetry in the way he . . .

I like a walk
I like a drink
I work –
I worked –

I work –
I worked
– for the sugar industry.
But my . . .
My great-great-great-great grandfather . . .

*'There is certainly something in the amiable simplicity of unadorned
nature, that spreads over the mind a more noble sort of tranquillity,
and a lo-lo-lo*

Enough!

*and a lo-lo-loftier sensation of pleasure, than can be raised from
the nicer scenes of art . . .'*

Argh

At first I just . . .
At first I just . . .
To be rejected so gently,
So absolutely . . .
*Took a little comfort – hell, not ashamed to admit it – in the
embrace of the bottle*
The lovely bottle
And Gillian with herpes
From the PR
The PR
The PR . . .

Depart

Not enough

When they caught him . . .
After he stole the fucking . . .
The fucking pond . . .

Not enough

He was everything I ever . . .
He was . . .
He had . . .
He disregarded . . .
He thumbed his nose . . .
He trampled . . .
He turned his damn back . . .
And I
He –
I –
He hated him for that

Had to keep an –
An –
An –
An eye . . .

Keep track

First the private detective, just to keep a few . . . a few . . . a few
tabs . . .
The mounting ex-ex-ex-expenses

The baby

God

Am I . . . ?
Could I . . . ?
Did my in-in-in-infidelities . . . ?

And Bethan told him –
me –
him –
me . . .

It's him or me, Arthur
It's him or me and our little . . .

little –
little –
little –
Fucked up

Baby

Look

I'd love a drink
A short
A shot

I'm over it.
I'm honestly . . .

Look!

Arthur put out his hand towards the limp body. He could feel a shoulder, a face . . .
Was he awake?
He could feel his . . .
His hand –
That wounded hand
That trade-mark hand
How small it is

– then the rope. Twisted . . . he felt for it . . . still looped around him and then over a . . .
Beam?
Rafter?
Plank?
Log?
. . . holding him down. Stopping his escape. Deer at the other end.
Yanking. *Yanking.*

'Rise to the surface, Arthur
This is your Father speaking
I think you probably need something we people call oxygen'

Just a small twist, a jerk, a pull. He would be free again . . .
Shall I leave him?
Arthur turned –
The hand tightened in Arthur's hand –
He was awakening –
Arthur tried to see him –
Could almost see him –
Waited for the entreaty –
Help me!
Save me!
   But then it dawned on him. He wasn't actually clinging on so
much as pushing . . . pushing *away* –

Can't be!
– he was –
Not begging but rejecting . . .
– He didn't . . . he didn't *want* to be free. He wanted to . . . to . . .
to *stay.*
He's planning to stay here, like me
He's planning to finish his journey in this place
At this time . . .

The swine!

To be trumped here? In death?
Even in death?
By Wesley?

Arthur found the snag on the rope, unlooped it, tugged –
Tugged
Then the deer did his work for him – dragged Wesley towards the
surface like a sprat on a line . . .

Wesley roared –

Urgh-argh-urgh-urgh!

Threw out his arms, grabbed Arthur's shoulder . . .
They embraced each other . . .
Kicking . . .
Bellowing . . .
Flailing . . .
Rising to the surface like a self-hating eight-angry-limbed octo-octo-octo . . . *pussssssssss*

Punctured balloons, deflating

HUUUUAAAAHHHHHRRRRR!

Air

The deer dragged them to the bank, two pegs on a line; two knots in a lace; two rattles on a snake . . .
Breathing
Gasping
Chattering
Pumping

Life

They clung together; tight as a couple of sharp notches on an old, leather whip. Caked with hair, sweat, blood.
    Two ugly, trusty outboard motors, their cords held and pulled . . .
    The wonderful stop, restarting with a roar.
    The wonderful *stop*, restarting.

The boy stood by the trolley stroking the Old Man's left foot. The Old Man was still missing a shoe. His foot was clad in only a thin, clean, white cotton sock. Slightly too big for him. They were in casualty. There was currently no bed ready. The Old Man had seen a trauma specialist. Then he'd dozed off.

He hadn't noticed the boy's arrival (his hands clutching anxiously at the zip on his jacket, his thin neck, his grey skin, his eyes darting about him like two water-boatmen on the polluted surface of a dank river basin).

Patty was uncertain about the extent of the Old Man's injuries. He'd made several forceful enquiries on this subject upon his arrival, but had then promptly neglected to listen to the answers. Had simply moved on and enquired some more.

He was shivering. A kind-hearted nurse had brought him a cup of tea and he crouched over it, like a sullen rook after a rainstorm, its feathers all shaken out. The heat in-between his palms and fingers made his shoulders stiffen.

'Following's got so complicated,' the boy murmured to the sock, once he'd put the cup aside, 'but you're the champ at it, Doc. You're the whizz. You're the star. If you left us, Doc, it'd all fall apart. Because you're the champ, Doc. You're the killer.'

As if words alone could not convey the violence of his emotions, the boy began twisting Doc's white-cotton-clad toe, at first softly, then with an ever-greater voracity.

'I love you, man. You're the bloody-fucking-whizz. That's for certain. I even love your dog, although it pissed on my boot when I first joined up and everybody laughed at me. And that wasn't actually very funny. I didn't like it. And you didn't like me either, back then, Doc. But I think we've grown to mutually respect each other. But you're still the champ, man. You're still solid, man. *Rock* solid, man.'

Doc sat bolt upright.

'*Ow!*'

The boy sprang back.

'You're alive again,' he whispered, plainly awed.

'What are you doing to my bloody foot?' Doc asked crossly.

'Nothing.'

'Then what have you done with my bloody shoe?' Doc asked, crosser still.

'Nothing. It must've fell off.'

'A likely story,' Doc harrumphed.

'I thought you was dead,' the boy muttered.

'You thought I was dead so you stole my damn *shoe*?' The Old

Man felt around inside his pockets, 'What else did you try and nick, you little monster?'

Doc pulled himself stiffly from the trolley. 'Not dead yet, boy,' he mumbled darkly, starting to walk, gingerly, 'still too much to do.'

'Your dog's outside,' the boy followed him through the ward, 'he was tied up at the Turpin house, so I brought him over. Just in case you . . .'

Doc turned and looked down at the boy. 'What're you waiting for?' he asked gruffly. 'You've had your moment, now *sod off.*'

On his way out, the boy dumped his half-full paper cup onto the desk at the nurse's station. 'I *hate* fucking tea,' he yelled, then nudged it and tipped it up and ran out laughing.

When the back of the pick-up was fully loaded and the tarpaulin was pulled over to protect its contents, Dewi opened the bonnet and inspected the engine. He checked the water, the oil. The oil was low. He carefully added some.

He was ready to go.

But first . . .

He'd seen Josephine Bean leaving at full tilt on Katherine's bike. He'd heard a certain amount of commotion. But he refused to . . . he couldn't . . .

He sniffed and pulled up the collar on his coat.

The sleet was setting in; there'd been a slight change in wind direction. He glanced over towards the smashed bungalow window. He frowned. He scratched his head. He turned and disappeared inside his own bungalow. He re-emerged, minutes later, holding some strips of polythene and some masking tape. He crossed the road. He began to hold up the polythene to the window frame . . .

He scowled.

He returned to his van, pulled back the tarpaulin, located his tool box, removed a small hammer, a chisel, a little hand-brush . . .

He climbed in through Katherine's window. Katherine was sitting on the sofa, wrapped up in a duvet, quietly watching him. He gave her a blank look, as if all remaining traces of affection had been scoured out of his eyes, his brain, turned, and gently began tapping out the worst of the glass.

But he was a perfectionist. Soon he was tapping out all of it, even chiselling out the bits inside the frame. When it was clean, he climbed outside again. He began sticking the plastic up; it didn't take him long.

Then he was ready to go.

But first he went and found a broom and began sweeping up the exterior glass. He went and grabbed an empty, heavy brown-paper potato bag – *Bonzer Potatoes; Desiree* 10lbs – and poured the glass remnants inside it. Folded the top over. Once. Twice. Sealed it with tape. Put it next to the gatepost for the bin-men to collect.

Now he was ready to go.

The hydrangea was still on the pavement, though. He went over and fetched it. He inspected it for root damage (extensive, no matter what the Bean girl'd said). He went into his back garage and found some compost, a fork, a watering can. He carried them over to the bungalow. He turned the soil over, fertilised, replanted the hydrangea, watered it.

Now he was ready to go.

First he needed to wash his hands, though. He went back to his bungalow and washed his hands. Dried them. Strolled out onto his verandah. Noticed that the hydrangea was tilting in the wind – to the left. Went and found a stake in his back garage and some rope. Staked the hydrangea up and tied it into place. That was better.

Yup.

He dusted himself off.

Now he was ready to go. He put the keys to his house into a brown envelope and pushed the envelope under the doormat. He straightened up and looked around him for the final time. The last, the very last time. He walked down his steps, along his path, through his gate (which clicked shut behind him then opened again. He turned and clicked it properly shut). He climbed into his van. He put on his seat belt. He adjusted his rear-view-mirror. He pushed his keys into the ignition. He fired the engine. He waited for three minutes exactly. Then he drove off.

He was gone.

*   *   *

'It's *your* fault.'

Wesley was standing on the bank, dripping wet. He was pointing at Eileen who was holding onto Sasha for support. Clutching at her. Or perhaps it was the other way around. He couldn't tell. He didn't care.

He was angry. He was cold. He was alive.

Eileen was shaking. The box of eggs lay open on the floor.

'Pardon?' the little girl said, her eyes moving religiously from his face to his hand, his face to his hand.

He tried not to look back at her. When he looked at her he felt an uncontrollable urge to slap her face, then his own. So he tried not to look.

'You sank my father's boat,' Wesley snarled (ignoring the girl's intervention), 'and that was *all* I had left of him.'

Eileen was terrified.

'It was only . . .' she kept saying, making a pathetic throwing movement with her hand, 'just a tiny . . .'

'He's being *ridiculous*,' the girl murmured, '*ignore* him.'

Wesley took a furious step forward, lifted his bad hand and slapped his own face.

Clap

Arthur turned, from the bank, to apprehend this act. It was the first time they'd made eye contact since they'd been on dry land. Arthur watched him, half-smiling. There was almost . . . almost *pity* in it. Wesley saw the smile, recognised its meaning, felt a surge of rage rise within him. 'I should've left that damn canister,' he spat. He immediately regretted it. So much so that he held his breath –

A stillness

Arthur frowned. The deer made a grunting sound. He turned back towards the water. Sasha gave a low cry and moved towards the bank. Eileen remained where she was.

Wesley began breathing again. He shuddered. He saw his knife in her hand.

'That's *my* knife,' he murmured childishly, '*give* it back.'

She held it out to him, terrified, handle first. He snatched it from her, picked up the vixen, slung her around his shoulders, then pointed with the knife to the eggs, which were still on the floor where she'd left them. 'There are two cubs,' he said, 'in a den under the flyover. This was their mother. A car killed her. The eggs are for them.'

He began walking.

'What about the deer?' The girl turned from the bank. 'What about *Brion*? He . . .'

Wesley blanked her out. Walked on.

Once he reached the flyover he clambered up onto the road and headed along it. Away from Canvey. The first dwelling he came to, he knocked at the door and asked for some dry clothing. The oldest son in the house obliged him, gave him a mug of coffee, a piece of toast. He brought out a spade and they buried the vixen together, under an old cobnut tree at the far end of the garden; Cooper – a grey-muzzled brown labrador – officiated, accompanied by a tunelessly raucous starling choir.

Fifty

When the first police car roared past her, she pedalled faster and
followed it, remembering the details Arthur Young had unwittingly
let slip on the phone in the smoky bar the night before – he'd referred
to some kind of . . . of *craft* –
Hadn't he?
– and he'd mentioned the flyover.

She overtook the agent's Fiesta (not recognising it), kept going,
felt the sweat freeze on her. A fire engine. Siren howling. Then an
ambulance. She jumped off the bike at the back of a ludicrously long
line of emergency service vehicles, sprinted to the base of the bridge,
leaned over it, fingers spread, elbows rigid, *gasping.*

A crocodile of people – mostly uniformed – were slowly advancing
along the river path. On the river itself; a noisy, motorised, marine-
rescue dinghy, two men in black rubber, a diver, a series of disparate
objects floating on the choppy surface of the water.

On the bank . . .
Where was he?
She saw Arthur Young –
Oh thank . . .
Thank . . .
– wrapped up in a blanket, staring down at . . .
A prone deer?
With . . . with . . . with antlers?
Could that . . . ?

She blinked. For a moment she almost believed that Wesley'd been
transfigured. That it was him. That he was it. In form. In fact.

She blinked again –

No

– her eyes jinked left.

A child stood next to Arthur, holding onto his arm. A girl. Dark (was it *his* child?). Dangling from the fingers of her other hand, a long, rather distinctive, fluffy orange . . . *uh* . . . scarf?

No . . .

A fox's tail?

Am I . . . *?*

She blinked.

Could that . . . *?*

There was another person –

Yes

– a third, possibly a vet – down on his knees, trying to help the stag, clearing out its airwaves, blowing onto its nose, rubbing at it violently with a towel or a sack.

The child – the girl – seemed in a state of some distress.

Josephine's eyebrows rose in sympathy, but only momentarily. Soon her focus shifted again –

Where was he?

Where?

Towards the front of the line she saw the agent comforting the librarian. The librarian was blowing her nose while holding – and very nearly dropping, before the agent considerately intervened – a large box . . . an *unwieldy* box of . . .

Of eggs?

Jo jumped over the concrete partition, clambered down onto the bank and ran to join them. Eileen saw her first. 'I threw . . . ' she spluttered, 'and the *whole* thing just . . . it just . . .' She made an expansive gesture with her hands.

Josephine ignored the hands, the words, yelled straight into her face, without restraint, '*JUST TELL ME HE ISN'T DEAD.*'

She was almost screaming – shocked herself, in fact (had no prior conception of how agitated she was feeling).

'He *isn't*,' Eileen said (in a slightly resentful tone – as if a tragic fatality might've helped all those involved to feel marginally better).

Josephine grabbed the agent's arm and shook it (as though Wesley might fall out of his sleeve, his jacket, if only she persisted). 'Where is he? Has he gone? Did he hurt anyone? Was *he* hurt? What happened?'

She began coughing –

Not enough breath

'He's *fine*,' Ted gently removed her hand from his sleeve, squeezed it, released it. 'He climbed up onto the main road, turned left. Ten minutes ago. Fifteen . . .'

He pointed towards the little girl, 'That's his daughter. He wasn't especially happy to see her. He took off.'

Josephine nodded repeatedly at what he was saying, but she wasn't focussing. She was staring wildly around her, looking for scraps, for clues. 'Was there some kind of . . . of *craft* here before?' On *craft*, Eileen's face crumpled. She clutched the egg-box to her chest, lifted her lime green mud-encrusted pixie-boots and tottered unsteadily off.

Josephine stood still for a second and struggled –

Struggled

– to remember the landscape of her past.

The boat. The *craft*. Tried to recollect . . .

'I had a feeling it was you,' Ted murmured – in a soft conspiratorial tone – once Eileen was out of earshot.

She stared at him, blankly.

'I have re-lived that event in my mind . . .' he continued, with a smile (almost of relief), 'a thousand, a *million* times over.'

He waited for some kind of reaction from her, but none came; she was studying the river again, closely scrutinising the three remaining struts of the walkway still poking out of the water.

'I knocked, but just gently . . .' he continued, hardly caring any more, simply telling himself now, as much as her, 'because I didn't really *want* him to answer . . .'

He re-enacted that gentle knock; 'I'd been involved in a scuffle during PE – totally out of character – but another boy – a boy called Bo – you might possibly remember . . . ?'

Nothing

'Well he threw my uniform into the toilet; pissed on it . . .' Ted shrugged, defensively, 'I waited outside his office, but no answer, so I knocked again – louder – and still nothing, so I took a deep breath and I . . .'

He re-enacted opening the door, walking in, his eyes widening in horror, 'You were perched on his knee with your arms around his neck. I only saw you from the back – your hands, your hair – he was sitting in his chair, at his desk. I thought about . . . I almost . . . I tried to . . . I . . .'

He shook his head, 'I was just a kid. I was stupid. And Bo – of all people – was directly behind me – and when he saw my expression, he asked what was wrong and I just . . . I *blabbed* . . . and that was . . . that was *it*. It was . . . it was *out*.'

He stared at Josephine, hoping – perhaps – for understanding. Sympathy. Fury, even.

But nothing

Her focus had shifted again, back onto the dark-haired child and the skinny, enigmatical Arthur Young.

'Katherine found me,' he continued, 'a few days after. Took me aside and swore it was her. Said I'd *misconstrued* . . . made me believe her. Made me *swear* . . .' he shook his head, dazed. 'And you know what?' he chuckled dryly at the extent of his own folly, 'I *wanted* to believe her. I was weak. I wanted things to be clean and right and proper. So I made my apologies,' he shrugged, regretfully, 'and that was my mistake. Because I'd entered the lie. I *became* the lie. And for one reason or another – I don't really know why – I never stopped apologising after that.'

Ted looked down at his hands. His fingers and his nails were absolutely filthy, and there was a wide slick of mud – he observed irritably – across the middle of his tie. A few feet away, some encouraging progress was suddenly being made with the exhausted brown stag; Brion slowly lifted his head, coughed, kicked out a front leg . . .

Sasha squealed and threw both of her arms around Arthur. He held onto her, stiffly (like an exhausted swimmer embracing a buoy), smiling embarrassedly.

Josephine smiled herself, in reaction, then turned back to face the agent again, her expression rapidly degenerating from cheery to stony. 'That's all ancient history now, Ted,' she told him bluntly, 'get over it. Move *on*.'

*   *   *

'You need a drink,' Katherine murmured, staring at him sympathetically – although sympathy wasn't really her thing, was an unfamiliar visitor to her emotional vista (so she made its acquaintance tentatively, unconfidently, and it was a stretch – took moral effort – which was exhausting for her).

She was tired –

Tired

He was still shivering, although he'd had a warm bath and was wearing her father's old clothes – wearing them exceptionally well, as it transpired (every item but the shoes fitting perfectly).

His arm had been bandaged by the mobile doctor. She idly recalled the Bean girl having a bandaged arm, earlier (the right arm). She presumed it was some kind of Wesley-based phenomena – that these were copy-cat injuries; imitative woundings of a sympathetic nature. She *loved* this idea. She was sick. It amused her.

'I don't really know why I'm . . .' Arthur glanced around the kitchen. Everything seemed – if possible – even more sordid than when he'd been there the night before, '*imposing* on you like this . . .'

He rubbed his hair. It was lank and soft thanks to the tiny splash of geranium oil she'd applied to his bathwater.

'A warm berth,' she gave him a salacious look. Didn't quite pull it off, '*bath*,' she adjusted, hiccuped.

Blinked –

Pine

She filled the kettle. Arthur walked over to inspect her chinchilla.

'Was the girl alright in the end, though,' Katherine asked, 'the daughter?'

He nodded, 'As well as can be expected. It was all slightly . . .' he sniffed, 'traumatic.'

'Was she sweet?'

'Very. Hard-nosed. Funny.'

'Was she like him?'

Arthur frowned, scratched his head again, slowly, 'Yes. *Yes*. I suppose she was, really.'

Katherine plugged the kettle in, turned it on. 'And what'll happen to her now?'

'The mother's been called back from her honeymoon in . . . in . . .' he grimaced, 'and is driving down to fetch her.'

'*Wow*,' Katherine sighed, as if delighted – by proxy – at the trouble Sasha had caused everyone.

Arthur cautiously pushed his index finger through the bars of Bron's cage. Bron froze and stared pointedly at the finger, his whiskers vibrating crazily.

'Does the rodent have a name?' he asked.

'Bron.'

'Really? What's the background on that?'

'*The Tomorrow People*. Bron is a magical creature who possesses the special gift of transforming himself into the one thing each person most loves.'

'Ah.'

Arthur stared at the rodent, unlovingly.

He suddenly felt . . . was feeling . . .

What was it?

Empty?

Bereft?

Ever since . . .

'And the deer?' she asked.

He turned and stared at her, intently. Surely she must be feeling it too? He hunted for the signs. *Longed* for them. Saw none.

'Tough as old boots,' he eventually murmured.

Katherine nodded sagely,' That's why Santa favours them over the motor scooter.'

He didn't react. He was inspecting her boiler suit. The poppers. The length of the arms. The traces of sick down the front.

'So what will you do now?' she asked, slightly disconcerted by the attention he was paying her (she didn't remember asking for it, but attention – she supposed – was always rather like that).

He shrugged, 'Haven't decided yet,' then smiled. 'I thought about you,' he said thickly, 'all night long, in the dark.'

She scratched her chin, uneasily. She didn't believe him for a second.

'But I don't know anything about you . . .' he continued.

'Apart from . . .' she interrupted, widening her eyes, 'the *obvious*, obviously.'

He nodded but looked vacant.

'The fold-up bike,' he suddenly said, as though snatching this

522

abiding image straight from the ether.

'Yes.'

'And the sex.'

She picked up a couple of mugs from the work-surface, turned her back on him.

'So you work locally?' he asked.

She rinsed the mugs in the sink, her mouth tightening at its corners. 'I do.'

She faced him again, her countenance scrubbed clean. 'I sprout beans for a living.'

'Really?'

He struggled to concentrate. He was remembering . . .

That gas canister

That cold water

'Yes. Mung, aduki, alfalfa . . .'

They stared at each other.

'Lentils, chick peas . . .'

The kettle boiled, clicked, sighed.

It started to rain again outside.

The chinchilla yawned.

Her stomach rumbled –

The sheer . . .

The infernal . . .

The unbelievable mundanity of it all . . .

'I can spare you thirty quid,' she said briskly, 'and a coat, and a hat too, if you have need of it.'

They crouched quietly under the flyover in the comforting semi-darkness, hoping – waiting – for those tragically orphaned cubs to make an appearance. He wrapped his arm around her. And when it grew too cold, she borrowed his jacket, inspected the seam-work, and even in the half-light, saw that it was perfect.

'You're fantastic, Ted,' she said.

And he nodded. Because he believed her. Because he knew it.

*   *   *

He needed to walk it off –

Just to walk

– but his shoes weren't right – a fraction too *loose* – so he stopped off at Saks to pick up a tissue or something –

A napkin

– to shove down the back. He took the money Katherine had given him out of her father's old tweed coat pocket.

This is a new lease of life, he thought, I am re-invented. There are things that I don't need to understand or regret or explain any more. Because I am over it, I am . . .

I am . . .

But the words wouldn't come.

To fill up this temporary mental vacuum – this space – this confusion – he walked over to the counter –

The sound of my own feet

What a blessing

– and when he arrived there, he ordered a vodka.

Once the money'd run out, he produced his own wallet, opened it, pulled out Dewi's wet notes, the damp picture of his kid, propped her up against an empty glass, toasted Dewi, toasted Sasha, toasted Katherine, toasted . . . toasted . . .

God this took some doing

– toasted Wesley –

And that fucking gas canister

– toasted himself, toasted her . . . until his arm couldn't toast anyone – not anyone – anymore.

'What did you forget *now*?' she asked, in a tone which implied that he'd have forgotten his own hair if it hadn't been well-rooted.

'I forgot you,' Dewi said grimly, 'go and get the chinchilla and we'll be off.'

She shrugged, went through to the kitchen, brought the chinchilla cage back with her. He took it, held it primly aloft.

'Good.' His tone was crisp.

'I suppose I'll need a change of underwear,' she ruminated. Her voice was uncertain – as if only half of her was involved in the current transaction; the less contentious part (the troubled side was off on sabbatical; perhaps swearing at a kindly nun, or giving hand relief to a total stranger with not-quite-clean-enough teeth in a not-quite-deserted-enough railway compartment somewhere).

'No.'

He opened the front door, drew a deep breath, and gravely made his peace with this other, rather more rambunctious, rather less *appealing*, absent part; 'Katherine Turpin I *like* . . . I *accept* . . . I *love* your stink,' he told her.

She caught up with him on the hard shoulder. The boy – the oldest son from the house – was still walking alongside him, accompanied by his grizzled but genial stiff-limbed brown labrador.

The boy's name was Peter. He was fifteen. He wanted to be an astronaut (way off, though; *way* off in the future). He was exceptionally athletic; currently Canvey Athletics Team's 100 metre champion (and a mean hurdler, a good walker – a keen hiker, he told Wesley) but scientific, too; had attained the top grades in his year for physics, maths, biology, chemistry . . .

He was deadly serious about everything, himself especially.

'To pursue my dream,' he said, 'I'll need to get some kind of scholarship to America. The British Space Programme's just a joke, but it's an entirely different kettle of fish over there . . .'

'Space is relative,' Wesley teased him, his eyes scanning the path as he walked along, 'and all creatures are travellers. The most important journeys are the interior ones. The most important and the most hazardous.'

Josephine snorted at this, under her breath –
God
He was so full of . . .

The bike's front wheel suddenly hit the kerb and the whole structure folded – in the middle – where the join was. It was definitely a design fault. It just needed some kind of . . . of *clip*, maybe, for when the bike wasn't being ridden but was still in . . .
In motion

Wesley heard this slight commotion and glanced over his shoulder.

525

His face snapped shut when he saw her. His mouth tightened. Then he turned back around and simply walked faster.

'I know about *Gumble*, Wesley,' she said tiredly – not shouting over the traffic, but speaking quietly, within her normal range. He continued walking, though, as if he hadn't heard her. 'I know about *Goodwin*, Wesley,' she said, slightly louder.

This time it was the boy's turn to swing around and stare. It was a haughty look –

Keen

Jealous

Josephine dropped the bike with a clatter. 'Doc's been in an *accident*,' she observed stridently, then paused, speculatively, 'although whether it's entirely accurate to actually *call* it that . . .'

She had his attention. Wesley stopped, turned to the boy. 'I need to talk to this person,' he explained, 'but we can still meet up in Tilbury. Around six. Outside the pub. Like we discussed.'

The boy nodded. 'I'll bring your rucksack,' he said, 'I know where the house is. I've got the address.'

He tapped his back trouser pocket. The labrador drew closer – sniffed – as if there might be something for him in it. Wesley leaned down and patted the labrador's smooth, wide head. 'There you go, Coops,' he said, then straightened up, smiled, 'I'd appreciate that, Peter. Thanks.'

Used the name

The boy shrugged, grinned, called the dog, moved off. As he passed her by, he shot Josephine a small, sharp look.

Wesley observed her reaction to it (the angry blush) as they stood and faced each other, unable to speak at first thanks to a powerful blast on the bullhorn of a juggernaut.

Wesley waved his bad arm, tiredly – like a thoroughly world-weary celebrity of the roadway. Two consecutive horns sounded. He grimaced.

'Didn't take you long,' she said eventually, tipping her head towards the kid, struggling –

Battling

– not to sound like her nose was out of joint.

He was a tart. A *flirt*. What else did she expect?

'You may not be aware of this fact,' Wesley murmured, 'but I don't often *speak* to the people Following. It's my . . .' he paused, 'it's my tick, my *trademark.'*

His tone was ironic, but he was obviously serious.

'You're pathetic,' she observed coolly, holding her neat chin up.

Wesley turned side-on and stared into the hedgerow, as if determined to prove it.

'So did he survive?' he asked idly.

Doc

She could've sworn she saw hope –

A glimmer of it

– in his profile.

'Do you secretly wish he hadn't?' she asked, shocked.

Wesley chuckled at her reaction, 'Of *course* I do, stupid.'

He seemed buoyant. Unhindered.

She was infuriated by his frivolousness, but she wouldn't –

Couldn't

– give in to it.

'So you've set up some kind of company,' she began, calmly, 'to buy out Arthur Young and control the Following. You got the confectionery people to help you – part of the original deal, I imagine – used them as intermediaries because Arthur Young has some kind of long-standing grudge . . .'

Wesley raised his eyebrows, watched a sparrow flit out of the hedgerow and onto a muddy furrow in the bare field behind. 'It's always been a labour of *love* with Arthur,' he interrupted, 'and that's part of his charm.'

'So you signed an exclusive advertising deal with him under the guise of a company called Gumble Inc,' Jo continued smartly, refusing to be drawn by him, 'beguiled him, hoodwinked him, gained his trust. Then, once you were certain that you'd managed it, you withdrew. You knew all about his sick kid – that he really needed the money – that he was desperate . . .'

Wesley shook his head, tolerantly, 'You've got it all back to front, Bean; I contacted the confectionery people *because* of Arthur Young. He used to work for them. They still pay him a pension. He suffers from an illness related to an extreme form of alcoholism . . .'

'You sent a letter to Katherine,' she continued tenaciously (ignoring his intervention, simply determined to disgorge her own side of the story, before it either imploded, evaporated, or totally eluded her), 'warning her off Arthur because you knew for a fact that she'd do exactly the . . .'

'Flattered as I am by your *unshakeable* conviction in my boundless ingenuity,' Wesley muttered, adjusting his damp trainers as they hung around his shoulders, 'even *I* can't understand why I'd've bothered to do that. My agenda has always been to keep Arthur Young at a distance. To draw him closer would've been counterproductive . . .'

'You have some kind of *deal* with the confectionery people,' Josephine battled on. 'I don't understand all the ins and the outs of it, but you're intending for Hooch or Shoes to pick up the prize on Goodwin and then to re-invest the profits into Gumble. You're planning to fleece them. It's going to be your great revenge on them, your ultimate coup . . .'

'What?' Wesley gasped in pretend shock. 'To make money out of . . . out of *myself*?' He threw up his hands. 'But that's absolutely *scandalous*, Bean.'

She didn't respond, at first.

'Perhaps you prefer the idea of me,' Wesley continued, provocatively, 'as some kind of limp commodity which other people can simply pick up or drop or exploit, at will, whenever they feel like it?'

She looked confused, momentarily, so he pushed home his advantage, 'But can't you see the irony in that, Josephine? Can't you understand – even after everything you've been through with Katherine – can't you understand how *demoralising* it is to have other people consciously exploiting your mistakes, your energy, your weaknesses in that way?'

Josephine stared at him, her brown eyes narrowing slightly, 'You *knew* Katherine wrote the graffiti?'

He shrugged, bored, 'Who else would've cared enough to do it?'

'So all that stuff in the book was just . . . just *bullshit*?'

'No,' he smiled. 'It was a gift. I gave her exactly what she wanted. I *magnified* her self-hatred. I tested it. That's my flair – or as Hooch would say – my . . . my *knack*.'

'That's cold,' Josephine murmured, shaking her head.

'It's disgusting,' he nodded, 'but so what?'

He turned away from the hedgerow and glanced covetously up the road again. She could tell she was losing him, and that once he was lost, she would never get him back.

'You *love* the Following,' she murmured, 'you pretend to hate it but the truth is that you *thrive* on it. Hooch was right, you're terrified of letting anybody get too close. It isn't grand or magical, it's just pointless, slightly neurotic and not a little sad.'

He shook his head, smiling contemptuously.

'You're out of your depth, Bean,' he warned her.

'If you did actually hate it as much as you profess to,' she said (refusing to be warned), 'then all you'd actually have to do is to *stop*. But for some crazy reason . . .'

He stiffened. She suddenly had his full attention – couldn't be entirely certain *why*, exactly, but she took a chance, anyway . . .

'Just *stop*.'

She said it again. This word seemed to have a remarkable effect upon him. He finally made eye contact with her. His eyes were burning. She saw him reach out his good hand towards his bad.

'I can't.'

He turned and began walking again. She followed.

'Why can't you?'

He ignored her.

'*Why* can't you?'

She grabbed his arm. He lurched away from her, pulling his arm free. '*Why the fuck should I?*' he yelled, then immediately struggled to kerb his temper, as if he'd let something loose, given something away. 'It's my *right* to keep going,' he said emphatically.

He walked on. But he was shaken. She could tell by his uneven gait, the way he swung out both of his arms with a disproportionate vigour.

'I regret mentioning the gas canister,' he suddenly spluttered, 'everything was fine before . . .' He shook his head and walked even faster, as if trying to escape this unhappy fact. 'But when I saw the girl,' he told a passing bus, 'and she looked so . . . she looked . . . something just . . . this *fury* . . .' He put his hand to his neck.

'Which gas canister?'

She was struggling to keep his pace. She was confounded.

'*Which* girl? Your daughter?'

He stopped walking. 'I like you,' he said, drawing a deep breath, 'and it's incredibly sweet, this need you have, to tidy everything up. It's very . . .' he struggled, 'very *quaint*. And I'm sure it's an extremely *helpful* quality – up to a point – in terms of your medical career, your finances and all the rest of it. But as a *philosophy*, as a way of *life*,' he stared at her, incredulously, 'it's just . . . it's fucking *tripe*. It's *shit*. Because things don't automatically fall into place, Bean. Things don't automatically make sense or add up . . .'

'I don't care what my weaknesses are,' she said staunchly, 'I still think I deserve better than that.'

He was silent for a moment, as if struggling against the over-powering urge to indulge her. 'What you need to understand,' he explained, giving in, momentarily, 'is that there was an *integrity* to that Loiter . . .' he paused, 'and a *sacrifice* on my part . . .' he paused again, 'because I felt nothing but *sympathy* for Arthur's situation, and I knew – I understood perfectly well – why he . . . why . . .' Wesley tipped his head stiffly to one side, as if – contrary to his words – he *didn't* really understand; couldn't . . . hadn't . . . didn't *want* . . .

He closed his eyes, shrugged, 'I played a joke. I taught someone a lesson. It was years ago. I was vulnerable. I needed to prove a point. I took it too . . .'

He opened his eyes again, as if already dismissing this theory. 'But when the boy died,' he rapidly continued, switching his focus, almost burbling in his desire to be done with explaining, 'I knew I was fucked. The whole joke had turned sour. That the thing I'd done to help, that the move I'd made to . . . to . . .'

He scowled – as if still in dispute with himself on this matter –

'But life *is* sour, and jokes are . . .' he stopped himself, shrugged, 'I saw what it did to the Old Man. He was a bad father. He *knew* he was. He cared too much. It ate him up.'

'The point is,' Josephine interrupted gently (as if flattered or satisfied in some way by the neatness of it all, the way the puzzle had slowly started to fit), 'that he got what he wanted. His son won. Just like you said. Because when he died, Doc finally took notice, and that was all he'd ever really . . .'

Wesley scowled. 'The Loiter's become a compromise,' he said coldly, 'and I won't compromise the Following just because a large corporation is afraid of a little negative PR.'

Josephine frowned, 'But you're going along with it.'

'Really?' he cocked his head to one side. 'Who told you that?'

He smiled at the look of shock on her clean face, 'I'm blackmailing the company. I see the drowning as an *opportunity*. I'm demanding major environmental concessions to keep quiet about the whole affair.'

Josephine tried to make sense of this.

'They don't believe I'll jeopardise the feelings of the Old Man,' Wesley shrugged, 'but they're wrong.'

He shrugged again. It gave him away.

'But they're *right*,' Jo contradicted him, 'you *wouldn't* jeopardise his feelings.'

'So I came down to Canvey,' he continued, ignoring her, 'to shake them up. But they called my bluff. They sent Arthur Young in as a warning. I don't know how they managed it, what they've told him or how it'll affect the situation . . .'

Josephine frowned, shook her head, 'I'm still not . . .'

'I set up Gumble to launder the cash I was paid with for the *Loiter*. I fed it into the Behindling site through sponsorship. I thought if Arthur made enough money through the Following that he might finally re-evaluate his feelings on the situation. He could help his kid, rebuild his relationship with Bethan, go off and do his *own* walking, his *own* writing . . .'

Josephine smiled, 'You thought he might give the whole thing up . . .'

Wesley smiled straight back at her.

'But you were wrong.'

He nodded, 'And then the company re-activated Gumble to try and win me over. Started all this buy-out bullshit, involved Hooch, Shoes – superficially to protect Doc . . .'

'If Arthur doesn't sell, would they hurt him?'

'Maybe,' Wesley scratched his ear, 'depends how badly they want to fuck me over.'

'But they sent that letter,' Josephine jumped in, 'implying all kinds of stuff about . . .'

Wesley looked tired, 'Things can't always fit together like a jigsaw, Bean. And nor should they.'

'Why not?'

'Because it'd be a kind of *hell* if they did.'

He began walking again.

'If Arthur found out that you were behind Gumble,' she said, 'that you knew about him, about his kid, that you'd given him the money, that he'd turned down the chance to make everything right out of . . . out of what? Some pathetic sense of . . . of *spite*? That you *knew* he had, that you were suddenly enjoying some kind of serious moral *advantage* over him . . .'

'Arthur needs to hate me,' Wesley interrupted. 'If he gives up the site . . .'

'And what if he *can't* hate you any more?' she butted in. 'What then . . . ?'

Suddenly – and with no prior warning – Wesley turned and strolled casually into the middle of the highway. Two cars narrowly avoided colliding, trying to avoid him. He bent down. He picked something up. He was fearless. It was terrifying.

When he returned to where she was standing she saw a snail held between his fingers. He placed it gently into the long grass.

'You've got to stop,' she said.

That word again.

'Why?'

He was buzzing, full of an uncontrollable exuberance. He laughed at her expression, clutching his stomach. 'D'you have something *invested* in making me give up, Bean?' he asked cruelly. 'D'you think this is love? D'you think we should move in together? That I should get a proper job? Settle down? Get serious? Relinquish everything and betray everyone, after one single, dismal, meaningless *fuck*?'

She shook her head, opened her mouth . . .

'Shut up,' he raised his wounded hand, '*enough.*'

'If you'd only just . . .'

Still she persisted.

'No.' Wesley pointed behind her. 'Look,' he said, '*there's* everything you need to know. *There's* all your answers . . .'

At first she thought it was a trick, that he was going to swipe her or shove her or run off. She hesitated. But then she turned, very slowly . . .

In the distance; Doc. The young kid. Hooch.

'You're running away,' she said miserably.

'No. I'm just running. I *like* to run.'

He clutched at his stomach again. She saw that his nose was dripping, that he was shaking.

'You want to stop,' she said calmly, 'and you can.'

'I can never stop walking,' he whispered, drawing close to her, staring at her cheek, her ear, as if he longed to touch her there. 'Not now, not ever.'

She turned, tried to speak. He stopped her. 'The boy is dead,' he said softly. 'He is *dead*. Nothing we can do can bring him back. Doc has nothing left now but the Following. It's his mission. It's my *legacy*. He will die behind me. On his feet, struggling. On duty. In service. I am . . .' he almost laughed at his own verbosity, 'I am the Colonel of his undoing. I am his reaper. That's my obligation. It's the law. It is written. I can't . . . I can't . . . I *can't* . . .'

He couldn't even say it.

'Which boy?' she asked flatly.

'What?' he did a double take, was immediately furious. 'This is the end, Bean, aren't you even listening?'

'Your brother,' she said, 'Christopher.'

Wesley's left hand lunged towards his right.

But she stopped it. She grabbed a tight hold of it.

'No,' she said, 'he's *gone*. Your brother is gone. Christopher is *dead*. You can't bring him back, but you can . . . you *can* stop.'

He slapped her face. His fingerless hand. *Hard*.

She released his other, in shock, clutched at her cheek.

'I'm a vessel,' he said, falling backwards, reeling away from her, 'they inhabit me. They find a home in me. I give them breath. I give them meaning. I am . . .' he started laughing, indicated down towards his body, almost tripping with self-disgust, 'there's nothing *left* of me. I'm what remains on the beach after the high tide. I am the flotsam. I am gathered up. I am spat out. I am redundant, surplus, *debris* . . .'

'*Rubbish.*'

'Exactly!'

He pointed at her, howling.

She frowned, 'That's not what I . . .'

But he'd turned and was walking again. With wide strides. Joyously. Like a whistling lumberjack in a mature pine plantation. Like a cowboy in spurs at the start of a long cattle drive.

'*I am the fucking*,' he suddenly yelled, then started running.

She knew she'd never catch him, then.

'*I AM THE FUCKING.*'

He was abandoned

He was delirious

He was un-stopped

He was *begun*

Then a car pulled over, onto the hard shoulder. Two men piled out of it. She had never seen them before. But they were entirely at their ease here. They were familiar. They set their faces, established their paces. And suddenly they were Following. They were . . .

I am the FUCKING

She could hear him, still shouting, and then clapping his hands and laughing.

And soon the boy drew adjacent with her – then Hooch – then Doc – just one shoe on his foot – the little dog – they drew abreast of her, they drew ahead of her, they pulled away from her.

The *fucking* . . . ?

She shook her head.

The fucking *what*?

She stood. She stood and waited –

Just waited

– frowning.

She waited for an end to it –

She waited for a conclusion –

She waited for a rounding off – a flattening out – a consummation –

She waited for a termination – an ultimation – a comeuppance (*Oh God, yes, please, anything*) – a noun – a verb – a full . . . a full . . . a full . . . a full . . . a full . . .

Stop

*With special thanks to **Mr Alvin Toffler** for his widely celebrated genius, **to Mr Vic Chesnutt** for his unabashed lyricism, and to **Bill Menniss** (proprietor of the incomparable Landgate Books, Rye), for laughing so mercilessly at my origami.*